TO BE A PILGRIM

Joyce Cary

Tom Wilcher is a miserly lawyer deeply at odds with the modern world. On the verge of death, as he plots to run away and marry his former housekeeper Sara Monday, he reviews his life and times, looking back on the bloody conflicts that ushered in the twentieth century and on the varied fortunes of the close-knit family that he both resents and adores. *To Be a Pilgrim* is a study in contradictions, the confession of a political radical turned reactionary, of a religious man and sometime sexual offender, of a landowner who is also a passionate defender of the beauties of an English countryside threatened by unlimited economic development. But Tom Wilcher, for all his disappointment and anger, is at the same time a pilgrim, searching for redemption almost in spite of himself.

"Cary has a gift of humanity. . . . His humor shows no traces of carrion under the fingernails. His prose . . . suffuses his perceptions with all the vitality of a language well used and hard thought over."

SIDNEY MONAS, *THE HUDSON REVIEW*

COVER: Illustration by Brian Cronin

TO BE A PILGRIM

Joyce Cary

■

Introduction by

BRAD LEITHAUSER

NEW YORK REVIEW BOOKS

New York

THIS IS A NEW YORK REVIEW BOOK
PUBLISHED BY THE NEW YORK REVIEW OF BOOKS

TO BE A PILGRIM

Copyright © 1942 by Joyce Cary
Introduction Copyright © 1999 by Brad Leithauser
All rights reserved.

Reprinted by arrangement with the Trustees of the J. L. A. Cary Estate

First published in Great Britain by Michael Joseph Ltd 1942

This edition published in 1999 in the United States of America by
The New York Review of Books
1755 Broadway
New York, NY 10019

Library of Congress Cataloging-in-Publication Data
Cary, Joyce, 1888–1957.
    To be a pilgrim / by Joyce Cary ; introduction by Brad
Leithauser.
        p.   cm.
    Sequel to: Herself surprised.
    Sequel: The horse's mouth.
    ISBN 0-940322-18-8 (pbk.: alk. paper)
    I. Title.
IN PROCESS PR6005.A77 T
823'.912—dc 21   99-15896

ISBN 0-940322-18-8

Printed in the United States of America on acid-free paper.
October 1999
www.nybooks.com

To My Wife

INTRODUCTION

ALTHOUGH IT RUNS only two pages, the first chapter of *To Be a Pilgrim* discloses a great deal about its narrator, Tom Wilcher. He's a rich old English gentleman. He has just suffered the traumatic loss of Sara, his housekeeper, who was sent to jail for robbing him of "some old trinkets." He doesn't fault Sara but himself for the theft, which he assumes would never have occurred had he offered her an adequate salary. He hopes to marry Sara on her release from captivity. He is himself a sort of captive, tightly supervised by his niece Ann, who "could lock me up for the rest of my life, if she chose, in an asylum." He is "suspected of being insane." He wears a "curly-brimmed bowler," believing that hats "are getting more degenerate, more slack, more shapeless, every day."

From those two pages we might hypothesize as follows: Tom Wilcher is an old man, but not so old he doesn't yet dream of romance. He's tight-fisted and self-reproachful. He's in love with tradition—perhaps something of a slave to the past. He dreams of freedom. He's a bit of a paranoid.... All these suppositions would be correct.

Continuing on, reading between the lines, we might surmise that Tom's posed helplessness in his niece's hands is something of an act—that he's a sly and manipulative old dog, as much a jailer as a prisoner. That he's fond of lamentations and is often more feared than liked. And that he holds within him more than his share of guilty secrets.

These suspicions, too, would eventually be borne out, for reading *To Be a Pilgrim* is largely a process of growing confirmation. Chapter by chapter, we observe with engrossed satisfaction as Wilcher, in his chary and unforthcoming way, corroborates our suspicions about him—suspicions which he himself has planted.

And the guilty secrets he harbors? Chief among them is that this proud and wealthy and august gentleman is in truth someone else as well—he's that figure commonly condemned and ridiculed with the phrase "a dirty old man." Wilcher's life follows a downward spiral. Even as he should be entering a stately old age, he seems to have less and less control over his urge to make obscene propositions to young women and to expose himself in the most public and dangerous places. He is a sex offender awaiting, with fascination and horror, the pounding of the constable's billyclub on the door.

As depicted by another author, Wilcher's increasing nakedness—both psychological and literal—would likely be the point of the tale, as all those trappings of respectability to which he clings are revealed as a sham. But such was not Joyce Cary's way. The individual power and pathos of *To Be a Pilgrim* lie in the equal weight and reality Cary accords to both the carnal and the spiritual hungers bedeviling Tom Wilcher.

As a man of the flesh, Wilcher is not merely one of those pariahs whom society lumps under the term sexual deviates, but a figure of almost humorous indignity and contempt—the sad little old exhibitionist in the park. Yet as a man of the spirit—as someone who has dreamed since youth of the life of a missionary, and who even in old age still yearns *to be a pilgrim*—Wilcher is someone on an intense and lofty quest.

For even while succumbing to his basest and most foolhardy urgings, he is also seeking to arrive at some living accommodation between past and future, between his longstanding Liberal politics and a shifting, unrecognizable electorate, between a fading and an emerging England. His devotion to an ancestral world—symbolized in his attachment to Tolbrook, his country estate, and to his persnickety clothes, including that outmoded curly-brimmed bowler—is so fervent as to leave him terrified of most forms of change. Visions of a future in which the traditions and keepsakes he reveres are no longer valued paralyze him. He's a man in the paradoxical position of loving the world so much that he grows to dislike it; its perishability renders it treacherous and inimical.

To Be a Pilgrim, first published in 1942, is the middle volume of a trilogy that begins with *Herself Surprised* (1941) and concludes with *The Horse's Mouth* (1944). The narrator of *Herself Surprised* is that larcenous Sara whom, at the outset of *To Be a Pilgrim*, Wilcher still hopes to marry when she's sprung from jail. *The Horse's Mouth* is narrated by the great love of Sara's life, the penniless painter Gulley Jimson, who likewise knows the inside of a prison cell. A pair of irredeemable outcasts and outlaws, hopeless with money, hapless and intemperate and misguided, Sara Monday and Gulley Jimson are ultimately lovable and irresistible figures. Wilcher, by contrast, is hardly lovable and quite resistible. Leaving aside his unsavory sexuality, he can be a stiff, avaricious, pontificating, and manipulative man.

As such, he is the boldest of the trilogy's three creations. When he began drawing up the character of Gulley Jimson, Cary knew he could bank upon the reader's indulgence and goodwill. In the case of Wilcher, though, Cary had to overcome our resistance. He had to make us care about someone we might not ordinarily care about, and sympathize with someone we might naturally find unsympathetic.

What is so impressive about *To Be a Pilgrim* is the painstaking patience with which Cary works. You might well have expected him to give Wilcher short shrift—to employ him chiefly as a foil for those characters intended to be far more easily endearing. Yet Wilcher's extended apologia forms much the longest of the three books, as well as the richest and most many-tiered portrayal of family, place, and the passing years. Neither Sara nor Gulley has much interest in politics, despite the Depression at home and the ascendancy of Hitler on the Continent. It is left to Tom Wilcher to give the trilogy a sense of historical moment and political depth.

Of the three novels, *To Be a Pilgrim* is by far the most somber. It is one of the trilogy's many quirks that the book in which the hero publicly suffers the least has the most tragic tone. Both Sara and Gulley lose whatever fortune they have and wind up penniless; Wilcher holds on to his money. Both Sara and Gulley more than once misstep and wind up in jail; Wilcher somehow stays one step ahead of the bailiff. And yet there's a weight and a tragedy to his life not borne by those two ne'er-do-wells with whom his fate is intertwined. For Sara and Gulley have both lived fully—if foolishly—and Wilcher has somehow been hamstrung all along, crippled by an innate reserve that has disengaged him from others and left him overly connected to furniture and carpets, knickknacks and banknotes. At the close of *To Be a Pilgrim*, Wilcher is struggling—touchingly, perhaps fruitlessly—to open up his soul, even as his body is closing down.

In the eyes of the world, Wilcher is something of a great man. When he dies, respectful obituaries will be composed for him—unlike Sara and Gulley, who can expect to slip unremarked into paupers' graves. And yet they have lived teeming lives on that earth that will soon embrace them—whereas there's a part of Wilcher that will go to his maker still looking to be born.

—BRAD LEITHAUSER

TO BE

A PILGRIM

PREFACE

This book, the second of a three-piece that began with *Herself Surprised*, is about the Wilcher whom Sara, of that first book, served and robbed; and fancied as a cherishable husband for her middle age; a dream suddenly blown away by Wilcher's heirs.

But by the time Sara goes into Wilcher's service he is old and battered by life. He is deep into his own dream, which is chiefly of the past. He has been, as a young man, the plodding younger brother, with strong affections, but no very strong ambitions. And he has grown up, like many Englishmen, Liberal by conviction but Conservative in heart. In him, that is, the attachments of sentiment, which are the perpetual root of Conservative feeling, are stronger than the drive to adventure. He has a passionate love of home, of his more brilliant sister and brother, who use him and trust him and laugh at him; of the home fields and the manners and values of his youth.

Yet he knows, with his sound education and evangelical protestant training, that he must not set his heart of worldly things; that history is always a turmoil of change; that there is no rest for the soul except in the love of God, and His beauty and His justice; that man is condemned to be a pilgrim in an unexplored wilderness; that all the schemes of politicians, with their promises of security; all the near paradises of the churches, are fraud or delusion. The best that can be hoped from any government is that it will navigate among unknown rocks and unexpected hurricanes without sinking the ship and drowning the crew. The most that can be hoped of a church is that it will neither fossilize into dogma without inspiration, or dissolve into frenzy without sense; that it will, in short, develop without losing its coherence, without ceasing to be a church. Wilcher perfectly understands this truth, but he does not like it, and so he suffers frustration and loneliness.

The background is historical change seen through the eyes, not of Sara, who knows it only in people and in herself, or of the artist Jimson, who sees it as the battle of aesthetic ideas with each other and with a public always blind and self-assured, but of the man of political and religious intuition. The tragedy of such a man is that he sees the good for ever being destroyed with the bad; especially that irreplaceable good, those graces and virtues of life that depend on tradition, on example, on that real education which lives only from mind to mind, and cannot be even described in text books, despised by cheap fools or going by default in mere ignorance. What is worse, he sees these true civilized virtues so tangled into evil practice, idleness, stupidity (even of their inheritors) and conceit, that they are for ever in danger (being eaten hollow by selfishness) of falling into elegant affectations or the tricks of a set. Their beauty is like that of the top of a wave. The sun shines through it for a moment and makes it a jewel, but only because it is so fragile, because it is just going to topple over and die into the sand.

—J.C.

1

Last month I suffered a great misfortune in the loss of my housekeeper, Mrs. Jimson. She was sent to prison for pawning some old trinkets which I had long forgotten. My relatives discovered the fact and called in the police before I could intervene. They knew that I fully intended, as I still intend, to marry Sara Jimson. They were good people. They saw me as a foolish old man, who had fallen into the hands of a scheming woman. But they were quite wrong. It was I who was the unfaithful servant, and Sara the victim. It was because I did not give Sara enough pay and because she did not like to ask me for money that she ran into debt, and was tempted to take some useless trifles from the attic.

I was very ill on account of this disaster to my peace of mind, and the family put me in charge of my niece Ann. I say in charge, because Ann is a qualified doctor, and has power over me. People boast of their liberties nowadays, but it seems to me that we have multiplied only our rulers. Ann, aged twenty-six, could lock me up for the rest of my life, if she chose, in an asylum. This would not alarm me so much if I could make out what goes on in the girl's head.

When I asked her to be allowed to see Sara in prison, she answered only, "We must see how you are."

And the very next day she said: "What you really want, uncle, is a change at the seaside."

"What, at this season?" I was startled by such a suggestion. The girl kept silence. She had no more expression, behind her round spectacles, than a stone ink bottle.

I do not like this girl. I prefer my other niece and several of my honorary nieces. I haven't seen Ann since she was a child. She has lived much abroad, and she never troubled, during her medical training, to visit me.

She had been chosen to take care of me because she is a doctor. But she is a stranger, and I can't tell how dangerous she is, how obstinate. Old men don't like strangers. How can they? For how can strangers like old men. They know nothing of them but what they see and imagine; which in an old man cannot be very pleasant or entertaining.

"If you take me to the seaside," I said to Ann, "I shall go mad. Or perhaps that is the family's plan of campaign."

"You must have a change, uncle."

"Do you think I am mad?"

"No."

"It wasn't you who tried to get me shut up?"

"Cousin Blanche may have—no one else."

"Why? Because I wear a queer hat? To me, you know, it isn't a queer hat—it's a sensible hat."

"I think you're quite right to stick to your own fashions."

But I could see very well that she doesn't like to go out with me.

This is a small point, of course, but it shows the peculiar

difficulties of my position, as an old man suspected of being insane. If I ordered tomorrow a young man's suit, with enormous trousers and a tight waist, and put on my head a little American hat like a soup plate, or one of those obscene objects called a Tyrolese hat, I should look and feel so disgusting to myself that life would not be worth living. Yet when I examine myself, as now, in a long glass, with Ann's eyes, I see that I must be a queer object to a stranger, and a young stranger.

My hatter tells me that there is only one man in England besides myself who still wears a curly-brimmed bowler. But he agrees with me that there has never been a better hat, that hats, in fact, since the last war have gone to the devil. And are getting more degenerate, more slack, more shapeless, every day.

"If you don't like going about with me," I told Ann, "you can walk behind or on the other side of the street and watch me from there."

But this suggestion was badly received. The girl did not answer at all. The effect was quite that of a keeper in an asylum. I was upset, and after a little consideration I said that I should go to the seaside if she insisted.

2

But after all, we did not go to the sea, for suddenly Ann said that the sea might be bad for my heart; why should we not go instead to my house at Tolbrook, near Dartmoor. "It is nice and relaxing," the girl said.

This sudden and extraordinary change of plan seemed to me even more suspicious than the first suggestion.

Tolbrook had been let for years, and the question at the moment was whether to sell it for the price of the materials or to find another tenant stupid enough to take a place in such bad repair.

"Tolbrook won't suit you at all," I said to the girl, "and the worry of it has been the curse of my life. In the autumn it is a perfect hole, damp and drafty. Far better go to some seaside town, with concerts and hospitals and libraries for you, and central-heated rooms for me."

"I haven't seen Tolbrook since I was a small child, and I've always wanted to see it. There is a kind of staff, isn't there?"

"Yes, a caretaker and one or two maids. The gardener's wife will always help."

"Then let's try Tolbrook."

"I can't understand why you want to go to Tolbrook."

"It will give you an appetite perhaps."

"And take me farther away from Mrs. Jimson."

"Yes." The girl was not at all disconcerted. "And perhaps you won't worry about her so much."

"I don't worry about her, but about myself. She is happy wherever she is—she is saved. But I miss her very much. It is too easy to forget what people are in themselves when you can't be with them."

"Sara seems to have got a hold on you, uncle."

"She is a remarkable person."

"She rather affected the religious, didn't she?"

"No, you are quite wrong. She never affected anything, but she is deeply religious. She is one of those people to whom faith is so natural that they don't know how they have it. She has a living faith."

"She seems to have looted you pretty thoroughly."

I said nothing more. I looked at the girl's uncheerful pale face, so confident in its uncheerfulness, and thought, "I might as well talk about grace to a Choctaw Indian."

She drove me down next day in her own car. She drives fast and dangerously. Her driving terrified me and gave me a pain in my breast. But I thought perhaps she liked to frighten me and so I said nothing. I resigned myself, I relaxed to this pain and this old man's fear, and, what was strange, when we rushed into the narrow lanes of the West and I began to recognize a cottage here and an inn there, they seemed not only charming but new, like a foreign country recognized from photographs. I was not the exile returned for a brief sad visit but the visitor from another world.

Tolbrook Manor house has no beauties except two good rooms by the Adams brothers. Although it stands high, it has little view. It is an irregular house: a three-story block with one long east wing and on the west an absurd protrusion, one story high, ending in a dilapidated greenhouse. It has a two acre field in front of it and a farmyard behind. A small old topiary garden, called Jacobean, had been restored by one of the tenants. The crooked drive is more like a farm lane than a drive. Elms and oaks stand along it as if planted by chance in a hedge; here, three in a row, then a gap, then a clump, then two great elms so close together that one could not squeeze between them.

They talk of the deep country. In the early evening, as we drove through the lanes, I felt these words with a new force. The tall banks and hedges, the great trees in their autumn colors, seaweed green against the clear green sky, all gave me the sense of passing beneath enormous depths of silence and loneliness.

And when we were in sight of the old house, so hated and so loved, I found myself laughing. Its very chimneys, of all shapes and sizes, seemed comical to me. And its solitude, its remoteness from all rational beings, now gave me a lively pleasure. For I thought, "At least I'll get some peace here. I shan't have to feel every moment, as I used to, 'the next budget will take all this away,' or 'how senseless to spend all one's life in patching up these old walls.' "

"It's not much of a house," I said to Ann.

"How do you feel, uncle?" She had not even looked at the house, in which she had declared so great an interest.

"Very well."

"You are rather breathless. Is your chest all right?"

"I had a little pain just now."

In fact, I found myself so exhausted that Ann had to pull me out of the car. She gave me some of her bitter medicine and refused to let me go upstairs. She sent for an old carrying chair that my mother had used, and had me carried up to bed.

It would seem, therefore, that the girl did not drive at eighty miles an hour in order to kill me. Though I can't make out why she has chosen, in that case, to bring me to Tolbrook. Perhaps in order to get me away from the rest of the family. There is I know some anxiety about the future of the property. I have two nephews and a niece, all with equal claims. Perhaps Ann, having been almost unknown to me, now wishes to make up for lost time. I do not blame her. She has every right to her share of the booty.

3

I had been brought to my old room. Indeed, I had asked for it; a small room, once the sickroom on the nursery floor, with two round-topped windows looking out upon a great lime tree, and, to the left, the yards. And my feeling, as I was laid, already drowsy, in the iron servant's bed which had served us, as children, for measles, scarlet fever, so many illnesses, was one not of returning home but of discovery. "So this is what it was— this dismal little room, this lumpy mattress." Mattresses have improved in the last ten years. Everything had improved except people, manners, dress, etc.

"Good night, uncle," Ann said, "and if you want me, I'm on

the other side of that door," pointing at the door of the nurse's room between nursery and sickroom.

"I think Robert will want that room," I said. "It was his room before he went abroad."

"When is he coming?" And in the tone of the girl's voice I seemed to hear a particular interest.

Robert is my nephew, lately returned from South America. I dare say the family sent for him to prevent my marrying Sara Jimson. But Robert is an old friend of Sara's; she mothered him in his boyhood. He quite approved my intention.

Robert and Ann had met in my town lodgings. And they had not had much to say to each other. Robert, to my surprise, had been shy of his cousin; and Ann, who can spend a whole evening with her nose in a book, had been at a loss with a young man who had read nothing more recent than Dickens or perhaps Kipling.

But now it suddenly struck me that Ann's decision to come to Tolbrook had closely followed upon a telephone message to me from Robert, asking if he might visit Tolbrook before his departure.

"You like Robert," I said. And the girl answered me, in an indifferent voice, "I did rather fall for his nice eyes."

I was so startled by this news and the manner of its communication that I did not know what to say. But at last I ventured to hint that Robert was not a literary or artistic person. "Neither does he care for classical music. Nor, if you'll excuse me, girls in spectacles."

Ann was silent, and I saw that she did not wish to pursue the subject. To my relief. For I felt that I had discharged my responsibility.

And before I was aware of it, the girl had left the room. She is, I must admit, very quick and neat in her movements. A trait she inherits from her father, my eldest brother Edward. But one that commends her to me more, no doubt, than to a boy like Robert.

Now that I begin to get used to this girl, I see that she is like Edward in many ways, even in looks. Her plainness is merely a veil drawn over Edward's handsomeness. You can see his features beneath. Her eyes are not blue like his, but smoke gray; that is, a shaded blue. Her nose is not fine but flattened and broad, like Edward's delicate beak pressed down and coarsened. Her hair is a dark yellow, old straw to Edward's bright new straw. She has what Edward had, the look of breeding; but subdued, as breeding should be. Put one of the Velasquez infantas into round spectacles and send her to a medical school, and you would have Ann. Even to the melancholy, the look of a doomed race, lonely and burdened. But all these girls nowadays, after their first twenties, have that look. Sad and responsible.

When I see Ann, daughter of that gay, that brilliant Edward, going about as if her life were finished, I want to stick pins in her. But what can I do? No one could plant happiness in a soul that rejects all faith.

4

I slept deeply, my first good sleep for months, and when I waked, early as usual, a short inquiry revealed that I was still in good health and excellent spirits. Neither Tolbrook nor Ann had upset me. On the contrary, I was excited by the thought of exploring the old house, after so many years. I opened all doors to these memories, from which, in my late mental anxiety, I had fled, and at once my whole body like Tolbrook itself was full of strange quick sensations. My veins seemed to rustle with mice, and my brain, like Tolbrook's roof, let in daylight at a thousand crevices.

It was a breezy morning, and every knock of the blind on the window ledge brought something fresh and gay and austere into my spirit. A sensation from the past, which I could not place. Why so gay, and why so austere? I opened my eyes and looked toward the window. The curtains were some light cotton stuff, spotted with small flowers, and the old yellow blinds behind them were transparent.

As the blind flapped, the curtains bellowed into the room, and cold drafts struck my cheek. I could not resist those beckoning curtains, the fresh chill of the breeze. I got up and went to the window. With precautions, not to attract my nurse's attention, I released the spring of the blind and let it roll itself up.

A pale green sky, as brilliant and cold as sea water in winter sunshine, stood before me, infinitely high. The top twigs of a great lime outside the nursery windows, swayed gently and threw off another few leaves. They were almost bare already.

I stood and wondered at myself. "You old fool, you'll catch cold." But my excitement increased. I seemed to be expecting something.

"Of course," I said, "I am simply a child again. This expectation is the feeling of getting up in the morning. I am getting well after some illness and waiting to join the others in the nursery."

I went down the passage into the old day nursery, next beyond the nurse's room, where Ann had chosen to sleep.

The room had been used by the tenants for a maid's dormitory. There were two beds in it. But the old table, cut by knives and burnt by hot smoothing irons, stained with ink and paint, stood uncovered between the windows; and over the mantelpiece hung the old steel engraving of Raphael's Dresden madonna. I stood waiting and listening.

Ann, who must have the ears of a roe, came suddenly into the room. She never runs, but for all her smallness she moves fast and smoothly. She said in her professional severe voice, "What are you doing, uncle? You'll catch your death."

5

It was true that I was in pajamas, but I had not meant to go out of my room. I said that I had thought to hear voices in the nursery.

"Voices," she said, and blushed. She always colors when she thinks me strange or mad. She tied up my pajamas, which were falling down, and said: "You mustn't go about like that— I don't mind, but the maids might, and you know we had trouble in town."

Ann, whose education is like a set of boxes, all neatly arranged in a filing cabinet, has put me in a box labeled "Exhibitionist."

It is, I gather, one of her Viennese or German boxes, which she brought back from her medical studies abroad. Next year there will be a new set of boxes, and poor Ann's will be out of date and useless.

But Edward's daughter ought to have more sense than to put people into paper boxes, and if I like to startle her sometimes, it is for her own good.

"Now back to bed," she said, trying to lead me out of the room. "Or you won't be allowed up to dinner."

"It was my own voice," I said, "as a child, and your father Edward's and my brother Bill's and my sister Lucy's."

"You are dreaming, uncle."

"No, they were here—this was our nursery, you know."

She decided to change the subject. "I wouldn't choose a room facing east for children."

"We got the morning sun here. That's what I remember; and running out of bed straight into the sunlight. My dear child, you must allow me to wait here a little longer in case the others want me."

Again she looked sharply at me to see if I were playing some trick on her. And of course my words were half-joking. I thought, "She hasn't got a box for this emergency." I said then, downwards and sideways, as if speaking to a child at my elbow, "Lucy, you called me—have you heard that Tolbrook is being sold, to be pulled down? I am escaping at last from my prison."

Lucy had been my dearest friend in life; dearer than any friend. And as I pretended to listen, I was startled to find that I was holding my breath.

Now, I do not believe in ghosts. They are, I believe, uncanonical. It was, I consider, merely the name Lucy, uttered aloud in the old nursery, which had a certain effect upon my nerves and threw me into confusion. Certainly my pulse raced, my ears drummed, and my head sang. I felt very queer indeed. And then all at once, something happened which caused me a severe shock; much more than I had bargained for. The voice of Lucy spoke to me. But not from a child's level. It was into my ear, and a phrase that I did not invent: "To be a pilgrim."

The voice was not that of Lucy as a child, shrill and always full of passion, excitement; but of the young woman Lucy, at twenty or so, a girl I had forgotten. It was gay and coquettish. And the words had actually been spoken in that room by that young woman, long vanished even in Lucy's lifetime. It was a phrase private to us two, for a private reason. Sometimes a joke and sometimes serious. I had written it, as a boy of fifteen, on the flyleaf of my confirmation prayer book, under my mother's inscription. I had read it there ten thousand times since, and sung it, from the well-known hymn, but I had not understood it for many years.

I was so taken aback that I did not know where I was until I found Ann helping me back into bed. She was reproaching me, in her patient and bored manner, and saying that if she would stand nonsense, my heart would not.

I murmured my apologies, for I did not want to lose my discovery. A real discovery is not a thought; it is an experience, which is easily interrupted and lost. "Yes," I thought, "that was the clue to Lucy, to my father, to Sara Jimson; it is the clue to all that English genius which bore them and cherished them, clever and simple. Did not my father say of Tolbrook which he loved so much, 'Not a bad billet,' or 'Not a bad camp?' And Sara. Was not her view of life as 'places,' as 'situations' the very thought of the wanderer and the very strength of her soul? She put down no roots into the ground; she belonged with the spirit; her goods and possessions were all in her own heart and mind, her skill and courage."

And is not that the clue to my own failure in life? Possessions have been my curse. I ought to have been a wanderer, too, a free soul. Yes, I was quite right to break off from this place. Although I have loved it, I can never have peace till I leave it.

As for my age, did not Caxton begin to learn Greek at sixty in order to translate books for his Westminster press? Even doctors prescribe a change of scene for the sick body and mind. As if the very mold of man was that of the Arab, the wanderer. "Yes, I must go," I thought. "I must move on—I must be free."

6

Robert came today, as always unannounced, and as usual at an awkward moment. I was holding a conference with the garden boy among the trees near the main gate when Robert strolled in. He saw me before I saw him.

Now my business was private. The truth was that since my illness I have had a mysterious difficulty in getting cash. And what is a man without cash? His self-respect, his faith oozes out at the bottom of his empty pockets. But when I have asked for a checkbook, Ann has forgotten to order it. I wrote for one and it didn't arrive. So yesterday I made up a bearer check with a postal stamp, and sent it by the garden boy to Exeter. Not Queensport, which is full of family spies. I told the boy to get silver. I have always liked some silver by me. And he had brought me, to my great delight, twenty-four half-crowns, which he had barely transferred into my pockets when Robert's voice sounded at my shoulder. Between the doubt whether he had seen anything suspicious and delight at seeing him, I was highly confused, and perhaps talked some nonsense.

As Lucy's son, Robert is very dear to my heart. That is to say, whenever I see him my feelings are thrown into an affectionate agitation which is almost painful.

"My dear Robert," I cried. "At last," and so on. I could hardly express my delight. And the weight of silver, combined with the weight of excitement, filled me with anxious foreboding.

"Oh yeah, it's good to be here again—and how are you, uncle?" Robert said, shaking my hand and taking me affectionately by the forearm. "O.K. I hope—you look just wonderful." He is, I think, fond of me, in his way. Though probably he would like me out of his way.

Robert has come back from his ten-year exile both better and worse. His manners have improved. He is more polite. But I feel that he is, in reality, more pigheaded than ever. Almost as pigheaded as his mother, in her worst days. You can see it in his face, even when he smiles.

I was shocked when I first saw Robert on his return. At twenty-eight, he looks like forty. His face is like a peasant's, thin and hard, colored liked the inside of an old rein and seamed as if by cuts.

But even when he does not smile, he has always a smiling air. He has the habitual expression that I saw once on the face of a successful young pugilist, at Paddington Station. He was going to some fight in the north, and he was surrounded by a group of admirers, who continually talked about his prowess, not to him but across him, reminding each other of his feats and illustrating his blows; as, I am told, the courtiers of some barbarous chief flatter him, not directly but to each other, surrounding him with a glory which seems to him, since he contributes nothing to its production, like the natural and proper atmosphere of royalty.

Robert has the little smile of that scarred young boxer, at once melancholy and knowing; as if he said, "All the same, I do the fighting."

An obstinate smile, which alarms me. But I am resolved not to quarrel with Robert. And when now he remarked, in his usual way, that some of the trees in the drive were pretty rotten and ought to come down, I answered only, "They'll last my time at Tolbrook," and changed the subject.

It has been suggested to me, by my niece Blanche, that Robert would like to get hold of Tolbrook for his own purposes. No doubt. I understand that he has brought back nothing from his ten years' farming in Canada and South America. He lost his inheritance in bad speculations, and he has not stayed long enough in any job to save a new capital sum.

"Is old Jaffery still running the place?" he asked.

Jaffery is the estate agent in Queensport, and my local manager.

"Yes, yes, more or less," I said. "Did you know Ann was here?"

"Well, I knew she'd be with you. But I came to see you, uncle—and the old swamps and weeds that Jaffery calls a farm."

"Ann will be delighted to see you. She is really a good-natured girl, and clever, they say, at her doctoring."

"Well, uncle, I certainly found Ann an interesting girl to meet, but she didn't seem to take to me—she thought me a hick."

"Not at all—that's only her modern way," etc., and so on.

"Now there's a tree that ought to be felled. An ash. Get a good price for an ash."

"Yes, yes, but it's not your tree, Robert; that's my tree, or rather your Uncle Bill's tree—he planted it for the Jubilee of '87—excuse me, I think I see Ann now," and I hurried into the house. I had not seen Ann, but I perceived that Robert meant to worry me about the trees. A bad beginning.

Even as a boy Robert always tried to alter our arrangements at Tolbrook, which caused many disputes and much exasperation.

As soon as I had put my change in a safe place, I hastened to find Ann. "Robert has arrived. He walked from the village and his luggage is coming by the van. You must go and entertain him. Get up some beer."

"Whisky is what he likes—but I was just going into Queensport for shopping."

"You mustn't do that—you must go down to him and keep him amused—and tell him not to worry me about the trees and the farm, and so on. Tell him I can't stand it. What have you done with your face?" Ann always powdered too much. I had not meant to pester the girl about this idiosyncrasy. Girls resent such criticism. But now, seeing her with a dead-white face, lips painted blood color, and a pair of enormous black-rimmed spectacles, I suddenly found myself exasperated into speech. I could not bear to see the girl, who is, after all, Edward's daughter, making a repulsive spectacle of herself before young Robert.

"My face, uncle isn't it all right?"

"No, it is not—it looks like a chamber pot crudely daubed with raspberry jam. I cannot conceive how you can make such a fearful object of yourself. But excuse me," for I was horrified at my rudeness and lack of tact. "Of course I don't know anything about these modern fashions—I may be wrong," etc. I was afraid that I had hurt the poor creature. But she answered gravely that it was very kind of me. "I'll do what I can about the face," and she seemed to bear me no malice.

It is true that she did not make the slightest change in her make-up. Indeed, I thought at luncheon that she was powdered a little whiter and had made her lips a shade darker. But I may have been deceiving myself, because her spectacles also looked larger and blacker, and I can't believe that she went to the expense of new spectacles only to spite me, unless she had a blacker pair by her, ready for such an emergency. And I thought better of Ann after this incident. It is a merit perhaps, in these modern girls, that they are not, on the whole, so touchy as those of our generation. Though, of course, this virtue probably has it own defect, in a general coldness of disposition, and other faults of a graver nature.

7

When Ann came to put me to bed, take my pulse, mix me a draft, and so on, she began to ask me about Robert and his side of the family. "I was always told that Aunt Lucy was rather fierce."

"Fierce. At your age—no, six years younger—Lucy was one of the belles of the season—a charming girl. But she had a strong will. So has Robert. I suppose Robert has already been telling you that this place is badly run. Don't you listen to him. Robert is the kind of boy who never did, and never could, leave well alone."

"Is it true that Aunt Lucy ran away with a butcher?"

"Not at all. Brown was at one time a small farmer who may have killed his own beasts. But afterwards he was a preacher—a very good preacher."

"How typical of Robert to say that his father was a butcher."

"Quite so. It is typical of Robert. Though Robert was very fond of his mother. She died when he was twelve, but it was a fearful blow to him. I'm not surprised. She was a great woman. Or, I should say, she had the quality of greatness, like

Brown himself. He was perhaps a rough customer. But a touch of real greatness."

"I don't think I should have liked him very much."

"No, you would not have liked him. Neither did I. But perhaps we ought not to boast of that delicacy and refinement. Perhaps we don't like him because we are small people. Small people never like great people. Small people are people who follow the fashion and live like frogs in a ditch, croaking at each other. When a real man comes near, they are all silent. If baggy trousers come in, all the small people will get into baggy trousers like that old fool Jaffery, who looks like a dwarf with elephantiasis. And if painted faces and long bobs come in, then all the little girls paint their faces and wear long bobs, even if it makes them look like clowns with hunchbacks. The people of character stick to the shape and color given them by nature— to reason, and truth."

"Perhaps we have talked enough, uncle—if you talk too much you won't sleep."

"I don't mean to sleep."

But she took away the tray and I was glad. For I had been thinking of Lucy and Brown all the evening, and I wanted to be with them. I had not thought of Robert's father for years. But though I had called him great somewhat hastily, now I felt that I was right. He was a truly great man, who had failed to get worldly honors only because he did not seek them.

The proof was that only by thinking of the man I felt the excitement of his presence when, for the first time, I stood below him.

He was preaching on Tolbrook Green, from the tail of one of our own wagons, which apparently he had commandeered from our horseman by the right of a prophet.

His short squat figure stood black against the crimson sign of the Wilcher Arms, hanging behind him. Its gilt lettering, sparkling in the sun, made a kind of glory round his head and shoulders; the shoulders of a giant, or a dwarf; and the face of a prize fighter, pug nose, jutting brows, thick swollen lips, roaring over all the noise of bullocks and sheep.

> No foes shall stay his might,
> Though he with giants fight;
> He will make good his right
> To be a pilgrim.

At these words I felt my heart turn over, and I drove away as fast as I could. I had meant to claim the wagon. But I was afraid of Brown; I thought he could convert me, and I was enjoying life then as never before, in my first year at Oxford. Why was I afraid of Brown? I was a clever young man who was reading Kant. Brown had no arguments that did not fill me with contempt. But when he sang these verses from Bunyan, his favorite hymn and the battle cry of his ridiculous little sect, then something swelled in my heart as if it would choke me unless I, too, opened my own mouth and sang. I might have been a bell tuned to that note, and perhaps I was. For the Wilchers are as deep English as Bunyan himself. A Protestant people, with the revolution in their bones. Who said that?—Cromwell, Wycliffe, and Stiggins. Our grandfather was a Plymouth brother; he was converted by one of the Wallops, and there are Quakers, Shakers, fifth-monarchy men, even Anabaptists, on the maternal side. I did not know it then because I knew nothing and nobody real, only knowledge about things. I knew no living soul, not even Lucy, until I knew Sara, and found in her the key of my own soul. A key forged in English metal for an English lock. At that time my own English spirit, like Lucy's, was a mystery to me. I fled from Brown because I felt that if I did not run he would get me. I remember that when I reached the stable yard, in the dark, Lucy came out and called, "Is that you, Tommy, you're very late." I did not answer, but waited for a strapper to take the mare's head; and got down in silence. I did not quite know what had happened to me. But when I came into the lower passage by the yard door, under a lantern which always hung there, Lucy said in a startled voice, "What's wrong, Tommy; was Jinny too much for you?" Jinny was the mare. She took my arm and said, "You oughtn't to take Jinny—you're much too blind. Promise me you won't be dared by the others."

She knew I was afraid of betraying my real fear of horses.

"The Benjamites were having a meeting," I said, "and I had to turn back in Hog Lane. I think it must be a new preacher."

"Oh, yes, a man like a pug dog with shoulders like a fire screen. He makes a noise just like the bullocks."

"I don't think we can afford to laugh at the Benjamites, Lucy."

"Of course we can't," she said, taking off my box coat. "But I have to laugh in case they might catch me."

I turned to her in surprise. "Do you feel like that?"

"What?" she said laughing. "Have they converted you, too?"

"But you mustn't laugh. I'm not joking. I have had a very queer experience."

"My dear Tom," said Lucy, "we've all had that experience."

"You can't have felt what I've felt tonight."

Lucy smiled at me and took my arm. I had forgotten that. But now suddenly her arm glides into mine and I perceive how I loved Lucy then, with a love belonging only to that time, when we were both amusing ourselves with life. It was a love such as can exist only between brother and sister, who, because they are brother and sister, do not suffer the exasperation of the flesh. We never wished to play the martyr. We gave each other freedom to be in love with others, and even discussed our flirtations. Yet our tie was stronger than all. There was but one cause of bitterness between us, my jealousy of Edward. But that was not recognized; I did not allow myself to be jealous, and admired Edward quite as much as Lucy herself. I only did not like to see her run to him and throw her arms round his neck; to see her so deeply concerned in him that, when he was at home, she thought of no one else.

Luckily Edward was seldom at home, and so in those days I often had Lucy to myself, as on this evening, when she received me with that charming affection of which Lucy alone had the secret. Her very gesture of putting her hand in my arm threw a spell upon my spirit, so that I began to smile, without reason, and without any regard to the conversation.

Lucy smiled also at me, but she was not laughing at me as she did so often. "My dear Tom, you are blinder than I thought —you never seem to know anything that goes on. I have been converted by the Benjamites—really converted—at least three times. And the last time was only last year. Didn't you realize why I was nearly not presented?"

"I thought it was because father didn't want to open No. 15." This was our old London house, in Craven Gardens, shut up for years.

"No, it was because I didn't want to be presented or be brought out or to have a season—I wanted to go on the roads with Mr. Pugface and sing 'Come to Jesus' outside the pubs. Father and I had the most terrible row about it."

These words gave me a great comfort. Not because they answered Brown, but because Lucy's voice and smile carried me back into the world which made a joke of everything except friendship and amusement. "Yes," I said, "of course it's only tub thumping."

"Well," Lucy said, "we'll call it that or he'll get us. And I should hate to be a Benjamite."

Both of us were silent for a moment. And I felt as if some internal Brown were trying to pop out of a dark hole in my own mind.

Edward used to say that the effect of a Protestant education was to make people a little mad. "It throws upon everyone the responsibility for the whole world's sins, and it doesn't provide any escape—not even a confession box."

> Mad Englishmen. Why not? Whose Sunday bells
> Ring in raw beef and fifteen different hells.

8

Ann did not allow me to go to church on Sunday, but I had prayers in the dining room. And Robert did not come. I told him afterwards that he was no son of his father's to stay away from a Christian service on Sunday. He answered that he had meant to come "only I was having a look round Tenacre and forgot the time." And then he began to urge some changes in the fields at Tenacre, which is a detached part of our home farm, and also in the byres.

"You'll get it all back, uncle. Why, you've got ten cows, and you're buying milk."

"I really think, uncle, that some of the cows are not earning their keep," Ann said.

"I did not know," I said, "that you were an expert on farm management." For I have been astonished at her duplicity. During the last week she has been going about the fields and the yards with Robert, in mud and rain; and at table she talks about cows, crops, as if she had been brought up to be a farmer.

"I don't know anything," she answered me. "Robert is the expert."

"Expert in what?" I asked. "I think you are both experts in making fools of each other," and I took occasion to say, when I found the girl alone, that a farmer's wife in the remoter parts of the world had the hardest and roughest kind of work of any woman. It was work only for a peasant brought up to it.

"I wouldn't dream of marrying Robert," the girl said. "That would be quite fatal."

"I should think so indeed—but, of course, it's none of my business."

For I perceived very clearly that if I began to worry about a silly flirtation between two young people cut off from other amusements I should get no peace at Tolbrook—or anywhere else. It is such petty worries that have wrecked my whole life and prevented me from all achievement, all happiness; from men and from God.

"No, no, you old fool," I said to myself. "Let them alone—let them play. Let them make fools of themselves if they like. You can't stop them."

But at two in the morning I am brought up sitting in bed by a creak in the passage.

"That's not Robert going from Ann's room—he said good night at the door, two hours ago. But if it was, what does it matter to you. Go to sleep, you old fuss-pot. Or if you can't sleep, think of your death, and the judgment. Something that really matters."

But I can't go to sleep. I cover my head with the bedclothes, but still my ears strain, my heart beats; I catch myself holding my breath.

It is the misfortune of an old man that though he can put things out of his head he can't put them out of his feelings. Now, when my eyes and ears are failing, some deeper senses become every day more acute. And so I feel in these children, even while they are not in the room with me, something which makes me as uneasy as if I were full of jumping fleas.

Some secret excitement, some cunning passion, evil and treacherous, infects the whole house.

"You mustn't worry about us, uncle—I'm twenty-six, you know, and I've been responsible for myself since I was seventeen."

Ann said this to me today, apropos of nothing. It seems that she also has the family sensibilities. So much the worse for her.

"Responsible for yourself," I said. "But unfortunately you're my niece and Edward's daughter. No, it isn't matter of sentiment. How would you feel if someone stuck a knife in your leg? I suppose you would say that the leg could look after itself. As a scientist—"

Someone began whistling in the yard, and I knew by her face that it was Robert. I said, "Run along and play. God knows which of us is the madder."

9

When you are old, they throw "conservative" at you as a reproach. But I can remember very well when Robert himself, as a small child in this very house, would not go to bed without a certain lump of wood, the remains of a toy horse, in his arms. He loved his horse, and to protect that horse he would fight with his own mother, whom he also loved.

I remember a riot in our nursery when nurse attempted to abolish our silver bowls for earthenware, saying that the crockery was easier to clean. Dorothy, my youngest sister, who died a child, set up a yell as if she were being murdered, and Lucy flung her spoon on the floor.

I dare say Lucy was not more than six. And this is my earliest recollection of her fury in its true quality. But I knew even then that she was something more than a nursery rebel. She had the genius of a leader in revolt, full of malice as well as rage.

I saw the spoon go down, and heard it ring upon the floor,

with childish delight. But it was with more than childish delight that I watched Lucy, when the nursemaid stooped to pick up the spoon, deliberately and skillfully pour the bowl of scalding bread and milk over her hair and neck and then bonnet her with the bowl.

I felt then a devilish thrill, the thrill which, no doubt, has fixed that moment in my brain forever.

But Lucy, the rebel, began in revolution against the new. She did not think that all change was progress. She discriminated, even at six. She knew the value of order, of a routine, even in our rebellious nursery. I dare say nature had taught her that it is precisely the stormiest spirit which needs, upon its rough journey, some rule of the sea and road. "The love of routine," a scientific friend said to me once, "is nothing to be ashamed of. It is only the love of knowing how to do things which Nature plants in every child, kitten, and puppy."

As I stand here at the door of the nursery staircase, collecting my strength for the climb, I hear Lucy's voice screaming to me furiously, "Tom-my, Tom-my. Aren't you ready?" She is disgusted by my irresponsible conduct. She darts round the corner, a rosy child in a white fur tippet and a blue coat. She seizes my hand, jerks it violently, and yells, "No, he isn't ready —and his face is *still* dirty. Oh, you are a nuisance."

The jerk still jerks me now. But apparently it did not cause me any distress, for I remember nothing else until I am walking along the drive, through red mud, with my hand firmly locked in Lucy's. I wear a long yellow coat with large buttons and a round hat. Edward in a bowler and a smart overcoat, Bill in a cape, swaggering his broad shoulders, walk in front. Edward I think is even carrying a walking stick. My father, in a flat-topped felt hat and my mother, in a tight-waisted sealskin and little round ermine hat, are already fifty yards down the drive. My father holds himself very upright but rolls a little on his short thick legs. He is still a soldier in his back, but his legs are growing farmerish. My mother glides in her long skirt, which seems to hide a machine designed to carry smoothly forward the molded body in its tight jacket.

Lucy is still abusing me. She shakes my hand up and down, and I hear the words, "stupid, naughty, a perfect nuisance to everybody."

My attachment to Lucy was a country legend. I see myself joined to her as if by a string—a small ugly child with a round red face, a snub nose, black hair growing out of his round head in tufts, like that of an old-fashioned clown, and iron spectacles. I am always running at her heels, clasping at her hand; or anxiously hunting for her, with the anguish and despair of a lost dog. I cannot be happy without her.

But to her frequent abuse I pay no attention whatever. I am pushing my new boots into the soft bright mud, and I am full of a deep content, which is a child's happiness. This content is made up of several different parts in which Lucy's hand, the boots, the hat, the mud, the familiar ceremony of going to church, and the prospect of spotted dog for Sunday dinner all have place. My enjoyment of the moment, impressed upon my memory only by Lucy's violence, is so profound that even now it gives me a sense of peculiar happiness. For though I have no happiness now, except in memory, it says to me, "Happiness is possible to man among the things he loves and knows." And it comes apparently from the touch, from contact, from a presence in the air. I was happy with Lucy because all about was a familiar world, not especially friendly to me, but understood.

An old house like this is charged with history, which reveals to man his own soul. But I can't expect a boy like Robert to understand that.

1 0

"What you have to remember," I said to Ann, "is that Robert has a devil, an obstinate, destructive devil. Eight years ago he wanted to pull down half this house and make farm buildings of it. And when I wouldn't let him, he threw up a good job and went to Canada."

"Robert isn't spiteful. That's his great charm."

"I don't know what he is, but he has a devil. He wants his own way, and often it is the wrong way. He's like his mother."

Ann seemed to reflect, but I don't suppose she is capable of reflection at this moment. She goes about the house with the face of a sleepwalker. She said to me, "Why were you sitting here? Isn't it rather late for you?"

I had been sitting in the old high-backed nursery chair which I had discovered that morning in the back kitchen passage. It had been our nurse's chair and also our ship, our castle, our throne, and pulpit.

But I didn't want to talk to Ann about chairs private to myself. And I got up and went with her.

"Why did you leave us alone in the dining room, uncle?"

"So that you could make eyes at each other if you liked," and so on and so forth, etc. "I'm not going to chaperon you. I don't believe in chaperons, whatever you may think. I'm not so hidebound. I've been a Liberal all my life, as you well know. I was one of the strongest supporters of the emancipation of women," etc., and so on, while she was leading me up to bed. "I believe in progress, but progress upwards."

She was perfectly grave, but I could see that she was laughing at me, and this made my head swim. But I said to myself, "Serve you right, you old fool, if you drop down dead. Don't you know how to mind your business yet? And what if Robert does go to her room? Does that prove that he goes to bed with her? What do you know about this new world of morals, or immorals, which has floated out of the German boxes, like the ghost dancers of the high moor, who, they say, come smoking out of the earth on mid-winter night, to prance and jibber round the standing stones of phallic cults older than the human brain?"

11

And when she had put me to bed, with her usual expertness, she said in her mild and inquiring manner, "I thought, uncle, you were fond of Aunt Lucy."

"Of course I was fond of her. She was my sister. What's that got to do with it? That didn't prevent her from having a devil. And it won't prevent Robert from breaking your heart," and so on. A fit of temper which cost me a sleepless night.

But Ann, of course, only looked more grave, and laughed the more inside. She is as full of laugh as any bride in the first week of her honeymoon. "But, of course," I said, "you don't believe in the devil. Though, God knows, I should have thought there was plenty of his work to be seen at the present day—are you going to let that boy spend half the night in your room again?"

"Certainly not, uncle, I want to go to sleep. And you ought to sleep." And she wished me good night and went out, quite delighted with the whole world. You could tell it by the way she moved her legs. Going to the devil as fast as she could fly. And never believing that such a thing existed as the will to evil, to cruelty, to humiliation, to lust for the spite of lust; to treachery for the pleasure of destroying faith; to malice for the delight of stabbing innocence in the back. A devil now gathering power every day, while he quietly undermines the walls of freedom, the order of our peace.

I never hated anyone as I could hate Lucy; and I was right to hate her. For what I loathed in her was the devil. That destroyer, when you see him face to face, is always terrifying and hateful.

My battles with Lucy were a family joke, and even I could not understand why I fought her; why once, at six years old, I tried to kill her. Indeed, I often tried to kill her. But the reason was that she made me murderous with her devil.

"What an extraordinary boy you are, Tommy." Her voice flies at me out of the dark like a snake out of ambush. Devil's words. For Lucy did not believe them; she meant them to stab me, to destroy my faith in myself, and to increase her own importance.

"Let me alone, Lucy," I say.

"Well, I'm only being nice."

We are in the nursery and Lucy is holding my hand. But already I feel from the hand a kind of electricity which secretly alarms me. I want to be at peace, and to think out something which puzzles me.

A bright fire burns and snow is banked smoothly on the window sill. There is a sense of comfortable joy which belongs to all snowy days, when one is kept indoors and there will probably be muffins. But Edward, wearing an old alpaca coat of my father's, as Geneva gown, is preaching over the leather back of the old nursery chair. And I am perplexed by something queer in his voice and manner.

"I stand here as the heir of Wycliffe and Cromwell and Stiggins."

We were fond of preaching and funerals. Such games were probably traditional with us, like family prayers, and meetings. My father, as colonel of his regiment, had held prayer meetings for his officers during the Crimea. I was accustomed to play at church. But now I did not recognize the service. What are these Stiggins, mysterious word, pronounced in an unexpected tone? Suddenly I feel that I have lost all clue to what is happening. And now Edward, pulling a long and hideous face, lets out a nasal howl, quite senseless to me. I cry out in terror, and Lucy draws me aside, exclaims with a look of wonder, "What's wrong with him now—really, Tommy is the most extraordinary boy."

She pities me; or rather, she practices her pity on me. And since that, for a child of five or six, is consolation enough, I cling to her. Her rosy lovely face leans toward me, and I think she is going to kiss me and comfort me. But suddenly when her lips are within an inch of my cheek, she bursts into cries of laughter, and I see that all her front teeth are missing. Her look has changed in one second from impulsive affection to that of a little demon. She is delighting in Edward's blasphemy, with wicked joy.

My tears of fright change to yells of rage. I seize Lucy by the hair, she claws my face. The boys laugh. And my mother comes in hastily, but already with an anxious and despairing look.

My mother, gentle, witty, unable to hate, was helpless before brutality. I think she was perplexed by all her children except Edward.

"What is it?" she says to me. "What has happened? Don't shout so much, Tommy—I can't understand what you say."

How can I explain what Lucy has done since I have not the faintest notion of it myself? I do not know even what has happened to me, or why I am suffering from this agony of shock and rage.

"She laugh-ed," I shrieked. "She laugh-ed at me."

"Did you laugh at Tommy, Lucy?" my mother asks, patiently.

"I never did," Lucy shrieks. "He did it for nothing. The liar, the beast. I'll kill him."

"How can you say such things, Lucy? Let go of him at once."

"I won't. I hate you."

Nurse appears, a countrywoman, low built and broad. She

tears us apart with her powerful arms and says, "That's enough —I've had enough, thank you. The third time today, mam, and I couldn't say which was the worst. I was going to speak to the colonel as it was."

My mother protests. "Oh, I don't think you need do that, nurse. They're going to be good now."

My mother could not bear us to be whipped. Especially she was made miserable by the very idea of Lucy being whipped. In her own east country family of scholars and Quakers, the idea of beating any child, but especially a girl, would have seemed an outrage. Yet at one time she had forced herself to be present when Lucy was beaten, out of loyalty to her husband.

She gave up that duty only after Lucy herself, just about to be whipped, had screamed at her, "Go away, go away. What are you looking at? I hate you."

After that my mother had thought it better to stay away from our punishments. She intervened only to prevent them, when she could.

And even for that she had no gratitude from Lucy, who would say, "Mama leaves it all to Papa. But of course she's only a Bowyer," meaning that she didn't belong to the family. And even I could see that my father, by his abrupt decisions, at once dissolved our deadlocks; while our mother, with all her scrupulous anxiety to understand our troubles, was at a loss among the violence and confusion of nursery affairs.

But though she saved us perhaps from two-thirds of our just punishments, she could not abolish whipping altogether. Nurse and my father, and the fear of hell in combination, were too strong for her. So now she was driven from the field into her room, where, I dare say, she passed moments much worse than ours, while we were dragged still howling to my father's study. Nurse, gripping us one in each hand, would knock on the door with her elbow.

My father, as I remember him on these occasions, is sitting

at his enormous flat desk, before a heap of papers. He looks across them with an expression of resigned duty—the face of an old soldier in an orderly room. All his wrinkles seem to deepen and at the same time his lips compress themselves beneath his big white mustache, causing its drooping ends to move slightly outwards.

"What is it, nurse?"

Nurse pours out a long story about our crimes, fighting, swearing. We are brought round the desk and my father interrogates us.

"What is all this?" in a patient tone.

We begin together our incomprehensible stories. After five minutes, when everything has become still more obscure, my father says, "That's three times this week."

Our father never went into final causes. His idea of religion was that of Confucius, rules of conduct, carefully taught and justly administered. Prayers were at a fixed hour. And it was a crime to be late. All quarrels to be made up, and all repentances spoken, before the last prayer, at the bedside, on penalty of drumhead court-martial—that is, an immediate slap on the behind, so conveniently reached at that hour. And three complaints from nurse in one week meant a whipping.

"Three times—I shall have to whip you."

"Oh, please, Papa," we both begin to roar. This is almost as much routine as the other. And Lucy shouts, "I won't be whipped, I won't."

"It's no good saying that, Lucy," my father says with mild surprise and impatience. "You know very well that three time means a whipping. If you don't want to be whipped, you must be a better girl. Give me the stick, nurse."

Nurse brings him a short piece of cane which he uses for riding and folds her arms. She always stayed to see us whipped and used to apologize to my father, between the blows, "I'm sorry, really, to put you to so much trouble, sir."

She sympathized with my father's feelings in these trials; she would also exclaim at Lucy's rage, "Tch-tch—there you are, sir, her temper is a cross to us all."

Lucy, before a beating, would always scream, "I won't, I won't, I hate you." But while she was being beaten, she didn't utter a sound. Indeed, I think she gripped her teeth and held her breath from the first blow, and at the last, she would fly out of the room so that no one, especially not my father, should see her cry.

My father beat according to the merits of the case. Three or four light strokes for quarreling or fighting but more severely for lying, stealing, or other moral offenses.

I used to roar through the punishment, but only my mother pitied me. And I dare say I roared the louder to obtain that pity, and consolation in her sitting room.

1 2

That room was forbidden to us by my father, who understood my mother's need of a refuge from her family. It had for this reason a powerful attraction for us. It seemed to me, with its austere neatness, its hangings in white and brown, the most delightful room in the world. It had a quality that I can only describe as blessed.

My mother asked us there only one at a time, making it our refuge. For I have no doubt she could not have allowed herself a privilege; unless she had made it also a privilege for others. Even Lucy, tempted by sweets and a large book of Crimean battle pictures, would sometimes accept an invitation to spend an hour in its quietness. I went whenever I could contrive it, especially in winter, when I could take the armchair, in brown velvet with brass nails, before the bright grate, in polished brass with a fender before it of semicircular brass walls, like the golden bib worn by certain ancient prophets. In all this brass the fire sparkled at me, with a wonderful gaiety of intimacy. It was, for the moment, my own fire.

I, with my special book, some volume of engravings only allowed to me in that room, or on Sundays, would feel such intense delight that often I could not read. I would fidget, scratch myself, look about me, suck acid drops. I would think, "Aren't I a lucky boy?" or "I wish it was further off from teatime."

I would spring up to stroke my mother's cat, Gray. Gray avoided us children in the house, but in that room she accepted us as visitors. And we would stroke her in a special manner and even with a special expression, anxious and attentive like that of rustics who finger the curtains of a palace. We felt that she was a special cat, quite different from the kitchen and yard cats, which we chased over walls, scratched with sticks, or stroked with a violence which caused them to give at the hocks and switch their tails, unable to make up their minds whether they were enjoying a pleasure or a torture.

The presence of Gray, calm and trusting, was another sign of my privilege, and an additional pleasure. I seemed in that room to be existing within my mother's being, an essential quality, indescribable to me then and not easy to describe now; something that was more grace than happiness, more beauty than joy, more patience than rest, a dignity without pride, a peace both withdrawn and sensitive; but for me, as a child, beauty, grace, and distinction. Even young children understand and love distinction of the soul, because it speaks from mind to mind and gives them confidence in the world.

Yet in that retired and peaceful place for some reason I always got into my worst mischief. I spilled the flowers, broke the vases. One Sunday afternoon I managed to set the rug on fire. And I still remember my mother's face when she came in, to see on the carpet a spreading stain of red ink from a bottle which she herself had never seen before. As if by a supernatural power of mischief, I had caused it to fall from the air. It was, in fact, from one of the servant's rooms, and I myself had no idea why, in a fit of the fidgets, I had brought it down in order to give Garibaldi's heroes, in one of my father's books, real red shirts.

My mother's expression of wonder was mixed with resigned amusement. She translated my own feeling into speech. "The wonderful ink," she said, "how did it get there?" And if it had not been my father's book I had damaged, I should probably have escaped even without a scolding.

I stand in my mother's room now. It is a small room opening out of the big state bedroom on the second floor. It is the only room in the house which remains as it was. I stipulated that it should be left untouched.

I believe my tenants showed it off as a Victorian relic. But to me it is a holy place. In this cold morning light I look at its faded hangings, its worn carpet with the sense which only the old can know, of a debt that was never acknowledged and can never be paid, not only to my mother, but to a whole generation. Of storied richness which can return to the spirit only in the form of the things it touched and loved.

13

But of course small-minded people hate what is rich to the mind. They hate the past, not because it is old, but because it might give them something new, something unexpected, and disturb their complacent littleness.

Jaffery, my agent in Queensport, came to see me today. I had written to him about an alteration in my will. For I felt I ought to make some special provision for Ann. And suddenly he proposed that I should allow him to advance Robert three hundred pounds for improvements to the farm and repairs in the house.

"Nephew Brown is a real go-getter," he says to me in his disgusting lingo. "And a good head, too."

"Robert has been to you, has he? I haven't heard anything about it."

"Just met by chance in Queensport. The two young things." And the old fool nearly winked at me. "Nice couple they make—and we had a chat. Very striking the way that boy has got round the place in a fortnight."

Jaffery is older than I am, but he affects the young man, wears a light suit and probably a body belt. I have even seen him in an open-necked shirt, without a tie, a ridiculous object, like a beadle in fancy dress. He does not understand that an old man belongs to his own age and should not ape the dress and manners of another, where he appears like a foreigner. In foreign places, a visitor who tries to seem like a native only makes himself despised.

Jaffery has an expression of absurd self-confidence on his old red face, wrinkled like a fried tomato. He speaks to me as to an invalid, gazing with discreet but sharp curiosity, as if asking, "Is he really as mad as they say? Did he burn his house down? Does he want to marry his cook?"

"Since we are leaving the place, it doesn't seem worth while to spend money on it," I say to him.

"It'll pay you, pay you," Jaffery says, with the brisk air of imitation youth. "All the time. Get it back three times over. A little cleaning up on a place like this is like a coat of paint on an old car—puts up the price at once—yes, and cropping and stocking—nothing looks worse than empty fields full of thistles—people say they're derelict, derelict."

"My nephew wants to make a lot of changes."

"No, no, not at all. Put in a new bathroom. Plow up Tenacre

perhaps—quite time—take down a few old trees—dangerous. Clear the ditches and drains. Get a few beasts in."

"I'll think about it."

"No time to waste if you're going to do anything with the farm next year—ought to be at it now, now."

I am silent. He gives me a cunning glance and says, "Shall I tell him to leave the house alone, and not to touch anything near the house? Then you won't see any difference, not a thing."

Jaffery is the kind of man who, at seventy, has never known a true attachment, a real loyalty, who would sell his dearest friend for a few pounds.

"I don't suppose," he says, "that you have been up to Tenacre for twenty years"; his impudent glance means—"and you will never see it again."

"It's a pretty part, near the moor. And always more valuable for its beauty than its crop. Poor land." But seeing that he is thinking me merely obstinate and obstructive, I add, "I shouldn't let that stand in the way if we had the money."

"Then that's all right. The money will be in the bank this week."

A trick. A plot between Jaffery, Robert and Ann. And I had given myself into the hands of the Philistines by my own dishonesty of mind. Proof again that hypocrisy, even in an old fool, is the worst of folly.

"You have been very smart, Jaffery," I said, "but I'm not dead yet, and Robert need not think so," etc., etc. "Perhaps after all I shall decide to get rid of the place. It's always been a curse to me."

I thought that Jaffery would not like losing the agency. But he only smiled. Whether in cunning or senile imbecility, I could not discern.

But suddenly I remarked to him, "You know, Jaffery, I often think it would be a good thing if this place were burnt down, like the London house. It would save me from being driven distracted by all you people who keep on pestering me about a lot of damned old chairs and tables and cows, which are, after all, not very important in comparison with a man's immortal soul," and so on. Very dangerous kind of talk from a man under suspicion of being a little cracked, to a man like Jaffery, who thinks that everyone who does not love money and property above everything in the world is certainly cracked. Highly dangerous, but extremely effective. Jaffery's smile soon faded away. He began to look queer. His cunning eyes lost their assurance, and looked like all such eyes when they encounter something a little unexpected, completely imbecile.

And when I began to shout that I knew all about his plots with Robert and Ann, to put me out of the way and get hold of my property, he was fairly beaten. He jumped up. Ann came quickly in with a look which meant, "There; he is insane after all, what a bore." And Jaffery retreated at full speed. But I could tell by the way that he moved his turkey's neck that he was frightened. Which gave me some satisfaction. And it might give me some more, if they lock me up. Who can tell?

14

I frightened Jaffery, but I gave myself a heart attack which kept me in bed two days. I told Ann Tolbrook would kill me, and I was right. I have never had peace or comfort in this house. I have been too fond of it. To love anything or anybody is dangerous; but especially to love things. When Lucy took my books or broke my toys, I tried to kill her. And when Edward mocked at anything I was used to, anything I loved, I hated him. All children hate and fear mockery. For it is aimed at the very soul of love, which is always a serious passion.

Ten years ago I would have told you that my childhood was

peaceful and happy. At that time, a very unhappy time in my life, I often took refuge in the idea of my happy childhood. But an old man's memories, like his bones, grow sharp with age and show their true shapes. The peace of the nursery, like all my peace, dissolves like the illusions of my flesh.

Now I see our childhood like the life of little foxes, wild cats, hares, does, in their savage and enchanted world. They are surrounded by marvels and enormous terrors. Their eyes and ears, their secret senses, quiver to impulses unfelt even by the vixen and the doe. They dart into the earth at a stroke of fancy which, to their mother, is beyond even explanation, since she herself has lost the idea of it. They rush at each other with bared teeth; they sulk; they starve themselves; they accept; they embrace the fate of the outcast, all in the same unreflective dream.

> Children forget their wrongs; a happy set
> Were we; or if we weren't, children forget.

I thought this couplet in Edward's first book of epigrams a typical piece of his cynicism; but now I see it's truth. The secret of happiness, of life, is to forget the past, to look forward, to move on. The sooner I can leave Tolbrook the better, even for an asylum.

1 5

I open my eyes, but it is still dark. There is silence throughout the house, but it is like a threat. It says to me, "The plot is made—there is still time to escape." I could get up now, dress and slip away. I know every back lane for fifteen miles, for I always preferred their quietness to the main roads. I could be at Queensport in time for the seven-ten to Paddington. But where then? My family would simply hunt me down and have me locked up in an asylum.

The only person in the world who can save me is Sara Jimson. I must wait for her, and keep myself sane for her. In less than thirteen months she will be free, and then she will set me free. Married to Sara, I can snap my fingers at the family, because she will testify for me.

No doubt they will fight. They hate and fear Sara. And nothing I could do or say would make them understand how much I owe her. All of them, including, I suppose, Ann, accept the vulgar story that I was a wicked old bachelor who lived with his cook-housekeeper. They see Sara as a fat red-faced cook of forty-six. And they believe that this cook, a cunning and insinuating countrywoman, who had deceived two men before, swindled me and robbed me, and so enslaved me, by her sensual arts and smooth tongue, that I promised to marry her. They flatter themselves that by employing a detective they stopped Sara's wicked plot, found her out in her robberies, and sent her to prison for eighteen months. This is what they believe, and the facts are true; yet they believe a lie. The truth is that when Sara came to me I was a lost soul. I had become so overborne by petty worries, small anxieties that I was like a man lost in a cave of bats. I wandered in despair among senseless noises and foulness, not knowing where I was or how I had got there. I loathed myself and all my actions; life itself. My faith was as dead as my heart; what is faith but the belief that in life there is something worth doing, and the feeling of it?

And it is true that I lived with Sara more than ten years; and that Sara welcomed the arrangement; perhaps encouraged me to make it.

But what is forgotten is that Sara was a living woman, with a certain character; she saved my soul alive. What I had heard of her, when Jaffery hired her, was this, "A widow who has been living with a painter and when he deserted her tried to pass off bad checks. A very doubtful character, but clean, good-tempered, and a good cook. She'll take a small wage and you can always lock up your checkbook."

And I admit that when I first saw Sara at Tolbrook I felt some curiosity and a certain attraction. Every fallen woman attracts men. And Sara, at forty-six, was still a handsome woman, fresh, buxom, with fine eyes and beautiful teeth. Her broad nose, that mark of the sensual temperament, did not displease me. I was not then fifty, and my blood still had its fevers. I thought of Sara, "A nice armful, and no doubt ready for anything." Then when I saw her excellent old-fashioned manners, I thought, "And she would know how to keep her place. I could have her without upsetting the household," etc.

I will admit that in that time of my darkness Sara, at first sight, made my fingers, etc., tingle to pinch her, and so on. But I did not do so, in case, after all, Sara should misunderstand me and give notice, and leave me once more without a housekeeper, when I was almost driven mad with domestic responsibilities.

So I had time to notice how well Sara looked after both my houses, how she cleaned and polished them, and how she cherished them and loved them. Yes, she loved them. I remember still how, within a week of my coming to Tolbrook, she showed me a table in the salon which had been scratched by some careless maid with a gritty duster.

"It ought to be seen to, sir. It's such a lovely polish," and she passed her hand over its surface in a caress.

"Yes, yes, Mrs. Jimson," I said, "that's a very fine table—a very remarkable table. It's been in this room more than a century, since it was made for this very room," and I saw again, I rejoiced in the beauty and distinction of the old table. Sara had renewed to me that joy which is the life of faith. And so in those days, while she cleaned the house and set it to rights, after many years of lazy and careless maids, I came again to feel its value, to enjoy its grace.

No doubt any connoisseur, any collector, some bored old millionaire when he shows off his treasures, is seeking in your praise the resurrection and the life. But he could not get the kind of appreciation which Sara gave, out of her generous and lavish heart, to my old things at Tolbrook and Craven Gardens. She delighted in caring for them as if they had been her own.

We say of such a one as Sara "a good servant," and think no more of it. But how strange and mysterious is that power, in one owning nothing of her own, to cherish the things belonging to another.

16

This week next year, when Sara comes out of jail, shall see my salvation. As I wrote to her last night, "With you I can make a new life, and unless life be made, it is no life. For we are the children of creation, and we cannot escape our fate, which is to live in creating and re-creating. We must renew ourselves or die; we must work even at our joys or they will become burdens; we must make new worlds about us for the old does not last," etc. "Those who cling to this world must be dragged backwards into the womb which is also a grave.

"We are the pilgrims who must sleep every night beneath a new sky, for either we go forward to the new camp or the whirling earth carries us backwards to one behind. There is no choice but to move, forwards or backwards. Forward to the clean hut, or backward to the old camp, fouled every day by the passers," etc.

Or did I write this? It is always difficult for me to remember whether I have actually written to Sara or only composed a letter in my head. This letter has a quality which in old days I would not have approved. I would not have cared to write in so romantic and poetical a vein; it would have seemed to me dangerously open to misconception and perhaps a little inclined to encourage rebellious and destructive ideas.

But Sara has that quality that I can say what I like to her. Possibly she does not always listen or understand; but neither will she think evil.

17

I am now quite used to hearing Robert and Ann muttering together behind the door at two in the morning, and I say, "What matter—I'm off." As for the house, my poor Tolbrook, it is infected with lies and deceit from top to bottom. The cousins are in a state of infatuation, to use a polite word for that excitement. And their every emotion is simply a new lie. Ann, who hates dirt and dirty work with her whole soul, goes with Robert to clean out the byres; and all her gestures, her way of pushing a squeegee, as if she wanted to make a hole in the floor, are imitated from Robert. Even her face is like Robert's, when she thrusts up her jaw and says, "It's not good enough." And in the evening Robert listens to Beethoven on Ann's gramophone with a rapt expression, and says, "Very nice—I like that—it's quite a tune."

"It's funny," I say to him, "that you've become so musical. You used not to know 'Home Sweet Home' from 'God Save the King.' And your mother was the same."

Then he looks at me and Ann looks at me as if I had said something quite beside the point, and Robert says, "Well, uncle, I like this man Beethoven."

"Music often comes out in people quite late in life," Ann says, with a solemn face. And the same night they go to bed together. That, of course, *is* the point.

18

It is extremely dangerous for anyone to get the feeling that somebody is plotting against him, even when the plot is quite obvious and the plotters conspire in the next room. It is a feeling that drives men mad. It leads to hallucinations. And I have always been subject to anxiety.

To Edward, Bill, and Lucy my anxiety was a joke. They laughed at my caution, at my hiding my pennies under the chest of drawers, and down the crack in this very floor, in the bell trap, where for years afterwards, and even now, I like to keep a little change in silver. They would tell how I never entered a strange house without peeping through the doors and hesitating on the threshold. They forget how often my pennies had been borrowed by Lucy, who, like many people with small value for money, never remembered her debts; and that the tins full of peas, etc., placed by Bill on tops of doors to fall on Edward or Lucy, usually fell on me. Bill's shout of laughter which always burst out too soon, a fraction of a second before his practical jokes took effect, warned the quick Edward and Lucy, but never me.

When I awoke last night, at half-past four, and found myself alone at Tolbrook, I felt that I should have to get up and knock my head against the wall.

The wind was blowing gusts so hard that the dead leaves were carried through the top of my open window and slid down the inside of the blind with a noise like a cat's claws. After each gust, doors rattled and windows murmured. And I distinctly heard Ann's voice say something about the time. "Perhaps," I thought, "she is talking to herself; and in any case, I'm not going to expose myself to ridicule by any further interference with these children. They have their own ideas about things."

But a moment later, to my own surprise, I found myself in

the passage, at the door of the nurse's room. I opened it quietly and turned on the light. There were two heads on the pillows of the narrow bed, and before I had time to turn off the light and withdraw, I saw Ann start up.

I felt a great relief. "That settles it," I thought, as I went back to bed. "Now I need not bother my head about the girl. I shall get some peace at last."

But when Ann, at eight, came in to take my pulse, etc., I could not even look at her.

She undid my jacket buttons, put the thermometer under my arm, and said in a tone of amusement, "I told Robert he was making too much noise."

I could not answer her. I thought, "Whether I am an old fool or not, this house has changed. It is not for me any longer. I shall gladly leave it."

"I'm afraid you are rather shocked at me," Ann said then in a tone like a little girl who has been stealing the jam. But she was laughing at me.

But I was determined not to be angry with her. I said, "I suppose it is a modern custom. Do you go to bed with any man who offers?"

"No, uncle, truly, it is the first time."

"The first—don't you think it's a pity—and that perhaps some of these old conventions about chastity and so on were designed for the happiness and protection of women?"

Stooping for the thermometer, she murmured something about science, which did really shock me. "And what will your mechanical devices do for you if Robert walks off and leaves you?"

"We've discussed that," Ann said. "We're not going to be too tragic."

"How do you know what you're going to be?" And as the girl, full of that elation which she can't hide, went out of the room, humming to herself, I thought with pity and astonishment, "She doesn't even know she's a woman—that's something these chromium-plated schools don't put into their test tubes."

1 9

Now that I cannot bear the sight of Ann, she is beginning to run after me. She kisses me good morning and shakes up my pillows. She takes me for walks and tries to amuse what she thinks are my prejudices. She has brought up the old nursery chair from the back passage to the day nursery, and cleared out the beds, saying, "We'll make it as it used to be, and have it for our own sitting room." But all this affection does not deceive me. It is one more symptom of her infatuation.

> She's true; for proof, today she cuts me dead,
> And headlong throws herself at Papa's head.

And when she tries to make me talk about her father and Lucy and all those relations whom she has forgotten for twenty years, and disgraced, I keep silence, unless she drives me out of all patience.

"After all," she will say in a humble and apologetic tone, "Daddy was not so strict." And when I do not answer, she hints, "And you told me yourself that Sara Jimson was as good as a wife to you. Of course, I'm not blaming you, uncle—quite the other way."

"Then you ought to—I did wrong—a terrible sin. It is fearful to think of my responsibility."

"But, uncle, you shouldn't let that get on your mind. You were so strictly brought up. And that always produces a reaction."

I do not answer this folly.

"Is it true, uncle, that grandfather used to beat Aunt Lucy for not being able to repeat the sermon?"

Now of all things I find most unbearable the worst is the injustice of one generation to another. Say that it is inevitable. Say that children cannot know what they are talking about until they have lived their lives. Meanness is still atrocious. At Ann's words, I felt such a pang in my breast as if I might die, and I shouted at her, "You have no right to say such things even if you believe them. My father was the noblest and kindest of men, and your Aunt Lucy worshipped him."

"But, uncle, I didn't mean—"

"And what is this fearful rubbish about natural reactions— heaven knows life is bad enough without having such imbecilities rammed down my ears."

"Uncle, uncle, you mustn't be so excited." The girl was alarmed. She bent over me, holding my hand. "Please, yes, I understand exactly."

"You understand nothing—nothing at all, and I don't think you ever will. Unless Robert gives you a baby and I hope he does. That will teach you a lesson," etc., etc. I was rude and quite ashamed of myself. But I could not stop because the girl was so upset. Upset people always make me upset. It's catching, especially between the sexes. "And as for our childhood, what does it matter whether we were smacked or not? So long as we knew we deserved it, and nobody thought we were martyrs or heroes or any more of your textbook rubbish. Our childhood was good for us; whatever it would have been for you ninnies in your fog of flummery, it was perfect for us—I could not wish anything better for any child. We knew where we were and what we had to do, and what was right and wrong—all the things you silly geese have muddled up till you don't know your etc. from an etc." A very coarse comparison, such as never before, except when I was in the army, had I used to a woman, much less a niece, however disreputable. It shocked me so much that I was left speechless. Ann ran off and I thought that she was disgusted with me. But she returned at once with some medicine which she made me drink. And then sent for Robert and had me conveyed back to bed. They appeared to be deeply concerned for me. But that is a bad sign. Young people in the first rage of animal passion are always very humane; at least, in each other's presence. All the beggars in town know that, and thrust out their hats before every bride and bridegroom, into every hansom turning out of Leicester Square.

2 0

It is no good talking to children like Ann because they have no education; only information. They are like wastepaper baskets full of exploded newspapers and fraudulent handbills. They don't mind going to bed with each other, or talking nonsense, or making a pigsty of the world. But they are shocked that a bad child should be punished with the rod.

It would be useless to tell Ann that I and Lucy, whom she pities for our hard upbringing, probably had greater happiness in our childhood than she and Robert, in the same nursery, twenty years afterwards.

They cannot understand the virtue of law, of discipline, which is to give that only peace which man can enjoy in this turmoil of a world: peace in his own soul.

The first time I was beaten by my father I was surprised immediately after the punishment, and when I had barely dried my tears, to meet him in the passage and hear him say, "Run along and fetch my hat, Tommy, there's a good boy."

I was startled by this easy greeting after what had seemed to me a tragic and even awful episode. There was, I suppose, something of my mother in my constitution. I was even offended, and I did not run for the hat; I walked. But on the way, hearing my father call, "Can't you find it?" I broke into a run, and bringing the hat, I shouted all the way in my natural voice, "I've got it, Papa—I've got it."

"Thank you, my dear," he said in his usual placid tone. "Tell your mother I'll be a little late for luncheon." And he went out to get on his cob and ride off somewhere across the fields. He left me in so easy a mood that when I discovered that my bruises were still burning, and I tried to recall some appropriate bitterness, I could not do so. I found myself simply a little boy with several new and useless weals on his behind. I made no profit at all out of my sufferings.

Certainly my father's battles with Lucy were often terrible to them both. For though my father by sticking to the regulations erected between himself and conscience a wall of irresponsibility, yet he loved Lucy, and hated to punish her, and feared the consequences. My father and Lucy were devoted to each other. My father would boast that Lucy could climb and ride and shoot better than any of us. He delighted in her beauty and cleverness. And to Lucy he was the bravest and noblest man in the world. She loved to talk about his Crimean battles, and all the history she ever learned was army history, and especially the Crimean campaign. And in the village she visibly delighted in saying to the villagers who complained of any misfortune, "I'll tell the colonel about it." As if her father could have brought back a bad daughter from London, or cured a stroke. But to Lucy an opportunity of saying "the colonel" and enjoying in that word her father's glory was not to be missed.

Yet her rage against him when she had to be beaten was fearful to see. And under his code she had often to be beaten. She was a demon of mischief.

I'll never forget the day when she challenged him, with all the cunning of her malice, her devil, to a final battle of wills, counting, as she always did, in all her battles, upon the very virtues of the enemy to help her to destroy him and triumph over him. She said in effect, "You can kill me, if you dare; or own that you don't dare, and submit to me."

She was twelve, but already a woman in all the essentials of her craft and strategy. Lucy had not then gone to school. She had governesses, with whom she battled day and night. At this time the governess was a certain Miss C., a fair, pretty mild creature, who was some distant relation of my mother's family. She was musical and clever and, I think, rather High Church.

Lucy despised her and made her life a misery. Miss C. would weep and complain to my father, who would then punish Lucy, not very severely, I think, until Lucy performed, on the same day, two crimes which deserved the severest punishment. The first was an act combining blasphemy with indecency. One of little Miss C.'s holy pictures was found in the chamber pot. So Lucy had expressed her contempt of High-Church religion and Miss C. in one act, probably the impulse of a moment.

But the two offenses together formed, in my father's code, a very serious crime.

My father, as I say, loved Lucy with pride as well as joy, that love which is the noblest, as well as the most demanding, form of the passion. He wanted for her every virtue of body and spirit. His code for women was high; not higher than for men, but different. He looked in women, above all, for the peculiar grace which inspired all my mother's acts and moods; a grace of spirit as well as body; a charity of soul which affected even her carriage and her voice. Edward used to laugh at our mother for the way in which she would caress a handsome piece of china, a cup or a plate, with one finger, while she sat at table. But the gesture was a true expression of her character, full of a sympathy which belonged even to her senses, and extended to all things.

My father, unlike his daughter, could appreciate my mother's quality as well as Lucy's. His mind may have had an inflexible character, but his sympathies were pliant and comprehensive. He understood and valued my mother's peculiar sensibility and her gentleness of spirit, as well as Lucy's courage and passion. But coarseness and brutality in a woman was to him a sin against Nature, as well as his code. He thought of women as the guardians of a special virtue given them by God. If he had passed over Lucy's crime without the most determined punishment, he would have felt guilty before God, and even perhaps before some power more universal to his feeling: Nature. Lucy's crime was unnatural in a woman, and he beat her severely.

On the same evening Lucy did not appear at prayers, and a maid was sent to fetch her. It must have been on a Sunday when some of us had not gone to church, perhaps because my mother did not feel able to walk the two miles for a second time. For it was only on a Sunday at home that we had prayers before supper, and I remember that the sun was shining across the floor while we waited for Lucy.

I remember still my feeling of suspense at Lucy's absence from the chair beside me. I had already a warning, in my nerves, of the conflict.

Lucy returned a message that she wasn't coming to prayers; she would never again attend prayers or go to church. Miss C. went up to reason with her, and Lucy gave her reason, that she hated God, who was nothing but an old Jew.

My father then sent an ultimatum to which Lucy answered that she hoped she would go to hell. The devil was a devil, but at least he was better than God. And she did not care for anybody or for anything they said to her.

This, of course, was a direct challenge to my father, and all of us understood very well that he would not care to beat her twice in the same day; that such a beating might have serious consequences for Lucy and therefore for him and for all of us; and that Lucy was counting precisely on that point to defeat him.

At that age, I could not describe Lucy's mind, or the complicated politics of our nursery, but I knew them both very well. I can't say whether I was more horrified by the crisis which Lucy had deliberately provoked or interested, from a professional point of view, by her moves in the game. My father meanwhile continued with prayers; but I thought he was slower than usual to find them, and my mother remained on her knees for some time after the last amen. Possibly she was praying for Lucy and her husband; and also, I think, she was trying to appeal to him, by this indirect method. But he probably did not notice this maneuver. He had no subtlety. He was putting away his books, again, I thought, with unusual deliberation. His eyebrows, already white, were arched, so that his blue eyes seemed more prominent than usual at the bottom of their round hollows. This gave him an expression of surprise, mild alarm, and resignation, as if he had just discovered a large plum stone halfway down his gullet.

He seemed to stoop a little as he went out, as if to push his way through some opposing obstacle. A minute later we heard him going upstairs to his study on the second floor. Then Lucy's voice suddenly screamed out, "I won't," and the door closed.

I ran out of the house—why, I did not know. I felt oppressed, and I was panting as if I wanted to cry. I flew from the house as if it might fall on me. But a moment later I was standing at the bottom of the nursery back stairs, straining my ears for the sounds of the beating, or a cry. I must have been eleven years old, but I was still attached to Lucy in the manner of a small child, almost as if I had been part of her. I could not separate myself from her; I wanted to know what was happening to her, as if it were to myself. And my sensation, while I stood, hardly breathing, was not of sympathy but only tension and fear, as if I myself were to be beaten. My teeth clenched together, my lips opened. Suddenly, without warning Lucy came rushing round the corner of the stairs, her hair flying, her face, usually rosy, as white as a candle, her eyes wide open and staring in front of her like a lunatic, her lips parted as if to scream, and yet uttering no sound. She came at such a speed I wondered she did not fall, and what especially frightened me was the movement of her hands. They were tearing at her clothes as if to pull them off, and yet she seemed unconscious of the rapid frantic plucking. She darted straight out from the passage door, called the children's door, at the bottom of the stairs. Some inspiration or mere attractive impulse made me run after her, and I saw her rushing across the rose garden toward a coppice where we often played and where, too, we sailed our boats in a shallow branch of the lake, a muddy pond. As I came through to the coppice, I heard Lucy cry out, a high screech such as I could not have believed could come from any child's throat, and I ran faster, now terrified, breaking through the scrub. I saw her close to me, and she was now tearing her clothes, not tearing them off, but tearing them away from her body. She was already half-naked, and I could see the blue and red marks of the stick on her thighs. I shouted after her, "Lucy, Lucy," and she stopped for a moment and half-turned, still tearing. I caught her arm and said, "Did it hurt badly, darling?" But she screamed, "No, he couldn't hurt me—never, never—he couldn't if he tried." Then suddenly she rushed into the pond and disappeared.

Neither she nor I could swim. Only my brother Bill of our family ever learned to swim, and that was at Woolwich for his army training. My father could not swim and never went near the sea if he could help it. Our holidays were spent at home or, for a treat, on visits to some big town, for the theaters and museums.

Luckily, when I screamed, a gardener was near, and he came running. He was in his Sunday clothes, a dark-blue suit and a bowler hat; I suppose he had been strolling in the garden, as gardeners do on Sundays, to admire his own work. He stood for a moment on the edge of the water, glanced down at his clothes, as if asking himself what would happen to his best suit, then handed me his bowler, turned up his coat collar and waded into the muddy water up to his neck. Apparently he couldn't swim any more than I. But he ducked down his head, where I pointed, felt about till he found Lucy, and carried her out. She was not even unconscious, and as soon as she had choked up the muddy water from her mouth, she began to kick and struggle, saying, "He can't hurt me—never—never."

The gardener, puzzled, I suppose, by this violence in a girl who had always appeared so sensible and dignified, set her down with a respectful gesture. She ran at once back into the pond, but the man caught her before she was beyond her knees.

The fact that Lucy had been beaten twice in the same day became a family joke, which Lucy herself repeated with pride. This humorous memory was all I had kept, and in its light I had recollected the event. But now my heart contracts with pain, as it did when, as a child, I stood and watched Lucy struggling in the hands of the puzzled young gardener, and heard her scream, "I will—I will." That is, she would kill herself.

I stood helpless and accepting my fate. I had even then, I suppose, a lack of resource. I couldn't imagine any way of preventing Lucy from doing what she liked. I felt as if suspended in air; but in some unfamiliar empty space, empty of Lucy.

Now Edward and Bill came strolling toward us. They had been to evening church. The evening sun was slanting from the side under the branches of the trees and penetrated even the Gothic arches of the hedge timber.

Edward and Bill both wore bowlers, but Bill, as usual,

looked as if his clothes belonged to someone else. He grew
more square and bulky every year. Edward, on the other hand,
was slim and smart; even at sixteen he was already dandified.

"Hullo, hullo," Bill shouted, staring at us with round eyes,
"what's up, I say—has Lu been getting it again—poor old Lu."
He approached with a sympathetic expression, but stopped
suddenly when Lucy shrieked at him, "Go away, you fool, or
I'll kill you."

"Well," said Bill indignantly, "what have *I* done—that's stupid. All right then, I *will* go away." He was aggrieved. Bill was
an affectionate friendly soul. He had all Edward's good temper
and my strong affections. But he was easily hurt in his feelings.
He walked backwards, rounding his eyes and saying, "All
right, all right then—if I'm not wanted."

Edward meanwhile asked the gardener, who was still, with
some difficulty, holding Lucy by one arm, what had happened,
and heard my hasty explanation. Lucy muttered savagely,
"And you're worse, you conceited beast—go away—what's it
got to do with you? Shut up." With another scream, "Shut up."

Edward, having gathered all the facts available, smiled
down at Lucy with a condescending air and said, "You do look
a comic cut."

To my surprise Lucy stopped screaming and answered, "I
don't care what you say or Papa does."

"A very good thing," Edward said. "It's quite time you
stopped making eyes at Papa—you're getting too old."

Then he strolled away, and to our surprise Lucy ran after
him, and a moment later we saw them talking together.
Edward was trying to wave Lucy away from his new suit
while, dripping with mud and slime, she threatened to take his
arm. He walked backwards fanning her off with his stick. At
last she ran into the house, and in her way of running we could
see that she was in good normal spirits.

In fact, she never showed the smallest ill effects of this

nervous crisis, and almost at once began to turn it into a joke and a kind of glory, both for herself and my father. "When Papa beat me twice in the same day."

But none of us was encouraged to self-pity, the disease of the egotist. Religion was not our comforter. How could we be comforted by hell-fire and individual responsibility for sin? We lived in the law, the ark of freedom. A ship well founded, well braced to carry us over the most frightful rocks, and quicksands. And on those nursery decks we knew where we were; we were as careless and lively as all sailors under discipline.

2 1

In the morning I lie half-asleep, and the pillow frill tickles my neck. Lucy returns to me, no longer a savage with gap teeth, wriggling with mocking laughter or shrieking in rage; she is a warm presence. We are lying in the dark, in this old iron bed where I lie now, and she is saying, "They said I mustn't see you, so I just came. How are you feeling, darling?"

I have been ill with measles or chicken pox, and isolated from the rest.

"Haven't you been awfully lonely?" Lucy asks, and I answer, sleepily, "No, but I wish I had a book. I'm not allowed to read."

"I'll bring you a book this minute—which would you like?"

She brings a book and lights a candle to read to me. I do not remember what she reads, but only the sight of her sitting up beside me in bed, in a flannel nightdress, with her dark hair falling in two tails down her shoulders. She is absorbed in her task, which she finds hard. She has to spell out all the long words. Lucy could not read so well as myself.

But now I was stirred by a feeling that I cannot describe. I lie beside Lucy with my arm round her waist and not listening to the book, but watching her and saying within myself, "This is Lucy—isn't she nice. Isn't she being awfully kind to me. I love her awfully—I can't say how I love her."

But suddenly my love seemed to expand and burst into a fit of laughter. I began to squeeze Lucy and punch my head into her chest, and all the time I am laughing. The shy serious little boy, making his anxious and careful way through a world full of older brothers and sisters all capable at any moment of the most unpredictable fits of violence or mockery, gives place, like a magic-lantern slide, to a stranger. I see the serious face split by an enormous demoniac grin; the tufted hair speaks no longer of disability and ugliness, but of an unruly coarseness. I am full of violence and rebellion. I don't care for anybody; and when Lucy says indignantly, "Am I reading to you, or aren't I?" I answer with another senseless laugh and another butt.

This is the very phrase and manner of our old nurse who used to protest, "Am I dressing you, or aren't I?"

Lucy is acting nurse, and because of my exuberance I am not afraid to tell her so. "You think you're like nurse. But you're not a bit. Nurse reads like this." I try to take the book from her and, amidst bursts of senseless laughter, cackle like a hen.

Lucy, astonished by my behavior, lets go of the book, gazes at me, and says at last in a dreamy wondering voice, "The boy really is quite ma-ad."

Suddenly she throws back the bedclothes and tries to jump out of bed. Nurse's step is heard in the corridor. But I still hold on to her, laughing; and when she tries to drag herself away, I grab at her nightdress.

"Let go, you id-i-ot," she whispers, spitting out the sylla-bles like a furious cat. Her anger pleases me in my lawless mood, and gives me even now a shock of pleasure as if once more I come close to Lucy. She jerks at my grip.

Nurse's voice says outside, "All right, Miss Lucy—I hear you—your Papa shall know about this."

I know that I shall not be whipped while I am ill, so I do not care. I am still grinning, full of delight, of the mysterious senseless glory which issues in my laughter and violence. I take a firmer hold, and Lucy, beside herself, beats at my face with the book. Suddenly the flannel gives way and leaves a huge rag in my hand. Lucy, half-naked, flies to the door just as it is opened by nurse; she is carried off at once to be smacked, and I am severely lectured. But I am still full of that glory. I don't care for anybody or anything.

22

The very idea of Lucy goes to my head. "There aren't such people nowadays," I think. "And what if she had a devil? She did God's work. Out of devilry. She made something good and noble of her life. As I might have done if I had not been turned into a family drudge. If I had been allowed to go upon the Lord's work."

"And what," I ask, "are you doing now, you old fool, what would Lucy think of your worries?"—and such is Lucy's power that twelve years after her death she can raise me up out of the darkness. For the last two days I have been a new man. I laugh at the children. "For heaven's sake," I say to Ann, "what's wrong with you this morning, you look as if you had taken a horse pill. But I suppose Robert has been showing a little independence. I'm not surprised if you go about with that face."

For I notice that Robert, as one might have expected, had suddenly grown tired of classical music. He sucks his pipe in the evenings and reads the paper. Also all day the cousins are disputing. That is, their good nature has deserted them, and they have reverted to their own natures, which are highly different. But I must not say "I told you so."

Robert came in yesterday morning, picked up Ann's book from the arm of her chair, and said, "What's this you're reading?" And she answered, "Something you wouldn't care for—it's quite good."

"You mean it's muck."

And then they quarreled for the whole of lunchtime about books. For Robert, as one might expect in Lucy's son, had always a great disgust for what he called modern muck.

And Ann, in her quiet voice, which she never raised even in anger, answered that Robert, no doubt, wanted a censorship to suppress everything modern or civilized.

"I'm just a rube, I only know what stinks," Robert said. "I wouldn't know about this civilization."

"How could you if you're intolerant, and you like being intolerant. Civilization is tolerance—and that's why I hate all this censorship."

"You're telling me."

"Oh, no, Robert, no one could tell you anything."

"They could tell me muck wasn't muck, but my nose would still be a born fool."

"Not only your nose."

The cousins speak so mildly to each other that it is hard to tell when they are disputing. But I could see now that Ann was trying to hurt Robert, and that he was annoying her by his indifference. As Lucy used to enrage me.

"Don't you mind what Robert says to you," I told her. "Laugh at him."

But the girl looked as if she were going to cry, an expression which enraged me in one so young. "It's your own fault," I said, "if Robert has the power to make you unhappy. Robert is like your Aunt Lucy. He will be cruel if you don't stand up to him. Lucy hated weakness in anybody or anything. She was so strong herself."

"Yes, that's what I hate in Robert."

"Then you are very foolish. Robert has very good qualities—above all, he enjoys life. Like Lucy. And he makes other people enjoy it. Lucy had a hard life, goodness knows, but she never moaned or groaned," etc.

But the next day it was the same. Robert disappeared to fetch some new engine that he had hired, and Ann walked about the house with a miserable face. "Good gracious," I said to her, when we met for our morning walk, "no wonder Robert runs away from you—it's a sin for a girl of your age to be so wretched, even if it is your own fault."

The day was cold and the sky broken with cloud. A sharp wind was driving from the sea and whirling the red oak leaves from the drive right over the roofs, so that, looking up, one saw them floating among the white gulls like small agitated birds. It was so strong that Ann had been in two minds whether I was to be allowed a morning walk, even so far as the lodge.

"Robert is like his mother," I said, "he can't bear to see people moping and mumping about nothing. Of course, I don't mean to say that what you have done is nothing—leaving out any moral question, it is a piece of disastrous folly. But, relatively speaking, when you consider the state of the world and all the misery and folly going on everywhere, it is nothing much. And as for my walk, if you don't come, I am going by myself, and I don't care if I drop dead. At least I shall die with my boots on, as Lucy did."

Ann gave way then and put on her coat. But we had not gone ten yards before an enormous traction engine appeared in the drive and rolled toward the yard gate, where it stopped. I could see that it was making big holes in the gravel, but I thought, "Who cares? Holes can be filled in. I'll tell the garden boy to see to it." I could not help feeling how Lucy would have enjoyed such an engine. Its size and power made the weather seem exhilarating. And I said to Ann, "What on earth is Robert doing with that machine?"

"I don't know what Robert is doing—he doesn't tell me."

"Because you take no interest. Where is all your enthusiasm for farming?"

"I suppose he is going to break down something somewhere—that's what he really enjoys."

"Robert is a regular son of his mother—he's always full of energy." And I thought, "He is worth six of you, you poor thing. He may be obstinate and troublesome, but he knows what he wants, from girls to traction engines."

And going up to the yard gate, I called out, "Where did you get this new toy? Out of a circus—"

"Oh, yeah, uncle," he shouted down from the cab where he was standing with the driver and stoker, "that's it—out of the circus at Queensport. It was laid up for the winter."

I was astonished. For when I looked more attentively, I saw that the traction engine actually was from a circus. I could not help laughing at this surprise. "A circus engine at Tolbrook." Now when I stood close to it, I saw how big it was; as big as a cottage. Its wheels, covered with gilding, were eight feet in diameter. Its cab was so high above my head that Robert might have been in the howdah of an elephant. Its funnel was blowing black smoke full of smuts as big as flies into the second-story windows. But I thought, "Who cares, curtains will wash, and they are only new curtains."

And as this great engine throbbed and jerked and rumbled with steam, making the ground shake and the windows rattle as if in a bombardment, one felt that majesty of power which had caused the maker and architect of the creature to decorate it in every part with painted giltwork and glittering brass. The great wheels were painted scarlet and green, and the hubcaps, as big as beer barrels, were sunflowers of gilt with silver petals. The rivets on the fender were golden roses, as big as bath buns, so bright that you could barely look at them. The pillars of the cab were twisted brass, like those of a little temple; and on the top of the funnel there was a brass crown with long spikes, such as befitted the king of the road.

And everywhere one perceived the delight of the maker in his creation, which is, precisely, the joy of the Lord; and I thought, "How Lucy loved a fair and the roundabouts. How she would have loved to see Robert up there, with his dirty face, so calmly smoking his pipe, in command of the monster."

"And what's this piece of nonsense?" I shouted. "What are you going to do with this plaything?"

The engine was making such a noise that I could not hear Robert's answer, but Ann said, "He's going to pull down some of your trees."

This alarmed me a little. And I waved my hat and umbrella at Robert to show that I must have an answer.

Then Robert bawled out something and Ann said in my ear, "He's going to Tenacre—shall I say he mustn't?"

"No, certainly not—I gave my word. Some of those trees at Tenacre must be rotten, and Robert is quite right to want to clear them out," and so on. And when they started to move the engine, I took off my hat to it and waved my umbrella to show that I thoroughly approved of his plan.

"You ought to encourage Robert," I said to Ann. "After all, they're not your trees. It wouldn't cost you anything to show sympathy with the boy—and if you want him to marry you, you can't afford to irritate him in trifles. Obstinate silliness is the one thing that never goes unpunished in this world."

"But he has married me, uncle, or I've married him."

I didn't believe her till I found, from Robert himself, that the couple had actually been married at Queensport registry office, nearly a week before.

I could not understand this marriage. Robert had had what he wanted of the girl. He knew she was useless as a wife—why then did he need to marry her? Unless, of course, in pursuit of some other purpose, such as a general plot, with Jaffery, to get control of Tolbrook.

"Why on earth," I asked him, "did you marry a girl like Ann, who will be perfectly useless to you?"

"Well, uncle, it was just an idea we thought up. We thought we'd see how it worked."

"And is Ann going to Brazil with you?"

"Why, uncle, we haven't talked over our plans, and we couldn't go yet awhile—she wouldn't leave her job till she's seen it through. So I've put it off for a bit—till spring, anyhow, and maybe harvest. I'd like to see my job through, too."

"Seen it through" was the only phrase that carried illumination. It meant, I suppose, that Ann was waiting until I died, and the context seemed to show that I was not expected to last beyond the spring, or, at worst, September.

23

But even if they are waiting till I die, and even if Jaffery has promised them Tolbrook, I cannot understand why a clever girl like Ann should throw herself away on a rough boy like Robert. "This marriage is a perfect puzzle to me," I told her. "Your reasons can't be moral reasons because apparently you have no moral scruples in such a case."

"I'm surprised, too."

"Is Robert in love with you?"

"Oh, no, I think he just lost his head."

She was knitting and reading, at the same time, in a chair by the parlor sofa. Her whole pose and expression, with her spectacles, her middle-aged gravity, were domestic, and afforded a strange contrast with the child's paint and powder, her peculiar attitude of mind.

"You'd better pretend to be in love then, if you want to be happy."

"Do you think we could be happy, Robert and me?"

"If not, why in heaven's name did you marry?"

"Well, uncle, Aunt Lucy wasn't happy with her butcher, but she fell for him."

"No, she did not fall for anybody. She would not even have understood that horrible phrase. She made her own life."

"Then why didn't she make it happy?"

"It was a happy life, though I suppose you can't imagine it—neither could I. But then I was a young fool myself at that time. I didn't know how to be happy."

"How is it done?"

"You must have an object in life—something big enough to make you forget yourself."

The girl went on knitting and reading her book under her knitting. She said at last, "But suppose you can't find one."

"There are plenty to be found—or there were plenty in my time, if you looked for them."

"Would you let me have that photograph of Aunt Lucy from downstairs?"

"Lucy's photograph won't do you much good"—and I was going to say that what she wanted was Lucy's spirit of life and joy, and confidence. But I stopped myself. For how was I going to bring to Ann even the idea of that spirit nourished in faith?

24

I let Ann have my own photograph of Lucy, from my mantel-piece. It is better than the one downstairs. And I don't like photographs. They are dangerous. They serve only to hide the real people from me. When I look at Lucy's picture, faded and pale, she disappears behind it. But if, when I lie in the dark, I only think the sound of her voice, she stands before me, warm, breathing; and always in some unexpected appearance, so that often I cry out in surprise, saying, "I had forgotten."

We are at a picnic on the moor. I cannot remember the year, but we are both grown up, and I see Lucy's green frock and the sky behind her head full of round clouds like new-washed sheep, pink and soft. She turns to me and I notice, as she laughs, that her mouth is slightly crooked. One corner, the left, is longer. I am so interested in this discovery that I don't hear what she is saying.

We are walking in the drive, under autumn trees, when she takes my arm and suddenly utters a coo-ee to Edward, far off at the house door. I remember a pang of indignation because I feel her woman's malice. She wants to feel my jealousy of Edward.

And on the fatal night when she ran away. It is after dinner, late in the evening. She has come suddenly to the nursery where I am pasting photographs into my album; and her smile makes me think she is up to some mischief. She has played some new trick on a neighbor or one of her lovers. And I catch that smile. It flies to my lips, out of her secret mood, before I know it is there.

She says, "Tommy, darling, will you do something for me? Go to father's room and get the key of the stable yard."

"What on earth for?—you don't want the trap at this time of the evening."

"Never mind. But if he catches you, say I want my bicycle to go to the vicarage."

"But where are you going, Lucy?"

She looks at me with that expression of an elder sister for a small boy who asks silly questions, and quotes our old catch-word "to be a pilgrim."

"Don't be silly, Lucy. If you don't tell me, I won't go for the key."

"Oh, please, darling." She takes me in her arms and pleads,

kissing me, with the gestures and tones of a loving compliant girl asking a favor. But on her lips the smile of the woman who knows her real power and could command if she chose. In spite of my real terror of having to tell a lie to my father, and perhaps losing his esteem, I go for the key.

In the same way she makes me help her to harness the mare. It is while I am holding up the shafts of the gig, for her to put Jinny in, that she answers my repeated questions. "I am going to be married."

"Don't be silly, Lucy. Tell me. Is it some joke with the A's?"

"No, it isn't a joke. I'm eloping."

"Not by yourself?"

"Yes, by myself. He said he would send for me when he wanted me, and I had a message tonight; half an hour ago, to be exact."

"But that's nonsense—no one can be married at ten o'clock at night."

"Oh, we shan't be married tonight, nor even tomorrow."

"When is it to be, the happy event?" I said, chaffing her.

"We must wait for the sign, the second sign—and the third sign. At the first sign we are pledged, at the second sign we shall be married."

"And what will happen at the third?"

"You're asking too many questions, Tommy—hold up the lanterns while I hook the trace."

"And who is it to be?"

"Brown, my dear, Puggy Brown." She laughs in my face with a triumphant air of mischief and joy. "Who else would want three signs before he married *me*?"

"What rubbish." But I feel a half-belief. I catch from her being, not from her words, a tremor of excitement and fear. I know she is at some crisis of her life.

I plead with her not to do anything hasty, to think before she commits herself, and so on. Using all those phrases which must be used on such an occasion because they alone express a plain meaning in plain words. But she smiles as if delighted by her plan, and answers, "No, I won't think any more. I don't need to think, thank goodness. You see, I've promised."

"But Lucy, you're not going on that—one of your whims. Who is it—it's not Captain Frank?"

"My dear Tommy, Captain Frank. I would rather run away with a cold mutton chop. Come now, be good and help me with Jinny."

It should have been a romantic scene and so I have thought it since. But now I know that it was not so. A clear dark sky, no cloud or wind; a warm night. Not a dog barks, and we can hear the maids rattling their everlasting cups in the kitchen. My senses will not rise to tragedy and separation in this quiet yard, among familiar things. And Lucy herself, standing so close that, by the light of the match with which I am about to light the gig lamps, her old tweed driving cape, with crossed bands over her breast, her smile, her look, the feather of her breath on the night air make elopement seem like family routine. She climbs into the gig with her usual agility, which, like an acrobat's, seems always to delight in itself, and calls to me, "Good night, Tommy. Don't look so stupid. And you'll find the gig at the Crown at Queensport. And if they ask you where I am, say that I'm off to sing for Jesus."

"But Lucy, for God's sake, be serious. This is some of your nonsense."

"Yes, it's some of my nonsense."

For of course I was quite right. Even Lucy knew it was some of her nonsense. To amuse herself or to shock us, or both at once.

"Then tell me the joke. I'll not say a word."

"I told you the joke, Tommy. Puggy Brown has called me, and I'm going to him."

"Just for fun—that's impossible."

"Not a bit. It's quite easy. Just look," laughing down at me as she drove off. And I never saw that Lucy again, the pretty lively young woman with the indescribable charm of her innocence. I had not appreciated her; and I did not understand her nonsense. For Lucy's nonsense was her own nonsense, and therefore it had courage and faith. It was set off by a devil's whim, but it flew straight forward, it broke a way through walls. And now I think, "How did Lucy know at twenty-one, even in her whims, what I don't know till now from all my books, that the way to a satisfying life, a good life, is through an act of faith and courage?"

But then, where was my faith? I was a child and my faith was a child's; it was my world and not my possession. And when my world shook in some earthquake, I, too, trembled.

I got up to steal down into Lucy's room, a great state room on the first floor. It is refurnished, but it still has the iron basket grate before which I sat with her on so many evenings and the view from the windows: the paddock, the green line of the ha-ha ditch, a corner of the lake, the woods beyond, and above them, the high moor.

She delighted in that view, the best from any room in the house. As her room was the most luxurious. No one appreciated comfort and luxury like Lucy. But she left them in a moment. Why? Not for love; not for charity. Not because her conscience troubled her. Not for the sacrifice. But for the adventure. Lucy was one of those whose faith is like a sword in their hands, to cut out their own destinies. That faith has come to me now. At least, I hope so.

"Who are you talking to, uncle?" I am sitting in Lucy's armchair looking at Ann in a blue dressing gown. The room is filled with a blue-gray light, as pale as her eyes. She seems to be only a little more solid than the light. She looks like a ghost these mornings with her gray-green face and transparent eyes. She is certainly ill, and I tell Robert that she ought to eat porridge and cream, and plenty of red meat. But he won't interfere. He does not perceive that, clever as she is, she is a fool in marriage.

"Was it Aunt Lucy? This was her room, wasn't it?" And when I do not answer, she says, "I suppose she felt it was religious duty to get married and give up her life for that brute."

Her voice is like a ghost's voice, talking from another world, fifty years away. I don't speak to her because she cannot understand me or the real solid world, where Lucy and I loved and fought.

She feels my arm and says, "You are quite frozen. Shall I bring you a rug if you don't like bed?"

I should like to tell the girl that I am sorry to see her so unhappy; but I am afraid that if I encourage her to talk, she will chatter about Lucy and Bill and Edward and drive me mad with her incomprehensions.

25

I did not yet believe that Lucy had run away from us until she was missed, the next morning, and I told my father, as a joke, that she had spoken of joining the Benjamites.

My father turned that dark purple of an old man who has had a shock, and said, "So that's the end of Lucy."

He sat down in the nearest chair, and I saw his hands and knees trembling. "I thought it was that."

"But you don't think she could really marry Brown?"

"Why not—why not—she won't turn back."

And instantly I saw that the marriage was possible. I said, "But she must be stopped—it can't be allowed."

"Nothing to be done," my father said. "He's caught her."

My mother, who blamed herself for Lucy's flight, as for all

our faults, tried to console us. "We oughtn't to grieve for Lucy. She has been called to a good work, God's work."

"God's work," my father would say, flushing more deeply. "Brown's work isn't God's work. It is devil's work."

My father made many and nice distinctions, not clear to me, between different sects of the Christian Church. To him the Church of England, the Presbyterian, and the Wesleyan stood apart as churches of the true God. After that came other branches of the Wesleyans, the Congregationalists, the Scots Free Church, and the Baptists. The Quakers stood in a separate place as innocent eccentrics; the Unitarians as vain and foolish word spinners, harmless only because of their poor grasp of final things. The other free sects, of all kinds, belonged to the devil. They were egotist, anti-Christ, and the worst of them was that of the Benjamites. And he could not console himself, like my mother, whose sensitive nature perhaps needed that defense, by saying that "God's will was not to be opposed, even by repining."

His strong courage penetrated to every part of his nature. Even if he had seen God's will in Lucy's flight, he would have suffered, because he had no idea of escape from suffering. His feelings could not deceive themselves or be deceived.

"We'll be lucky if we ever see her again," he said to me.

I felt now very angry with Lucy for inflicting so much misery on me and on her father; and also for some other crime, which I can only describe as giving trouble. Like all young men, I detested people who gave me trouble.

"I'll go and find her," I said. "I'll go to the police, if necessary."

It did not prove so hard as I had expected to trace Lucy. The Benjamites in the village promised to find out for me where Brown was, and after ten days' delay, while, I imagine, they were writing to him and getting his leave to give the information, they sent me an address near Birmingham. I set out at once, full of indignation and confidence. "She'll be sick of them by now," I said. "You know Lucy's whims, they don't last long."

But my father answered only, "Mind they don't catch you, that's all."

"Me?" I cried.

"Might catch anybody," the old man muttered. "Why not?"

"I thought you were against the Benjamites."

He shook his head. "They're very catching—they make it so easy."

Brown had left Birmingham. But I was directed to his next stopping place.

I had always imagined the Benjamites as passing from village to village, squalid in their lives but at least among the distinction and fresh beauty of country scenes. I found them now in the back street of a large industrial town, squalid beyond my imagination or experience. I saw this wretched place on a day of late autumn when, at Tolbrook, the eye was enriched at every glance by the beauty and majesty of oak, elm, and ash in the magnificence of their age. Here the narrow pavements flowed with a mud which seemed thick with a hundred years of foulness, the house fronts ran with a dark ooze, a sky like the arch of a sewer dripped the condensation of filth upon garbage buckets.

I knew London dirt, but I had seen it as the antique crust upon classical dignity or Gothic vigor. I had never before known a town in which the dirt clung to meanness even more disgusting than itself, where the larger buildings, with architectural pretensions, grew only more ugly with size, where the middle-size houses had the air of bankrupt brothels, and the back streets, like this one in which I sought Lucy, were like the corridors of a prison, a catacomb. In these fearful gullies a pale dwarfish people moved, through the slow rain, like prisoners condemned for life. I was a small man, but among them I felt like a giant among cripples.

Here I felt for the first time the presence of that devil of which my brother Edward had spoken in a speech bitterly attacked at that time. "If the devil is known by his work, then you can find hell all over England. Every great industrial town is a candidate for the honor, and improves its chances of election every year. The accepted plan is to place as many people as possible in the most hideous and wretched surroundings, and give them no food but adulterated rubbish and no pleasure but drinks. It is highly successful."

Edward's speeches had often startled us by their violence, but when I criticized them he would say, "The only question is, Tommy, do you want your throat cut neatly by a civilized reformer, or do you want to be hacked to death with rusty knives by maddened savages? I leave out the moral arguments because they are not convincing."

When Edward spoke so, he gave out a ruling thought of that time and of our class. Then much more than now, people feared revolution, but in secret, often so deep in their soul that their minds did not know it. For, in that time, the rich men were still boundless in wealth and arrogance; the poor were in misery; and neither saw any possibility of change without the overthrow of society. The Tories said, "Give the least concession, and they ask for more. Concessions were the fatal weakness which opened the way to the French Revolution"; and the Communists, the Socialists answered, "Nothing from the enemy but their blood."

I was one of those who supported Edward. "We have a magnificent opportunity," I said. And like other young men, I was impatient with the government for not immediately bringing in the new world. I was amazed at their blindness in not seeing the danger of revolution.

But in this midland town I was conscious for the first time of a deep anxiety, an oppression that became almost unbearable. As I knocked on the door of Lucy's lodging, I felt not only guilt but terror, as of the wrath to come.

It was as if I, personally, had raised this hell and peopled it with savages; and that, in justice, the savages would destroy all that I valued in the world.

26

The door, after long delay, was opened by a short plump girl with round, pale cheeks. Her eyes, too, were pale.

"Mr. Wilcher," she said to me at once.

"You come from Tolbrook?"

"I lived there for a while." She spoke in a calm and sad voice, but her eyes gazed at me with a peculiar boldness. This glance was a mark of the Benjamites. It meant, "You think me low and contemptible, but I know you are beneath contempt, one of the vilest of the vile, a dweller in the sties of the world." This look usually offended me, as a young man, conceited in his youth. But in these streets, before this house, I felt humble and apologetic.

"Miss Wilcher?" I asked.

"Sister Wilcher. She is here."

"May I see her?"

"That's for the master to say," and she shut the door in my face.

I rang again, but the door was not opened for several minutes. Then Brown himself stood before me. He was wearing his usual dress, long black frock coat, tight black trousers, white shirt, but neither collar nor tie. He said, "What do you want, young man?"

"I've come to see my sister, Mr. Brown, if you please."

"That depends on her. Perhaps she does not want to see you."

"I think she would like to see me."

"I will ask her."

But at the same moment the young plump girl returned and said, "She says, send him in."

Brown threw back the door and said, "Go in, young man, your sister is in the back kitchen." He laid a peculiar weight on the word "sister," as if to say that Lucy was now a sister in another and more religious sense.

I went through another passage into a kitchen smelling of dirt and soap. There in the middle of the floor I saw Lucy scrubbing. A stretch of wet tiles lay between us.

"Stop," she cried, sitting back on her heels. "Don't step on my floor."

She was laughing at my surprise. I had never seen her look more beautiful than in her apron of sacking, with the soapsuds running down her arms.

"When will you be finished, Lucy?"

"Not for a long time. I still have the passage and then all the potatoes for supper."

"Are you a kitchenmaid here?"

"Well, you know the rule."

"What rule?"

"The Benjamite's rule—work and obedience. And I was never taught to cook or dressmake. So I wash the floors."

Once more she began to scrub. The curls of her hair, lank with steam, clung to her forehead and cheeks. The veins of her pretty arms were swelled with hot water, and her nails were broken back to the quick. I felt pain and fear as I watched her toiling in that foul air, among mean streets and barbarous people.

"Did you run away from us to scrub floors?"

"Oh, no, Tommy, you know why I ran away—"

"Lucy, you don't really mean to marry that man."

"That is for God to say."

"You mean for him, Brown, to say. Do you know what he is with women, what they say about him in the village—he has a new woman every time he comes there."

"Now Tommy, that's enough. We'll never understand each other on that subject, and I'm too busy to argue."

But it seemed to me now that I understood very well. The idea of Lucy in the arms of Brown gave me horror, and in that horror was my understanding. The words came into my mind, "And she shall be offered for a sacrifice."

Lucy suddenly began to laugh at me. She got up, put a chair for me and a newspaper under my feet to keep them from the floor.

"You must stay with us, Tommy."

"What me—be a Benjamite?"

"I should like to see you happy."

I began to argue very reasonably about the wrongness of the Benjamites, pointing out the danger of a religion which appealed only to the feelings and the nerves. But Lucy continued to scrub; she said, "When shall I see you properly? I shall be busy till six getting tea, and then there is a meeting, and after that I must get supper, and then wash it up. And at ten I shall be sent to bed."

"Sent to bed?"

"Oh, yes, Puggy is very particular about bedtime—the night prayer is at a quarter to ten, and we must be in bed by the hour."

"When am I going to see you?"

"Come to the meeting at eight, and perhaps I shall see you for a little before supper."

I went to the meeting and found Brown at the corner of the street. He was speaking from a box to a small crowd of silent unhappy-looking people. The Benjamite traveling party, three young men and five women, including Lucy, stood behind the box against a wall of rusty iron. While Brown was speaking they listened, and often exclaimed, in their quiet voices, Hallelujah, or Amen. I saw Lucy utter such an ejaculation, and it gave me a sense of horror and disgust. When Brown knelt to pray, they all knelt down in the mud and raised their faces and their hands toward heaven, bowing up and down in the strange manner which he used. When he turned to them for a hymn, they sang without book or accompaniment, in loud but uneven voices.

After the hymn, or one verse of a hymn, Brown would speak again, usually about grace, or the hardness of heart which refuses it.

Grace was thus explained to me by an evangelist, an American, who made a fortune by conducting religious meetings. "Grace is a feeling inside you that God is there all the time, to help. So all you've got to do is tell these poor sinners that they've got the feeling, and they always believe it. Why, if you told them they'd got a pain, they'd soon find it for you, show you the exact place. So when you tell 'em they've got a feeling, they soon find one. And then you only got to tell 'em what it's saying to them. And they're yours."

"What do you tell them that it says?"

"That they got to stop worrying about themselves and their troubles and hearken to the voice of the Lord."

"And do they forget their domestic anxieties and responsibilities so easily?"

"They just do. Why, the most of men are just about halfmad with worrying. They're just delighted to hear there's anyone to tell 'em what to do."

"And what does the Lord, that is, what do you, tell them to do?"

"Young man, I tell 'em to do the Lord's work in love and charity."

"It is not always very easy to know what is the Lord's work."

"No, young man, it is not. They got to wrastle and pray for it. And they do wrastle—"

"So they're just where they were at the beginning."

"Not so, my young friend, for now they wrastle for the Lord, and so they get grace—that makes a difference, believe me."

But like a young man I had always an answer to one who would teach me. I quoted Edward to him.

> "Grace, Lord, I crave. Answer thy servant's question:
> Is this Thy grace I feel, or indigestion?"

Then the American evangelist looked at me and answered, "I pity you, young man, you are like the ass who was too clever to walk upon the beaten path."

"What happened to that ass?"

"He stuck among the thorns and no one listened to his bray. For he was a useless ass."

27

After the meeting I did indeed see Lucy, for five minutes. Another party of the Benjamites had come from a distance, to see the master, and she had to find lodgings for them and prepare a supper.

"But have you no rest?" I asked her.

She answered me laughing, "No, but I have the joy of the Lord."

And this phrase had so strong an effect upon me that for a moment I scarcely knew where I stood. I seemed to enter into the meaning of Lucy's life, and to understand her happiness; that it was a real, a lasting joy.

Lucy herself felt some change in me, for she suddenly laid her hand upon my arm and said in a tone more gentle than I had ever heard from her before, "Stay with me, Tom, and you will find the answer to everything."

"Is there an answer to everything?" I said. But I think there is no doubt that I should have been converted, if it had not been for an incident on the next day.

Lucy persuaded me to remain that night, in order to be with her.

"If you could stay to Saturday, you would see me and you would see that I am good for something more than dishwashing. I am the forerunner."

"The forerunner?"

"I go to the next week's camp and find lodgings for the master and his disciples. Everyone agrees that I am much the best at the job. Stay to Saturday, Tom. You can come with me and see the fun."

I stayed, and on Saturday Lucy took me by train to a little town distant about forty miles. She was smartly dressed and wore gloves. "I must cover my hands," she said, "for they mustn't see that I'm a char. I am a lady today. Rather reduced, but still a lady, who wants a quiet lodging for herself and friends—and you mustn't mention Brown, Tommy, or Benjamites, or say how many friends I have."

"Why?"

"Landladies don't like us. We have rather a bad name among lodginghouse keepers everywhere," and she began to laugh. "Wait and you'll see, Tommy—but not a word about Puggy or his crew. My crew."

We got out at one of those small country towns which is growing fast but has not yet lost its character. It had still dignity and beauty. Its church spires and towers were still to be seen over all, giving scale to the shops and warehouses, and meaning to the whole design. But already in the back parts were found long streets of brick boxes, in which the workers lived, packed like the products of a factory.

Lucy, having walked up and down in these streets, chose a terrace, six houses in a row, with bay windows and small gardens in front of them. Three of these better houses had letting cards.

"Which shall I choose, Tommy—the one with the brass steps, or the one with the new-painted door, or the one with the pink bows on the curtains? The brass steps are a good sign, but new paint is better, I think, especially when only the door has been painted. For that means the tenants have done that work themselves. I votes for new paint."

She knocked, and we found in the house a very clean buxom woman, full of house pride, and a little husband, with a pale thin face and a long gray mustache. He was a retired clerk, shy and modest.

The goodness of this couple, the affection between them and their pride and love of home, drew me to them, and I took occasion to say how much I admired the neatness and cleanliness of their rooms.

"Oh, sir, but if you knew what a difference this new factory has made—with all the smoke. I'm afraid you've noticed the curtains in the sitting room, but they were clean up only last week."

"They seem spotless to me, Mrs. Jones."

"Oh, sir." She shook her head, smiling as one would say, "You're flattering me." But her round face was blushing, full of pleasure, and afterwards I saw that both she and her husband, when they spoke to Lucy, kept looking at me. Indeed, I felt our common sympathies. For the house pride of simple people struggling to make a perfection within their small reach has always affected me to a deep respect.

I thought, "These people are now not far from death, and the slums are creeping up to them on every side, but the drawing-room curtains must still be spotless, the front door shining in new paint."

"It's a great shame," I said to the husband, "that factories are allowed in a town like this."

"Well, sir, they do bring a lot of smoke and noise, too. But we needed the employment. We mustn't complain."

"You could complain of the smoke. I hope you have complained."

The man looked at me and smiled as if to say, "That wouldn't do much good." He said mildly, "Well, they do say something might be done. But they don't seem to do it."

While he and I talked in this way, Lucy saw the rooms and asked many questions. She must have three bedrooms, at the least, and four beds.

"How many are coming, ma'am?"

"That depends," Lucy said, "but we'll need all your beds."

"I don't think I could manage for more than three visitors, ma'am, or four, with a married couple in the double room."

"Oh, no, we won't ask you. If there are more than four of course we shall give help. We could do all the cooking if you liked, and we'll make our own beds."

"I don't allow the cooking, ma'am, in my own kitchen. But if you could help with the beds . . . Are they schoolmistresses, ma'am?"

"No, why do you think so?"

"I thought perhaps so many ladies together and not knowing how many might come."

"Well then, the three bedrooms and the sitting room, for a week from Monday, and if more than four, to give help. You wouldn't mind two ladies sleeping in a single bed, if they can't get in otherwise?"

"No, ma'am, if it's all right for them. But I hope it won't be more than five."

I had now begun to suspect, though I hardly believed it, that Lucy meant to bring the whole party to this little house, and I said sharply, "I hope not, indeed." Lucy instantly turned to me and we exchanged angry glances, like those which we had not used since childhood; hers meaning, "How dare you, what impudence," and mine, "You think I am a fool, but look out."

Lucy then smiled at me and said, "You're not joining

the party are you, Tommy, or are you going back on your promise?"

This speech, cryptic to the woman, was meant to remind me that I had promised not to interfere in Lucy's negotiations. She turned her back on me at once, and said to the landlady in a cold voice, "I can't make any promises, but we might pay a little more if it's over four to cover extra work. Say another five shillings."

"Five shillings each, ma'am?"

"Good gracious, no. Five shillings for all extras."

"I'd rather say so much a head, ma'am."

"Very well, half a crown a head."

The landlady hesitated and looked from Lucy to me. But I was tied by my undertaking, and I was not even sure of Lucy's plans; and so I made no sign. Lucy then said suddenly, "Very well, Mrs. Jones, I see you think our party might be too much for you. And the place is rather small—perhaps I'd better try elsewhere."

I had often seen Lucy make such a stroke in our private battles. Her tone, her manner were perfectly polite, but both of them had the power of throwing an opponent into confusion. They were like a pistol suddenly brought out and aimed at his head. They caused a kind of panic. As Lucy turned away, the landlady said quickly that she would agree at half a crown a head. The bargain was struck, and Lucy said again, "Half a crown a head for extras, and I'm not promising that there will be any special number."

"No, ma'am, but I've no more beds and there's only two will take double."

"And the sofa, of course, for one. Now about supper—"

We stayed the night, and the next day, by the first train, a crowd of Benjamites arrived, with a cart full of luggage, sacks, great rolls of bedding, Gladstone bags, cardboard boxes, Brown's box, from which he preached, now filled with his books, flags, and flagpoles. The disciples came together and poured into the little house like an army, while Lucy, standing on the narrow stairs, called out directions. "You three men, on the sitting-room floor; you can put the bedding under the sofa for now. You, Master [this to Brown], in the front single room, first floor."

I saw the Joneses, swept to the back of the hall, looking on in horror and amazement; and feeling suddenly that I was taking part in a crime, I pushed toward Lucy and called to her, "Lucy, you're not bringing them all in here to stay—it's impossible."

"Lots of room," Lucy said. "I allowed for fifteen." And she called, "Put that box in the place under the stairs."

"You can't do it, Lucy—it's a mean trick. You know the Joneses never expected anything like this."

"Go away, Tommy, I'm busy. You elder sisters, back room, double bed—it doesn't really need a mattress. Two of you put the mattress on the floor—the other two can have the bed with some extra blankets on the springs. Mr. and Mrs. Black—single room on the top floor; it's a three-foot bed. Ellen, Daisy, and Margaret, double room top front, in bed. May and Mabel on the floor. Ella, in the top passage."

The thickest young girl, whom I had known before, answered from behind me in her slow calm voice, "I was in the top passage last time."

"Well, you're in the top passage this time, too," Lucy said. "Hallelujah, praise the Lord."

She uttered these words in Benjamite style, that is, without emphasis, as if saying, "It's a fine day."

"And where are you, sister?" the young woman Ella replied.

"I'm in the first-floor passage."

"But I'd rather have the first-floor passage—it's warmer, and it has a carpet."

"But I have to be ready for the master's call."

Ella answered that all of them were ready for the master's call, she hoped, hallelujah. But at this moment Brown himself, who had gone into his room, thrust out his big head and said sharply, "Sister Ella, I want you." At once he vanished again, leaving the door ajar.

"Oh, dear," Ella said. "Oh, dear." And her voice was tearful. "There I go again, upsetting the master. Oh, dear, what a turble bad heart I do have."

It was strange to see this stout country girl faltering toward Brown's door as if she were ready to faint and could barely carry herself upright. When she had nearly reached the door, Brown suddenly threw it back. Then she fell down on her knees, and crouched so low that I thought her face touched the threshold.

I was moved to excitement and horror. I was in pain to see a human being brought so low, and yet I could not turn my eyes from the scene until Lucy, carrying a large bundle upstairs, said to me in a sharp voice, "Get out of the way, Tommy, if you can't find anything to do."

I noticed then that no one was paying the least attention to the scene upon the landing. Women and men of all ages continued to pass up and down with their bundles within a yard of the crouching, weeping girl.

All, too, young and old, with the exception of Lucy and one of the young men, a mere boy, seemed to wear the same expression which I had seen in Ella, and which I might call placid truculence. Three older women, bent, pale as turnips, who passed up the stairs, did not even look at me, and their air as they pushed me to the wall, murmuring softly together, seemed to say, "We are the humblest of the Lord's servants, but who are you that dares stand in His way?"

This look among the Benjamites, the humiliation of Ella, as well as Lucy's conduct, now filled me with something more than disgust. I felt afraid. I made my way to the lower passage, meaning, if possible, to escape.

But when I struggled to the door, I saw that the little front garden was choked by a thick crowd, treading upon beds, grass, flowers. A drizzle of rain was falling, but it did not seem to trouble these devotees, who, bareheaded, now struck up the hymn:

> Who would true valor see,
> Let him come hither.
> All here will constant be
> > Come wind, come weather.
>
> There's no discouragement
> Shall make him once repent
> His first avowed intent,
> > To be a pilgrim.

The swelling voices, the sight of these rough people, let out I suppose for a dinner hour and still in their working clothes, again made tremble in me that nerve which always responded to the ancient call of the apostles, "Leave all and follow after Christ."

There was a silence, and I heard Brown's great voice rolling out, I supposed from the first-floor window, "Brothers and sisters in Christ—"

Some fell on their knees in the road, raising their eyes to the window, and I saw right in front, close to the door, the girl Ella, kneeling with her hands pressed together, her face, stained with tears, turned up with an expression of such humility and adoration that my knees faltered beneath me.

I turned and hurried down the passage, meaning to fly by the back way from this dangerous contagion.

28

But when I opened the kitchen door I found Mrs. Jones in tears. Mr. Jones was blustering about the police. I sympathized with them. "I am very sorry this has happened to you—"

They would not look at me. They blamed me also for the disaster that had befallen them.

"Don't take on, Polly," the old man said, "it's a police job. I'm off to get them now." But the old woman leaned back against the table and let her tears run without an attempt to wipe them away. She shook her head.

"No, no, Willy, how can we tell if it isn't God's work they're doing? We daren't do nothing against them. And well they know it."

"They're going to learn better then."

"No, don't be silly, dear. Oh, my poor house. It was Mrs. Fredericks last time, and they fairly ruined everything she had. Oh, but I mustn't complain, must I, it's God's work perhaps"; and she fell down in the chair and threw her apron over her head and broke into loud sobs.

I ran to find Lucy. She was still on the upper landing, busy with beds and bedding. And I told her that Mr. Jones was about to call the police.

"He can't do that," she said, "they would laugh at him. Besides, the Inspector is one of the disciples."

"You've done these people a great wrong, Lucy."

"Nonsense, it's good for them. You're always so sentimental, Tommy."

"Good for them to have their home wrecked?"

"Well, look at the way they live, like bugs in the wallpaper. They think of nothing but making themselves comfortable. What are they good for—nothing at all."

"Is that a Christian way to speak?"

"Here you are, sister—a towel for your room. It will have to do for all of you."

I was angered by her coolness and said, "I suppose Edward is right—you must have a new thrill, and you were tired of hunting."

"Poor Edward, I'm afraid he's awfully in debt again."

"You must have your thrill, even if it kills father."

"And here's one for the master's room," Lucy called.

"The master, what blasphemy it is."

"Why Tommy, he is our master, under God."

At these words, spoken in a peculiar voice, I felt another moment of fear. It was as though a dark wave had stretched itself before me in a bright and calm night, inviting me to approach.

"Master," I said. "Puggy Brown, the butcher."

Lucy started up from her heap of bedding and said, "Come, I'll see these Joneses for you." Her face was red, and her eyes glistened with anger. "You are a soft fool, Tommy, and you will never be anything else."

"And what are the poor Joneses—bugs in the wallpaper."

"Yes, you are all bugs in the wallpaper—coming out in the dark to suck somebody else's blood."

She was running downstairs. I ran after her in fear that she would say something spiteful or cruel to the Joneses. But when I came to the kitchen, I found Lucy holding Mrs. Jones with one hand and Mr. Jones with the other. They were gazing at her with round foolish eyes, like sheep at a sudden fire, and Lucy was saying, "A great and wonderful day for us all when the master comes when we hear the call of grace in our hearts. Do you not feel it?" She spoke to Mrs. Jones. "Ask of your heart—don't you find it there—something which says to you, 'A wonderful and strange thing has happened to me'— there, I see you do feel it. You're lucky, Mrs. Jones; be wise and don't fight against this great new happiness. I fought it for many days, like a foolish child that does not know what is good for it. Tommy," she turned to me, "put me out of your heart—put all that anger away and ask yourself if you know where you are going or what you are doing. Are you not lost and bewildered? Do you not say to yourself every day, 'Who am I—what am I seeking?' and can't answer yourself? Let us all kneel down and confess we are stupid lost creatures whose lives have been nothing but self, self, self."

"Don't you listen to her, Mrs. Jones," I said. I was quite furious, so that I hardly knew what I was saying. I felt such rage against Lucy that I could have beaten her, and yet I know that half my rage was fear. For her words, her voice, her look filled me with the same weakness which had seized upon me before, at the sight of Ella creeping to Brown on her knees, and again at the sound of the hymn. I say filled with weakness, because it was a positive thing, a feeling as if some spirit had entered into me, cut my sinews, and dissolved my self-will. While I was warning the Joneses, I was defending myself. "You saw how she tricked you yesterday—don't trust her now."

Lucy raised her voice and began to sing, joining in the middle of a verse. And now I heard the crowd in front of the house singing. They were singing so loud that the whole little house was shaken and seemed about to be torn up and carried away on the great waves of music and passion like a hut lifted off a river bank by a rising flood. Lucy and the Joneses suddenly knelt down together on the kitchen floor. Mrs. Jones was weeping and singing at once. She raised her face to the ceiling in a mournful expression, like one defeated. The old man was not singing, and he looked from Lucy to his wife with pursed lips and raised eyebrows, surprised at what he was doing.

Lucy fixed her eyes on me and smiled as she sang. And in her smile I saw the mischievous girl who had so often, in so many ingenious ways, used me and made a fool of me. It was that smile which saved me, or damned me, I cannot tell which. I shouted at her, "Yes, and this is another of your devil's tricks," and rushed out of the house. I did not even wait to get my hat or my handbag, and when, seated in the train, I realized the fact, I said, "Never mind, I couldn't have borne that place for another minute, the hypocrisy, the self-deceit, and Lucy at her worst."

So, too, when I came home and related the story to Edward, I made it out a victory for myself, as a reasonable, a civilized person, a lover of justice and decency. But, in fact, I had not dared to wait another moment in case I, too, like the Joneses, had fallen on my knees and confessed myself a miserable sinner. The dark wave was rising over me, and I had longed to drown in it, to get rid of self; to find what? A cause. Excitement. The experience of suffering, of humiliation, so attractive to my sense. Above all, an answer to everything.

But when, three months later, we heard that Lucy had married Brown, I spoke again scornfully of her, in my grief, and said, "That's not the way to do good in the world—she had better have been a district nurse."

"Though I suppose," Edward said, "it wasn't the district nurses who cut poor Charles's head off or drove James off the throne."

"You back up the Benjamites because they vote Radical, and you think they're going to vote for you."

Edward was standing for Queensport at the next election.

"One hand washes another," Edward said.

"Not if they're both dirty."

Edward laughed and raised his eyebrows. He was obviously quite surprised at my wit. And I was gratified even by his surprise. Edward was then my model as well as my hero. And perhaps my refuge from Lucy's Lord.

29

The Benjamites and a dozen other strange sects did vote for Edward, in force. They seemed to like his violent speeches, his denunciations of their political sins, as much as they enjoyed the hell-fire threats of their preachers. And Edward, like his grandfather, became member for Queensport. He was twenty-eight, but already known as a first-class election fighter, especially against strong opposition.

The Liberals were broken and divided. But as Edward said to me when I visited him in town, soon after election, "There are two ways of making a political career. Joining a party in opposition and taking a strong line, or joining the party in power and taking the modest and useful line."

But I did not want to talk politics with Edward. In my first year at the varsity I had become a dandy, or, as we said then, masher. At twenty, I was ambitious to be a man of the world. And I wanted Edward's advice about women.

I visited Edward three or four times in town, from Oxford, before, one night, I found the boldness to say to him, "Do you keep a mistress, Edward?"

"No," in a gloomy tone, "I'm afraid my life has been a little irregular."

"But Edward, I heard you were rather intimate with a certain lady."

"Most of them are only too uncertain."

We are walking down Bond Street on a winter evening, about five o'clock. I smell the sour chill of the mud and see the yellow gas flaring through misted windows. Hansoms float past on their rubber wheels faster than cars of today, and the flash of the spokes trembles on the golden fog.

"What about that divorce case which you were going to be involved in?"

"What case?" Edward has forgotten this special fear, born of some former depression. But he adds, "I might be involved any day. But I don't think I'd mind very much."

"What nonsense. It would ruin your career."

"I'm rather skeptical about this career that Lucy and you have invented for me. One thing at any rate is certain, I'll never do much in politics."

"Now why on earth should you say that when you've already had such a success?"

"Anyone can make a beginning in politics—it's the finish that kills."

But I am thinking all the time, "I must get Edward onto women. No one else can tell me how one sets about getting a mistress. And it's probably quite time I had one. At the very least I ought to have a woman."

The young man who, not a year before, had nearly been on his knees to Puggy Brown was now seriously considering adultery or seduction.

I remember very well that I discussed with several Oxford friends the question—ought one to keep a mistress? Our argument was that in all the great civilizations, in Greece, Rome, Italy, France, mistresses played an important part. It was only in the more barbarous countries that they weren't prominent.

If no one kept mistresses in England, I thought, would not something be lost? Would England not lose her place as a civilized nation? Would not literature and art decay?

And had I the right to enjoy this art and literature, this civilization, if I did not undertake the risk and burden of a mistress?

For some months I was obsessed with this question. Something within my own mind accused me night and day, "You are a coward, a parasite—you neither denounce mistress keepers nor join them. You are Mr. Facing-both-ways." And I felt both guilty and resentful in the presence of those men of the world, like Edward, who had taken a decision.

"This Mrs. Tirrit whom we are meeting this evening. Is she an intimate friend?" I ask him.

"She's a clever woman, and she thinks she can make use of me to pick out a good speculation in pictures—have you seen the Academy?"

"They say at Oxford that you and Mrs. Tirrit are

extremely close friends and that Colonel Tirrit is making trouble about it."

"The poor chap is at Carlsbad most of the time—he has some liver trouble. He's there now, so you needn't be anxious. I was going to do the Academy with you, but it isn't really worth while. English art died with Turner and Constable," and he began to talk about art, in which I had small knowledge and less interest. "Look at French art," he says. "What gives it such amazing vitality—among so conservative a people—with such a miserable constitution?"

"French politicians are greatly influenced by their mistresses."

"Are they?" Edward says dryly. "I don't know any of them personally—do you want a buttonhole?" He sees that I am bored with art.

A flower girl is offering her tray.

"Does one wear a buttonhole in an overcoat?"

"I don't, but you might like to try it. No—" and he gives the girl sixpence and we go on.

Both of us are dressed in the extreme of fashion. Our overcoats are long and tight waisted; our top hats have fall-to sides and curled brims; and we wear little curled mustaches. Mine is black and coarse; Edward's fair and fine. In our hands we carry ebony canes; mine with an ivory head; Edward's with a gold head.

At that time I copied even Edward's clothes. At college I sought to be of that group of rich young men who were scholars and dandies at the same time; who could talk both philosophy and horses; who pursued actresses and carried a Homer in their pockets. Edward was still remembered among them, and his name gave me admittance to their company. But though I was a scholar of my college, I had no quickness of mind; and I perceived already that these brilliant young men, like Edward, found me dull and foolish. I could never hit upon the right tone with them. For I was either too serious or too jocular.

This was the time when Edward, visiting our club, made a speech, defending dandyism, and quoted:

Memento mori, spite of Keats and Kants,
God strikes and strangers see your winter pants.

There was much laughter, but many of the young men, my companions, had a thoughtful air, even while they laughed. To them, as to me, it seemed that there was a deep significance, a whole philosophy of life, in the words. And afterwards, proudly putting my self forward before the club as Edward's brother, I said to our great man, "That was a wonderful couplet—the best you ever did. It's so true and it goes so deep."

Then I saw Edward smiling at me, and I was confused. I knew that smile which meant "Poor Tommy, he is always blundering into some nonsense."

Fortunately another young man now took up the word and agreed with me, saying, "That's just what needed saying, sir— that the dandy has the highest standards right through, I mean, even to his underclothes, which nobody sees. That's the real point of dandyism, and where it has such importance. It's really a practical Christianity—I was thinking of the Sermon on the Mount. Blessed are the pure in heart."

And of the young men standing round our visitor, most were listening with those anxious faces which seem to ask of some inner being, "Is this true? Is it what I am seeking? It may seem ridiculous but so do so many profound ideas. I must not be frightened by the absurd." And of the rest, only one was grinning, the foolish grin of the man who sees only the surface of things.

Edward looked around at our serious faces, and I could see that he was surprised and ready to make some joke. I was afraid he would make some ribald joke. But suddenly his face changed and he said in his pleasant good-natured voice, "I suppose there is religion in everything if we like to put it there," and, changing the subject, he began to talk of French painting, and Whistler.

When I remember those days and my friends of the D'Orsay Club, I have called myself a worthless young fool, but I do not think now that we were worthless. Edward was right. The tight-waisted coats, the French hats, the ebony canes, which, in the old novels, make the young men of my youth seem empty fools, were often a kind of religion.

> Adultery, sport in France. In England shame
> Unless designed to glorify God's name.

This, too, was a couplet of Edward's which we took seriously. I remember discussing it for an afternoon walk through Cumnor with a friend who maintained that love, if true, is always from God, and therefore conferred the right and duty to break all human laws.

30

We enter a gallery where, under shaded lights, there is an exhibition of French prints and pictures. Edward presents me to a small ugly woman with a snub nose and brown eyes. I notice her bad skin, pale and covered with small pits, her prominent chin and her darting glance. "Mrs. Tirrit—my brother Tom." She raises my hand in the air with a quick pressure, and then looking sharply at me says, "Not the soldier."

"No, this is the one who is going into the law or perhaps the Church."

"Into the Church," and her voice, like her glance, conveys

an intense curiosity. I no longer see an ugly little woman with prominent brown eyes, like a French bulldog, but the friendly glance, the eager expression which says, "Tell me." I feel that here is someone eager to be my understanding friend, and I open my mouth to explain that Edward is wrong and that I have by no means decided to be a lawyer, when I find myself looking at the lady's back. Her glance is turned to Edward, her hand is on his arm, and they are going past the curtain which divides the outer gallery from the inner. I have been dropped. But I still feel an extraordinary excitement, as if a new land of discovery has been opened to me. I wait impatiently for another glimpse of the face, whose ugliness now seems to me a charm. I turn the corner of the curtain and see a tall man walk up to Edward and Mrs. Tirrit from behind. He says something to them. They turn round, and I perceive that they have had an unpleasant surprise, that this new arrival must be Tirrit mysteriously returned from abroad. I am so astonished that I stand without movement, and yet full of horror, thinking, "So Edward is lost."

But no one raises a hand or stick. The three are talking together. I go up to them and Edward introduces me. "Colonel Tirrit—Mr. Tom Wilcher."

"Who is going into the Church," Mrs. Tirrit says.

The colonel shakes hands with me, pressing my hand. He is tall and heavy. His face is long and yellow, deeply folded; that of a very sick or unhappy man. Edward waves his hand toward a picture and says to Mrs. Tirrit, "That's the only kind of Corot for me—Italian period."

The two walk over to the pictures, and I notice in Mrs. Tirrit's walk a new spring, as if she is acting a part, and enjoying it. The colonel says to me, "You're going into the Church."

"It isn't decided yet. I am still in my first year at Oxford."

"It's a serious step."

The colonel says no more and we walk in silence after Edward and Mrs. Tirrit, who stop at every picture. At last they come back to the entrance door and a cab is called. Mrs. Tirrit, standing among us on the pavement, makes to each, like a queen, the appropriate remark. To Edward: "After all, you're quite right about what's his name—the splashes—I shall buy that picture." To me: "You must come and see me, and don't wait for Edward to bring you. I don't want to see Edward, but you. So come by yourself." And then unexpectedly to her husband: "My dear Johnny, you look wretchedly ill. I shall have to send you to bed." And in each phrase she expresses a kindness, a sincerity, which is the more convincing because of her tart humorous tone. The cab arrives, her husband opens the door, and Edward hands her in. Edward stands hat in hand—the colonel looks straight in front of him, from his corner, with his hat on. They drive away.

"I understand now why you like her so much," I say to Edward. "She is perfectly charming."

"You saw what happened?" Edward is once more gloomy and depressed.

"No."

"Tirrit came up and said he was going to knock me down."

"Nonsense."

"I suppose he came home just to make a row. I asked him to wait till we had looked at the pictures, and as you see, he didn't do anything after all. Lost his nerve, poor chap. Or too decent."

"Poor Mrs. Tirrit, what a scene."

Once more we are walking down the pavement, in the golden fog. Edward says, "Yes, I'll bet ten to one she planned the whole thing."

"Does she want a scandal?"

"No, but she's bored and whimsical like all these women. Too rich. And no children. And a devoted jealous husband. Yes.

They mean to make trouble, between them. He's a fool, and she's capable of anything to amuse herself."

"He couldn't divorce her, could he?"

"Why not? He will if she makes him. And then I shall have to marry her. A nice prospect."

"Then I can't understand how you let yourself be compromised, I can't understand how you can have anything to do with such worthless selfish people."

We are back in Edward's room among his beautiful books, his first editions, his ivories and china, his French impressionist pictures which seem even to his friends still an affectation. It is not a large room, but its contents are worth some thousands of pounds. Edward is in his shirt sleeves. He has meant to put on a smoking jacket, but he has not troubled. He sits over the fire with the poker in his hand. Now he taps a coal, seeking for the grain, in order to break it with the lightest blow, and says, "Angela Tirrit is one of the most charming women in London."

"How can she be charming?"

"How is anyone charming? She has the special charm of being—what shall I say? Civilized is the nearest word. Yes, she has taught me a lot."

"A woman who deceived her husband and wants to ruin you out of pure selfishness?"

But as I abuse Mrs. Tirrit, I imagine her pursuing me, driving me into all kinds of scandals, causing me the greatest misery, and finally involving me in her divorce, marrying me and using me. Using me, is the idea that occurs to me. I remember very well that I did not think "I ought to take a mistress," but "How I wish some clever woman, older than I, ruthless, corrupt and fascinating, would seduce me, ruin me, and carry me off to this mysterious and exciting world where Edward is so much at home."

"A horrible woman," I say.

"The question is, of course, whether life is worth living," Edward says. I cannot see the connection of this remark. But I know that Edward is speaking as he has never spoken before. An hour of confidences has struck.

"What," I say, astonished. "You to say that; why, even if Mrs. Tirrit did drag you into the court, you would still have a dozen other careers open to you."

Edward pays no attention to me. He taps the coal again, a big coal which ought to be left alone. A bad and extravagant trick of Edward. And in my surprise and alarm at his strange mood, I say sharply, "Don't spoil the fire—I never knew anyone waste coal as you do." Edward pays no attention to me. He reflects a moment, letting his cigarette hang crookedly, and then gives the coal a sharp rap. "That's it, Tommy—is life worth living? Give a man everything in the world, give everyone everything they think they want, and they might still ask that question. Judging by my experience, they might be all the more ready to ask it."

"Do you believe in God, Edward?"

"Oh, yes; I mean I believe in His existence. But how does one keep up one's interest in Him?"

I am inexpressibly shocked. "Edward, think of what religion means."

"And how does one go on being interested in life? That is the important question which governments will soon have to answer. How do you maintain the vital spark? It isn't a matter of health. A perfectly healthy world would probably die out like the Polynesians. And look how poor Papa clings to life—I've always envied him."

"He does really believe in God—and heaven."

"But then you would think he would be willing to go to heaven. And look at Lucy, she doesn't believe in anything."

"She's given up everything for God."

"Do you think so? My impression is that Lucy hasn't

any religion at all. But she has a great sense of class. She has turned herself into a char because she feels that her own class is finished. She doesn't feel grand enough as a mere lady. She has flown to the arms of Puggy to give herself the sense of nobility."

"I think that's nonsense."

"Yes, quite probably—like most other things." And having tapped the coal on all sides, he gives it such an expert stroke that it flies into thin pieces. I see him still, in the glow of the blaze, smiling at his own feat, with the air of one who laughs at his own childishness.

31

I did not find out how to get a mistress. But I did learn from Edward that, according to his man, the between-maid at home was not entirely virtuous. And when I went home, I permitted myself to knock into her, with such a sense of desperation as still makes me say, "So does the soldier of the Lord disembark on an unknown shore among cannibals." I tremble again before that little maid whose very name has gone from me. She was a little fat creature with a face like molded soap and the nature of a bird in a cage, chirping with all domestic music. You heard her voice everywhere but always with some other voice, or the sound of a kettle singing, a grate being scoured. And our love passage was a short and confused interlude when all romance vanished in her giggles and her expertness.

"How did I do it?" I ask myself. "How was it possible?"

It is not yet eight o'clock and still gloomy; a cold winter morning, but I cannot stay in bed. I get up and go along the corridor to the linen room. The baskets ranged beneath the shelves, and the linen lying in the close warmth of the pipes, have the air of all things seen at night, of having been interrupted in their private thought and memories. "It was on that side," I thought, "under the window, where there are no shelves and the baskets made a kind of couch." But how did I dare? So wicked and foolish an act.

But at once I remember that I had not dared. It was the little maid who contrived the meeting. So suddenly and unexpectedly that I still wonder how she divined wishes which were scarcely clear to myself. I was walking in the passage, when she started in front of me from the nursery. By an effort, I said something to her: "Where are you going?" or "What do you want?"

Suddenly she darts aside into the linen room and, as I come to the door, opens it a few inches and looks up at me with an indescribable look of mischief and challenge. Then runs back into the room. And I follow as if drawn by an elastic. The young man of my memory, serious, burdened, prematurely anxious, whose very dandyism was a moral inquiry, changes into somebody quite different, a boy who at twenty-one was utterly unsure of himself. So shy, so clumsy beneath his careful manners, that he was scarcely responsible for his own vices. Moved this way and that by every voice of power, by Pug Brown, by Lucy, by Edward.

It was some impulse far deeper than physical desire, the wish to suffer some new, some profound experience, that brought me to this room and the scene of a strange humiliation, where rules were suddenly reversed and the servant became the master, commanding with authority, and the master became a shy foolish creature who could not even find words or manage his own buttons.

"Do any ee be afeared," the girl says, smiling, but not at all in scorn. She is full of sympathy. The shy servant who could not raise her eyes above the master's waistcoat buttons, nor speak to him above a whisper, is now, in one moment, become the superior, responsible and confident. She takes charge, and is only puzzled by my increasing helplessness. In fact, it is her competence which has increased it.

She pauses suddenly in her arrangements and says as if in doubt, "He bees and he bant."

This was a variation from a local saying about a girl who could not make up her mind whether to give way to her lover or remain "a maiden still."

Her words, her shrewd smile, fall upon my trance like raindrops and light on a curtained glasshouse; they do not move or warm a leaf within. Yet I am sharply aware of them.

A psychologist, explaining to me once the extraordinary failure of a public man, famous for his resource and courage, said to me, "He was in two minds at once and that means he had no will, for the will is only the servant of a desire."

It was not fear, it was a conflict of desires, a paralysis of will, which made me feel so foolish and helpless in the hands of the little maid. Fortunately, I suppose, she had the native wit to perceive my condition and to understand that the success of the enterprise must depend upon herself. I should have kissed her little red hands, swollen and glazed with washing soda, for that instinct of sympathy, like a bird's or a cat's, which perceived that I could not go back and carried me so kindly and adroitly forward, even with compliments upon my manly powers, to the only possible solution of my deadlock. I wonder still at the goodness of that soul, so understanding, and ask how any can deny the love of God who have known, even in so trifling a passage, the unbought kindness of the poor and simple.

And the next day when I had to pass in the corridor, she pressed herself against the wall and looked at the floor. We were alone, and there was no reason why she should have behaved so respectfully, except her own idea of what was right and proper. I felt then for her an impulse of gratitude and affection, so strong that I feel it now. It is a true and deep love; the love which is full of respect. For I perceived in that moment that there was to be no difference in our relations, no upheaval in the order of life at Tolbrook.

When Edward knew the story of the maid, though I told it as an exploit, he laughed and said, "I thought she would seduce you—was it very alarming?"

Edward thought that I had been the timid victim. But Edward had not much penetration into character. He was too clever. He never understood the force of moral conviction in certain souls, or its variety of forms.

32

"The young people think me an old fossil," I thought, moving along the passage wall to find the place where the girl had stood aside, in modesty and subjection. "But what I am now I was then. Even as a child I had a passionate love of home, of peace, of that grace and order which alone can give beauty to the lives of men living together, eating, chattering, being sick, foolish, and wicked, getting old and ugly. I hated a break of that order. I feared all violence."

I found the place, just opposite the newel of the stairs, and leaned against it. It was, of course, an illusion that the wall was still warm.

Passionate Lucy threw herself upon the dark wave of fate, of God's mysterious will; and in the presence of the little maid, part of me cried, "Foolish and wicked boy, you are destroying the peace of your home and your heart." And another part, "Be reckless, have faith—take no thought for the morrow—cast your bread upon the waters."

"Hullo, uncle, I was wondering where you'd got to." Robert stood before me, but his eyes did not look at me. He did not wish to show any surprise at my position, with outstretched arms against the wall. "It's about the power line for old Raven. The electricity people say they can do it for fifty pounds if we decide today, while the gang are working in the village. But to-morrow they'll wind up, and after that it will cost a hundred."

"Old Raven is eighty," I said. "What does he want with electricity?"

"You won't see the wires from the house."

"No, but they'd go across the meadow behind the drive—they'll spoil the view of the church."

I was struck by the boy's rough appearance. He had not shaved for the last two days, and his open shirt was filthy. He looked like a laborer. His rubber high boots were caked with mud. I felt that for his own sake I ought to tell him that his appearance must be painful to Ann. But I was unable to do so. I felt, too, far away from Robert and his plots with Jaffery.

"Sorry to bother you, uncle," he said, "but about this power line—it seems a good chance."

"I'm afraid we haven't the money," I said, for I knew it was waste of money to give old Raven power. He would never use it except for a few lights. "Were you coming to prayers—you remember that you used to like morning prayers."

"Yes, uncle, but I just have no time at all."

I went into the old day nursery where for the last week or so I had been reading prayers in my dressing gown. I had not meant to start this old custom again until the housekeeper, Mrs. Ramm, one day told me how she missed it. Agnes Ramm had been at Tolbrook twenty years, and I remember her when she first came, as kitchenmaid, a round, blooming young girl. Agnes had turned out a good maid, but not of the best character. She had had two illegitimate children before she was twenty, and once at least she had attempted some approach to myself. A hussy. But now at forty-six, after severe illness, a sad woman with strong religious feeling. I was glad at her suggestion, and since Ann made no objection, Agnes and a niece of hers, who was the housemaid, attended every morning in the old nursery for morning prayers. This had become a great pleasure to me and to poor Aggie, who would often say how she had missed the comfort of it in the years when Tolbrook had been let to "those heathen from London."

I scarcely expected Robert, who was truly a heathen, to come to prayers; but I thought I preferred his bias to Ann's indifference. For Ann, it seems, is pregnant. And it shocks me to think of any girl undertaking the great and awful responsibility of motherhood without religion of any kind.

33

I could not speak to the girl directly on the subject because it would have involved some reference to her condition, which might have embarrassed her. But on one of our afternoon walks I took occasion to remark on the importance of religious education for young children. "They cannot, of course," I said, "understand the *arguments* for the existence of God, simple and irrefragable as they are. They can be taught only to recognize the *experience* of God, of goodness in their own hearts, and in other people's acts, so that when they grow older, they are ready for those proofs upon which faith must stand, unbreakable and triumphant."

"Do you believe in the afterlife, uncle?"

"Most certainly. I don't know how anyone can bear to live without such a belief." But remembering that she might have certain fears, I changed that subject quickly and said, "And why shouldn't it be true? You young people choose to disbelieve it just as you tie handkerchiefs over your heads to play at being peasants. It's a fashion to attack the Church."

"Oh, but I'm not against the Church, uncle. As I tell Robert, it seems mean to attack the poor old dear, when she's so weak."

I was just going to answer with some indignation that the Church was very well able to look after itself, when the young woman went on, in a thoughtful voice, "Today is like the picture in the back passage, isn't it—with the old squire and the little girl," a remark which, referring apparently to a steel engraving beside the kitchen door, entirely threw me out, and scattered my ideas.

It was a January afternoon, with a sprinkle of snow, and the gray fields, the silver sky, the cottages seen at a distance through the fine lines of the branches certainly made a scene just like the engraving. And for a moment as often at such unexpected strokes of imagination, I did feel like the old man in the picture, whose hat and cape coat, wellington and stick I had often examined as a child, climbing upon a chair to discover, with my shortsighted eyes, whether the stick made real holes in the snow, and whether the artist had put in all the footprints.

"And this girl," I thought, "who is holding my arm, she is rather like the little girl in the picture. She has the same short skirt, and she wears a handkerchief tied over her head. Ann is like a peasant again, going back to the soil. She is even gray-faced like the little girl, with the big eyes that old-fashioned artists gave their little girls. Her eyes seem bigger since she began to be so ill." And for a moment my feeling was that reality had actually disappeared out of the world, and that such an absurd appearance from the past as myself, and so flimsy a being as Ann, the peasant from Kensington, were simply figments or phantoms.

"Did it always hang in the back passage?" Ann said. "I don't remember it there. I thought it was upstairs somewhere."

"It was in the night nursery. But what does it matter where it was, and I don't think this afternoon is at all like a picture. It's a real winter day of the best kind—the kind you get only in England—where human beings can still go out and enjoy themselves," and so on. For I felt indignant with the girl for her romantic stuff which was trying to deprive me of life. I thought, "I may be old, but I don't belong to the past. It is this sad gray-faced little girl, the imitation simpleton, who has gone back into the past, the most primitive past; she lives in a perpetual winter, austere, colorless; a cruel and bleak winter; quite different from this glorious and encouraging scene."

"We are lucky in our dry weather," I said.

"It is nice to look at—out of our parlor window."

"But you must take exercise. That's doctor's orders."

"Robert's orders."

"Robert is becoming a good husband. He takes great care of you now."

"Not of me, but the baby. I am only the box labeled 'fragile, with care.' "

"Robert is right. You carry a great responsibility."

"I suppose so. But I don't feel like that."

"Don't you want to have a child?"

"Yes, I think I do. I suppose Nature is at her old games."

"God's will is not an old game."

"I'm afraid, uncle, I can't think God had much to do with it. It seems too natural."

"What has the love that God puts into a woman's heart for her child got to do with your ideas of Nature?"

"But do women always like their babies? I remember two cases in Paddington." And she would no doubt have told me about these miserable cases had I not changed the subject by remarking that it was about to snow. For I did not want any more nonsense. I am too old to be bothered with it.

34

Ann talks of our parlor. Perhaps to flatter me. But, in fact, I was glad when she brought the parlor into use again. The parlor was our family room, where, for many years of my youth, I could always be sure of company.

It is a small square room with two tall windows facing west. Its carpet has always been shabby, its chairs worn, its pictures, the outcast portraits and old prints which will not do elsewhere. A large fly-blown print of the Derby finish hangs over the chimneypiece. It has wanted a glass ever since Bill, sixty years ago, put a slug from his air gun through the finishing post.

It is a darkish room, occupied always by a brown shadow which Edward once likened to the spirit of gravy. "I always feel," he used to say, in the parlor, "as if the Sunday joint were going to walk in and take the best chair by the fire."

Yet Edward, too, loved to stretch himself in the parlor, with unbuttoned waistcoat and his feet as far as they would go up the side of the mantelpiece, while Lucy, perched on the arm of his chair, would tease him or comb his hair.

There in wet weather we used to play whist for matches; there Bill organized picnics, gathering together the luncheon baskets, the sandwiches, the rugs, the dogs, and shouting furiously, "Where on earth is Lucy, where is Mama, where is the French mustard? No, I want to see it. Very well, the basket must be unpacked again."

And after our father's death it was the smoking room, where we sat till the small hours, in that community of gossip which is the ground of family life.

Now in these winter afternoons, when Ann reads and smokes on one side of the fire and I on the other, the parlor is again the parlor. True, we converse little, but there is comfort and company in the air. For while two of us sit in the old room, it is again a family room. It gives out again, like a dried flower warmed in the hand, its essential quality, a rich ease.

And Ann, with her unexpected power of knowing my feelings, if not my thoughts, said to me one evening, "I wonder will this baby be sitting here in another fifty years or seventy-one years."

I was surprised by such an idea in Ann's head. But it gave me a keen pleasure. For I had wondered already if perhaps Robert and Ann would not decide to settle at Tolbrook, either as tenants or as my managers.

"Tolbrook has been a great anxiety and burden to me, and I am leaving it," I said, "but Robert seems to enjoy estate work, and he will not find a prettier piece of country or better land."

"Wouldn't you like to see the house stay in the family?"

"Yes, of course I should. Though I don't know if that isn't perhaps a weakness on my part."

"The trouble is Robert," the girl said. "He is too fond of the place."

"It was his own home—the only real home he ever had."

"Yes. But Robert is the kind of man who would always be cruel to what he loves."

35

This idea, that Ann herself might be inclined to set up a family line at Tolbrook, occupied my mind with such force that for some days I thought of nothing else. And the girl's new domesticity, suggested, I suppose, by her condition, encouraged me to speak of a matter even closer to my heart, the religious education of her child. I pointed out that Tolbrook had always been a religious house, and that the whole value of its tradition, to a family, lay in that fact. "And what can be more important to a child than a religious education? It's the first years, too, that count—that give direction to his whole idea of the world—his whole *feeling* about it."

It was just before tea, and Ann, with her spectacles falling down her nose, was reading, smoking, and knitting. She looked reflectively at me and said, "Yes, I suppose that is true," and then asked me what a chaise was like.

"A chaise?" I think my surprise was justifiable.

"I always thought a chaise was an open carriage, but here is Julia Bertram in Mansfield Park talking about being boxed up in a chaise."

"You may be surprised to hear that chaises went out thirty years before I was born. Do you feel no moral responsibility at all toward your child?"

"I expect I shall feel too much. Yes," and she blew a cloud of cigarette smoke, "I'm terribly afraid I'm the type that makes rather a fussy mother."

She was wrinkling her forehead, a bad habit; but I thought it the wrong moment to warn her of it. I was gathering up my forces.

"This poor child," I thought, "is lost already—she is blinded by prejudice and ignorance. And if I speak to her of God, she probably imagines an old man in a gray beard and a very bad temper. It is useless to appeal to her on religious grounds. But there are others." And drawing up my chair, I said, "My dear, I understand your difficulty about religious instruction. But let us make a bargain. If you will allow this child to be brought up in a reasonable Christian faith, I shall settle two hundred a year on him, in your trust. Yes, and you know," I said, "he would have a very good claim to Tolbrook. I might even undertake to leave the place to him. I should be glad to find in Edward's and Lucy's grandchild a successor," etc.

"But I'm not sure if I want him to be a Christian," Ann said.

"Wait a minute," I said, perhaps too hastily. "Of course, you won't be forgotten. Not at all. I have already made some provision for you. But in a case like this, I should be prepared to go much farther."

"Made provision for me," the girl said, in a most rational tone. And I, thinking I was on the right track at last, explained my recent instruction to Jaffery which would be communicated to her in the next week or two, etc. That she was to have a thousand pounds on my death, and a hundred and fifty more for every year I should live after her undertaking the care of me.

"So the longer you live, the more I shall get."

"Yes, and I might increase that amount."

This, of course, was a delicate point, apt to be mistaken. And I added that I believed it was a not unusual provision and only just, having regard to the time she was sacrificing, etc.

The girl seemed to meditate. But when I expected an answer, she exclaimed, "It's time you had your tea, uncle," and rang the bell. Neither did she refer to the matter again that day.

36

The feeling. What is this feeling that I talk about to Ann, and how can she know what I mean, when I barely know it myself? When I, with all my churchgoing, my prayers, lose it so easily. One would say I was a dead frog, which shows animation only at the electric spark from such as Lucy. The touch of genius; of the world's genius. And when that contact was withdrawn, I became once more a preserved mummy.

As soon as Lucy went away from me, and I lost the feeling of her, I began to mummify. I called it growing sensible, responsible, etc. At Lucy's return from the Benjamites I did not even recognize her. It seemed that we belonged to different worlds.

I was coming down stairs into the hall one winter evening dressed for dinner, and probably much pleased with myself. I was no longer the youth who had almost fallen on his knees in the Jones' kitchen. Neither was I a dandy. I was a young man, in his last year at Oxford, serious even in dress. At home, I began to take an interest in the estate and the people. I taught in

Sunday school, and helped my father with the estate work. And when I heard, from some cart-tail on market days, the peculiar hollow shouts of the open-air preacher, I would think, "Yes, it's all very well to talk about God's laws and renunciation of this world's goods, but where would you be without the magistrates? And what do you say when somebody walks off with your sheep or rifles your potato clamp in the night?"

I had not set eyes on Lucy for nearly four years. And when, in the dim-lit hall, I saw near the door a poorly dressed woman standing in silence, I took her for some beggar or gypsy, come to ask a favor. She had the look of gypsy women as soon as they cease to be girls; thin and nervous. No one can tell what age they are. At twenty they have the thin dry wrinkles which will only be deeper when they are eighty, and show already bitter experience and strong will.

This woman under the hall lamp, which made deep hollows in her cheeks, looked at me, in my dinner jacket and white shirt, as gypsy women look when they beg from the gentlemen on Epsom Downs. Their hard filmy gaze puts gentlemen into a glass cage like wax figures in a museum.

"Good evening," I said. I meant to save my father a troublesome petition. But in the same moment that secret nerve moved, I knew Lucy, and I was shocked by the voice of my good evening, which had seemed cordial and now seemed distant and cold. In one instant I ceased to be the young master, the serious man of affairs, and became Lucy's young brother. "Lucy," I cried, "have you been ill?"

"You didn't know me," Lucy said. "I'm not surprised. And look at my hands."

Her hands were like the little maid's, but darker and more chapped. The finger tips were cracked and gray.

"That work is killing you, Lucy," I said.

"Yes, it was killing me. But I knew the rule. It's not because of the work that I've come home."

And she told me that Brown had taken the girl Ella to his bed. "Six months ago, before my baby was born."

"I didn't know you'd had a baby."

"It was born dead. But I didn't want it to live and be a Benjamite."

"Poor Lucy, but you're not going back to those savages."

"Never again. Brown has broken his own precious rule, and now I want a bath."

My mother and myself were horrified by the change in Lucy. My mother hastened to bring comforts and new clothes, the most eager sympathy. My father, who had showed his delight in Lucy's return by a sudden gaiety I had never seen before, took no account of her sufferings. And when I spoke to him of her lost looks, he answered only, "She's young." I could not understand then, as I do now, that to the old, a broken marriage is little more than a broken knee in a child. When they see a daughter worn before her time, they think only, "She must have come to this in a few years, and she is still young. That is the great thing."

And Lucy, even more than before, sought her father's company and avoided her mother. A situation which my mother's tact at once accepted. While Lucy was at home she effaced herself as much as possible from our family party.

37

To our pleasure, Lucy was quite ready to be distracted. She had always delighted in luxury, and like Edward she seemed to enjoy it in the idea, as well as in fact. The sense of luxury about her, of wealth, of good servants, of expensive carpets and hangings, things which after a few hours one does not notice and which add much more to one's cares and burdens than one's comfort, gave her deep pleasure. She loved sheets of the thinnest linen, and Paris clothes, with the finest sewing in inner seams never to be seen by any except herself and a maid. But though Lucy bought new clothes, though she went to parties with us and romped and danced and flirted as before, she did not lose her haggard cheeks and hollow eyes. She could not sleep, and she used to come to my room in the small hours to make me talk or read to her.

It was on these nights that she made me feel the inadequacy of my life, so respectable and proper. For Lucy carried a nervous force which charged the air about her so that, when I waked to find her in my room, I was suddenly carried out of its narrow domestic comfort and security into that mysterious universe of passion and faith in which she lived.

"I can't sleep," Lucy would say, touching my forehead, "so I came to you."

Nothing gave me more pleasure than such words from Lucy, which meant, "I need you." I sprang up eagerly. "Shall I read to you? Get into my bed, while it's warm—and I'll find a book."

"No, you stay in bed and I'll roll up in your counterpane—read me about Pigg and the cupboard."

I kept all Surtees in my room for Lucy, who, when she read at all, desired only her old hunting books. And so I read to her as she demanded, the celebrated passage in which Jorrocks and James Pigg drink healths in turn to each of the hounds; and James Pigg, being asked what sort of a night it is, puts his head out of what he supposes to be a window, and answers, "Hellish dark and smells of cheese."

At this point I waited for Lucy to laugh, but she remained silent and said only, "Go on about the rain, but you can leave out the poetry."

What went on in Lucy's head while she lay beside me, wrapped up like a white mummy in my counterpane, with her black hair, already full of gray, falling in two pigtails across her shoulders? Probably very little. She was not used to reflect upon things.

"You must hunt again," I said.

"I don't know. It's really rather a bore. It takes such a lot of time."

"But now you have plenty of time to enjoy yourself."

"To bore myself, too."

"But you will love it—don't you love your Jorrocks?"

"Yes, but I know every word of Jorrocks—read me again the bit about the hound that was as wise as a Christian."

I read the passage and said, "It's true—a hound does know how to live and be happy."

I spoke from that excitement which Lucy always brought to me. But Lucy answered only, "Oh, nonsense, Tommy—a dog's a dog. Go on with the next chapter—the day in the forest. Wasn't it Pinch-me-near?"

And when I had finished she would stretch herself and say in a dreaming voice, "How gorgeous that is—how lovely to be Jorrocks on a day like that. Read me the bit about the morning again, with the drops like diamonds on the bushes."

I read the piece of description, commonplace in every word, but because Lucy felt it, an experience which made me long to get up at dawn. It still delights me in my memory.

"I'll go cub hunting with you, Lucy, if you will hunt."

"And put some cobbler's wax on your saddle? You would hate it, Tommy, and so should I—to see you in agony."

"Then go with Edward. That would be real hunting."

"Yes, perhaps I shall go with Edward. Though I wish he wouldn't waste his time and his money on all that nonsense."

"What, do you call hunting nonsense?"

"It is nonsense for Edward with his brains."

Lucy adored Edward and would never allow him to be criticized, even by my mother, whose favorite he was. When my mother said, with her gentle irony, "His majesty is coming to see us tomorrow and commands that the carriage be sent to Totnes," Lucy would flush and answer, "Why not, mother— it will do Wilkins good to have a little work for a change." Wilkins was our old coachman.

38

When this same year Edward was threatened at last with the Tirrit divorce case, and Colonel Tirrit fell dead in the street on the day after his lawyers had filed suit, Lucy said that it was the judgment of God.

"Nonsense, Lucy." I was shocked by her superstition. "It is just Edward's luck."

I told her that Edward was already entangled in another affair, with a young actress called Julie Eeles. "But perhaps you think providence arranged that, too."

"Yes, I think it might be so."

"What nonsense, Lucy."

"I hear Mrs. Eeles is a very nice woman and she has helped Edward a lot in his worries."

"But surely, Lucy, you don't approve of Edward's taking her from her husband."

"If her husband is such a ninny, he deserves what he gets."

"I thought you were a Christian, Lucy."

"What's that got to do with it? And if you do go into the Church, Tommy, I hope you won't be canting humbug. I'd much rather you were the real old brandified kind like that man at Combe Barten. They say he has children all over the county. But I don't suppose you'll ever get married. You're a born old maid."

Lucy would never talk religion with me, though often she talked of Brown, giving me strange pictures of her life with the Benjamites.

"When he took that bladder of lard, Ella, into bed with him, he made me sleep on the floor and serve Ella as a handmaiden. I washed her clothes and emptied her slops. And didn't she glory in it. She would say, "Sister Lucy, praise the lamb, could you brush out my hair now, hallelujah, and please don't pull, or I shall scream."

"I wonder she dared."

"She knows how I hate her. But that sort of creature enjoys being hated. If you knew what a set they are, Tommy. The mean jealousies and dirty little spites that creep about in them like worms in a dead rabbit. You think they're alive, but they're only rotten. Except Ella. She's alive, like a weasel with dropsy."

"How could you wait on her, Lucy?"

"The master commanded, and I obeyed. It was the rule— the rule." Lucy repeated the word in a voice of mockery.

"But you say he broke the rule. It is against the rule to take another wife."

"Not if God commands. But God did not command him to take Ella."

"How did you know that?"

"One day it was revealed to me and I told him. And when I pressed him, he began to doubt. I said to him, Master, will you swear that it was not the voice of the devil speaking to you in the lust of the flesh; and he would not swear. God stopped up his lips. And though he prayed all night and all of us prayed, that the truth might come to him, he could not tell whether it was God who had commanded him to put me away, or the devil, who had made him lust after Ella."

Lucy spoke this language of the Benjamites without any change of voice, and on her lips the Biblical words did not make me smile.

Lucy laughed and said, "How would you like getting out of bed at three in the morning, Tommy, and kneeling down on the oilcloth in your nightshirt and howling to the Lord for a couple of hours, to save your soul from hell?"

"Did you get up always at three?"

"No, we got up whenever Puggy had a fit of the horrors and shouted at us to pray, pray, pray, against the devil."

"What a queer kind of religion it is," my mother remarked, when she heard these stories.

"Do you think so, mother?" Lucy would answer. "But you know, it does work—it does keep the devil away. Sometimes at least." And then she burst out laughing, "But you ought to hear the moans and groans when we all have to get out on a cold winter night. And you ought to see fat Ella tumbling out of bed like a bagful of turnips—how she does hate it. You can see the spite boiling in her little green eyes. But she has to pray louder than anyone or Puggy might have a new revelation and take another wife—and then she'd have to sleep on the floor again and empty slops."

"I'm glad you're not going back," my mother would say. "I don't think Mr. Brown's religion makes anyone much better or more charitable."

"Good Lord, no," Lucy would answer. "Puggy doesn't bother much about tea-table virtue."

Lucy was strange to both of us. And yet, as I say, every word she said, however unexpected, found in me a response; some secret nerve within me was excited. To what? I was going to write, to the love of God, of religion, to some grandeur of thought. But now, as I pace restlessly through the lower rooms, I feel it as something deeper, more passionate. The life of the spirit.

39

I found myself in the dining room, which still has its old chairs, too big and clumsy a set for a modern house, and I began to hunt for those two at which Lucy and I, side by side, always prayed. For each of us had our own chair, and many times, when my father was waiting with his books and the servants were already filing into the room, Lucy or I would discover by the minute signs known only to ourselves that we were at the wrong chair and would get up hastily to look for the right one. Then if my father said, "Sit down, children," and we had to use a wrong chair, we would feel so restless and exasperated that, as Lucy said, she felt the devil tickling her all over. Once at least she was beaten for toppling such a wrong chair right over. The crash makes me start again. I begin to laugh, and it seems to me that I am grinning that demon grin of Lucy's childhood.

Here is my chair with a mark in the mahogany like a long narrow eye, a snake's eye, and a chip on the near hind leg. I kneel at it for a moment. Suddenly I feel that somebody is present, and getting up I see Ann at the door.

"You didn't take your medicine." She looks embarrassed. And I am angry at being watched.

"No, I forgot."

"You don't really think I am trying to poison you, uncle?"

In my astonishment I jumped to an unlucky conclusion. I said that she had no business to read my notebooks.

"I don't read them," she answered. "Have you written me down as a poisoner?"

"Certainly not. I wouldn't dream of such a thing."

"Do, if you like. You ought to write everything down. It's good for you. I kept a diary myself once, and it was so awful I had to burn it. But it did me lots of good."

"Good for what? Is this some more of your German boxes?"

"No, I meant only it's natural to want to give yourself away—"

Then I was sure she had been reading my books, and I said, "I never thought you were deliberately giving me the medicine too strong—I only thought that you might say to yourself, 'It's better to keep him quiet than to prolong his life, which is a useless one.' "

"And that's why you arranged that settlement to pay me for keeping you alive."

"My dear child, you and I are sensible people—we know what the world is. And I am a useless old man. While you are strong and eager for life, for travel, for lots of things, that only money can buy. I don't say that the idea occurred to you that I would be better out of the way, but if it had, I should not blame you. It would be very reasonable under the circumstances," and so on, saying no more than the truth. But all at once the girl exclaimed that I could do what I liked with my property, she didn't want any of it. And she got up and walked out of the room.

After a moment, when I perceived that she was angered against me, I hastened to find her. But it appeared that she had gone out. Her hat and cloak were missing from the back hall. And it was a cold day, with squalls of rain, as green as ice, moving continually in from the sea. When I imagined Ann, as usual insufficiently clad, lingering about the fields in this weather and endangering not only herself but the child, I was ready to beat my head on the walls.

I felt so ill that I lay down in the salon, itself bitterly cold in its dismantled state. And the idea occurred to me that I might actually be in some measure possessed by an evil will, by the devil.

"If that is so," I thought, "and I am really an exceptionally wicked man, it might explain my fallings away from Lucy, and also my bad treatment of Sara. It would also explain why this child Ann appears to be shocked by conclusions on my part, which seem to me only logical."

40

A heavy depression fell upon me, and I was in a most unhappy condition when I thought, "Such unsystematic argument leads only to confusion. Let me see how I stand—let me draw up what I might call a balance sheet."

I then took paper and noted down rapidly in pencil the opposing arguments thus:

1. My past blindness and failure of understanding with Lucy, Sara, and Ann.

   My present comprehension of these failures and desire to amend them.

2. My love of an orderly and settled life, my too great reverence for tradition, etc., and the family possessions that represent tradition in material form.

   My resolve to leave it and to leave Tolbrook.

3. My suspicion that Ann and possibly Robert would not be sorry to see me out of the way.

   The truth that such a wish on their part would not be unnatural or incompatible with dutiful feelings, etc.

4. My provocation of her by hinting about the will, etc.

   This is wrong, but it is difficult to find out what is going on in these children's heads without provoking some expression of feeling.

5. The possible injustice of suspecting her of interested motives.

   This is a crime which I must at all costs avoid. I have too often behaved unjustly before.

Conclusion, that though I am not a good man, I need not fall into the vanity of supposing myself a monster. I have lived a futile and foolish life and done many things of which I have cause to be ashamed; but I must not allow myself the luxury of those romantic ecstasies by which an Alfred de Musset makes of his common and vulgar sins a special glory. They would be out of place in a retired English lawyer of seventy-one, suffering from a diseased heart.

Let me rather, in the way of my fathers, soberly resolve to do better. Let me reflect in Sara Jimson's own words:

> A miserable sinner is the devil's pet,
> Two sins got in one bed, a worser to beget.

41

And the very thought of Sara as usual brings me peace. For that was Sara's quality. Not the passion of Lucy which transported the soul out of darkness; but the tranquil light, like that of an English morning, which disperses shadow out of all corners.

I remember Sara dropping a china sauceboat on the stone passage floor at Tolbrook. I was close to her. Indeed, my sudden approach had perhaps startled her into letting the china fall.

Both of us were struck dumb at this accident, for the boat was old Spode, a family heirloom. And indeed I was depressed all that evening until, going to the kitchen for some trifle and consulting with Sara about the disaster, I heard her say, "It's bad enough, sir, indeed, but it might have been the tureen. I had that in my hand not two minutes before."

The very idea shocked us, and I suggested that it might be better not to use the Spode tureen.

"No, indeed, I think we'd better not," Sara said, "except when the bishop comes to dinner, or the baronet. And I'll have to do with one boat then. Though they say, indeed,

> 'Tis not so bad as judgment day,
> And who can tell but that's today."

And so, in a moment, by that country rhyme, I was brought to mind of the four last things, beside which even the tureen, unique as it was, seemed a trifle. I could smile at my fears for it. Though after all, if we feel no anxiety for a beautiful and unique treasure, we may want feelings which supply more important virtues.

Two more different women than Lucy and Sara never lived; Lucy, proud, contemptuous of the people, ignorant, and strong willed; Sara, compliant and shrewd, a born intriguer. But both, born in neighboring parishes, had the same power of bringing before one's eyes the Pisgah sight of wider landscape than a provincial drawing room or a London square.

42

Ann suddenly appeared from the garden to ask me if I wanted tea. And as she seemed in very good spirits, I asked her if it was wise for her to be out in such a wind. "It's not me but you," she answered. "How is the enemy behaving?" meaning my heart.

She then took my pulse and sent me to bed, saying that I had thoroughly upset myself. I obeyed without protest. For I still felt guilty before her. It is always dangerous to forget that in every human soul, however irreligious and irresponsible,

God has planted some spark of altruism, some kind and unselfish feeling. I believe Ann to be, at bottom, a good creature, spoiled only by a bad education.

This impression seemed to acquire some support when two days later she began to attend morning prayers. But I said nothing, and I soon discovered how wise I had been in that prudence, when the young woman asked me if the prayer book had been changed since the days of Mansfield Park.

"So you come to prayers as a literary amusement?"

"No, uncle, I just wondered."

I was about to tell her that if she wished only to amuse herself with antiquarian pursuits I had rather she did not come at all. But I restrained myself. For I thought, "Even if the mother only plays at the forms of religion, these very forms may save the child. As a bad priest can still be the means of grace—and dogma carry the living truth," and I took occasion to say to her that Jane Austen had always been a favorite of mine. No writer of her time had shown so true a picture of English Christianity in its good sense and social dignity.

"I used to think *Pride and Prejudice* best," she said, "but now I like *Mansfield Park* better."

"You are quite right— it has a far deeper and truer experience of life—it is a book for the adult."

"Yes, I suppose I am growing up, or old, as well as fat and stupid."

4 3

March weather like this was Lucy's delight, with all the moor streams full and roaring down the stones, and winds blowing up the clouds and the rain together, so that the clouds pour along the sky and the rain showers sail along in mid-air, like enormous cobwebs, at the same pace. The sky and Tolbrook

River flow the same way, and you seem to stand between two rivers, one above and one below, whirling foam and glittering bubbles to the east, till they fall over the horizon together.

Bill came home on leave that year of Lucy's return and took us walking even in the pouring rain. Bill was now a captain of Engineers and an expert on tropical barracks. In that time of little wars he was seldom seen in England. And we had prepared to entertain him.

But it was Bill who entertained us from the first hour. "Who's for the moor? I say, who's been planting daffodils along the drive, good idea, what?" Bill, who did not spend a week at home in two years, knew every corner of the house and would at once perceive the smallest change. "Who chose the new carpet in the library—it won't stand the sun, you know. Blue is a very bad color for the sun. I say, did the woodpeckers nest in Tenacre last year?"

He had grown almost as broad as he was tall, a square red-faced man with a ginger mustache and eyes like a retriever, pale brown and transparent; and now he had begun to show that thirst for exact knowledge which, as with many soldiers of his corps, grew all his life. Bill was always anxious to get to the bottom of things. Yet he would never read the books we recommended to him. He was suspicious of learned works. And I think he was impatient of reading. He fired a hundred questions at Lucy about the Benjamites, to which she answered but shortly.

"Scrubbing floors," he said. "Well, it's a new idea." He pondered it. "Probably a good idea."

"You should try it, Bill."

"Well, dammit, I'm Church of England. But if I were a Benjamite, I suppose it would do me good. Scrub for the glory of the Lord. Why not?"

"It nearly killed Lucy," I said severely. "Look at her."

"I don't see much change—blooming as ever."

I was angry with Bill because Lucy refused to recover weight and still could not sleep. It had already been resolved that she must have a long change. My mother was to take her abroad.

But Lucy, to my delight, had so contrived it, through my father, that she should go alone with me. For, as she said, "Mother will worry about me all the time, but you will only worry about the tickets and the fleas."

Our plans were already made, and Bill himself, as soon as he heard of them, at once forgot his sympathy with the Benjamites and strongly urged Lucy to go as soon as possible. He got out a map, sent for railway guides, and organized the whole expedition. "Pisa—I did Pisa between two trains on the way to Brindisi."

"But I want to see a lot of Pisa," I said.

"Every day at Pisa is a day off Rome. Take your choice—but according to the guidebook, and after all, it's supposed to know what it is talking about, half a day is quite enough for Pisa."

"We'll spend a week at Pisa if Tommy chooses," Lucy said.

"A week—what on earth will you do for a week in Pisa?"

"Me, I don't care what I do. But Tommy wants to study the cathedral or something, or the place someone was starved to death in, and I'm not going to have you organizing him out of it."

"All right, all right, just make up your minds, that's all." Bill was always perfectly cheerful when his advice was rejected. He had the good temper of a modest man who does not set a high price upon his own ideas. And in twelve hours, that is, on the second day of his leave, he had already arranged our trip and written for tickets.

But on that afternoon, a very wet one, while I was recounting to my mother in the salon how wet it had been and how wet we had got, I heard a strange man's voice from the hall. He was talking to my father. "I'm afraid it sounds like Mr. Brown," my mother said.

"Why afraid?" I said, annoyed by her tone of resignation. "If it's Brown, I'll kick him out."

"Yes, but he must have come to take Lucy away."

"He can't do that," I said, lowering my trouser bottoms, which I had turned up to show her how muddy they were. My mother, with her high-arched brows which expressed so much sadness, answered only, "Lucy will do what she feels right." She laid a slight emphasis on the *she*.

I went out into the hall and heard Brown say to my father that he had come to fetch his wife. My father stood at the bottom of the stairs. Lucy, still in her wet ulster, had retreated three or four steps upwards, but now stood half-turned, looking down at the two men with a critical air.

My father did not seem to know how to answer, and remained silent, and as if mildly confused. But this appearance was habitual to my father, who had long since lost all resemblance to a soldier and was more like an old-fashioned countryman, short, bowlegged, plump, with a bald head and a pink face, in which his pale blue eyes were like rain puddles reflecting a pale spring sky from the pink Devonshire earth. He had still a large mustache, but now, snow-white and drooping over his mouth, it gave him a sheepish rather than a fierce look. After a long pause, he muttered to Brown something like, "Er-r, yes, er-r, yes."

Brown thought that he was not understood and said loudly, "I said, Colonel Wilcher—I've come to fetch my wife and no one has the right to keep her from me."

Brown, as I say, was an ugly man, all body and no legs, not very short, but shaped like a dwarf. His head was extremely big, and he had the face of so many great orators and preachers, advocates and demagogues, a political face: short pugnacious nose, long upper lip, huge thin mouth, heavy but shallow chin, deeply cleft, hollow deep-set eyes. He was as formidable as a gorilla, and seeing his threatening movement toward my father

I ran between them and said, "But she has every right to stay away from you, Mr. Brown."

"Er-r-r," my father said. "No one is keeping wives from you, Mr. Brown. I am the last man." And then he turned to Lucy and said, "If you don't want to go back, Lucy, stay here—you're free, you know. Do what you like."

Although he spoke in his usual quiet voice, we knew by his flushed forehead that he was very angry. But I don't think this was why he had taken Lucy's side. Our father had two contradictory views about women: one, that a wife must cleave to her husband at all costs; the other, that a woman, as a living soul, should have all freedom. Many of his generation held the same contradiction; they were Christians as well as Whigs. But in practice this enabled them to use their judgment, and my father plainly judged that Lucy had every reason to stay away from Brown.

To my surprise, Brown did not thunder at us, but turned to me and spoke in a reasonable and almost polite tone, "Excuse me, young sir, but she is not free,—she is under God's law like every one of us here; and by that law, she must serve Him and obey Him and humble herself before Him."

"That does not mean before you, I suppose," I said. I was in a great rage with Brown and wished to provoke him.

My father said, "Er-r, no right to speak like that, Tom," but then suddenly walked away into the back hall and left us.

Brown spoke to me in the same earnest way. "No, young man, and if you know me, you would not make so blasphemous and foolish a charge. God knows I have tried to serve Him, in agony and sweat, and if I have failed, then I shall answer for it to Him. Lucy, I have come for you in His name."

He called this upstairs, and turning, I saw that Lucy was walking away upon the upper landing. I was glad that she had escaped, because I could speak freely. I told Brown that he ought to be in jail. He had ruined my sister's health and then betrayed her. "Do you deny that you have taken another wife?"

"Not so," he said. "Ella was given to me by the Lord and it was by his commandment that I took her to wife, and put Lucy away for a season. And it was His command, too, that she should serve Ella on her knees and be a servant to servants, that grace might come to her and that she might know Him at last, by His spirit."

I answered that I took no interest in his cant and that he had better go. He would never see Lucy again.

I left him and went upstairs to Lucy. I was afraid that she would be put out. I found her on her knees, packing her box.

"What are you doing, Lucy?"

"Where is he?"

"I told him to go."

"Run and stop him—tell him I'm coming."

These words, so totally unexpected, threw me into confusion and anger. I felt that Lucy, as my mother said, was beyond us; an unreasonable creature. I said, "You can't go back—what has happened to you?"

"Run along, Tommy, quickly—you'll miss him."

"Are you afraid of him, or what?"

She looked up at me and I saw again the gypsy face, calmly impatient of the protected, the comfortable, the self-deceivers. "You know very well he's right—I am a spoiled and selfish woman. I have always fought against God, and it's my plain duty to do His will and go back to the master."

"And what about the rule—about God's command?"

"I don't need God's command. It's common sense."

"And this woman Ella, are you going back to be her servant—it's revolting."

"It depends on how you feel," Lucy said. "What right have I to be jealous and spiteful? I've known I was wrong the whole time. It has poisoned every day here. Silly old Dr. Mac thinks it's my innards are wrong, but it's not my bodily inside keeps me awake. It's God's anger and grief. Now, Tommy, please don't pester me with any more philosophy."

Lucy always called my arguments with her philosophy, and nothing made me more angry. She always had the power to enrage me, and now I raged at her and said that she was quite right about herself, she had always been spoiled and selfish.

"If you won't go for the master, I must go," she said, and began to get up. But just then Brown himself walked in and said, "Are you coming, Lucy?"

"I'm getting ready as fast as I can."

"Do you not ask for forgiveness?"

I was told afterwards that Brown's disciples used to ask his forgiveness on their knees. But Lucy certainly did not do so then. She answered only, "I shall ask when I've time." Then she pointed at a pair of boots under the dressing table and said, "Put those boots in the bag on the bed."

Brown, to my surprise, obeyed her with the quick humble movement of a meek husband; and Lucy continued to order him about, in a very sharp manner. At last she got up and said, "Now you can strap this trunk and mind you don't nip that petticoat."

I perceived then once more how limited was my imagination, and how little I had understood either Brown or Lucy; how little Edward understood them either. And in truth, as I learned at a later time from one who had been a Benjamite, Lucy was a terror to Brown; she treated him often with such cruel and bitter contempt that he would howl to be delivered from her. She had brought him publicly to tears on more than one occasion. It was no wonder, this observer said, that he preferred other women from the sect; such as the sheepish Ella, to whom he was a god.

"Why then," I asked, "did Brown take her back?"

"It was God's command," said the ex-Benjamite, who was

still, apparently, a Christian of the simplest order. "I have been told he wrestled many days on his knees before he submitted, and I think we can see what God meant. For your sister was a great power—she gave him strength."

However Lucy and Brown suffered by the other in their partnership, she was, at that time, sure of her duty; and the moment she had bowed herself to it, she was at peace. She went to Papa and made him so affectionate and tender a farewell that the old man was in tears. And to me, when she said good-by, she smiled once more in her old kindness, as she had never smiled during her visit, and tapped my cheek and said, "Don't look so surprised, Tommy. It's all quite reasonable—as you will find out for yourself—or perhaps not."

Even to Bill she was charming. For Bill, who had been forgotten, suddenly appeared at the moment of farewell.

"Hullo, hullo," he said, staring, "where are you off to?"

"She's going back with her husband," I said bitterly.

"And a good thing, too. She's quite right."

"You know nothing about it, Bill."

"Dammit, you don't want her to separate from her husband, do you?"

"No, of course not. Bill is all for a wife's duty, aren't you, Bill?" Lucy was laughing at him. "Like all bachelors."

"That's not my fault, marriage is marriage." And he added, "I've always meant to get married, you know."

Lucy kissed him, avoiding his mustache, and said, "Good-by, Bill, bless you."

"Good-by, old dear. But you're doing the right thing. Sure of it."

Brown was seen at the turn of the stairs, carrying a large trunk upon his back, like a professional porter. Lucy called out to him sharply, "Careful—don't break the balusters." She spoke as to a slave. But Bill, exclaiming, ran to take one handle of the trunk, and said, "You mustn't do that, sir. Let me help you." He was full of compliments and apologies, and when they had brought the trunk to the hall, he reproached the visitor. "Shouldn't have done that, Mr. Brown—a great effort—but you might have strained yourself."

He laughed and straddled his legs like one talking, not perhaps to a bishop, but to a dean, a reverend person who required special treatment, special protection, but not the highest kind of respect.

When the Browns had left and I understood that again Lucy had gone from me, I turned my anger upon Bill. I asked him if he had not seen the change in Lucy: if he understood how greatly she had suffered.

"Was she changed?" he asked. "Well, we're all growing older. Poor old Lu. But she knows what she's doing all right. Trust Lu. She's always taken her own line, and she likes a stiff one." He laughed and said, "I'll bet she keeps him in order."

I began to laugh at Bill, and the laugh still mixes with the memory of my bitterness when I canceled the holiday with Lucy. I had looked forward to it with joyful hope so that even now I carry in my mind pictures of Rome and Venice, and only recollect with an effort that they were always pictures, anticipation, and never a reality. For I have never found time to go abroad. Indeed, I have never been out of England in peacetime, except once to Paris, Edinburgh, and Cardiff.

44

But I know why Lucy went back to her hard life and why Brown took her back although she was his scourge. They were both people of power; life ran in them with a primitive force and innocence. They were close to its springs as children are close, so that its experience, its loves, its wonders, its furies, its mysterious altruism, came to them as to children, like mysteries, and gave them neither peace nor time to fall into sloth and decadence.

No one can understand that private quality of life, the very spring of faith, who has not known it in himself or in some other, like Lucy or Brown or Sara, one of those whose life overflowed to all about them. I feel that energy in Robert, but not in Ann. And so I am afraid for her. She is listless and careless. Like other doctors, she will not follow a proper regimen. When she should be taking exercise she leans over the parlor fire, and when it is cold or wet, she goes out without a coat to the garden or the yards. And if she is not watched she will sit down on the stone seat.

According to Robert, it is especially dangerous for her to sit on stone, in case she should catch cold below, which would be very dangerous. But he says to me, "It's no good me talking to her, uncle. She just naturally doesn't do anything I say. She'd die first. So if you would just take a look out of the window now and then and see that she's being reasonable."

But when I tell Ann about the danger of sitting on cold stone, she answers: "Robert is talking about cows. He is clever with cows, and with me, too—he has got his calf. But if I am to be a cow, he will have to give me some more legs, for I can't carry so much of myself on two."

In fact, she has now got very big. It is astonishing that so small and thin a girl can be so big. And I feel very anxious for her. A fall, for instance, might be disastrous. I have seen so many families afflicted by a half-wit, and there is no more terrible misfortune. Yet it is risked a dozen times a day by the carelessness of young women like Ann. Or perhaps by something worse than carelessness.

"Just cussedness," Robert tells me with his mild cheerful air. "But women are cussed creatures, especially when they're that way. Trouble is, I've no time just now to run round her—so she's bent on going out alone and falling in some ditch."

So I find myself with a new and heavy responsibility, which keeps me at the window nearly all day. And it is true that the girl is cussed. She dodges out when no one is looking, or hides from us in some corner. Just now I missed her, and it was ten minutes before I caught sight of her from the nursery window. She was among the little apple trees which Robert has planted in the rose garden, drifting about like a fallen leaf. And as usual without a coat. I seized a coat and hurried out to her. She looked at me with a bored, indifferent face.

"It's all right, uncle."

"It's not all right. You're frozen—your face is blue."

"I meant your baby is all right. I'm keeping it warm."

"It's not my baby—it's Robert's, or you might say it is Edward's and Lucy's and Brown's. You don't realize perhaps that this baby of whom you are so careless ought to be a very remarkable man."

"Or woman."

"Or woman. I do not mind in the least. Another Lucy or another Brown—you couldn't have a better stock."

"You don't mean Robert's father. I thought we both detested him."

"What do you know about him?" I said, startled to think I had prejudiced her already against Brown. "He was a great man, a great Englishman, in the line of Bunyan, Wesley, Booth. What a preacher." And I began to explain to her the absolute necessity, to a living faith, of the new revelation. That such as Brown and Lucy, who can give the experience of grace, are the very founts of God's revelation, etc., and so on.

"And did he really make Aunt Lucy scrub the room for that other woman, and sleep on the floor when they were in bed together?"

"What did it matter? What is going on in your head now? Don't you see that Lucy enjoyed it?"

"Do you mean she was happy with that brute?" in a tone of mild surprise, which is as much as she has ever shown.

"Happy? Yes, of course, and you ought to be a very happy wife."

"I'm sorry, uncle, but you know Robert and I never had many ideas in common."

"What does that matter?" I asked her, quite horrified by her ignorance. "Good gracious, what is going to happen to you? You didn't get married because you liked each other's ideas."

But then Robert appeared suddenly beside us and said, "Excuse me, uncle, but I think it's time this girl was taking her milk and malt. I don't want to spoil your walk, but the wind is a bit sharp this morning, and there's a lot of flu about."

"Why not bring me my bucket here?" Ann said. "The other calves get it put under their noses."

And she began to talk about dairy bulls and milk records.

When the child speaks so, I cannot listen to her. For it seems to me that she is trying to hurt herself, as Robert takes pleasure in destroying the old trees in whose shade we used to play.

"Do you *want* to spoil your life?" I asked her. "Of course it's none of my business. But why else do you say what you don't believe? Surely you know that you aren't a cow. Cows don't read pathology. Though I suppose it is just as well for them and for us."

"But don't you think it will be better when marriage is arranged more on stock-breeding lines?" and so on. All very reasonable and scientific. And so, as Ann, I suspect, well knows, the more upsetting to me.

"Eugenics is the next great step forward," she says, in her dreamy voice. "Don't you think so, uncle?"

"A great improvement would be made, certainly," I answer,

"for instance, in discouraging the mental defectives from marriage," and so on. But all the time I am getting more and more upset, until at last I am finally driven from the field. I have to take refuge in my room, which is very cold this weather. Ann, to do her justice, wants me to have a fire, but I have never cared for fires in bedrooms. A needless and enervating luxury.

4 5

Ann would say that on the subject of marriage I am a sentimental old Victorian. But what is sentiment? It is only a feeling about life. Every age has its feelings, and if they are strong and good feelings, surely they are not disgraceful. And what Ann thinks a sentimental idea about women was only one part of a whole collection of feelings, which made up the spiritual life of a whole society.

When Bill came home in '89, and announced that he wanted to be married, he was not in love. His feeling was that he ought to be married.

Edward asked him if he had anyone in mind. But he answered, "No, that's the problem."

"Then why do you want to get married?"

"Well, old chap, I'm going on for thirty, and if I don't get married soon, I'll turn into a damned old bachelor. I'm a bit that way already."

"What are the symptoms?"

"Why, getting finicky about things—and turning against the whole idea, too. In another two years I shan't be able to face matrimony at all."

"Why should you?"

"Why should I?" Bill was surprised. "What, not get married? Well, dash it, what would happen if no one got married?" He was indignant with us for taking the matter so lightly.

"And besides, it isn't natural to be single. But you know that as well as I do. And it's the happiest kind of life."

"Why is it the happiest kind of life?" we asked him, for it was the rule to draw Bill out.

"Why," said Bill, turning his indignant eyes upon us, " because it's natural. But the trouble is, I thought I'd get six weeks to be hitched, but I only got a fortnight on account of this new fuss with the old Mahdi. So I shall only have time to look round. Are those nice girls, what's their name, still at Rose Hill?"

"You mean the Farrens. No, two married and one's dead. Good heavens, you didn't think of them, did you? There are dozens round here far better-looking than the Farrens."

"Yes, but they wouldn't have me in a fortnight, or their mothers wouldn't."

"Of course they would," Edward said. "They'd marry any-one to get away from their mothers. And you're the hero of the day—the girls would draw lots for you."

"What girls were you thinking of?"

"There's Amy Sprott for one—I saw her looking at you yes-terday," Edward said, using the first name that came into his head.

"Amy," Bill said, "what Amy?" frowning and trying to rec-ollect the girl, whom he had probably never seen.

"Daughter of old Sprott in the I.C.S."

"Is she pretty?"

"Depends on your taste."

"All the better if she isn't. The pretty ones are generally spoiled," Bill said. "Amy, Amy, I seem to remember an Amy, brown eyes and rather good at croquet—or was it tennis?"

"Blue eyes, but she does play croquet."

"Oh, but she wouldn't have me—I mean not right away."

"I wouldn't mind a bet on it."

"It's not a thing to bet about."

Bill said no more upon the matter until the next afternoon when there was a tennis party. By that time both Edward and I had forgotten the conversation of the day before. We were arranging matches and talking to the guests, especially two very pretty girls, the daughters of our neighbor Sir T. A. There was a special relation between us and these two girls, because it was known that the parents on both sides were anxious that one of us should marry one of them. Suddenly Bill drew me aside and asked which was Amy Sprott.

His gravity frightened me. For the first time I thought, "Can he be serious? Suppose he really married that dumpling Amy Sprott, because of our stupid joke, and ruined his whole life." "My dear Bill," I said, "you don't need poor Amy. You have half a dozen of the prettiest and nicest girls in the county to flirt with."

"Yes, but which is Amy?"

I laughed. "But Bill, we were only joking about Amy."

Bill looked at me with an absent-minded stare which was a trick of his. It showed not anger, but obstinacy. "Come on," he said, "introduce me."

"She isn't here. I expect she stayed away because she knows she can't compete. Besides, she's fearfully shy. She's really only a schoolgirl, and gauche at that. Come." I took his sleeve. "I'll introduce you to a really charming girl."

Bill jerked away his sleeve. Now he was angered. He said sharply, "I wish you'd mind your own business, Tommy. Can't I choose my own friends?"

"But you've never seen Amy in your life. Edward was pulling your leg."

"Kindly shut up and put your silly head in a basket." He walked off, furious. And I saw him speak to Edward, who at once sent off a note to the vicarage. Amy was staying there with her uncle, for her father was in India. Half an hour later, too late for tea, we saw her approaching, with the old gentleman, from the drive. The whole party gazed at her, in her dowdy cotton frock, like a servant's print, and a straw hat which was visibly her school hat with a new ribbon. The girl was crimson with heat and embarrassment.

"Is that Miss Sprott?" Bill asked. He jumped up, walked across the ground and presented himself. He then spoke to the uncle, who nodded several times and came toward us with a benevolent smile. "So you wanted to see me, Mr. Wilcher," he said to Edward.

Edward, much amused by Bill's strategy, invented a question about the political feeling in the village. For the Gladstone government, which we all supported, was then in opposition.

We were gazing at Bill. He spoke to the girl, and we saw her start and blush and stare. She came quickly toward her uncle. But Bill, following at her elbow, continued to speak.

She was now close to us, and even our visitors noticed that something strange was happening. As for me, I have never seen a more candid expression upon a girl's face, the round red face of a countrified miss which I had thought so inexpressive of anything but the crudest feelings—joy, greed, embarrassment. You could see that she was amazed and unbelieving, and yet she was saying to herself, "But perhaps it is true, perhaps it could happen like this."

After all, if Bill at thirty, having lived in the service since he was eighteen, had an idea of a world as simple and clear as the field-service book, the girl, from the convent of an English school, was not much more wise. Bill continued to speak with energy and passion. Bill was never short of words. The girl hesitated, stopped, and for a moment stood on one foot. It was the pivot of her life. She turned suddenly and walked away from her uncle, with Bill beside her. The engagement was announced the same evening, and they were married by special license four days later.

This was no romantic freak. To Amy and Bill, I am sure, it

was the common thing. To simple-minded persons, miracles appear like nature. In the same way, they expected to be happy, to love one another, etc., and therefore they did so.

46

"A kind of faith cure," Ann said to me, and I thought I must have been speaking aloud.

"I don't know what you would call it." But I thought, "Not a cure for anything. It was the whole idea of an age, and how could I convey that, or its strength? For only the idea can fight against the cruelty of fate. It is in some strong well-founded idea that men and women, and whole nations, float as in a ship over the utmost violence of chance and time."

"It was very romantic," Ann said in her voice of a small girl who has a pain and knows that she mustn't eat cake.

"They were not a sentimental couple. Their arguments were a family joke. But they were devoted all their lives."

"Yes, I suppose romantic people could go on being happy—it was a kind of hallucination."

"You speak as if your uncles and aunts had been weak in the head."

"Oh, no, but Aunt Lucy and Uncle Bill do seem a little mad—with a good kind of madness."

"You think we're all mad. You think me mad."

"Never, uncle. You are much too clever at getting your own way."

I was astonished. "So you think me cunning. Lunatics are famous for their cunning."

"Well, look. Robert meant to go back to Brazil, but here he is tied to Tolbrook. And I meant to be a distinguished patholo-gist, and here I am, a silly little wife with a big tummy, also tied to Tolbrook."

"And I did all this—why, it's perfectly ridiculous."

"Perhaps you didn't know you were doing it. You only suggested that I should see Robert again if we came to Tolbrook. And you knew I had fallen for his nice eyes. And then you happened to catch us together. And then you gave Robert all these new toys to play with—a little at a time. Like giving cut wool to a kitten till it's quite tied up. And now you have got the baby you wanted and you have decided that it's going to be an Edward or a Lucy."

"What nonsense, what nonsense. Though these are good English names. And I suppose, if you have a son, he will be in the eldest line, and they are all Edwards."

For it was true that I had sometimes hoped for another Lucy or Edward. And I had perhaps shown my preference to Ann.

"But I'm not blaming you, uncle, for wanting the family to go on. The family is like you, isn't it, and of course you want to go on."

"Loftus and Blanche are carrying the family on, with their son."

"I'm not saying you meant to do all this, you know," the girl said, as if I needed assurance, and she began to talk about the unconscious will, and so on; unpacking some of her German boxes. "You know," she said, "I didn't think I meant to marry Robert, and yet I was mad to get him. I was quite in despair until you suggested that he might be at Tolbrook."

For a moment she made my head turn. Everything began to dissolve out of its familiar shade into a mysterious twilight like a witch night under summer lightning.

But I knew very well the danger of such notions to an old man. It was enough to make me mad. I answered, therefore, that she was talking nonsense.

"All this hairsplitting between a man's will and his deed

leads from one piece of nonsense to another. How can you tell what anyone's intentions are except by his acts?"

"I was thinking of acts. I know how I ran after Robert. It's frightful to think how scandalously I behaved. Poor Robert. I should be sorry for him if it weren't Robert. How we have taken him in, the pair of us."

"Don't say such things. How can you tell what we did or what Robert himself wanted? Who can look into others' motives? Look at your own achievement—that is plain enough. And look at Robert's achievement."

Ann, who was as usual dawdling over the fire, suggested that I had not yet seen all Robert's destruction.

"What has he destroyed?"

"You haven't been to Tenacre lately, have you?"

"But I am all for Robert's improvements at Tenacre. I thought his idea of the circus engine a stroke of genius."

"Well, you kept him off the trees here, and I'm glad—I don't want him to spoil our view."

"We mustn't get too fond of the view, as you call it—we have to move with the times. Or the time will move us. And modern agriculture shows a very valuable and interesting development. I'm all for the machine."

"But then," Ann said, "you're like me—you don't like horses," the kind of remark that always angers me.

"Why do you do the devil's work, Ann—trying to make me believe that there is nothing in the world but selfishness and self-seeking?"

And the girl answered me, apparently in all sincerity, "A world like that might be rather restful." A remark that drove me from her, in fear as well as anger. An abominable remark that tunnels like some devil's miner into the very ground of hope and love, to blow all up.

It kept me awake half the night, in wonder at this devil's power and terror of his persistence, his cunning. "But damn it all," I say, "you old fool, you know there is love, there is hope, there is faith. Does not everything in this house say to you 'God is'?"

47

The small, round-topped windows of my room are the last relic, so they say, of a priory whose ruins are built into this wing. They are perhaps seven hundred years old. The initials, W. A. W., cut by Bill in the keystone on the left, are already filled with paint, but from my bed I can see the faint shades of some of the downstrokes. I cannot remember why Bill and Amy chose this room, which was no longer the children's sickroom, and not yet my bedroom. But it was a favorite room with all of us when we came home, because it had a wide view and stood next the upper closet where there was a hot-water tap. And near the only bathroom.

Amy was seventeen at the time of her marriage in '89, Bill twenty-eight. Edward said that Amy had not yet taught herself to use Bill's Christian name before he was once more on the sea. She was engaged on Tuesday, married on the next Saturday, alone by Tuesday week, and a mother before she saw her husband again, three years later.

Bill was the joke of the family, but now I do not laugh at him. I think now, with surprise, that he was the best of us and that we laughed at him and at Amy because we could not see them in truth or know them as they were. It was a fashion to make a joke of them, and I followed the fashion all my life.

Bill and Amy had the unbreakable faith of children who come home every day to a new world; and from that faith they looked out, as monks once looked from this room, at the world as a spectacle. They did not need to think of themselves, for they knew exactly their purpose and their due. So, even on the last day of his leave, Bill spent half the night mending his mother's workbox, and Amy did not protest. She might not see him again for years, but she had undertaken the venture of Bill's wife. They were not a sentimental couple. Lucy used to say that when Bill left Amy for the first time, her last words, called after the railway carriage, through her tears, were, "Where did you leave my bicycle pump?" And that Bill answered at the top of his voice, "Don't forget you're punctured behind."

We were already laughing at Amy, as well as Bill, and we took her grief very lightly. I can remember Edward remarking that her swollen eyes and pink nose made her look like a sucking pig. "She only needs a good brown sauce and she would be quite presentable at the dinner table."

Yet Amy became a true member of the family. When she was at Tolbrook it was always the cry, "Where's Amy?" She was sent on all parish errands, and answered for everybody's buttons. If anything were lost, broken, torn, or forgotten, Amy was called to account. The very servants would say of any loss or any omission, "I thought it was Mrs. William, mam, who was looking after it." And this seemed reasonable and proper to Amy herself, who spent all day running up and down stairs, even when she was within a week of her time. She was used, I suppose, to the position of niece in houses where her presence was always a trouble or deprivation to others; where there were questions every day, whether she should be left out of a party to which the children of the house were invited, or if she could be asked to give up her bed for some valued visitor, and to sleep on a sofa.

Bill, when they were at home together, used to make the same demands upon her. Bill's shouts for Amy were louder than any others. On the other hand, he too was always busy with small tasks; he organized picnics, otter hunts, badger digs, rabbit shoots; he made Amy climb the local tors or bathe in the moor streams, which turned her nose so red that he would complain of it, "Look at Amy's nose. But she won't do anything about it. I don't believe she's taken a single cold bath since I've been away. Her circulation is disgraceful."

Amy, for her part, would try, without success, to make Bill wear mufflers and overcoats, which he detested. Both were stubborn and dogmatic. Bill was Low Church, Amy High Church, and they scorned each other's services. Bill would say loudly that Amy's parsons in petticoats could only catch women, who were idiots about religion; and Amy would answer that the parish church always sent her to sleep and gave her a crick in her ribs.

"You can't have a crick in your ribs. Don't you know ribs don't bend?" Bill would answer.

"I'm sure mine do."

"And you call yourself a Red Cross nurse."

"Well, there's a special bandage for broken ribs."

"But that doesn't prove that ribs have joints."

"I haven't done the joints, but ribs must join on somewhere."

"Listen to that," Bill would cry. "Well, damn it all. I give you up, Amy. You'd break the heart of a brass elephant. I'll never argue with you again—that I'll swear." But in three minutes he was arguing with her again. Bill lost his temper with Amy twenty times a day, and gave up forever; but they never quarreled. They were inseparable on leave, and one was never seen without the other.

I laughed at them when they were alive, but they always brought new energy to Tolbrook. Lucy came here only to escape from her life; but Bill, arriving from China or Lagos with silk robes or spears which no one wanted, was always like a small boy coming for his holidays. He had the same projects, impossible to fulfill; the same eagerness for news; and he had a small boy's astonished and aggrieved air when he discovered that we had not been shooting or fishing or picnicking lately and had not formed any plans for shoots or picnics. He made us see what was going on under our noses. "I say, what a gorgeous morning. What about the moor? I say, did you ever see such a sky? Quick—it's fading already."

When, on these mornings, the window arches of the old cell frame a cold spring sky and the first buds on the great lime, I think, "The medieval monks who looked out of these windows at sky and buds did not see them with clearer eyes than Bill's. Both looked out from a security and faith as strong as a child's surrounded by the unseen care of its mother. Bill's cry of 'I say, look at this, look at that,' had the same medieval quality of 'Loud sing Cuckoo,' that true lyric, which is a cry of delight and welcome."

The homeless priest with no part in this world, the homeless soldier without inheritance, had the same innocence, which did not even know its own happiness.

Bill's delighted "I say" and the monk's song make my heart beat. I find spring through memories and the ideas of a scholar. The life through the tradition. This morning, now that Ann has pulled my curtain, I see a sky as pale as Bill's eyes, or Ann's eyes, and three clouds like sheep in full fleece moving so slowly that they seem still to a single glance.

Ann has closed my windows. But the frames are loose and the gusts, which make the lime buds swing, blow through, as cold as the sky and quick with salt.

All about Tolbrook in this southwest country, March has always smelled of salt. Its sky has the translucency of an ocean sky where there is no dust, and all the birds are as white as foam. Gulls fly over our furrows all the year, but especially now, when the winds roll them about in the air like small boats in an offing.

When I look back again at the window the three clouds have jumped up toward the left-hand bow of the frame and the house seems to rock beneath me like a ship. I, eating breakfast in bed, and always the worst of sailors, feel as if I were at sea, as if England itself were afloat beneath me on its four waves, and making the voyage of its history through a perpetual sea spring.

> Faithful to ancient ways, the English crew
> Spread old patched sails, to seek for something new.

The monk, in his sleepy routine, who seduced my weakness just now, where is he? A new vigorous generation snatched his peace away; the generation of my ancestors, who made a farmshed of his chapel and bore their half-pagan children in his holy cell. Who once more pulled up England's anchor and set her afloat on the unmapped oceans of the West. Why do I ever forget that the glory of my land is also the secret of youth, to see at every sunrise a new horizon? Why do I forget that every day is a new landfall in a foreign land, among strangers? For even this Ann, this Robert, are so changed in a single night that I must learn them again in the morning. And England wakes every day to forty million strangers, to thousands of millions who beat past her, as deaf and blind as the waves. She is the true Flying Dutchman. "O Sealand, where do you travel on this voyage without a port, through countless sunfalls and day springs, with the wind in your face. And in your eyes, the blue of infinity, the changing clouds, the gull whose only home is air and ocean.

"As their feathers glitter with the crystal salt, so do your buds. The clouds light upon the rollers of your downs like Mother Carey's chickens, when they shut-to their wings on an Atlantic comber.

"Your ploughmen sight their first furrow on a lighthouse, and roll upon their sea legs like sailors. Your sailors, ploughing the sea for a crop of salted babies; born under the spray of a thousand bare-walled ports, dream of steeples like masts and church towers with fighting tops. Your bells, in this light air, sing like a ship's bell under the hand of a quartermaster, on urgent summons to duty, to watchfulness," etc. A favorite quotation of mine, but on the other hand the proper conduct of a ship requires a certain discipline, an order.

4 8

"Robert thinks there's going to be a war, uncle."
Ann, having brought my breakfast, balanced herself carefully on a chair.

"Does he mean in China?"

"No, he thinks Germany means to make war. Hitler, he says, is planning a war because we are so weak."

"Who is Hitler?"

"Don't you read your *Times*, uncle?"

"No, I haven't read the papers for a very long time. I'm too busy."

"Robert would like to go off to Brazil before another war. He says this country is finished—it's too soft."

"What do you say?"

"I think we may be a little too civilized for war, but perhaps that is what Robert means."

"You couldn't go to Brazil with a young baby."

"Robert thinks the baby a good reason to take me abroad."

"Brazil would not suit you at all. It is very hot; and all this talk about Germany's revenge is chatter. Germany is sick of war since her defeat."

"But Germany does rather believe in war, doesn't she?"

"So did France until 1870; that cured her of swashbuckling."

"The German general staff is said to be making an enormous air force."

"When I was a young man we all expected war with France.

It took us a long time to realize that France was tired of war. I remember that your Uncle Bill, before he was married, spent his leaves bicycling in France and studying the railway system and the ports. And he made your Aunt Amy learn French, so that she could come with him on his next leave. That is to say, he tried to teach her. He used to give her lessons. I can remember her walking up and down the library, with a distracted look, saying over and over again a long list of words beginning:

"*Wagon*—railway truck.

"*Wagon-écurie*—horse box.

"*Wagon-étable*—cattle truck.

"*Wagon-frein*—break van."

I would examine her and she always broke down. She would say to me in despair, "I'll never know it—he'll be furious." *He* was Bill; she was shy of calling him Bill to us. But it never struck her that learning military French was an odd way to spend time during a nine-day honeymoon. She was used, I suppose, to the idea of school life and quite prepared to find in Bill a severe master.

Yet, as I noticed, although she worshipped Bill, and seemed so submissive to him, she paid very little attention to his wrath when she failed in her French words. She would look at him with a round, anxious eye and a flushed face while he stormed at her, and say, "Your tie is crooked."

"Have you finished breakfast, uncle?"

I thanked her and she took my tray. But on the way to the door, she perceived that her mind had wandered, and she said, "So you think we are quite safe from Hitler."

"I think the Germans would hate another war."

"Which chair did you say was the nursing chair, uncle?"

"The little mahogany chair with the legs cut short, and the broken back."

"I must put it back in the nursery." She went out and I was

glad to be alone. For I had not before remembered Amy so well, and I felt that I had done her great injustice in her life.

49

It is strange to see how men's and women's lives follow their own separate courses in the midst of happy marriages. They are like two streams of different color, which can always be distinguished even in the same river. Perhaps at the first rushing together they seem to be one, but it is merely a single confusion. And almost at once the two currents reappear, crossing and recrossing in a continuous change of pattern, but always distinct. Amy's own life continued from the day of her marriage. Even in those few days while Bill could stay with her, she was asking his advice about her winter coat, and deciding for herself how she would arrange her room, with Bill's books on one wall and her Indian embroidery panel on the other. When Bill went away, she wept for two days but at the same time made herself new curtains for her room. I can see her now on the evening of Bill's departure. She is sitting in a dark corner of the little dining room, the tears in her lashes, discussing with my mother the best color for a bedspread.

"Blue is so cold for an east room," my mother says.

"It always looks clean."

"It won't match your pink curtains." My mother hated a clash of color.

"Blue is really almost my favorite color. But I don't know whether he likes blue," with a break in her voice.

"Bill? No, I don't think he does. He didn't like your blue silk, did he?"

Then there is a long pause while Amy struggles with her tears.

At last she says with a gasp like a sob, "Yes, I think I'll have blue."

Amy was pregnant for three months before she knew what was wrong with her. It was then discovered only because she caught influenza, and when the doctor came to see her she asked him about a lump in her inside. According to the family story, when the doctor questioned her and told her that she was pregnant, she answered, "Oh, it can't be that— my husband is in Africa." She had some idea that a baby could be hatched only by a continuous warmth of closeness.

Yet she showed neither surprise nor excitement. She only stopped doing her French exercises and began to sew baby clothes.

Amy, without mother or any relation in England save the old vicar and two maiden aunts in Yorkshire, was ignorant even for a girl of those days. But her ignorance did not oppress her. She advanced through life like an explorer through unknown country, ready for anything; not in conceit of herself, but in the belief which says, "It's all happened before, so it can't be so terrible." She expressed that very creed to my mother, before her lying-in. My mother wished to encourage the child, not yet eighteen, and said that she was sure everything would go well with Dr. Maccurdy.

"Oh, yes," Amy said placidly, "and I suppose it's all arranged for inside."

Amy took very little interest in her inside. She left it to God, who, in her view, had constructed it. But, what was strange in those first three months before she knew what was happening to her, she visibly changed from a schoolgirl, playing at various pastimes, into a woman of purpose. What Amy's purpose was I do not know, and she did not know any more than a bird, who begins, at certain times of year, to make certain arrangements; but even her walk and her expression were different while she went about the small trifling tasks which

seemed to fill her time. It was not perceived till long afterwards that in that first year she had somehow procured sav-
ings, a bank balance, an investment in Consols, an extensive
knowledge of private schools, taking sole charge of children, a
steamer trunk of a new pattern from America, and a complete
set of clothes suitable for the tropics. It was found also the she
had almost complete control of Bill's finances, received most
of his pay, and kept careful account of his liabilities.

<h2 style="text-align:center">50</h2>

Amy's son was born suddenly in May. The doctor was late, and
the girl had no chloroform—she suffered extremely. But when I
saw her afterwards, her first remark was, "That went off very
luckily, didn't it? I was sure it was going to be a daughter."

"But you wanted a son."

"Of course I did. That's why I was sure it wouldn't be. And
it worked beautifully. And they're getting the blue bows this
afternoon."

"Didn't you have some of both kinds ready?"

"Oh, that wouldn't have done at all. You have to be absolutely sure, or it doesn't work. I didn't even choose a name,
but, of course, it must be William."

Amy was a devoted mother; but again, in her own way. An
early question of hers to my mother was, "How young do
you smack them?" I remember her as she sat nursing her baby,
and looking down upon it with an expression I haven't seen
for many years; a smile of detached calm amusement, as if
the baby were a joke, of good quality, but too familiar for
laughter. And even as I look, her hair becomes white, her broad
cheeks darken; she is an old woman, looking, with exactly the
same smile, at another baby, whom I do not recognize, a small
sickly creature with bluish skin and eyes so pale that one

cannot call them gray or blue. This baby gazes upwards with a fixed look of grave curiosity.

Who is it? It could not be Amy's youngest, who died at three of Malta fever.

I went to look at the old screen, close stuck with family photographs, which once stood in the nursery, and now in the attic. It was not there, but as I went back along the corridor I was surprised to see it once more in the nursery. Workmen had been employed there for the last week; their trestles and buckets barred half the doorway. But their work was finished, and alone in the middle of the room stood the nurse's old chair, the old screen and the old high chair, consisting of a small armchair standing on a table, which all of us had used. I wondered where Ann had found it, and by what luck she had chanced upon a nursery wallpaper so like that of my childhood. I hunted the screen for Amy. Here was my mother in her furs, beautiful and sad; and I thought, "She has the look of an exile who can never go back, the one who has been turned out of paradise. All exiles, whatever they were at home, have the same look of angels deprived. As if exile itself refined the soul by giving it the love that can never be gratified." But here next her is Edward in an incredible bowler and a three-inch collar, which makes him look almost foolish. Here is Bill in uniform, with his mustache curled up at the ends. That was Amy's doing. She always admired the Kaiser, because of his blue eyes and because he was the Queen's grandson. And gradually she changed Bill's mustache from a set of bristles to something a little like the Kaiser's. And here is Edward again, old and worn, with his young second wife beside him, and in his arms the thin little baby whom I saw just now in Amy's lap—Ann, in her christening robe. And here is Amy at last, in a corner, between Heenan, the prize fighter, and Ellen Terry. She is in a form I had utterly forgotten; very young with round, frightened eyes, and balanced on her head an enormous hat covered with ostrich feathers. Even I can tell that she is dressed in the most fashionable bad taste. Bill is beside her in a cap three sizes too small, and his eyes jumping out of his head. He glares as if to say, "How dare you look at this lady. She's my wife." It was taken on their three-day wedding trip at Torquay.

But Amy's look pierces me. It says, "Why do you laugh at me?" I had forgotten that look. But I remember how, one evening after we had all been laughing at one of her unexpected remarks, at bedtime when I went to get my candle in the hall and found her there, she asked me, "What were you laughing at?"

"Nothing," I said. "A family joke." I could see that she was hurt and bewildered. And yet I went upstairs still laughing within myself, and it is not till now that I perceive our cruelty.

"Do you recognize the wallpaper, uncle?" Ann's voice asked me. She was standing at my elbow, but I did not answer her.

"We found some of the old original under the whitewash and they still had the pattern—at least they had the blocks and printed me a few lengths. Robert thought I was being extravagant, but I said it was a fancy. Fancies are often useful when I want to get my own way."

I took care not to answer her in case Amy should disappear from my memory, and I remained silent while Ann decided that I ought to go to bed, and put me to bed. I can tell that she thinks me madder, and she is even anxious about me, perhaps in case I am about to become violent and murder her. But I can't waste time upon this hypocrisy of trying to appear rational. I leave that to younger people.

I am an old man, and I have not much longer at Tolbrook. This is April, and before next April I shall have left forever. I want to use every moment of these last months at home with those I love, with Lucy and Amy, Bill and Edward.

51

In spite of all my precautions, when at last I was left alone in the dark, I had lost touch with Amy. I couldn't even recall the shape of her face or the dressing of her white hair. Yet her presence was close, and all night, while I dozed or waked, I felt as if she were in the house, upon one of her long visits.

"My dear," I thought, "if you were here and I could see you, I should ask you to forgive me—or perhaps you would not understand such a request. It might frighten you after all these years when our relations had been established in a certain form. You knew me even longer than you knew Bill. Yes, long before." Then to my surprise I thought I saw Amy standing before me, not as an old white-haired woman, but as the young, rosy, too rosy and too plump young girl, who had once romped with me at Christmas parties until her nose and her forehead shone like apples. She was laughing at me in a very unconstrained manner, and I remembered how once I had kissed her in a forfeit and suddenly felt an excitement, and I had thought for one moment, "I should like her very much for a wife," and in the next, "You might as well marry any plump milkmaid within five miles and get tired of her in a fortnight."

"Was I a fool, Amy?" I asked. "Or would you have been the same wife to me as to Bill? For he was noble and simple, and he expected a great deal from women; and I was suspicious and divided and asked nothing from anybody. I was shy and ignorant of women, too, like all sensualists, and Bill was shy of nobody and nothing. How much did Bill make your soul, or how much did the common soul of you and Bill arise from some accidental fitting together of your natures?"

The fat young girl looked at me and put out her lips as if to invite a kiss. Her little blue eyes were full of Amy's gaiety. Old as I am, I was moved and attracted by that gesture, always charming when it is good-natured; I put out my arms. But they were held back, and as I struggled I was annoyed and also I felt confused, guilty, as if I had been caught in some shameful act. Amy was still laughing, but her face had disappeared and gradually I perceived that I was struggling with my bedclothes and that some woman, not Amy, was talking in a soft voice outside my door. Her voice had that wavering rapid beat of a woman's who feels a desire to laugh or cry.

I put my hand under my pillows and rang my father's repeater. It was half-past six. I opened my eyes and saw that the room was full of light.

The chatter of the maids outside my door made me suspect that perhaps Ann had sent already for an asylum van, and that I was locked into my room. "She would be quite justified," I thought, "by my extraordinary behavior last night when I would not speak to her or even look at her." I got up carefully to try the door, and found it locked. This startled me so greatly that I felt extremely faint and hardly succeeded in reaching my bed.

But then immediately a terrible pressure departed from my blood. A pressure that I had not noticed before, and such peace came upon me that I was astonished. I thought, "I can do nothing more—everything is settled."

52

Such was my sense of peace while I waited for the asylum van to take me to that home of rest that I was resentful when suddenly Robert came in.

"Are you all right, uncle?"

"Of course I'm all right. You are up very early."

"No, I always get up at five. But I've been kept in this morning because Ann's pains have started and the doctor hasn't come yet. I think you'd better take your medicine. You look rather blue—what does Ann give you?"

At these words I felt that excitement which comes to me before a struggle. I knew that I should have to fight this child's battles.

"The yellow bottle. Supposing it is a son, Robert, I suppose it ought to be an Edward. As Ann is your Uncle Edward's only representative."

Robert said nothing and left the room. I saw that he would object to the name Edward. Now the drug began to take effect and I felt strong. I could not remain still. Nothing prevented me, in Ann's absence, from doing what I liked, and I got up and dressed and hurried out to obtain news and to find Robert. But when I discovered him in the yard repairing a tractor, he received me in an indifferent manner.

"Hullo, uncle, has the doctor come yet?"

"No, he hasn't come yet, and I'm sure Ann would like to see you. Has she talked to you about names?"

"No, I must go and see her. I'll go in as soon as I've found out whether this damn thing is going to let us down in harvest when it's too late to do anything."

But, in fact, when the baby was born, he was three miles away at a blacksmith's. I myself was the first to see Ann's son. He was a disappointment to me; red faced, with black tufts of hair. Exactly like myself as a child. But his eyes were blue, and I thought, "perhaps his second hair will be lighter, and babies' noses are always unpredictable."

"Well, uncle, what do you say? I have given you an heir."

Ann spoke as if laughing at me, but I was surprised to hear her speak. She was lying flat on the bed, so thin-cheeked and white that I was reminded of the thin baby in Amy's lap.

"Yes," I thought, going out to find Robert, "there is no doubt that the baby in Amy's lap is Ann. But when did Amy nurse Ann? When Ann was born, in 1910, Amy was in India. And she came to Tolbrook only in the next year. Edward and his wife had then gone away."

The problem agitated me during my drive to the forge, where I found Robert waiting his turn until a horse could be shod.

"Ann has a son," I told him. "His eyes are like his grandfather's, but his hair, at present, is dark."

"And how's Ann?"

I had forgotten to ask after Ann, but I assured the boy that she seemed very well. "Good enough," he said, "I'll be there in no time. I'd have been there before if it hadn't come so quick. Trouble is, this is about the busiest time for me, and I don't want anything to go wrong with the first corn harvest. It's a pity Ann couldn't have put off the baby for a month or two, till after the apples, anyhow."

I ventured to suggest that Ann might be expecting to see him, but he answered only, "There's one good thing about Ann —she's not so much of a sentimental girl. She'll understand I just couldn't be round the whole time. And I couldn't lose my place now when I've been waiting more than half an hour."

So we waited till the horse was shod and then Robert gave directions to the smith about the mending of a drawbar. "Sorry, uncle," he said, "but next week half the farmers round will be sending in their binders and tractors for new parts, and if I waited till then, I might as well wait till next year."

At last he was ready and took his seat beside me in the old motor which was used for farm work. "I remember that from the old times," he said, "when I used to see the road outside the smithy blocked up all harvest with these old cutters waiting repairs and horses wanting shoes. I always said if I had a farm I wouldn't stand in that row and look like a fool while the wise virgins were getting their stuff into the threshing yard."

"You've done good work here, Robert," and then I spoke of the need to choose a name for the boy, and to give some thought to it.

"A small point," I said, "but sometimes more important to a child than people may think."

"Just what I tell Ann," Robert said, to my surprise and pleasure. "If I'd been called William, I might be a soldier now, like Uncle Bill."

"Your Uncle Edward had great qualities."

"Yeah, Ann's set on Edward. But I seem to fancy my own father's name, Mathias."

"That's not a family name."

"Well, it's not a Wilcher name, but it's a Brown name."

"But the boy is more Wilcher than Brown. And suppose he was to inherit Tolbrook some day—just supposing it. How would he feel with a name like Mathias?"

Robert said no more. He always had that bad habit of breaking off an argument as if he did not care what anyone might say. He had made up his own mind.

He stopped the car to shut a gate, and I asked him, "Where are we?" For I could not recognize the fields.

"Tenacre."

I got out of the car to look for Tenacre—but saw only a large field extending over the top of the low hills which made the horizon. I could not find a single landmark. "Where is lover's lane where you and your mother used to walk on your way to church, and where the woodpeckers nested every year?"

"Well, uncle, all those beeches and elms were pretty rotten, and we wanted to put the field together, so we grubbed the hedges. I thought you knew. It was done last October. This field is fifty acres now and goes right down to the main road. We put in potatoes because it was too rough for roots. Not too good for wheat either. But all it wants is a little feeding—a ley next year and more stock."

I looked at the new broad landscape in front of me. Every landmark was gone. Not only the winding farm lane with its great trees, the beauty of this valley, but the very shape of the ground, once marked by the curve of hedge and shrub.

I saw that the boy had tricked me. But I said to myself,

"There's nothing to be done. Nothing is to be gained by anger. On the other hand, I can still save something by diplomacy, by tact." So I said, "It's a wonderful change—you have certainly done great things here."

"Well, uncle, I've done only just what I could to get the place going again. I won't say it was run down a bit, I'll say it was so dead you could smell it. And from what the old chaps tell me, it hasn't been a real going concern since Granddad's time. He cut some drains and built some cottages—and he made the first Tenacre out of a couple of yards and a bit of moor."

"Yes, yes," I smiled and looked about me at the strange raw landscape. "A fine piece of work. Edward would have liked it. He was all for modern methods," and I was going to mention the name again, and perhaps to make a definite proposal for a legacy to any Wilcher grandchild carrying Edward's name, when I began to feel very queer. It was as though the pain of loss kept on growing all the time in my heart. I paid no attention to it. I did not allow myself to think of that loss, but it kept on growing.

It was true, of course, that I had suffered a catastrophe far beyond Robert's imagination. A country landscape is not like a piece of town, where the streets seem to say, "We are thoroughfares, do not linger here." And the houses, "We are conveniences, don't stay too long. Somebody else is waiting." Here every field and hedge was an invitation to pleasure, not only of memory but of sight, of interest. In lover's lane, now abolished, generations of mothers had seen their daughters courting. For though it was a private lane, gated at both ends, the great trees made it a favorite tryst as far as the village. And all these trees, banks, and paths said to every passer, "Wait and you shall enjoy us." A great loss; and though I turned my mind from it, it swelled up of itself till suddenly, to my dismay and horror, I perceived that my heart was affected. I was going to faint.

I was obliged to turn to the car, but I could not find the door or climb into it, and Robert was alarmed. "Where's that bottle Ann gives you?"

Much to my surprise, there was a little phial secured by a piece of elastic sewn to my pocket lining. Robert drew it out and put it to my lips. I swallowed the bitter contents, but they seemed to have no immediate effects. My breast was contracted by a pain like screws clamped on my heart. My eyes saw darkness and my head was full of fiery confusion. Robert helped me into the car and made me lie at full length across the back seats. He appeared greatly concerned, and said several times, "You know, uncle, I wouldn't have anything happen to you."

Robert was fond of me, I knew, a good-natured boy. But an obstinate one. And now it seemed that he would win this battle, by the treachery of my miserable heart.

But I thought, "It is my own fault. Haven't I known all my life that it was folly to give my affections to sticks and stones and all that helpless hopeless tribe," etc., etc. It was all very well to philosophize, but there was that great swelling pain in my breast which I could not get rid of. It was as though the very spirit of those murdered trees had come to revenge themselves upon me.

Not upon Robert, you notice. Because they could not enter into that alien soul. It is only our nearest and dearest who can haunt us, and spite us.

53

My fainting fit, as usual, passed very slowly from that darkness and confusion of my whole body into a condition of tranquil weakness. I found myself lying on my bed in my own room behind the drawn blinds, in a twilight which seemed to belong to my spirit. The light from the July sky was warm, but it seemed that I lay in perpetual winter, frozen still, without hope of spring. I breathed in the air of infinite resignation, sad and clear, through which all objects appeared in their own colors, neither gilded by the sun nor glorified by autumn mist. All appeared small, distinct, separate; and charged with several mortality. "We die," they said to me, "we die alone and all our hopes die with us. Anger is foolish, struggle is useless, and self-pity is self-torture, for there is no help from anywhere." And I remembered the verse of Edward written in his own failure and despair:

> The art of happiness? High art it is
> To walk that tight rope over the abyss.

Love is a delusion to the old, for who can love an old man. He is a nuisance, he has no place in the world. The old are surrounded by treachery for no one tells them truth. Either it is thought necessary to deceive them, for their own good, or nobody can take the trouble to give explanation or understanding to those who will carry both so soon into a grave. They must not complain of what is inevitable; they must not think evil. It is unjust to blame the rock for its hardness, the stream for its inconstancy and its flight, or the young for the strength and the jewel brightness of their passage. An old man's loneliness is nobody's fault. He is like an old-fashioned hat which seems absurd and incomprehensible to the young, who never admired and wore such a hat.

One day, soon after I came down from the varsity, my father exclaimed to me, "An old man like me has no right to mind what anybody does." I thought myself a man of the world, but I was merely surprised and embarrassed by this ejaculation. My whole idea of my father, and with it my idea of the world, seemed to waver. I did not know what to say and I can still see the look of his blue eyes fixed upon me with the appeal which I cannot understand; and their profound sadness, as he turns away.

I wonder still why he confided in me. But the beloved Lucy was gone, Bill was in Africa, and he had never been close to Edward.

I asked my mother that evening after dinner, "Isn't Papa well?" But she answered only, "I think he may be worried about Edward's debts." Neither of us perceived the warning of change, of crisis. It seemed to us both a time of great and unexpected happiness.

Tolbrook had never been so gay. For during an important election some of the Liberal chiefs had chosen to hold council there. This was partly, no doubt, in compliment to my father, a devoted supporter; and my parents had gathered all the magnates of the county, with their wives, sons, and daughters, to meet them. Every day there were meetings, conferences for the great men, picnics, and luncheons for their ladies. And almost every evening, dinners and dances. And what delighted us, and especially my mother, was Edward's success. We suddenly perceived that he had become a personage. We had heard, of course, that he was a rising man, but as in all families some secret domestic acid darkened and dissolved the evidence of his triumphs until it was before our eyes in the deference paid to his opinion by others. But perceiving it, we were carried away. And all of us, as by a change of light, showed new characters. I felt my dignity as Edward's brother, and found myself raising my voice at the dinner table. My mother was talkative and, I must use the word, flirtatious. We remembered the tale that, at Cambridge, she had been a flirt as well as a belle, and we dimly understood the excitement of an old gentleman from the university who had described her as "the most enchanting girl I ever met—as clever as she was kindhearted, and twice as beautiful. But, of course, we were too dull for her. We weren't really surprised when the handsome hero carried her off under our noses."

My mother perhaps had not escaped dullness among the soldiers' wives or in a west-country manor house; but now, with the house full of clever and interesting people, and, above all, with her darling Edward beside her, she was so happy that her very step, her smile, her glance seemed different. As she said to me, with a moment's look of doubt, "You know your father doesn't like to worry me," Edward came smiling to her and with a very low bow asked her to dance. To which she replied with the radiant glance that I had seen before only in young girls at their first ball, "Is that a command?" And her movement, as she yielded her body, still slim and beautiful, into his arms, was moving. For after all, it was not that of a young girl, but of a woman in her fifties, who had suffered already great joys and bitter long-lasting grief.

I was smiling with pleasure in my mother's beauty and gaiety, and I myself was intoxicated as with a triumph. I felt for the first time that sense which belongs only to a successful family, as if life and even the capacity of pleasure were increased to that family.

The house itself, I thought, felt that happiness with us. The big Adams salon seemed, like my mother, to have been waiting only for this day, and now, while the dancers turned in the old Viennese waltz, already growing faster, I felt, in the spring of its floor, a joyful pulse, as of a sleeping beauty waking to a royal destiny. The great chandeliers, out of their covers for the first time since Christmas, trembled like the jewels on the ears and breasts of the women; the smiles of the marble fauns supporting the mantelpiece seemed to come to life under the jumping candle flames, as the bare bosoms of flushed and panting girls, whirling by, almost brushed their marble lips.

I was not a dancing man. I was both too clumsy and too shy. But to see others dance gave me a keen exciting pleasure. The music, the noise of feet rasping the ground in rhythm, the motion of the skirts swung outwards, above all the feeling, "All this happiness, this excitement, these flirtations, these thumping hearts, are a family event. Tolbrook and Edward have created them," went to my head. Even as I walked now and then through the passages, on a visit to the buffet, or to my room, in order to make sure that my hair had not started up into tufts, as it was apt to do, or to clean my spectacles with a silk cloth, I felt that the back parts of the house were full of pride and excitement. They were like children on party nights, waiting with patience but the keenest anticipation for a glimpse of some distinguished visitor in a red ribbon, some renowned young beauty in her satin and diamonds—above all, some dowager, combining importance with a splendid maturity, moving through our simple hall, and raising it, by the very movement of her body, the poise of her head, the sound of her voice, supremely confident and gracious in that confidence, to palatial dignity.

Dowagers permitted themselves to waltz at our country dances. My mother, perhaps because she herself adored dancing, always found, among the bachelors of the Hunt, some of those dancing men who, even in their sixties, will never consent to sit down while they can find a woman to hurl. My mother, at Tolbrook, gave them very distinguished partners, ladies who perhaps had not danced for years until they permitted themselves, in our remote parts, to be squeezed and tousled by farmer squires whose manners with ladies had long become adjusted to the tastes of farmers' wives. I heard one of them address a duchess as "You gels," and the lady seemed to enjoy it.

It was my special delight to see women such as these in the rich and brilliant dress of that day, frilled and flounced from hem to bosom, moving through the dance with stately impetuosity. They brought together in one vehement impression the sense of magnificence, power, and vivacity. The red coats of our bachelors, which were usually the most eye-catching ornaments of our ballroom, could not stand against the frocks, above all the shoulders, of these splendid matrons. Whiteness, by mere perfection, overcame scarlet tails and the rainbows of their own silks, as in spring the snowcap of some tor outdazzles the emerald grasses and jeweled flowers below.

And when I caught sight of my father wandering among them, like an old blind sheep lost on a familiar pasture, I felt only distress as at an impropriety. We had thought of our father as a man of the great world, the brilliant young staff captain from the Crimea, who had carried off a beauty; and I was shocked to see this confused old man, with round red face and wool-white dabs of hair, who wandered silent and embarrassed among the guests, like one of his own laborers brought in from the moor to celebrate some family anniversary.

I learned to avoid him, for when he caught my eye he would at once come toward me and say something incomprehensible. "Ridiculous," and he muttered something about Edward's support of old-age pensions, put before a royal commission that year. "Pauperizing whole country—" I knew that my father, a devoted Gladstonian, disliked all the ideas of the young radicals led by men like Lloyd George. And I answered something about moving with the times.

"Yes, moving where? Ruin. Turning good English workmen into parasites. And look at the price of corn—what's going to happen?"

I shook my head and looked wise.

His shaking hand touched my sleeve, as if seeking for comprehension. But I was merely alarmed. I said, "Let me get you something, Papa, something to drink."

He remained gazing at me for a moment like one who perceives that his language is not understood. Then he gave a long slow sigh and walked away, with his slow waddling movement. And I thought, "Poor Papa, I had never noticed how old and stupid he was getting."

Two days later, on the evening after our greatest party, the catastrophe fell. We were relishing that hour when, languid and sleepy, a family gathers for a last gossip before bed—when they enjoy at once the memory of keen delights, the anticipation of long and luxurious sleep, and the present comfort of restored privacy and unity.

We were in the parlor and Edward was amusing us with an account of some sharp exchanges between two ministers in the recent cabinet.

Edward was at his best. He was not a man who gave one quality of entertainment to his friends and another to his family. We knew that he forgot us as soon as we were out of his sight. He never wrote to us, rarely knew anything about our family affairs. But we perceived that, when he was with us, his affection was real and quick.

And perhaps that week, which had been so happy for my mother, was also the happiest of Edward's life. For what glory is so sweet as that rare but ungrudged admiration of one's own people? He delighted in our respect, our pleasure.

While Edward chattered and we laughed, my father was walking about the room, in his new restless manner. But we did not notice him, for my father's presence had never repressed our spirits. He was too gentle, too even tempered. Above all, he had no nerves. He did not mind noise or games, however boisterous, at his very elbow.

Suddenly my mother, with that mischievous smile which was peculiar to her when she spoke to Edward, brought a piece of newspaper out of her corsage and handed it to him.

"Is that yours?"

"What, has it got into the papers?"

"How strange," she said, "that it should reach the papers. The post office is so careless." Her voice had that lively tone of the coquette who is not afraid to wound, because she loves. Her stroke was a caress. Edward laughed. "But I didn't send it in to *this* paper, mama."

"What is it?" I said, and I was poking my face between their heads to read, when to the surprise of us all my father's thick little red paw intervened and carried off the paper. He put on his pince-nez, which dangled from his neck on a thick ribbon. His hand shook so much that this operation took some time, during which I think we all began to feel apprehension. He read the couplet and threw the scrap of paper into the fire.

"Rubbish," he said in a loud harsh voice which we had never heard before. "Dangerous, foolish," and I think he said "lewd," though, in my incredulity, I may have misheard. "I'm ashamed—any son of mine—bad enough to write such stuff—but to print it—"

The verse which caused this violent agitation was one of the few political verses which Edward allowed to get into print during his lifetime. It was a mild joke about Gladstone and Home Rule. To Edward, and therefore to me, Gladstone was an old-fashioned Whig, and already an obstacle to progress. We condescended to him as the Grand Old Man. It was not for many years that we realized how great he had seemed to my father's generation; a prophet, a leader sent from God.

My mother blushed a soft pink, her deepest sign of feeling, and said, "But my dear, Lord Rosebery himself showed me the paper. He was laughing and he said, 'I think this is something by your clever son, Mrs. Wilcher.'"

"No, no. All rubbish—disgusting, vulgar—but what does it matter? You'll never do any good." My father was purple and struggled for words as if choking. He stood before us, jerking his arms and legs like an absurd marionette on wires which can't resist their manipulation. "Rubbish. How can anyone trust a man who swindles his own family? Nobody can trust him. He's spoiled. We've spoiled him. And look at him. Doesn't even know what I'm talking about."

We stared in horror and astonishment. Even Edward was moved. His handsome face became a little pink. He got up and went toward the old man, saying in affectionate and contrite tone, "But Papa, I hope I'm not so bad as that. I've been careless perhaps—"

"No, no. Too late. Spoiled. What's the good of talking? I told you twenty years ago that he was getting spoiled." He made an angry gesture waving Edward back and suddenly shouted, "But he's not going to ruin you—I won't allow it. Lucy and Bill. And your mother. You don't care what happens to them. But I'll stop it—I'll stop it."

Suddenly he staggered back, put his hand to his head, and would have fallen. But Edward and my mother, who flew to his help, caught him in time. They laid him on the sofa, and in silence undid his collar, raised his legs. I was sent for the doctor. My mother came to give me some last instructions in the hall, and as I looked at her, still in her ball gown, with bare shoulders, I thought suddenly, "How old she looks," and I said, "Mama, you're quite worn out—go to bed and leave Papa to us. It's only a touch of heart."

For, of course, like other young people, I could not know the intuition which had told her already that my father, as she had known him, was finished. Nor did I know why she already blamed herself for his collapse.

She shook her head and said, "How could I go to bed, Tommy, when your father may be dying? Now remember that if you can't get doctor so-and-so," and repeated her careful rapid instructions.

The doctor came sooner than we had hoped. He diagnosed a slight stroke, and promised a cure. But though my father recovered his speech and movement, he was never cured in spirit. He became reclusive, and silent. He did not like strangers to see his shaky hands or to hear his faltering tongue. He still insisted upon managing the estate; but he handed over most of the outdoor work to me. And inevitably he became out of touch, and superseded. For it was often impossible to tell him all that was going on. There was no time for long detailed explanations.

5 4

A strange young woman in nurse's uniform came into the room, smiling. Even her walk was like laughter. She came up to the bed and said, "And how are we now, Mr. Wilcher?"

"I am quite well, thank you."

"Mrs. Brown sent me to ask and to make sure that you take your medicine."

"Tell Mrs. Brown that I have taken my medicine and that I am feeling very well indeed."

The young nurse was still smiling so that her plump rosy cheeks dimpled. It was obvious that she could not contain the energy and delight which throbbed in her healthy young body. "You don't ask after your grandson, Mr. Wilcher."

"My great-nephew. How is he?"

"He is just taking his first meal. He is a very greedy boy."

Her teeth flashed and her color deepened. She laughed and said, "Mrs. Brown says that he is biting her as if he could eat her."

"Please give my compliments to Mrs. Brown and congratulate her on this important event."

The young woman looked at me under her lashes and her smile said, "What a comic old thing it is." Then she answered, "And if you want anything, Mrs. Brown says be sure and ring your bell."

She went out with a rustle of her stiff skirt, opening and

shutting the door with a complete about turn, as if performing the figure of a dance. I heard her call out in her laughing
voice:

"It's all right, Mrs. Brown. He's all right."

I could not help smiling at the tone of this assurance. "A
charming child," I thought, "her face too square, her cheeks
too plump and rosy; but what a wife for some lucky man; what
a companion and a mother. It is a pleasure to have her in the
house." And as if the young woman's gaiety had been catching,
I felt a stir of pleasure "as English as this room, this weather,"
I thought. "How I should like to have her for a daughter or
niece-in-law, a piece of candor and simple woman stuff. What
babies she would have. What spring in her heels. I dare say she
has a temper with those thick eyebrows, but what is the harm.
Real women always have tempers because they are high met-
tled. Some farmer's daughter, I suppose, and nothing in family.
But what does that matter? All the better if she has had an old-
fashioned upbringing."

And indeed, the next morning, when, judging myself rested,
I went to take the prayers which by Ann's request were given
in the night nursery by her bedside, the little monthly nurse
attended and said her amens louder than any I had heard since
Sara's day. For Sara's amens had been the loudest of any housekeeper that I can remember.

The room was very warm and smelled of the baby, which
was lying in a peculiar cot, made of canvas, next Ann's bed;
a little thin creature with black hair and a sharp nose. He
was sucking his fist and uttering now and then an impatient
cry. The morning sun threw the shadows of the square window
panes upon the floor, and the bath and a towel-horse opened
before the fireplace. The nurse, in her blue print, knelt at a
chair and thrust herself out behind in a fervent manner. Ann,
wearing a lace cap which I had never seen before, and which
made her resemble the portrait of my great-grandmother,

propped herself on one elbow and kept putting out her hand to disentangle the child's fingers from the hem of his sheet.

From outside we could hear the hens clucking, and one of the men stumped across the yard in his long boots. A horse, standing, perhaps, by the gate, now and then threw his head and made a sudden loud rattle of trace chains. Now it happened that the day was that of St. James, and the collect that which describes how the saint left all to follow Jesus; but as I turned to it, I came in the page before on the gospel for St. John Baptist's day, and since it seemed to me appropriate to the scene, I read it. "Elizabeth's full time came that she should be delivered and she brought forth a son. And her neighbours and her cousins heard that the Lord had showed great mercy upon her; and they rejoiced with her. And it came to pass that on the eighth day they came to circumcise the child; and they called him Zacharias, after the name of the father. And his mother answered and said, Not so, but he shall be called John. And they said to her, There is none of thy kindred that is called by this name. And they made signs to the father, how he would have him called. And he asked for a writing table and wrote, saying his name is John. And they marvelled all. And his mouth was opened immediately and his tongue loosed, and he spake and praised God. And fear came upon all that dwelt round about them; and all these sayings were noised abroad throughout all the hill country of Judea. And all they that heard them laid them in their hearts, saying, What manner of child shall this be. And the hand of the Lord was with him."

5 5

Now though I had begun to read in a spirit of formal duty, to improve the occasion, the words took hold of me and carried me into grace. They opened for me, if I may speak so, a window upon the landscape of eternity wherein I saw again the forms of things, love and birth and death, change and fall, in their eternal kinds. I was reminded that the ordinary birth of a small and ugly child, so disappointing to me who had looked for a fair Edward, was a true miracle and mystery; the birth of a soul to which, however simple, was given a divine power. So strongly was I made aware of God's presence and visible deed in the quietness of the room, broken only by the clucking of hens outside, the snuffling of the baby, the sudden clank of the horse's chains, that tears were forced to my eyes, my voice wavered, and I was obliged to break off from my reading. I resumed it, but could not finish. It was with difficulty that I uttered the last prayers.

The nurse's amens, so charged with ardor, and Ann's silence appeared to me to show an equal emotion, and I felt it a duty and perhaps a great opportunity to speak to the young mother a few words such as might bring to her confused feelings a clear idea of the privilege granted to her by God and the solemn responsibility laid upon her, etc.

But before I had managed to rise from my knees, a difficult feat for my muscles, the nurse, having called out the last and loudest amen, jumped up and said in her gay voice, "Good gracious, isn't it half-past eight?" And Ann, smiling at the baby, began to unbutton her jacket.

I perceived that, far from being moved, they had probably not heard a word of either the gospel or the prayers. The nurse took me by the arm and guided me to the door. "Now, Mr. Wilcher, we're rather behind this morning." Before I had perfectly collected myself, I found myself in the corridor. But after a moment of surprise and indignation I reflected that the two women, in their present cares, were, in a measure, under continual inspiration. They were like those simple Indian nuns who, unable to comprehend anything of theology or even to read, nevertheless are often closer to God than the most learned professors. They are free, I thought; they have not given their hearts; and when I am free, with Sara, I too shall forget myself and my cares. And I sought Robert, to praise his work at Tenacre.

"He's in the salon," a maid told me.

I was surprised, for the salon, being disused, had been locked up for many months to keep out the drafts which blew through the house from its neglected windows and the cracks in its floor. I could not even find the key, and decided to go round by the garden entrance. I had not entered this part of the garden for a long time. And now, approaching the salon from the outside, I noticed a broad, muddy path broken through the laurels, reaching to the double French windows of the great room. The doors, enlarged by the removal of a central post, were open and inside on the floor of the room, under the white pillars and gilt decorations of its cornices, stood a new reaper and binder and a two-furrow plow. Sacks had been spread on the parquet below the machines, but the iron wheels had splintered the sills of the doors and broken the outer step.

I stepped into the room and looked about me. Rakes and hoes were leaning against the classic paneling, garden seats were planted before the inner doors, and a workbench stood under the great central chandelier of the three, under which, as my grandmother has recorded, Jane Austen once flirted with her Irishman. Upon the one chair remaining in a corner a yard cat was suckling two kittens. It needed nothing more to say that barbarians had taken possession. She did not even run from me, but lay watching, with up-twisted neck and the insolent calm ferocity of some Pict or Jute encamped in a Roman villa.

British country gentlemen of the fourth century were, I suppose, often more cultivated than ourselves. Their families had lived for two or three centuries in those beautiful manors, among an art and literature already ancient. Their comforts were beyond ours. And when we look at their bathhouses and see the marble steps worn hollow by the naked feet of a dozen generations, we feel so close to them that we suffer for them in their terror and destruction.

A gentle and quiet people, who loved home as no others, whose very gods were domestic. But this room breathes of a double refinement—the Roman art of life distilled through the long spiral of English classicism.

It has been our pride for a century. Even my father would boast of the architects who came from all over the world to photograph its decorative plaster and to measure its panels. Some have called it too delicate in its simplicity. But what beauty in its grace, its dignity; it is a room where no one could forget the duties as well as the privilege of gentle breeding.

But now I felt embittered against it. "Now you are crying out for help, too—you are jumping upon my back. And all your load of beauty is another burden. 'No,' I said, 'you can go to the devil. I have enough to do. If I can save this child's soul, if I can make his mother understand that he has a soul to be saved, then I shall have done quite as much as anyone could ask of me.' "

I heard Robert's voice at my elbow. "Hullo, uncle, I thought as we weren't using this old barn, it might do for some of our stuff. It will save a new machinery shed at least."

"An old barn," I said, for I thought that the boy was needlessly provocative. "It is a masterpiece."

"Yeah," Robert said, "I always liked this room best of any I know. It's grand. Good for dukes. Sixteen foot high, I measured it to see if it would take a thresher. I didn't tell you I was after a second-hand thresher—we'll have to put it somewhere out of the rain. But I won't do the building any harm, uncle. It's only temporary. And if we had to make a door for the straw we could take down a panel next the fireplace and knock out a few bricks."

"Thresh in here—you'll shake the whole house to pieces.

No," I said, "not while I live. And you're not going to kill me either, by giving me shocks. I'm not going to die yet for a long time," and so on. I lost my temper with the boy and told him to take his damned machinery into the yard.

And to my surprise, Robert was most agreeable. He apologized three times and we parted on very affectionate terms. True, that was a week ago, and I do not believe that he has yet removed his plow and tractor. But I do not care to look. I have laid down a rule: no threshing machine in the salon; and I should be stupid to fight about details. I should also be stupid to find him in default, for if I took no further steps, I should lose my authority, if, indeed, I have any.

56

And as for a plow or so, temporarily deposited in my house, why should I quarrel with them? Taken in the proper spirit, they can be an inspiration. I must not forget my first visit to Sara in her room at Craven Gardens. I was astonished to see that miserable attic in which she was living—the paper coming off the walls, a leak in the roof, a torn piece of linoleum on the floor, several handles off the chest of drawers, etc. The stove in the fireplace was broken and useless.

The only comfort to be seen was in the bed, which showed three mattresses, two of hair and one of feathers, and one of my best eiderdowns. The sheets, too, were my best linen. But even this luxurious bed had one caster missing. Its foot was propped upon two books.

Now it was true that just at that time, after the great strikes, I was obliged to use the strictest economies; my town house was in very bad repair. But I was shocked by this room. "Why," I said, "these are poor quarters, Mrs. Jimson. Can't you find any better?"

"Well, sir," she said, "I couldn't put a maid in here, or she'd go."

"But what about you?"

"Oh, I don't mind, sir, so long as it's somewhere to myself. And quiet for sleeping."

Then we both looked at the bed. But Sara did not blush. She said only "I was just dirtying out those sheets, after Master Robert went back to school."

And when I suggested that we might find a better piece of linoleum, she urged me not to waste my money "on fallals." I was pleased by my housekeeper's loyalty and economy. For I saw she identified herself with the interests of the family. But now, remembering that room, I realize for the first time that Sara slept in it, little changed, for nearly twelve years. I think the roof was mended, and I gave her a rug for the floor, but certainly she never had a fire there. Yet never once had she seemed to reflect on the hardness of her life. She seemed even to rejoice in depriving herself because it helped us both to save on the bills.

"A true soldier," I thought, "even to making herself comfortable. Bill would have appreciated her."

And I saw, as by a revelation, that deep sense from which Sara had drawn her strength and her happiness, the faith of the common people. That faith which is expressed in so many proverbs, "A great inheritance; two of each and one gullet." "Give me hands, give me lands." And I entered into the minds of those who for generations have known life as an enterprise for their bread, who do not think in terms of inheritance or profession, but of a temporary shelter and a month's wages.

Sara gave me that service, but she never unpacked her box. She was ready to move on, at any moment, to some other billet, and to begin life again under whatever conditions she might find there, whatever mistress or master.

I said to Ann, "Perhaps if you have Edward for the baby's name, Robert ought to have Mathias."

"I don't see why. To turn away bad luck?"

"How—turn away bad luck?"

"Because we are getting our way about the other names."

"What nonsense. No, I was thinking of Robert's father—a great fighter. Perhaps a boy, in this new world, might take some profit by his memory."

"I shouldn't like to have a preacher in the family."

"Why not, indeed?" I was surprised and shocked.

"There'll be nothing to preach about by the time he's grown up."

I answered that there would always be plenty to preach about. "And why do you suppose that the Christian faith is dying? Don't forget that Christianity has a way of reviving itself, of rising again from the very grave. It has done so a thousand times. For it springs out of the very roots of the spirit," and so on. And I convinced myself and said, "The baby must be Mathias as well as Edward. I shall tell Robert so."

But the girl answered with surprising warmth, "You are not going to desert me, uncle."

5 7

And, in fact, the boy was christened Edward John Wilcher. But the excitement of this victory, if it was a victory, was overcast for me by an unexpected misfortune.

Ann, as soon as she got out of bed, showed an unexpected energy. The lazy girl who had spent whole afternoons with her nose poked in a book, till I had been obliged to remind her that nothing is more disgusting in a girl than a stoop, now became busy and even a little troublesome. She was inclined to pester us all, with her spring cleaning and her punctuality. It was as though maternity, which had hollowed her cheeks and deepened her eyes and marked her body, had released in her a whole set of female instincts formerly hidden and suppressed in her soul under the heap of little boxes. She was rougher, ruder to me, and yet she seemed more affectionate, more like a daughter.

So one day when she found my bedside table full of unopened letters, she rated me, "Look at this, uncle. What are you thinking of? Some of them are eight months old."

Now the truth is I had not opened any letters from certain members of the family because I knew that they would be full of complaints against Ann. My niece Blanche had written such letters; and even my dear niece Clary, her sister, who had married, much against my will, a boy half her age and opened a shop, and sent me warning letters against Ann. It seemed that the whole family, having appointed Ann to look after me, now accused her of keeping me a prisoner.

This was probably true. But I was in no position to resent it and therefore I could not afford to be agitated by their charges. I was too busy. So I opened no more of their letters.

"I must have forgotten them," I said.

"But, uncle, you really can't ignore people like that. Here is Cousin Blanche's writing. Yes, she has written to you almost every week—there must be twenty from her alone."

"You read them for me."

"I couldn't do that. Cousin Blanche wouldn't like me to. She hates me, and I can't say I like her."

To keep the child quiet I promised to read the letters, but I did not do so. I put them into a broken ventilator and by God's mercy I forgot all about them again.

An old man is obliged to be a coward, not for his essential self, his mind and will, but for his body which may betray that will. He is like a general compelled to fight his last campaign with weak worn-out troops, badly equipped and likely to run away at the least reverse. He must use all his self-control, his ingenuity.

I had executed a skillful retreat. But I had not allowed for Ann's new coarseness of mind. Two days later she told me that Blanche was coming to see me. "I telephoned to her and said that it wasn't my fault if you refused to have anything to do with her."

"I do not refuse," I said. "A soldier does not refuse to be shot. But he doesn't desire it. No, I can't see her. It is impossible for her to understand me or for me to argue with her. She is as stupid as a horse."

"But, uncle, it's not fair to let her think that I keep her away."

"No, no, certainly not. But I can't see her—I have to see Mr. Jaffery first."

"I don't mind in the least what you do about your will, but you mustn't get excited. Having babies is too much for you altogether."

"I'm not excited. But I won't see Blanche."

"Well, I've asked her to tea with us today."

I said nothing. But I sent a wire by the garden boy to say I could not see anyone. I was in bed.

Yet Blanche contrived to see me, for as I was walking through the village with Ann she suddenly appeared before us, and Ann at once went into the village shop. Another of her plots.

5 8

Blanche Wilcher is a big and handsome woman. Her hair is still dark, and her cheeks are red. She has grown stout in late years, and it suits her big frame and upright carriage. I have always admired and respected her, though often I have found it necessary to quarrel with her. For if one is on good terms with her, she is apt to give too much advice. But she is a good Christian, a good honest soul, and now, kissing me on both cheeks, she said with emotion, "At last, poor uncle. How are you? You are terribly thin."

"How are you, my dear, I haven't seen you for a long time?"

"Tell me, Uncle Tom," she took me by the arm and drew me down the road away from the shop, "do you get my letters?"

"Yes, my dear. It is very good of you to write so often."

"Then did you really allow Robert to cut down the oak wood?"

"No, has he cut it down?"

"But I wrote about it long ago. Did you get the letter about what Ann was saying about you—that you ought to be shut up?"

"No."

"Just as I thought—the girl has been intercepting my letters. That is a criminal offense. I really ought to go to the police." Her face began to grow redder. "Don't you see, uncle, what that couple are doing to you? It's a conspiracy. They agreed about it before that deceitful girl accepted the job of nursing you."

"Yes, it's very likely."

"Is it true that they lock you up in your room?"

"Sometimes at night."

"It's incredible—terrible."

She was greatly moved and in spite of myself, I began to shake. I thought, "I have been foolish and unjust. I must make a new will. For Blanche ought to have the place. She is just the right person, a Christian and a parish worker, the perfect squire's wife. She has even put some backbone into that lazy fellow Loftus and made a magistrate of him."

"Would you like me to go to the police, uncle?"

"It wouldn't do any good. You see, Ann is a doctor."

"But she has no right to treat you as if you couldn't look after yourself. It's a scandal. It's got to be stopped."

"Stop what?" I said. For Blanche always upset me. So sure of herself. And besides, a reactionary of the worst kind. She belonged to the feudal age. I didn't object to a reasoned conservatism. There was, goodness knows, plenty to be said for maintaining such little civilization as we had accomplished. But I had no patience with the blind worshiper of exploded systems.

"Stop treating you like this."

"Well, you know, Blanche, I'm a bit of a nuisance. I am so restless at night."

"That's no excuse." And she looked at me with alarm.

"I dare say they think I might set the place on fire as I did to Craven Gardens."

Blanche became very red. "But, uncle, you never did so."

"Well, you know that the insurance company nearly didn't pay up."

"It was the electric wiring went wrong."

"Ah." And I grinned at Blanche so that she fell back a step. "But then I knew it was wrong. I even smelled that fire, and I could have stopped it. But I thought, I've never had any peace with this damned house—it's a perfect incubus, what with repairs and servants and wondering whom to leave it to. So I let it burn. I may even have assisted it to burn."

"Uncle, you don't say this kind of thing to other people, do you?"

"Oh, no, it's just between ourselves. If Ann suspected anything like that, she would send for the asylum van tomorrow. And then I couldn't marry Mrs. Jimson."

Blanche was quite taken aback. And I could see in her face the reflection of a terrible struggle. She was wondering whether it would be better to have me certified and so to save me from Sara, but to leave Ann and Robert in possession; or to get me away from them, at the expense of seeing me married to Sara.

"Of course," I said, "I should not think of setting fire to Tolbrook. It hasn't even occurred to me. The place has been a great nuisance to me, but since I am leaving it as soon as Mrs. Jimson is ready for me, I do not feel the burden so much as I used to."

This suggestion, that I might set fire to the house if I wasn't allowed to marry Sara, quite overwhelmed my poor Blanche. She became as red as beetroot and gave up the struggle. But to my confusion she was still more affectionate. "Oh, Uncle Tom, I do feel so worried about you—can't I help you in any way?"

Then I began to shake again, and I looked round for Ann. "Where is Ann?" And I went toward the shop, calling, "Ann, Ann." But Blanche kept beside me imploring me to be on my guard against both Ann and Robert. "They are simply robbing you."

At last I fairly bolted from her into the shop. I could not bear her kindly feelings. But Ann had gone out by the back way. It was Robert who rescued me. He happened to drive past in a wagon with two of the girls who, for the last fortnight, under the name of pupils, seemed to spend most of their time wandering about the yards in white smocks or carrying out cans of tea to the fields, where cutting had begun.

I hailed them, and Robert pulled up.

Blanche was now in tears. She kissed me, though I believe she would have liked to hit me at the same time, in exasperation; and she begged me to send for her in any trouble. Robert and one of the girls then hoisted me into the cart without much ceremony, and we drove on, leaving my poor niece in the road. But I felt such an attack of sympathy for her, so near me in my deepest feelings, in my love of Tolbrook and the old grace of life, in her Christianity, which is that of a country-woman, the simple calm faith of the village church, that I knew it put me in danger of a serious attack. I therefore removed her quickly out of mind and reflected on the charm of the evening, and upon Robert beside me, dirty and smelling of sweat. And I thought, "Now it is too late to change anything— I am committed into the hands of this rough obstinate boy—he is my fate. I have nothing to do any more with the farm. My trees are at his mercy."

It was a hot afternoon when the air, already full of chaff dust, itself seemed thick and sleepy. The very sound of ball upon bat from the village boys playing stump cricket on the rough field near the church came through this thickened air with a drowsy note. It reminded one of afternoons spent lying in the long brittle grass, between the tents, in the last day of some county cricket week. The trees, creatures so sensitive and quick, stood now motionless to their topmost leaf, dozing on their feet like horses. The wheat was as red as a fox's back, and the barley quivered as if transparent clouds of steam were passing over its awns. The hedges were covered with pale dust so that they were almost the same color as the hay which had been sticking among their thorns and brambles since June.

On summer days like this in harvest, the richness of the ground seems charged upon the air, so that even the blue of the sky is tainted like the water of a cow pond, enriched but no longer pure. It is as if a thousand years of cultivation have brought to all, trees, grass, crops, even the sky and the sun, a special quality belonging only to very old countries. A quality not of matter only, but of thought; as if the hand that planted the trees in their chosen places had imposed upon them the dignity of beauty appointed, but taken from them, at the same time, the innocence of natural freedom. As if the young farmer who set the hedge, to divide off his inheritance, wrote with its crooked line the history of human growth, of responsibility not belonging to the wild hawthorn, but to human love and fatherhood; as if upon the wheat lay the color of harvests since Alfred, and its ears grew plump with the hopes and anxieties of all those generations that sowed with

Beowolf and plowed with Piers and reaped with Cobbett. Even at my own last harvest at Tolbrook, nine years ago, the gardener's boy brought me from the field a little plait of straw. He did not know what it was or why he brought it, or that he was repeating a sacrifice to the corn god made so long ago that it was thousands of years old when Alfred was the modern man in a changing world.

The English summer weighs upon me with its richness. I know why Robert ran away from so much history to the new lands where the weather is as stupid as the trees, chance dropped, are meaningless. Where earth is only new dirt, and corn, food for animals, two- and four-footed. I must go, too, for life's sake. This place is so doused in memory that only to breathe makes me dream like an opium eater. Like one who has taken a narcotic, I have lived among fantastic loves and purposes. The shape of a field, the turn of a lane have had the power to move me as if they were my children and I have made them. I have wished immortal life for them, though they were even more transient appearances than human beings.

59

And I thought, "In fact, I have been ungrateful to these young people, especially to Robert. For he has at least set me free. I need worry no more about those old tottering relics in the fields. Let him respect only the house, for his own son's sake, and I shall be a fortunate man."

And I hastened down, after supper, to congratulate him. "You're quite right," I said, "about my father's changes. Revolutionary. I have been looking at the plans. And my grandfather actually pulled down the ruins of the old chapel to build a byre."

"What a pity," Ann said.

"But—what an act of courage, to destroy walls six or seven centuries old. A strong man. But he was the lay preacher who remembered the Wesleys. He was an Edward, too."

"I should think the place would have gone bust a good while ago if someone hadn't kept it on the move," Robert spoke in a sleepy voice; his face was hollow with exhaustion, and shone still as if varnished with sweat. He had not shaved that morning, and now his chin was blue. He was carrying a gramophone under his arm, and Ann had two lanterns in her hand, old and dusty. One had been patched with a piece of cracker paper pasted to the frame.

"It is as if Tolbrook itself were on a pilgrimage," I said. "It is like a gypsy van, carrying its people with it."

"You promised to go to bed, uncle," Ann said.

"Yes, I am on my way. What are you doing with the old lanterns?"

"We are going on the lake."

"You ought to send Robert to bed. He is almost asleep."

"It is Robert who suggested a water party—he found the lanterns in a cupboard. Are they the same lanterns that you used to have at the old water parties?"

"I don't know, but the lake has nearly dried up since the dams broke, and there are no boats."

"Robert had the old punt mended and there is still enough lake. You call it the pond. Shall we go, Robert?"

"Where's Molly?"

"Is Molly coming?" Ann turned her sharp, haggard look toward Robert. "I don't see that we need take Molly."

"We can't leave her alone all the evening. After all, she's paying us."

Molly was one of the two farm pupils. It seemed that both these girls not only worked for nothing in the yards, but paid for their teaching and keep. A stroke of genius in Robert, I thought.

But Ann had a different explanation. "They've fallen for Robert, and fat Molly thinks she's going to get him, too."

I thought this merely jealously on Ann's part and warned her against this foolish vice. Molly had been known to me from a child. A tall, fair, thick-set girl with a heavy snub nose and curled chin, daughter of a yacht chandler at Queensport. She had grown up a silent creature, who never spoke to me. But her family was highly respected, and I knew that she had been well brought up.

Robert was calling toward the back part of the house, "Molly," and at last she came with downcast eyes and the sly face which means only that a girl is shy. The three went out together. Robert and Ann looked already an old disillusioned couple. It was strange to see those three young people walking soberly across the dry short grass in the twilight on their party of pleasure, a yard apart, with bent heads, and uttering no word.

60

"When I leave Tolbrook," I thought, "I shall be beginning life again, where I should have begun it forty years ago when I resolved to be a missionary, to throw myself into that dark wave which had already carried Lucy away."

I heard the gramophone through my curtains, playing the water music. And looking out I saw that Robert had hung the lighted lanterns from sticks at each end of the punt and launched it upon the pond. He was pushing it forward with a crooked clothes pole, which still had its fork at the upper extremity. Between the stems of the alders I could see it floating in a clear space of water like a small gray cloud on a green sky. The long broken reflections of the lanterns were like flames wavering in the air.

Punt, lanterns, and music were insignificant in the great

space of the evening, and the three young people seemed to be performing a rite rather than enjoying themselves. The air was growing cool, and I knew the punt was leaky and rotten. Every moment or two Robert handed his pole to one of the girls in order that he might change the Handel records and wind up the gramophone. I thought of the children who play at balls or presentations in a stable yard, and sit upon the cold iron of an upturned bucket balancing a paper crown, only for the pleasure of the idea.

But who can say that our old water parties, with their dozen boats, their band, their decorated bowers on every island, were not acts of the same kind; realized romance, living poems? In which we sought for something ideal, something beyond the fact, some abiding place.

The last, the greatest of these water festivals was for the Jubilee. And I came to it unwilling from a party of young men who, like myself, thought themselves dedicated to God.

I was the eldest of them by two years. I had spent more than two years, since my father's illness, as his helper. The other three were still undergraduates; but in mind, I think I was still the simplest.

For forty years I have looked back upon that reading party as upon my happiest hour. I see myself climbing Snowdon by the long Pig Path, a slim young man in a straw hat and a dark-gray suit, carrying a long alpenstock in his hand, carved with the names of Alpine peaks, which he has never seen, and talking gravely to his friend. The friend is even shorter, but rather fat. He wears brown knickerbockers, a high collar, and a red tie, and a round cap with a glazed peak, like a yachting cap. The rest of the party follow behind in two pairs.

The alpenstock makes me smile, and yet I can enjoy my own affectation. For that young man has gone from earth even more completely than if he had died; and I can know him and value him as if he had been my intimate friend. He was grave and a little pompous; but the gravity was partly due to the knowledge that he was very plain, with an absurd ugliness. His red face, his snub nose, his stiff black hair, his round spectacles and peering startled eyes were comic in themselves. And when he forgot them and began to chatter, to wave his hands, he became at once grotesque. Yet he often did forget them, for he was greatly liable to enthusiasms. It was a common experience with him to burst into rhapsodies over a view, a piece of music, a face, a poem, and find himself surrounded by discreet smiles. He would then become dignified, until, in another few minutes, he would once more forget that Nature had cast him for the droll and not for the poet.

In this holiday, he was more than commonly excited by the mountains, by new friendships, by talk; by the vast and exciting ideas which in that Jubilee year seemed to infect the air itself with an intoxicating essence. I do not mean that we were carried away by the pageant of imperial triumph. We were all young Liberals, of a religious turn. But those who think of Jubilee year as a vulgar glorification of power and wealth forget or never knew its sense of blessedness. History does not move in one current, like the wind across bare seas, but in a thousand streams and eddies, like the wind over a broken landscape, in forests and towns. At one place, through some broad gap, it makes straight forward; in another, among the trees, it creeps and eddies. It flies through the cold sky at gale force; on the ground, a breeze scarcely turns the willow leaves.

We write of an age. But there is no complete age. In Jubilee year the old men remembered Peel and Canning and Cobbett; the old admirals had fought in sail; the old generals had been brought up under Peninsular colonels. Middle-aged men spoke of Dizzy and the New Tories; they had hunted with Trollope and Surtees; the young ones were full of Kipling and Kitchener, Lloyd George and the radical Chamberlain.

Men for whom the Empire had been a trust from God to

evangelize the world, Indian veterans who had heard Lawrence pray and Havelock preach, stood beside youngsters from the Kimberley mines for whom Empire meant wealth, power, the domination of a chosen race.

On both sides it was a battle of faith. Rhodes was already looking for the reign of eternal peace and justice under the federated imperial nations, and against him the Radicals passionately sought national freedom for all peoples. The first spoke in the name of God the law-giver, for world-wide justice and service; the second in the name of Christ the rebel, for universal love and trust; and both were filled with the sense of mission.

So in our arguments, our endless talk, we used often the words God, Christ, and value. We spoke of the crisis of the times and the duty of an imperial responsibility. We felt that our lives had fallen in an age of revolutions and heroic adventures.

The young man that I was then, in spite or because of his absurd looks and small size, had resolved upon the boldest adventure. Or rather, he found himself in such a mind that any other life was not to be thought of. But this ideal adventure had not yet taken shape, and he wavered between the diamond mines, some tropical service under the crown, in the remotest parts, or the missionary church.

6 1

My friend in the strange cap, which was a bicycling cap, was training to be a minister of some free church. He was poor, his father was a laborer; and he treated us with a ferocious contempt. I think his contempt of our wits was justified, for he had better brains and was far better read. His strength was in logic, and he asked always for definitions.

"If God is immanent in the world, then He is not only in

experience but in reason," I say, "for if we find Him in experience as love and altruism, it is only by reason that we distinguish this love, this goodness, and resolve that it is good, not only in itself, but for the world," etc., and so forth.

"What do you mean by immanent?" my friend demands. "Is hydrogen immanent in water? or the kernel in the nut? If He is like hydrogen how do we know Him as Himself? Hydrogen is lost in the water molecule."

"I suppose He must be like the kernel."

"Take the kernel out of the shell and you still have shell and kernel. They are distinct, and therefore transcendent to each other. But perhaps you meant that?"

"You can't deny that God is in the world or how do we know Him?" I am full of enthusiasm, and for some reason my friend's crabbedness increases it. I stop, mopping my face. "Glorious—what a view."

"The old ontological argument," says the other with fearful scorn, "which also proves the existence of double-headed eagles and green dragons. And how do you define 'in the world,' and 'I know'?"

I take off my coat and hang it from my shoulders by my handkerchief tied through my braces. This device gives me great pleasure, and I say, "It's easy to argue, but you know you do believe in God."

"Certainly," he answers. "But not from argument. No logic can prove the existence of God."

"Then how do you know Him?"

"By revelation."

"Do you mean in the Bible?"

"Certainly. And I know no other way. Or don't you believe in the Bible? If not, why do you call yourself a Christian?"

But I do not want to argue. I want to enjoy myself, and perhaps to be converted. I stop again and cry, "Look at those fields. Like jewels. Beautiful." And I say as if I had just thought of it, but in fact repeating something that I had heard, "Beauty is perhaps the happiness that God intends for us. Because love is a duty and not necessarily a pleasure. But beauty is pure enjoyment, God's happiness."

"What exactly do you mean by beauty?" the other asks. He has a small brown mustache and when he asks one of his sharp questions he points it at me like a weapon. "Is a cowpat beautiful?"

"No, of course not."

"If I say a cowpat is beautiful, will you contradict me?"

"Yes."

"Then who shall judge between us? Your beauty is a matter of opinion."

"Don't you believe in beauty?"

"Certainly."

"Then how do you know what is beautiful?"

"By revelation."

I admire him more and more, because of his fierce scorn, his sharp voice, his ferocious logic.

"You're as bad as all the rest, Wilcher," he says to me. "You won't face facts. Either the Bible is true—every word of it—or it isn't. Either you accept the God of the Scriptures, or you haven't got a God at all."

"But everyone interprets the Bible in his own way. And if every man did exactly what he thought right, there would be anarchy in the world."

"You mean religious liberty? Quite so, liberty or authority. God or the devil. And you can't have a little bit of both. You've got to choose."

"A world of anarchists would be full of evil."

"That's none of my business. If I am to preach God's word, the only question is, have I faith in Him or have I not?"

His words open before me dark pits which only serve to convince my enthusiastic feelings. I stop upon the narrow path a few feet wide, between two precipices, which leads to the mountain top, and tremble at the idea of falling, falling. Such heights make my head turn. And I say, "To believe in God is an act of faith. Yes, one must make the act."

62

As I say this, I feel the very presence of God, not only within me but in the whole surrounding air, as love, friendship, beauty, so that it is as if these feelings existed not only within me but in the nature of things; as if the mountains, the clear sky, the little fields below, my friends, were bound together not by my feelings about them but by a reciprocal character of delight and understanding. I think I know what it means to have perfect faith; and as I turn again to climb, I perceive that I belong to God. I must do His will, etc.

"I am converted," I say to myself, with that keen pleasure which comes from accomplishment. My excitement has acquired a meaning, and so I can understand it and respect myself as a reasonable being. What glory, for a small undignified person, at whom others were inclined to laugh, to be a missionary.

It was with this feeling that I returned home to entertain county neighbors and the lord lieutenant. I moved among the crowd with that sense of separateness and importance which one perceives still in young men at that critical age, when they attend parties in their own homes. They feel that they have better things to do than to gossip and dance and be polite. And perhaps it is true, for they are deciding the whole course of their lives.

Of course I enjoyed myself at the party; I enjoyed the ices, the strawberries, and even the sense of my own aloofness. It was with pleasure that I thought, "How ridiculous all this is—to spend two or three hundred pounds in order that we may be bored by the A's, the B's, and the C's." For in my new secret resolve to be a missionary I had a point of view. In the faces of the groups that passed I seemed to see the same reflectiveness, and I said to myself, "Why do we go to all this trouble, for nothing?"

Among the islands of the lake, each with its lanterns, boats crowded with young men and girls, in the full-sleeved bright dresses of the end of the century, floated like other smaller islands, or like great tufts of flowers, drifting in the water. One heard laughter and saw among these flowers faces that seemed to my short-sighted eyes beautiful and gay; but when I came near in my skiff, taking some message to the band on the largest island, or announcing supper to the boats, I could recognize Mary this or Phyllis that, plain and dull, and hear the forced sound of the politeness and the laughter, and catch at a yard's range glimpses of boredom and endurance. Mary was in the wrong boat with that intolerable Archy crushing her only frock; Phyllis, a parson's simpleminded daughter, was among a set of town visitors who ignored her.

"Why do they come—what do they want?" I thought. "They are all looking for something, some happiness; but they don't know how to get it. All this contrivance and expense is meant to give them the chance of this happiness and so they are delighted to come. But when they come, they are bored and frustrated."

I thought of haggard, unhappy Lucy, perhaps scrubbing a floor or cooking a meal at that moment. "She has found out what she wants, and so she does not even consider happiness."

Yet during these serious and important reflections, perhaps because of them, my excitement and pleasure increased. I paid compliments, looked boldly at the pretty girls, and ran about making myself useful and prominent. I caught myself smiling all the time and in the same way; I saw the most anxious and depressed look on some girl's face give place to a sudden smile. Everyone, every few moments, would glance about, even in the midst of talk, at the lanterns, the boats, the glittering water full of colored lights, and smile as if to say, "How glorious to be here on such a night. How lucky I am."

And the reflection "This is an occasion" passed at once to the exasperated thought, "But nothing has happened to me yet."

I felt now that I understood those looks of desperation which I had seen already a hundred times in young girls, at balls and parties, when they thought themselves unnoticed; a look which flashes into their youthful cheeks and mouths and eyes as it were from behind, and for a second makes them fierce and terrified. It arose, I thought, from the sense, "I have only this hour—nothing has happened to me yet. What if nothing ever happens to me?"

But I felt no sympathy, only, in spite of my importance, an answering quiver of the nerves. And sculling to another boat, full of old couples, rowed sedately by two footmen, and seeing the calm patience of their faces, I would think, "And I suppose they are pleased to be here because they think their children are pleased." But when at close quarters I saw the mild appreciation of their glances among the murmur of family gossip, so worn out that they did not trouble even to listen to it, but nodded their heads and smiled at the movement only of a chin, I would forget my adventurous vocation and say with envy, "Perhaps they are the lucky ones. They have got over their troubles, and only have to die."

"Supper, supper. Lady A.—oh, how do you do, Mrs. B?"

The news scarcely moves them except to polite nods and smiles. To the boats of the young people it comes like a message of reprieve to condemned prisoners. Each of them thinks, "Now is my chance to get another partner—I shall be in that other boat," or "No more boats for me. I shall stay in the ballroom." They row furiously to the shore, splashing frocks, shirt fronts. And suddenly the flower beds explode like rockets and shoot into the dark fragments of blue, red, white, and gold. I, too, my errand finished, hurry to supper. I do not care for any girl there; I abhor the dull ones, and I am fearful of the brilliant. Yet I have the feeling that next minute, the minute after, some extraordinary joy must come to me.

I did not reach the supper table because Edward pounced on me in the hall. "Just the man I want. Julie is here—she came with the Barrets. Apparently they know too little or too much. But she mustn't come to the house, and I want you to take supper to her on Lucy's island. That's where I left her. She's waiting for me. Tell her I got caught by somebody."

"Is Julie Eeles here? But she must have been recognized. The whole county will be talking about her."

"I dare say," Edward said smiling.

"But it's absolute madness."

"Run along and keep her amused till I come."

Such a mission filled me with panic. But I could not refuse Edward at a crisis. I thought, "It has come at last—the scandal that will destroy him."

6 3

We all say of certain men, like Edward, brilliant and spoiled by fortune, by parents, that they are rushing upon destruction. Yet when their destruction comes, as it always does to the spoiled, it is both sudden and unforeseen. We say, "Of course, that is just what was bound to happen to a man like that. It was in his character from the first." But we have never predicted just that kind of ruin for him. So all Edward's reverses to the final disaster took us by surprise. And now, while I hurried toward the lake with a basket of supper, I said to myself, "Julie. But she has been so discreet and so safe. She can't seek a divorce, and she hates a scandal." Julie was a Catholic, and we had always understood that she was very strict.

Julie had been separated from her husband, a police officer in India, within a few months of the marriage.

"But she has changed her mind or lost her head, as young girls do. Passion has carried her away," I thought. And I felt, "God is not mocked. Edward in his sin did not allow for all the consequences of that sin."

Julie had been Edward's mistress for two years. She was still very young, but she was described to us as an extraordinary person, the most beautiful and talented of her generation, who had conquered London in a few months, during a short Ibsen season, and then at once married and disappeared into privacy.

All that I had heard of Julie terrified me, and nothing but Edward's danger would have persuaded me to present myself to her. It was with a sense of one engaging upon a desperate enterprise that I took my skiff to the island.

We all had our separate islands. Lucy's, chosen in the first place for its remoteness, was at the far end of the lake, so small that it barely contained its bower, a kind of tent of willow branches set up against the stem of a weeping willow. It was lighted by three fairy lamps. And inside we had placed a rustic bench for two and hidden a box of chocolates, with a motto. I think it was, "Love looks not with the eyes, but with the mind," a favorite of my mother's.

Inside I found a thin pale girl, who jumped up and looked angrily at me. She seemed to me, as far as I could see in the dim light, very plain. Her pale hair was drawn smoothly back into a style quite new to me; her small round forehead projected in two shiny bumps, her eyes, very large and black, were also too prominent; and her nose was much too long. I presented myself and explained that Edward was kept for a few moments by family duties. We were to start supper without him. The girl listened in silence with her eyes fixed upon me like a tragic actress preparing for her great scene. I trembled. "Now for it," I thought. When I had finished, she gave only a little sigh and said, "I was wrong to come—I shall go at once."

"No, no. Edward will be awfully disappointed."

She gave another sigh and said, "I wish I could believe you. But I can see you are very good-natured. Must I eat supper?"

"Of course you must eat."

"Yes, I must, since you have been so kind. But I am only wasting your time." We sat down on the bench, which was like all rustic work, a torture to the flesh. We were sad, ashamed, formal. The girl sighed between each mouthful, and I tried to make talk. At the same time, of course, I was burning with excitement and curiosity. I thought, "This girl is Edward's mistress—I suppose she had a dozen lovers before. She is an expert in love, a courtesan." And the idea set me on fire. I no longer thought Julie plain, but beautiful. I pressed against her on the bench and at every moment my eyes were turning to look at her again.

"Why, of course."

"Do you think Edward means to come?" she asked.

"Why, of course."

"Why did he send you? I offered to go away. But he is longing to get rid of me."

"That can't be so."

"Oh, yes. I've been asked to tour with a company in America and he says it's my duty to go. So that he can break with me."

"I can't believe it."

"He's quite right. He's awfully in debt, and I simply don't know where money goes." She spoke as if musing on a bodily defect. "I wonder," she said, "if Edward has chosen you to succeed him."

"To succeed him?"

"Edward often sends his friends to me with that idea. It

would save him so much trouble if I fell in love with someone else."

I was shocked by such a notion. But Julie had the power, belonging to all those who stand outside convention, of making common moral ideas seem ridiculous or artificial. So a wild tree growing through a Roman imperial pavement makes it seem faded and paltry.

"He knows he can always find someone to love him," she mused, "and that he will love them, too, for a time; he has an affectionate disposition."

"Yes, he is very generous."

"If Edward does leave me," she said, "I shall go into a convent. I always meant to be a nun. And when I went with Edward, I was fearfully ashamed. Though my husband treated me so badly. I hid myself in the hotel. What peace it must be in the Carmelites—only to love and to pray. Which is love, too."

"What?" I cried. "A convent? Oh, no. To bury your genius like that. It would be very wrong. I think it's a great pity you ever left the stage. You were famous already, and nobody else could do what you were doing," etc., etc.

I had never seen Julie act, and I thought Ibsen revolting. I fully agreed with those who wanted to stop the production of the plays. Yet I was perfectly sincere when I urged her not to waste her genius. "It would be a perfectly wicked thing," I said.

"But you don't believe in God, and I do."

"I am going to be a missionary. I am preparing for it now."

"You Protestants are queer people—you say you believe in God, and yet you don't want to please Him."

"I suppose Edward has told you that they all want me to be a lawyer and look after the property. I loathe the idea."

"But if it's your duty—perhaps God meant you to be a lawyer. Perhaps that is the burden laid upon you, the test."

She was leaning toward me, resting her palm on the back of my hand and speaking so earnestly that I was enchanted. And suddenly I interrupted her, "I envy Edward very much."

She stopped. "Why?" But her expression had changed. She was not laughing at me, but even in the dim light I could see that look which means on the face of a pretty girl, "This man is in my hands."

Suddenly she was on her feet. "I am so glad we met tonight. I think God must have arranged it, don't you? But it must be awfully late." She went to the skiff. "You must come and see me—you must promise."

I promised. As I sculled out into the lake, whose water under the lights seemed like India ink splashed with quick fire, I heard her voice say with positive and earnest force which charmed me, "No, no, a missionary, that's absurd. When your duty is so plain."

From the beginning, I knew Julie's opinion of me. She saw me as a country cousin, a foolish ugly boy whom she could twist round her finger. She set to work at once to make use of me.

I saw this and I enjoyed it. How can I explain the strange feelings with which, after Julie's departure, I wandered about the grounds that night? I fancied myself Julie's slave, and my imagination went at once, without my volition, into humiliations of a peculiar kind. I wanted to suffer not only for Julie, but by Julie.

I exaggerated for this purpose Julie's strength and even her wickedness, saying, "A woman like that would stop at nothing."

Yet at the same time I was full of reverence for the girl. I said to myself, "What beauty, what sincerity, what true religious faith. And her life is a tragedy, she deserves every help."

Strange cries, like two or three people wailing and mocking, came from outside my window and startled me for a moment. Somebody was playing rapidly a broken rhythm on strings, and then again the voice cried "Wah-wah-wah."

I looked out and remembered that the children were on the lake. The punt was on the far side of the water, but it seemed to me that only two of the party remained in it, Robert and the Panton girl in her white dress. I thought Ann had landed on the island.

The water music, no doubt, had come to an end, and Robert had put on his gramophone some modern record of what he calls jazz. I hear it often from the separator shed.

"Ann hates that music," I thought. "She has left them as if to say, 'I don't care to enter into competition with fat milkmaids.' "

The music was astonishingly loud. The wah-wah-wah throbbed on the air like the cry of a giant voice. It fell upon my spirits like an extreme bitter sadness. I had never perceived before that the cries of the saxophone were like a human voice, the voice of one brought down to the lowest scale of human feeling, when human mocking passes into animal despair. Oh-oh-oh, wah-wah-wah. The thing was weeping and mocking itself. The voice crying in the wilderness.

The moonlight on the grass, like a blue rime, the leaves moving suddenly and then hanging still, the slow wavering of the quicksilver water seemed to lie under the spell of this sad and trivial music like simple creatures enchanted by some complicated foreign toy. And I thought of the words:

"Nevertheless, as concerning the tokens, behold, the days shall come; that the way of truth shall be hidden, and the land shall be barren of faith.

"And blood shall drop out of wood, and the stone shall give voice and the people shall be troubled."

At Tolbrook in that Jubilee year we were singing "Mandalay." It brought tears to my eyes. They say now that our tunes were sentimental like our religion. That already, as my angry friend on Snowdon so rudely declared, we were degenerate and self-deceiving, etc. And if I told these melancholy young-sters who now listen to mockery like a passion of the flesh, "On the day when I went to make love to my brother's mis-tress, I had in my pocket a letter to a missionary friend, prom-ising to join him in his work," they could well answer, "We are not surprised. Your whole life was illusion and hypocrisy."

But though I may have been a young fool when I darted through the sleepy dusty streets of Mayfair to Julie's flat, I was not altogether contemptible. I was not ashamed of my sentiment. I sought some ideal. And if I went seeking it in a frock coat, a tall hat, not very fashionable, and a new pair of gold-rimmed spectacles, I was at least sincere. When I thought, "Suppose I am refused the door," I felt as if I should fall dead.

But the maid did not refuse me. And Julie received me with warm pleasure. "My dear Tom, how good of you to call. I was so bored with my own company. Sit down while I make tea."

She puts me in a chair and disappears. I jump up, trembling with excitement and audacity, to explore the room. It seems to me beautiful and strange. On the walls, covered with a plain brown paper, are Japanese prints in white frames, and a few drawings, signed by the artists. A Beardsley, a Beerbohm print, an impressionist sketch by Manet. The floor is covered with Persian rugs. The chairs are upholstered in flowered linen. Along one whole wall a low white bookcase is full of books in bright bindings. I see a complete edition of the *Yellow Book* in its thirteen volumes, Beerbohm's works, Dowson's poems, Davidson's plays. And when I open them, I find many of them inscribed, "To dear Julie," "To dearest Hedda," "To my old friend, Julie," with the signatures of the authors and artists.

I had never seen a room with plain walls, plain curtains, with no gilt frames or silver ornaments, with no decorations but the austere prints. For even Beardsley in his black and white was priestlike. I thought, "It is like a cell, of one whose faith is in beauty and love, but a noble beauty, a proud and reserved passion."

"You like my Beardsleys, Tom?" Julie found me gazing at a strange drawing which would, I think, have shocked me in any other room. "Edward gave that to me."

"They say he is decadent and amoral."

"Poor Aubrey. He's dead. He died a month ago at Mentone. But he has been reconciled to the Church for a long time. He asked his friends to destroy drawings like that, and Edward said I might burn it if I liked. I had it in a drawer. But I have hung it up because I loved him and he was a great artist. Tom, I wanted to see you. I was going to write to you about Edward."

"Can you be a great artist and have no morals? I mean, in your art."

"Of course not. But his art is moral. It's a criticism of life. You know what Edward said about him." And she declaimed:

> "See funeral gondolas in black and white;
> Bury our Venice age, with Beardsley's rite."

I saw that she wanted only to talk about Edward. And I gave way to her for the pleasure of watching her lips. During the whole of our teatime she discussed the need of marrying her lover to some rich woman. "Someone like Mrs. Tirrit, who could entertain for him."

Julie was intelligent as well as beautiful, and her mind, at that time, had the same forms as her body—an austere grace, a balanced quickness. She had all the qualities of a great actress;

above all, that seriousness before life which we saw again in Duse. She had all, except ambition. Or if she had ambition, the other motives were stronger, especially that gravity which made her say so often, "But we must think."

I heard the phrase now for the first time when she said, "Edward won't think for himself. So we must think for him."

"You are the most beautiful woman I ever saw, Julie."

She turned her eyes to me with a grave earnestness; her usual manner of acknowledging a compliment. It seemed at once to thank me and to say, "But you and I have more serious things to think about."

She laid her hand on my arm. "If I go away, you will have to look after Edward," and then after a pause, "What shall we do about his debts?"

"They were paid last year."

"He must have a thousand pounds by next week. And he's no one to turn to, unless you help him. He's in despair."

Her face was close to mine, and her big eyes seemed to grow bigger. They say the eyes of a mesmerist appear enormous to his victim. I echoed, "I might try with Papa."

"Why not, Tom? You know how much influence you have with your father. Oh, dear, who is that?"

There was a knock on the door, and seeing that I must catch my chance before it was lost, I bent forward to kiss Julie. But she saw my intention and, to my surprise, advanced her lips and gave me a kiss, so light, indeed, that I hardly felt it. And then, springing up, retreated toward the door.

A woman came in, an actress friend, whose features had seemed beautiful to me in the photographs but now appeared large and coarse like the carving of a figurehead. She stared at me out of her greedy, disappointed eyes, like a dog at another's bone. I was seized with panic and rage, and took up my hat. Julie came to the door, pressing my hand, and said, "So it is a promise."

I ran down the street as if pursued. I could not forget Julie's kiss and her smile. The very smile of Lucy when she condescended to charm the ugly little brother. And what promise did she mean? I had never promised. It was a trick.

But I was full of elation. "How wonderful she is. How beautiful, how strong. She knows what she wants and she takes it."

66

But as it happened, Edward got his thousand pounds very easily. For my father, when I hinted that Edward had another debt, answered at once, "Yes, that woman wrote to me about it. Says it's all her fault, and she's leaving him. Going to America."

"But if she's going away, Edward may be more economical."

"No, no. It's not in him. But I'll have to pay. Or he'll go to the Jews." And he said again with bitterness, "Edward's got the whip hand of me. A waster with talent. Can't throw him out. Can't do anything with him."

To pay Edward's debts, old and new, my father was selling an outlying farm at Torcomb. He was ill with depression and I could not understand why the loss of Torcomb affected him so much. "It's a poor place," I said. "The land is third-rate, reclaimed moor."

My mother answered sadly. "Yes, your father paid too much for it. How could a soldier know about land? But it's always been a worry to him."

"Just as well to get rid of it."

But after the sale my father became still more helpless and dependent upon me. And he began to speak of his death. "Better clean up those papers, Tom. Lighten the baggage." One day, looking about his beloved room, he said, "Not a bad billet, but I've been here too long." He embarrassed me and he caused my mother great pain. I was sometimes angry with him and thought him inconsiderate. Now I understand his struggle and know he was only being frank to those he loved. We failed him because we were shy and could not speak to him of death.

Meanwhile, I had the whole estate work on my shoulders. My training at the missionary college had again to be deferred. But I prepared myself for my vocation. I read some theology. I wrote essays for old Stott, the vicar, who was a D.D. I gave addresses to local clubs, especially on India, which was to be my own field. I read and thought so much about India that it came to be believed, even in our own neighborhood, that I had been there; and I was asked to give lectures in Indian costume. As there seemed no reason to disappoint the clubs, I agreed to wear costume, and sometimes I stained my face, to agree with the costume.

"Here is our Indian sadhu," my mother would say, smiling. For I would often return in costume, to save the trouble of changing in our drafty parish hall. And because I was pleased to be stared at by the people. In fact, I looked much handsomer as a Hindu with a dark-brown face than in my proper form, with a red one.

"More like a sweeper," my father would say, "and boots on his feet."

"He is a good enough Indian for Queensport. And the dress suits him," my mother would answer. As a woman, she perfectly understood why I liked to keep my dress on, even though I might appear ridiculous.

And as I ambled through the lanes on the yard pony, I would say to myself, "Suppose now, instead of having two visits and a dozen trivial things to do before luncheon, I were an Indian sage, sitting in the dust of some holy city with my begging bowl beside me, and nothing to do but think of God's glory. No hair to cut, no farmers to interview, no shopping to do, no letters to write; no wretched little bothers or interruptions. But only peace and contemplation."

Then it seemed to me that I had entered into extraordinary happiness. That I was in a new world where the very air was peace and calm joy; and the ground of it was the eternal truth.

There, I thought, is the abiding place. And all I want to attain that blessedness, that everlasting security, is a single act of will. To renounce the shows of the world. And I would quote, "He who loveth silver, shall not be satisfied with silver. This day is vanity, if I have made gold my hope."

I would think often, To set one's heart upon the things of this world is the most plain folly. Because this world, solid as it appears, is a construction only of desire. All those cottages, those fields, and the very lanes are the deeds of desire. They are the spirit of man made visible in the flesh of his accomplishment. As he seeks, so he builds. There is the villa put up by old Stott when he retired from the parish, to grow his roses. And there is the wooden shed put up by old Brewer for his own quarters, so that he might marry his granddaughter to a man of family. The country people laugh at him and say, "All the striving and scraping of eighty years thrown away to catch a young fool of a clerk for an ugly girl." But so Brewer desired, and he sleeps under his leaky shed in triumph and joy because his granddaughter is married to a pretty man who sails a yacht and plays golf.

"Man lives by his ideas, and if his ideas be mean, then his life shall be mean. If he follow the idea of his body, then his life shall be narrow as one body's room, which is a single grave. But if he follow the idea of his soul, which is to love and to serve, then he shall join himself to the company of all lovers and all the servants of life, and his idea shall apprehend a common good. And if he follow the idea of the Church, he shall embrace the idea of a universal goodness and truth, which is the form of the living spirit. And its name is wisdom. And its works are love and the joy of the Lord."

"Good Morning, sir." Old Brewer is standing at his yard gate. He sings out the sir like a challenge. He has sent for me, but he does not open the gate for me. He leans upon it and stares at me out of his little blue eyes, which are like triangular splinters of bottle glass. His face is as hollow as a bowl. It is like the inside of a walnut shell, crinkled, dry, and yellow. His mouth is hidden in one deep pocket, his eyes glitter in two more. Every line is the track of cunning, avarice. And yet the whole map of the man, as drawn by eighty years of calculation, is now transformed like a dusty web caught in a late ray. The whole face is illuminated by triumph and pride.

"Yess, *sir*."

"About your parlor wall."

"Tain't a wall, *sir*. 'Tis a sponge."

"It was put right before. I see by the books you had a new drainpipe Jubilee year."

"Oh, Jubilee '87."

"No. Diamond Jubilee. Two years ago. Why, there's no pipe here at all. You've taken it away."

"It took itself away, *sir*. It fell down, 'twas nothing but a flake of rust."

"A cast-iron pipe doesn't rust away in two years."

Brewer pretends not to hear, and says loudly, "Nothing but rust. Fifty years old and more."

I know very well that the pipe is doing service, at this moment, somewhere about the farm; as a drain, or a feeder, unless Brewer has sold it. But I know that the old blackguard will swear he never had a pipe, or that the builders put in an old one.

I look at him, and he looks at me. I see his mean cunning, his fathomless cynicism; he sees my anger and hesitation. I don't know, in the face of such complicated impudence, what to do next.

All my fine thoughts are scattered. I am full of rage and disgust. Like other peaceful people, I hate to be swindled. I think, "You, damned old Barabbas, hell was warmed for you. And I should like to see you fry." But I am wary. In a country place, one has to be careful of one's words. With a strong effort, I keep my temper. I say only that perhaps I had better consult with the builder. And I take my leave, with polite inquiries.

The miserable old crook goes to open the gate for me. He did not open when I came because he was preparing for a conflict. He opens when I go because he has won the first battle. He thinks of me as a poor creature, to be laughed at. His politeness is a condescension, and he laughs up into my face as he shouts, "Fine day, *sir*, 'Member me to Colonel."

I remain in a fury all day, imagining fantastic means of bringing just punishment upon this slippery reptile. I find tranquillity at last only in writing to Lucy or Julie.

I write to them both every week. To Lucy about the family, to Julie about art, beauty, etc. To both about Edward.

Neither answers except at long intervals; unless by any chance I miss a post. Then Lucy sends me an indignant note, and Julie cables. In two years I have three cables from her, and two cards with Christmas greetings; one note asking for Edward's new address, and one letter of nine foolscap pages, analyzing, with a great deal of subtlety, Edward's feelings for her and hers for Edward. "He loves me better than anyone in the world, when he loves anyone, and is not more in love with some idea, or book, or picture, or horse. He is only tired of me because he can't expect anything new from me. He soon exhausts a woman's possibilities—he charms her to put out all her leaves and flowers and fruit at once, like a tropical sun shining on an English plant. And then he goes past. I often wish that he would make up his mind to leave me. The agony is wondering when the break will come."

Julie wrote that she loved America and she could never

come back to England and to Edward. But she begged me to continue writing to her. "For I know no one else in the world I can trust."

When I read this, I was well rewarded for my scores of letters.

68

Lucy in one of her rages accused me of stealing from Edward, both his inheritance and his mistress. It was a woman's stab, carefully poisoned with spite. No doubt I desired Julie and I was possessed by that desire, but I never said to myself, "I shall have that woman." And for six years she and Edward between them did their best to drive me mad. Julie suddenly returned to England, in the middle of Edward's most ferocious election. This was in 1900, during the Boer War, at Ragworth, near Liverpool. Edward had given up Queensport to M., one of his chiefs, because it was a safe seat. Ragworth was very unsafe, half-rural and half-urban, with many Catholic Irish dockers, nonconformist chapels, slums, a rich suburb.

No one can imagine the savagery of that election. I can still hear that terrifying noise, the yells of a mob, seeking to kill, to torture; not blindly, but deliberately; so that their howls were mixed with laughter and triumph. Nothing can make one understand, so suddenly and so well, the contempt of those who have loathed mankind, the fear of those who cling to authority, to some established church, which keeps, at best, order among savages.

And both sides were quite ready to organize violence. We encouraged the Irish to howl down the Unionist speeches. The Unionists told the women that we wanted the Boers to kill their husbands and sons in South Africa. Canvassers spent almost their whole time appealing to the worst instincts: fear, greed, hatred. The poor were told that the rich were monsters of cruelty and vice; the quiet little clerks in the suburb were told that the Radicals and the socialists were idle drunken brutes who wanted to take all they could get out of the country and give nothing back.

At first these tactics alarmed me. But when I hinted my doubts to Edward, he laughed and answered, "Politics isn't church work—it's a battle of wills."

Never had Edward seemed greater to me, or more brilliant. I saw his enormous energy, his resource, his courage, his good temper. I was moved, as never before, by his speeches. "They call our people savages," he said. This was after a policeman had been kicked to death. "But if they are savages, who made them so? They did not educate themselves and build their own slums. Millionaires don't break windows. Even clerks at three pounds a week don't break windows. On the contrary, they are more civilized than millionaires."

This was to the clerks. To the doctors, of course, he simply attacked the millionaires and the government. He told his canvassers, "Attack, attack—that's the secret."

And I was carried away. I was more ferocious than the dockers. I said of our opponents, "These devils must be fought with their own weapons." And I, too, assured workingmen in the back streets that all wars were started by millionaires, in order to make money and destroy democracy.

I was shocked and disgusted when Edward, after a meeting in which his eloquence had brought tears to our eyes, passed me this scrap of paper:

> Let tyrannies all to free republics pass
> The one by coppers ruled; the others, brass.

The chairman was still on his feet, asking for a vote of thanks to our "gallant galahad of freedom." And after the meeting I asked Edward how he could be such a fool. "Suppose anyone but me had got hold of that—it would have ruined you. This is not a time for cynical nonsense," etc. And when Edward laughed, I grew still more angry with him. For it seemed to me that here was a fearful danger to his career, and to our cause: his vein of rashness and cynicism.

69

And in the midst of a violent dispute with Edward about his habit of drinking champagne at dinner, a mad thing to do in such a constituency, I was thunderstruck to see Julie walk into the room. We were in Edward's hotel, which was also his headquarters and full of his canvassers and supporters; I had passed, two minutes before, three Baptist ministers sitting on the stairs together, waiting to obtain his support for their temperance society.

I was horrified, yet I was overwhelmed. For several moments I could find nothing to say. I was as confused as a boy in his first passion, who cannot speak, because he has no adequate word.

I had never seen Julie so beautiful or so magnificently dressed. She had had a great success in America. She had a new reputation, new clothes, new jewels; even a new appearance. She was heavier, more imposing. And her face had that special look which belongs to much-flattered women like the radiance of peaches which have been warmed in sunshine. I felt astonished that I had found the audacity to make love to this splendid being. At the same time, some deeper confidence returned to me so that I was filled with joy. As if the hermit in my soul had said, "Oh, man of little faith, see—your paradise is even more magnificent than your invention."

Julie pressed my hand affectionately and said, "How good to

see you. It was my friends I missed. I had to come home." And her eyes looked about the room, a private room at a mean hotel, with delight. "No, it was everything—everything here." She opened her palms downwards and outwards, the gesture of a woman who has just arranged some flowers in her drawing room. "I am longing to see my things again."

Edward, in a cool and rather bored voice, asked her to sit down and eat something. She looked at him and said, "I suppose I shouldn't have come—but I couldn't wait—after two years."

"I am delighted—charmed—if you could excuse me for a moment." He went out, no doubt to see the ministers, and suddenly to my own astonishment I said to Julie, "Of course, you can't stay here tonight—I'm sure you understand that."

"But why not, Tom? Who will know? I've signed myself as Mrs. Smith."

"And your picture's in this week's paper. Don't you realize that you might lose us the election?"

Julie gazed at me with surprise. And her surprise, my agitation, made me still more indignant. "It is really rather thoughtless of you."

Then she laughed and said, "How nice you are, Tom. I'd forgotten how nice—"

"But you don't seem to understand—how am I going to get you out of this place—we are surrounded by spies. All the publicans are against us."

And, in the end, I had almost to push her, wrapped in a man's mackintosh and wearing a cloth cap, down the back stairs. Yet all this time, while I bullied her and cajoled her, I was madly in love. I was seized for the first time by that kind of desire which is capable of violence. I adored her, I respected her, and yet I could not forget. "She is not a respectable woman." I did not think of possessing her; but her very flesh, because it was that of a mistress, gave fire to my passion.

Edward, so far from resenting my bold handling of Julie, congratulated me on getting rid of her. "I thought she had more sense than to turn up now, but I suppose she's one of those people who haven't got a political sense. They're common enough—after all. Either that, or she wanted to revenge herself for something. I have been rather slack about answering her letters."

"Julie is the last woman in the world to do a spiteful thing," I said angrily. "She's the most loyal and devoted creature in the world, as you, of all men, ought to know," and so on. For Edward's ingratitude enraged me. And though I persuaded Julie to retreat even beyond Liverpool, and found her quiet lodgings in Chester, I made Edward write to her every day. That is to say, I typed a letter which Edward signed. And with Edward's letters, I sent my own.

7 0

All these letters to Julie are now in my possession. And I notice that I always wrote to her of Edward as a hero, a prophet, and of myself as a poor fool and weakling. Why, I cannot tell. Except that all lovers seem to enjoy humiliating themselves before their mistresses.

It was true, of course, that at critical moments I was likely to do foolish things, or the wrong thing, or nothing at all. I was, too, a bad speaker; and my voice, in moments of excitement, rose to a squeak. For this reason and because of my general appearance I adopted usually a slow and rather pompous form of address, but forgot both my dignity and my measure as soon as I became excited by my subject. Thus my speeches in defense of the heroic Boers were described, fairly enough, by an opposition paper as a series of squeaks, inaudible to anyone but the reporters, and the policeman whose unhappy duty it was "to protect this miserable little Englander, little in every sense, from the just anger of decent people."

And I was often glad of the policeman. Yet I was glad, too, when his absence threw me into an adventure which brought me a compliment from Julie and even from Edward. Despite myself, I obtained the name of hero which reached even Bill in South Africa.

My glory was easily obtained. I mistook the time and place of a meeting and began to speak to the wrong audience in the wrong place, at the wrong time. That is, I attacked the Unionists before a Unionist crowd, just outside a Unionist public house, on the evening of market day, when the place, a small country town, was crowded with young farmers and laborers.

And when the crowd grew dangerous, I was first of all too blind to see that they had been reinforced by a band of hooligans, organized to attack our speakers; and then, when they began to press upon the speaker's cart, I was so paralyzed by fright that I stood my ground, and even continued to squeak. My committee ran away, but I could not move. And my feeling, when the mob seized me, passed beyond both defiance and terror. It became almost a sense of welcome as if my nerves cried out, "Yes, I've been waiting for this all my life. Get it over. Let us have some peace at last." I can't help remembering how tamely I submitted to the rude hands which took hold of my legs and arms and, what is worse, that I apologized all the time, especially to one great brute whom, by accident, I had kicked in the mouth as I was dragged from the cart with my coat over my ears and my trousers up to my knees. "I'm awfully sorry," I heard myself squeak. "I hope I didn't hurt you." And when I stuck between the posts of a railing, I apologized to the whole mob, "I'm so sorry—something has caught—I think it's my trousers." True, it was my trousers, which gave way just then and were torn almost off, whereupon the crowd, delighted, tore off the rest and most of my clothes. I was obliged to sit in the pond for several minutes, freezing, choking, and bleeding, until the rescue party of police could find a cape with which to cover my nakedness. A ridiculous and humiliating scene. But only the mob heard my apologies and no one attended to the mob. Everyone supposed that I had faced it with reckless courage and fought it like a warrior. The friendly papers made a fine story; and all my supporters regarded me as a champion.

From Julie, of course, I hid nothing. I may even have exaggerated my terror, the misfortune of my trousers, and my ridiculous appearance in the pond. But Julie agreed with Edward that I was a hero, and paid me this compliment: "Edward is lucky to have such a good brother."

In fact, my heroism didn't raise me very much in her estimation. She had the actress view of heroism, that it was something all men ought to possess, just as all women ought to be capable of devotion.

7 1

Edward won his election by forty votes. But I did not see the triumph, for two days before the poll my father had a third stroke, on a visit to Torcomb, and fell helpless. What was he doing at Torcomb, already sold? Apparently, having visited the hamlet once a week, at least, for twenty years, he could not break himself of the habit. He went to look upon the fields which were no longer his, the cottages which he had built; and climbing upon the steep moor sides on a hot day he had burst a blood vessel. He was brought back to Tolbrook on a cart and lived only a week.

He could not speak, but he could think and feel, and write, not very legibly. So on the last evening of his life, while I sat with him in his dressing room, he wrote for me these words, "Too long in same camp." But I did not understand what he meant. I thought, "His mind is wandering back to his soldiering days. The camp bed suggests this." For he was lying on his camp bed, which was kept in the dressing room for temporary use.

But when I had read the words and made no comment on them, he wrote again: "God's work—quite right, go into church. Set heart on God's things. Other things go from you."

I understood that he was thinking of Tolbrook, and it was hard for me to be patient with him. These slow long exchanges at his bedside took much time, and I was distracted with anxieties. Julie, for instance, had decided to take a flat in the same building with Edward, a huge mansion of flats, then not so common as now, in Westminster. I was writing, even wiring, to her daily. For I could not get Edward to be firm. And at Tolbrook one of our old tenants had gone bankrupt, owing two years' rent.

I answered my father, "But you have pulled the property together. Tolbrook is saved for the family."

He stared at me out of his blue eyes and made suddenly a violent effort to speak. His face turned dark, and sweat poured down his forehead. I quickly gave him pencil and paper again. But he could not write. He had too much to say to me. I thought, "Poor Papa, he is trying to tell me that his life's work has been wasted, etc., and that the only happiness open to a man is to set his heart on heavenly things," and so on.

I tried to soothe the old man, but I could not do so. His excitement grew worse, and I had to send for the doctor, who gave him an injection. I looked upon that operation with calmness. But now, when I remember my father's eyes as he watched the syringe brought toward his helpless body, I feel such a pang of grief that my own heart knows the pain of death. For I know what he was saying to himself: "Now they are putting me to sleep, because I want to tell them this thing, which only I can tell. Only a dying man, upon his deathbed, can know it. And because they do not know it, they don't know its importance, they don't want to hear it. And they will keep me asleep till I die."

At the first prick of the needle my father struggled again. Or rather, not he struggled, but something within him violently strove to overcome the weight and barriers of his dead flesh. Then quickly the morphia took effect. And during the night he died. Without knowledge of the agonies which life can bring, and of this last long agony in the presence of death, I could not understand the look on his face, and in his eyes. Only the old know enough to console the old; and then all their friends are dead.

7 2

My father altered his will, by codicil, at the time of the Jubilee. But afterwards he had rescinded the codicil. The will stood, which left all the real estate to Edward; a life interest from £10,000 to my mother, and £3,000 apiece to the rest of us. I resolved, with this money, which gave me a small income, to join our college mission, in the East End of London, as lay warden.

Whether I was attracted to this new career by the secret wish to be near Julie or by exasperation with the petty worries of Tolbrook and with Edward, I cannot tell. But I failed to escape because Edward could not be persuaded even to sign a new lease, or a check for the repairs. On the day of the funeral he disappeared into space. That is to say, we only knew where he was from the papers or sometimes from Julie.

In fact, having won his election, among the few Liberals returned that year, Edward was in demand all over the country. He was hated by millions and loved by thousands. He was known for the first time in every part of the nation, to those who never read the front page of a newspaper but hear, like their ancestors, political news only at the market or the workbench.

The manner of this fame startled me. But just because I was secretly alarmed to find that a man could become powerful only by being violent and singular, I would not allow any criticism of Edward. And when my mother, reading in the local papers of Edward, as "one of those Englishmen who have not forgotten their Liberal principles," etc., said, "I suppose this means notorious," I was angry with her, and said that she did not understand democracy.

I had found out that this statement always shamed criticism. No one ever asked me if *I* understood democracy. In the same way, when in my new responsibilities to the estate I was asked any question about business to which I did not know the answer, I looked resigned like a grown-up pestered by children, and said, "Well, it's rather complicated."

Or I would merely keep silence and assume a preoccupied expression. For I was distracted with worry. Responsibility is an idea. For three years I had made all decisions. But because I had acted in my father's name, I felt no burden. Now when I was asked to decide this or that, I hesitated. I lay awake at night under the burden of this thought, "Destiny, the happiness of others, depends on me." For the first time I understood that heavy word—"duty."

It was no consolation for me to find, in my first search among my father's papers, that he had felt the same burden, and also that he had made great mistakes. The Torcomb purchase had nearly been a disaster. He had spent thousands on draining and improving that wretched place, to no profit. But I said to myself, "If only luck saved my father, so careful and circumspect, what shall save me?" I felt as if the very frame of things in which I had lived so securely were falling apart, like broken screens; to show behind, darkness and chaos. Tolbrook suddenly appeared to me like a magic island, preserved in peace among the storms of the world only by a succession of miracles. As I walked through the rooms, the very chairs and tables seemed to tremble in their silence, like dogs without a master, asking, "What will happen to us now?"

73

And responsibility does not only weigh down the soul; as with iron chains, it divides. The man who makes decisions stands alone. He must be obeyed, but he is criticized, attacked, belittled. When Lucy came flying home to see us, I received her with love; but her first words were a challenge: "What are you doing about father's chair? He promised it to me. I must have something from father's Tolbrook."

"He said nothing about a chair, and it's Edward's now."

"It can't be Edward's. It's mine. Even Mama says I can have it."

"If it's yours, why did you need to ask Mama?" I went to our mother, who denied any agreement with Lucy about a chair, but said, "She ought to have it, perhaps."

"Why? You always give in to Lucy. You spoil her."

My mother was herself ill. My father's death, so long expected, overwhelmed her, almost as if she had caused it. She asked me once, "Why did you not fetch me that last time?" She meant in the hour when he died. And before I could say that I had not expected this death, she answered, "But perhaps he did not want me"; and then quickly, to ease my embarrassment, "To see him so ill."

For my mother, I suppose, a lack of sympathy between herself and that husband to whom she had been so devoted a wife had gradually become a sin to her conscience.

At that time she could not sleep, and I think, when we believed her sitting idly in some melancholy dream, she was often in prayer. But I, like Lucy and perhaps by Lucy's influence, was exasperated by her absent-mindedness, her lack of decision. "Do you want her to have the chair, Mama? What do you want?"

"Lucy was devoted to her father, and he to her."

"But about the chair; you understand it's Edward's chair, and we're responsible for Edward's property."

"Our statesman doesn't concern himself with chairs, except perhaps the Speaker's."

But seeing that I could get no support from my mother, I went back to Lucy and said, "Just what I thought. You never asked Mama for the chair—and as I'm in a position of trust—"

"Nonsense. You're in a position of grab. And you mean to hold on. Very well, then. Keep your old chair."

And thus began the battle of the chair which divided me from Lucy for eight years. For Lucy cheated me. While awaiting a letter from Edward, I came back one day from Queensport to find not only the chair but my father's camp bed, Indian pillow, and carpet being loaded onto a cart. I began at once to take the things into the house. Lucy met me with the carpet in my hands, and there was a kind of tug-of-war in the hall. Meanwhile the cart drove away.

"Really, Lucy," I said, "you have no conscience. You could go to prison for this."

"Then send me to prison, you wretched little pettifogger," she answered coolly. "I'm sure you're quite capable of it." And we parted in bitterness. Indeed, when Lucy found out, on arrival, that I had removed the pillow, she wrote me a letter so abusive that for years afterwards we had no communications.

Lucy could always enrage me by calling me a pettifogger. As I could anger her by calling her a hypocrite. For both words came so close to the truth of our natures that they took its light and cast a shadow on our souls. To Lucy, fighting pride with pride, it was easy to think that humility was pretense; and for me, clinging to order and rule in the turmoil of the world, it was easy to think that the word was greater than the spirit; that I valued not my father's memory, but a piece of property.

7 4

I was far from sleep. I got up and went downstairs into my father's study, which had long been mine. The chair was back in its place. Lucy had brought it with her when she came home for the last time. An ugly yellow chair in varnished oak. But now I saw it again with Lucy's feeling; I entered into her world, and I felt a strange sensation, a movement of the blood, a thrill in my breast. I felt my father's presence; and Lucy's thought of him; his innocence. He was present in his own being, as if Lucy's love had re-created him for me. I knew why she had wanted that relic of him, to give her faith in man's goodness.

The worn carpet had disappeared. I had expected to see it with the marks of my father's feet on it from door to desk, and I gazed with wonder at the bright new Turkey which covered the floor, a carpet which Sara had made me buy, to keep my feet warm while I worked on cold winter days.

I remember that I had asked for the old carpet to be renewed, a plain gray, and here was a Turkey of the most brilliant crimson. Sara had loved bright colors. I can't remember how she persuaded me to accept this atrocious vulgar object. But Sara was very persistent in getting her way and would wait two years, three years, for an opportunity only to change the stair rods or re-cover an armchair. And if she did not like a rug or a chair cover, it would soon look shabby, and even develop holes, as if the force of her dislike could destroy the material.

She had urged, I remember, "A nice red Turkey, to keep you warm, sir, for you know you feel the winter," as if the color would warm me as well as the pile, and put new blood into my veins.

And though I can't like its vulgar red, yet it makes me smile; it resembles Sara's rosy cheeks, her gaiety, her obstinate resolve that others should enjoy what she found good: warmth, food, affection, soft beds, a domestic sensuality about which her religion was like the iron bands nailed to a child's tuck box.

I was warmed by the very memory, and yet found myself shivering. Rain had been falling on the window for some time. But now I heard a call. I went to the window and saw that the night was clear. What I had taken for rain was pebbles striking the wall, and I looked down to see Ann standing alone under the window. From the lake I could hear, but now much fainter, as if the lid of the gramophone had been closed, a confused noise like jackals screaming and monkeys chattering.

Ann waved to me, and when I opened the window she called, "Don't do that, uncle. Go to bed at once. Wait." She came running upstairs and took my arm. "What are you doing here at this time? I couldn't believe my eyes when I saw the light. Do you want to catch pneumonia?"

"It is a warm night. Did you leave the others to look after me?"

"No, I left them. I don't like jazz, and I don't much like Robert's girls. If he wants to go off with that Molly, I wish he would do it."

"What rubbish," I said, for I was seriously alarmed. "Robert only feels a sense of duty to the girl because she pays a fee. He's quite right. And what do you do to please Robert, going about with that long face and wrinkles in your forehead?"

"Suppose Robert did leave me, uncle, would you let me stay on here? I should have Jan, of course. And I could pay my share. Young Dr. Mac is quite ready to take me as a partner."

They call the boy Jan, copying the local pronunciation of his name.

All this startled me so that I was confused. And perhaps I felt a temptation. But I told the girl she had no right to break her marriage. "That at least is plain."

"But it's failed, uncle. It's finished."

I thought by her voice that she was going to cry. Which alarmed me greatly. For do what I would, I had come to feel with the girl and I could not bear her unhappiness so close to me. Women's unhappiness is always more persistent and hopeless than a man's, especially nowadays when the poor things have lost God and all the powers of grace. When they have cast themselves loose on the world without even rules of conduct, good or bad, to hold them up against those terrible enemies, terrible especially to women, of time and conscience. "My dear child," I said, "your marriage has hardly begun—it hasn't had time to fail. And if you break it, perhaps you will break your heart, too. The only thing we can rely on in a tight corner is our duty. That's the only way out. Duty, duty, that's the salvation of poor humanity. Do your duty and then if everything goes to the devil, you won't have to blame yourself for your own misery, which is the worst misery of all. I think it is really what is meant by hell."

"I can't help that, uncle. I know I've deserved the worst. But I'm not going to fake anything. I can't make a pretense of marriage which isn't a marriage at all."

"Good God, you poor silly dunderhead. What in heaven's name do you think marriage is—a sugarplum dropped into your mouth off a gingerbread tree? It's you modern girls are sentimental."

But of course she did not listen to me. She thinks that because I am old I know nothing about the real world in which she lives. She kissed me suddenly and said, "So you will let me stay. I don't bother you too much," and went to the door. "But you can't trust Robert to do anything that suits you. And of course we won about the name. He can't forget that."

"Robert is not so small-minded."

"Names are not a small thing to Robert. Not when they are family traditions."

"Mathias is not a Wilcher name."

"That's why he wanted it. And that's why he wants to turn the Adams room into a machinery shed. There's a lot of Wilcher in Robert. He's a real old Protestant inside. He'd really like to make a whole new god for himself if he had the time after making me over."

75

When Amy was pregnant of her second son John, in the year after the Jubilee, and near her time, she had a wire at Tolbrook to say that Bill's troopship was arriving in Liverpool. He had been at Omdurman.

Amy's first child, William, now eight years old, was already at boarding school; but a second had been born prematurely, at sea, and did not live. Amy was therefore under strict supervision by the local specialist, a Queensport man.

Bill's wire seemed to cause her much perplexity. At intervals during the morning she was found wandering about the house, with the wire in one hand and some garment in the other, asking each of us in turn, "What shall I do?"

We all said that she must not dream of traveling; Bill would not expect her. The doctor had given strict orders that she was not to stir beyond the garden.

After luncheon, she appeared in a coat and hat to say good-by. We cried, "But what madness. And at any rate, you can't go now. It's too late. You couldn't get ready in time to catch the train." And it turned out that she had packed, ordered the trap, and looked up her complicated train connections during the morning. She left the house and caught the train with ten minutes to spare.

We laughed at this new evidence of Amy's oddity. "I suppose," I said, "she asked advice out of a kind of instinct, as a dog barks after rabbits in his sleep."

And the baby, as the doctors had foretold, was born on the journey, actually in the train.

This story, too, was treasured as a family joke. We told how Amy, her pains beginning, had asked an old gentleman in the carriage if he were a doctor. And upon his answering No, why did she think so, she had answered, "I didn't really think so, but I wanted to bring up the subject."

This tactful approach had had no results. The old gentleman simply returned to his paper. And Amy had been too diffident to make any further advance toward an understanding until it was too late even to stop the train. The old gentleman, seeing Amy collapse, and suddenly realizing the position, had rushed out for the guard, who then hunted through the train for a doctor. Without success. At last he brought her a very young man in a horsecloth waistcoat, with a gold horseshoe in his tie. He explained, with whispered apologies, that this was a student vet. "But it's the best we can do for you, mam."

"Oh," cried Amy aloud, "don't apologize. You couldn't have done better. I'd much rather have a vet than a real doctor." And then she explained to the blushing lad why she preferred him. "I'd be ashamed to ask a real doctor to manage in a railway carriage. But, of course, you won't mind, will you? You're used to cows."

And she took charge of him, reminding him to wash his hands and making him spread out newspapers, to save the company's cushions. And she made him get the newspapers from the next carriage. She would not give up her own *Morning Post*, which she was keeping for Bill. She held the

Post during the whole delivery, a very painful one, in order to make sure that it would reach Bill intact.

To Bill, of course, it was an episode which he used as a weapon against Amy. He never forgave her for endangering the life and, above all, the health of his baby by what he described as a "piece of her usual obstinacy." He would tell us that part about the old gentleman with extraordinary indignation even fifteen years later. "And she had only got to pull the cord."

To which Amy would reply, "The notice said it cost five pounds."

"It says, 'For use without due cause.' If you hadn't due cause, who has?"

"Well, I knew it might start before I started."

"What's that got to do with it?"

"It didn't seem quite fair to put it all on the railway, and you know we were saved a lot of expense. That nice boy wouldn't take anything but two glasses of beer at Chester."

"My God, and it didn't worry you that John might have been crippled for life."

We laughed at them both, but now, remembering Amy's untroubled expression before Bill's anger and terrible suggestions, I ask, "How was it that Amy always knew what she ought to do, and did it, and so calmly accepted the consequences?"

I thought her simple. No one is simple. But I can see now that Amy, in the very conflicts of her duty, as wife and mother, had strict though complex principles. Sometimes Bill came first, sometimes a child. But Amy was a woman of principle, and what strength that gives to the humblest soul, what wisdom to the most modest intelligence.

Edward used to say that Bill and Amy's conversation on any subject, but especially a political subject, explained to him the history of the Greek word "idiot." "They are the most private citizens I ever met, even in a village pub."

But it has struck me since that what I enjoyed in Bill and

Amy was this very quality of remoteness from Edward's world. Indeed, it was not long after Edward's election that I began to feel, in that world, an uneasiness which I cannot exactly describe and which has sometimes caused in me, I am afraid, an unworthy ingratitude toward public officials of all kinds.

It was this feeling which produced my first bitter quarrel with Edward, at one of his own political parties. The date must have been 1902, because I know that one subject of our interest was the peace terms after the Boer War.

I had been trying for some weeks to make Edward come to a decision on various points, such as Julie's debts, the agency which remained in my hands because he would not appoint a successor, and an IOU to Bill. Edward had already borrowed five hundred pounds out of that small legacy, which was all that Bill possessed.

I had resigned the agency by wire and by letter. Edward had answered neither. I came to the party, my first chance in three weeks of seeing Edward personally, determined to free myself from my servitude.

I found his big room, on the seventh floor, with an excellent view of St. James's Park, crowded, as usual at his parties, with very incongruous guests. Some, to judge by their uneasy and pompous solitude, were from the constituency; some, by their tweeds and ties and hair, from Chelsea; and some, as obviously, were ladies of the highest fashion moving quickly here and there and darting quick glances of recognition at nobody, to hide the fact that for the moment they knew only nobody. Two young officers chatted together like polite conspirators; a famous millionaire looked at the pictures with the face of one who asks, "Ought I to invest in these absurd things?" and two political groups, all of men, talked vigorously among themselves. All these latter, young and old, had the same kind of assured manner, which was quite different from the unassuming social confidence of the guardsman or the arrogance of the rich merchant. One could tell at once that they were all used to playing the statesman, in some circle, large or small, and to public speaking. They threw into their voices notes of geniality, indignation, and importance.

Edward's secretary, a very fair young man with the manners of a bishop, came up to me and asked me if I knew where he was.

"No, isn't he here?"

"He isn't at Mrs. Eeles?"

"No, I saw her just now."

There was a slight pause, as if we might come to some understanding about Julie.

Julie, after all, had taken a flat in the building at Edward's own request. Their only concession to public opinion was that she lived on a different floor. And I was still in daily fear of a scandal. I had not yet discovered that women were not to be Edward's ruin; that he was protected by one of those strange conventions of British public life, which prevents any reference to the personal lives of public men, however bad, unless they come into the courts. Even personal disfigurements must be respected. So that Gladstone's missing finger appeared in all caricatures, even by his enemies; and the newspapers never referred to the continuous drunkenness of Mr. A., a cabinet minister, or to even more scandalous liaisons than Edward's. He suffered more, with the party, by writing epigrams and collecting French pictures than by keeping Julie Eeles.

The secretary, though my ally in anxiety, was never equal to a private confidence with me. He was too loyal or too official. He regarded me merely as Edward's man of business. "How is she?" he would ask, with dignified reserve, meaning, "Is she going to behave?" And I answer it, "Quite well. But she won't be coming to the party."

"No," the young man murmurs, "I should hope not." As if an undergraduate had peeped out of the Bishop's window.

"Exciting times," I say, to relieve our mutual embarrassment.

"Oh, yes, this Williamson letter."

"I meant, about the peace," and as one of the political group turns to include the secretary, I say, "What terms are we going to give them?"

"Terms? No terms at all."

Another exclaims warmly, "I'm not going to deal with people who shoot our men under a white flag."

"Is it quite certain that the letter was meant to be private?"

The discussion breaks out again with still more energy, and gradually I perceive that it is all about a by-election, and some action by the other side which is considered unfair. A letter has been published showing that some Liberal leader disapproves of his own candidate.

"I was speaking of the end of the war," I explain.

"Oh, yes." They all look at me, and their faces say plainly, "A layman—an idiot." Then the oldest, a tall man who was afterwards minister, makes me a little speech. "In my view our policy should be to aim at so and so."

"Or the Welshman will give trouble again," another interrupts.

"But you mustn't forget the Roseberyites."

The door opens and Edward comes in with Bill. Edward is always late for his parties. He seems, as usual, both busy and unruffled. He carries a portfolio under his arm; but he is dressed as for Ascot, in a pale-gray frock coat, with an orchid in his buttonhole.

I push up to him and he greets me with an affectionate smile. "How nice to see you, Tom. You're staying?"

But I'm not to be cajoled any longer. I answer angrily, "Did you get my letter about the agency?"

"Just a moment." He turns aside and at once he is surrounded by the fashionable ladies, the young politicians. All but the two soldiers, the banker, and the two or three older men whom I take to be M.P.'s hasten toward him and enclose him. I salute Bill and ask after Amy, who has just had a baby, her third boy.

Bill, invalided with a wound and enteric, is still, after a year's sick leave, very thin. His mustache is already gray, and he looks ten years older than Edward. But he is full of life. His expression, the quick turn of his head while he looks round the room, even his attitude, incautiously curious, distinguishes him from all the rest. One says at once, "Soldier on leave from foreign service."

"Don't like these new coats much," he says. "Too tight." Bill's own coat, of the cut of 1894, is like a sack. "Who's the old bogey with the bow window?"

"Ah. He's a banker."

"Oh, I thought he might be minister for something. I say, Edward's getting on, isn't he? Is it true they've picked him for the next Liberal cabinet? Or is it just another yarn?"

"They'll have to give him something."

"If they get in. But I think they've finished themselves over this pro-Boer business. I told Edward so. But he says they had to do it. All the dissenters were against the war. Edward," calling out, "I was just telling Tommy that you're going to be sorry for all that treason you people talked while our chaps were getting scuppered."

Edward turns his affectionate smile toward Bill; a dozen other faces turn the same way with different expressions. The fashionable ladies with a smile which could stand, with very slight change, for congratulation or derision, as required by public opinion. The young political men with every shade of surprise and contempt.

"The fact is, Bill," Edward says smiling, "my constituency is full of treason, and as the representative of traitors, I—"

"You wait till the army gets back," Bill interrupts him.

The silence is broken at last by a young man with very black hair and gold spectacles. He says thoughtfully, "The army."

"Yes, the army," Bill says, looking round him like a bull-dog. "Doesn't that count for anything?"

"Not in a democracy, Bill—or I hope not," I say hastily. "The army, as an army, has no political power." I want to save Bill from exposing himself to these experts.

"Not even if it voted the same way. Because you see," the young man speaks as if to a child, "there's not enough of it."

"And besides," one of the M.P.'s remarks, leaning back and smiling down at Bill across his big wing collar, "the war is over—as a political issue, it's as dead as Queen Anne."

"Feeling at the moment is rather against the army," another says. "I noticed that particularly at my last meeting. There were two questions about the conduct of troops in the village."

"A good sign," says the first. "Getting back to sanity."

One of the country visitors, a little man with a hatchet face of which the cheeks are almost beet color, who till this moment has stood aloof, glaring at everyone, now flies at Bill and, shooting forward his head like a biting tortoise, exclaims, "So you're a soldier!"

"That's it," Bill answers, surprised. "Major Wilcher, at your service."

"Then allow me to inform you, major," and the little man stands on his toes like a gamecock about to strike. The crowd closes in as round a cockpit. I make a plunge at Edward, and say, "I suppose you're going to dodge out of everything again." I am furious with him, and my fury is the expression of my uneasiness for Bill. It is the revenge of the private citizen, the humble idiot, upon what is called a public man, with his special immunity. I want to break that shield of preoccupied egotism.

"Dodge out?" Edward looks at me in surprise. "What's wrong with Julie? Of course, something about a bill."

"She's had a summons and she's afraid your name may come out."

Edward's eyes wander, and his face assumes the look of a small boy on holiday who is reminded of some duty.

"Well, can't you do something about it? But I forgot, you've chucked up the job—wait a moment—I must see so and so." And he goes off to a new arrival. He becomes at once animated, charming, interested.

But I am suddenly so enraged against him that I forget myself. I push forward saying, "Excuse me, sir," and then to Edward, these words which astonish myself: "You great public men may be very important and all that, but merely private people do have some rights. And I want to know what you're going to do about the agency, and Julie's bills," etc., etc.

Edward takes this rebellion with perfect aplomb and good nature. "Julie? Nothing to do, old boy, I assure you. But I'll see her, if you insist."

"It might be a good idea," I say severely.

"Right." He turns and makes for the door. And at once, of course, I feel ashamed of myself. I reflect that Edward has, in fact, important responsibilities; that one must not blame him for a certain carelessness in domestic relations, since public men suffer special disabilities, etc., and so on.

"Oh, damn it," I think. "It's settled, at any rate." And I look round for Bill. I long to escape from all these anxieties and confusions. "Perhaps Bill would like a walk."

Bill is now fairly driven to the wall. The enraged evangelist is haranguing him like a murderer. An interested semicircle stands about them, gazing as at a cockfight. Bill, with an air of surprise, is saying, "Yes, yes, two sides to every question. Oh, yes, I'm not maintaining—"

And he seems astonished by the other's violence.

Suddenly Amy appears beside him carrying her baby in her arms. The politicians gaze at her in astonishment. She is dressed in electric blue, which gives to her high complexion the brilliance of a ribstone pippin. She is almost cubical in shape, as always when she is nursing; and her hat, of the largest size, is perched upon the top of a roll of hair so high that it is nearly as long as her whole face.

Amy looks with surprise from Bill to his antagonist, and gradually becomes redder. Suddenly her hat trembles, and turning to the evangelist she ejaculates, "Rubbish."

All are taken aback; not least Bill's opponent, who gazes at Amy with visible confusion. And through his eyes I see that Amy must now appear to strangers like a formidable person. A comical idea. At last the man collects himself, "Excuse me, madam, that isn't exactly an argument."

"Oh, yes it is," Amy says with royal emphasis. "It's my argument." And she walks off.

Bill, apparently shocked by Amy's intervention, follows her protesting, "But it's not rubbish at all. Lots of people have that kind of view— it's a religious view." Classifying the view under its proper head.

Amy, in this new role of the regimental matron, amuses me so much that I can't take my eyes off her. "I'm sorry that fellow worried you—a bit of a fanatic."

"Bill, listening to him like that. I've no patience. After the way they've treated the army."

Bill answers mildly, "My dear Amy, it takes all sorts to make a world. In a democracy—"

Amy is still moving away. She is now in retreat from a field of battle in which her own boldness has proved more alarming than the enemy. "And it's long after baby's bedtime." As if the democrats have prevented the baby from being put to bed.

"I notice that," Bill says. "I suppose you were showing him off again. No wonder he can't sleep. His nerves are in rags."

"Nerves! A baby of two months with a nervous system."

"Have you never seen that poor child jump when you drop something, or push the pram over a curb?"

"It may jump, but that's instinct. It's not nerves."

"Well, I give you up. But it's not my fault if the child has fits when it grows up."

Amy carries the baby away, but calls back in a warning voice:

"I can't wait." She disappears into a bedroom and Bill turns to me. "One doesn't expect them to understand politics, but babies, you'd think, would be safe with them. Not a bit, old man; not a bit of it. Women know nothing about babies. Like to see your new nephew washed?"

I go in and find Amy, in an enormous apron, sitting before a washbasin balanced on a piano stool. A battered uniform case, strangely painted with small red crescents, stands open beside her with various toilet articles disposed in the open lid which serves as a dressing table. Amy is undressing the baby, which is uttering loud furious cries.

We draw up chairs and I say, "I'm afraid it's very inconvenient for you here. They don't cater for babies. We could have sent you a bath from Tolbrook."

"We don't bathe him now, old chap," Bill says, warning me not to expect an important pleasure. "This is only a wash. Head and tail; how is the bottom, old girl?"

Amy turns up the baby which, head downwards, stops crying and makes desperate attempts to reach her breast.

"Better, I think," Bill says at last. "But I think I'd better do the powdering today. You want to give some mind to it." And he says to me, "All these creases. Marvelous legs, aren't they?" He takes hold of a leg and displays it to me. I am reminded of Edward showing a first edition.

"Come, we must get on," Amy says briskly, and plants the baby in her lap. It utters a yell of rage, then puts its thumb in its mouth and sucks loudly. Amy vigorously washes its head, causing its skull to roll about on the neck as if it might be dislocated.

Bill says, "Easy—easy—" The baby continues to suck its thumb as if its head is none of its business. It submits with the same indifference to having its nose and eyes cleaned. It screws up its face with a disgusted air, sneezes several times; one expects shouts of fury; but the moment Amy removes the towel the small features spring back, like India rubber, into an expression of dreamy greed, and the thumb goes back into the mouth.

"Quite good now," Bill says, in a tone of keenest satisfaction. "As a matter of fact, Tom, you couldn't have a better-tempered child when it gets a fair deal."

The baby suddenly takes out the thumb, doubles itself up, closes its eyes, and utters a long shriek of fury. Amy smiles, picks it up, turns it round, and drops it across her knees, to wash its back. Yells change to a modulated wail, like a slowly deflating rubber pig. But now and then, in the midst of this thin wail, it throws in a short phrase like the beginning of a song. It seems to be composing, and listening to itself.

"What a back," Bill says, spanning out the back with his thick, short fingers. "You won't see many better backs than that. You did a good job there, old girl. Set him up for life with a real good spine."

"I hope he'll have my digestion," Amy says. "That's the important thing—digestion."

"Nonsense. He's not a prize pig. Besides, you can't have a good digestion without a good back. No play for the stomach."

"Then I don't know why your digestion is so bad."

"My digestion is first class, except when I've just had enteric, or malaria."

"Look at the fuss today about the chops."

"Chops. You mean those raw horse collops. And that was

the first time in years. I never make a fuss about anything. If I did, I should be doing nothing else."

Amy is pulling on the baby's nightdress. The baby is now uttering a series of short loud yells and trying apparently to throw itself into the air. It bends its back, waves its clenched fists, jerks its head. Then sucks and pants, pushing out its tongue. It is a picture of frantic desperate greed. Amy says placidly, "That isn't good for you, anyway. You know how fuss upsets your stomach."

"Fuss," Bill says. "Fuss again. Good God." He utters a short laugh. "The joys of married life, Tommy. You don't know what you've escaped. Babies, schools, dentists, quarters, bills. And on top of it, you're told that you fuss."

"You're not going, Tom?" Amy says, warning me that she is about to feed the baby.

Bill says, "You're ready, are you? Come on, Tom. We'll scoot."

I should like to stay and see the baby fed, but Amy and Bill are firm. Amy, unbuttoning her bodice, calls after me, "But you won't go away, Tommy, will you? I haven't seen you yet."

And after the baby, now a mere bag of milk, has been put to sleep in the uniform case, which is its traveling bed as well as its campaign luggage, we go walking in the park.

Amy and Bill look about them with delight. Bill sniffs the air and remarks on the smell of narcissus, and the number of flannel suits, now in the park. "But I suppose this new Labor party has made a difference."

He stops opposite a flower bed and says, "Look at these trumpets. What's their name? I must really get up daffodils from someone who knows what's what in bulbs. Come in useful when I settle down."

I am still full of laughter at the couple. I have several stories to send to Lucy. But when Bill begins to talk of taking Amy back to the flat because she mustn't be tired, I support Amy's protest. I want to go on walking with them in the park. I feel with them a complete peace and confidence. I do not need to apologize, to defend, to rage against Edward's smiling selfishness or Julie's infatuated devotion.

It is true that Bill and Amy were private citizens, without ambition to be admired even in our own circles; but how delightful was their company to me, after political drawing rooms. With them I breathed an air free of self-seeking, as fresh as a spring day here at Tolbrook, where there are not even tourists to appreciate its candor.

76

Robert came to me this evening when I was sorting some of Edward's papers and said to me, "I don't want to be a nuisance, uncle, or ask too many questions, but I've been wondering just what your idea is in getting at Ann."

"What do you mean, Robert?"

"Well, I mean just the whole thing, uncle. First, it was the nursery chairs and the nursery wallpaper, and then it was the names, and now it's the kind of way she should bring up the boy. You've got her kind of switched back."

I was sitting in the little room behind the salon which used to be Edward's study, a high narrow room paneled in dirty white, with many shelves. Our tenants had used it for a store, and empty jam pots still stood on the upper shelves. In the lower there were those remnants of Edward's library, eighteenth-century novels in calf, French paperbacks, which had survived because they had neither interest nor value for servants or shooting guests. An upper cupboard had been used to store Edward's papers, and now, at Ann's suggestion, I was putting them in some order. She had brought down her father's old desk from the attic and found his study chair in the library. Her plan, indeed, in which I had warmly agreed, was to restore the room, which we both found one of the prettiest in the house.

On this winter day, with a big fire, and a new carpet on the floor, reproducing, as far as I could remember, Edward's French carpet, it was already, in spite of empty shelves and dirty paint, extremely pleasant; and I was possibly enjoying myself more than usual, humming, etc., over a task at once exciting and useful, when Robert made his unexpected attack.

He had just come from market and wore a blue suit with yellow shoes which, for some reasons known only to himself, he affects on market days. He looks more like a sailor on shore leave, or a commercial traveler of the humbler kind, than a farmer.

I was extremely startled by the boy's speech, and answered that he was talking great nonsense.

"How could I do such a thing?" I asked. "Ann is the last person to be influenced by anything anyone would say," and so on.

"Well, I don't know how it is. She's changed so much, and all the other way from me."

"But how am I responsible? I didn't do it. Every woman changes in her first year of marriage. It is a great experience for a woman, especially if she has a baby—far greater than happens to any man." I grew indignant at this attack. And I thought of Edward's saying, "Marriage, to a woman, is a conservative education."

"Of course," I said, "Ann has changed, grown steadier and wiser, more affectionate."

"Well, uncle, she may be more affectionate to some people, but she doesn't show it to me."

"Whose fault is that—you don't try to please her. You don't even shave every day. You may think that's nothing. But it's very important to a woman. If you have driven Ann away from you, it's your own fault."

"I didn't drive her to early service."

"Why shouldn't she go to early service—mustn't she have any religion of her own? I'm surprised at you, Robert. You young people talk about freedom, etc., and then you try and interfere with your wife's religious observance," and so on.

"I just wonder what she's playing at, and why you keep on at her. Whether you want us to split up and me to get out and leave her to it, and you to keep the kid."

"I never heard of such a thing." For now I was really upset. "Good heavens, is that the way you think about me?" and the rest. I spoke with energy, for the truth was, my conscience was disturbed. I had never dreamt that Robert would resent my efforts to teach Ann some rational belief. But I remembered that only that morning I had been speaking to her, perhaps too insistently, about the necessity of religion. "The world is senseless without faith," I had said, "a mere fantastic play of injustice and folly." No doubt true and necessary to the poor child's happiness, but possibly indiscreet to Robert's wife.

"I don't want to upset you, uncle," Robert said, having upset me extremely. "I'm not trying to make any sort of trouble between you and Ann; not at all. I've just been wondering, that's all. Especially since Ann grew all that hair. That seems to have made a big difference."

Ann came in with a stepladder and a paintpot, etc. She was about to paint the upper cupboards. She stood beside Robert during his last speech while he continued in the same voice, as if it did not matter if she heard it.

"You were pleased when I grew my hair," Ann said. Her hair was now in a neat bun. She showed me the paint. "Is this the color, uncle? Georgian green they called it."

I said that the color, in Edward's time, had been a little paler.

"I'll thin it," Ann said.

"I was pleased when you grew your hair," Robert said, "but I thought you were growing it from sense and not from some nonsense."

Ann climbed up her ladder and began to paint. She asked from above, "What sense and what nonsense?"

"Well, I should say it's sense for a woman to be a woman. And I should say it's getting on for nonsense for anyone to play-act being their own grandmother."

"Play-acting. But why do you think I'm play-acting? It's quite fashionable to do your hair in a bun and wear pork-pie hats."

"Well, perhaps it isn't play-acting, but I don't know whether I shouldn't be just as pleased if it was."

I was alarmed by his tone. The young people had had many of their discussions lately, and I had thought that there was more obstinacy and anger in their politeness than in their former rudeness. I said that Ann liked to be in the fashions, and I thought it a very nice womanly fashion, etc.

But I was so frightened that I could hardly breathe. I thought, "What is going to happen now?"

Luckily Ann, even without looking at me, seemed to understand my distress, for she suddenly came down the ladder, murmured something to Robert and took him out of the room. She then returned at once and said, "He hasn't worried you, has he? How's the enemy?"

"I feel very well."

"H'm, you've done enough for the day," and she made me rest.

And, in fact, I did not feel at all well. I was assailed by new fears. "Everything," I thought, "is going to be turned upside down. And whose fault is it, mine or Ann's or Robert's? Or the evil genius of the place?" I looked at Ann on her ladder, vigorously and skillfully painting the panels, and I thought, "Is Tolbrook claiming another victim?"

Government rascals! so cries honest Hob.
True, God made rascals; each man for his job.

Forty years ago, when I complained to Edward of my lost career, he smiled and said, "You've got what you wanted. You always meant to live at home. It's a shame the place wasn't
left to you."

I raged against him. To a man like Edward I was one of those
poor creatures, lawyers, bankers, the little clerks, who haven't
the spunk to take a risk. And what is the truth? That all
these quiet little men are the victims of ideals, of passions.
They are the lovers, the pilgrims of the world, who carry
their burdens from one disappointment to another and know
it is useless even to complain. For their own comrades will
despise them.

They are the private soldiers who do the hard fighting,
while the generals take the glory.

Bill used that very image to me on the evening of Edward's
party. "You and I are rankers to Edward."

But to Bill, of course, that was a natural and proper relation.
He had no envy, no grudge, in his composition, and no idea of
justice either. Bill, as he grew older, became simpler, and also
less consistent. Just as he surprised me by his respectful attitude to the pacifist, he now threw me into a fury by taking it
for granted that I should continue in the agency.

"You can't resign, Tommy—what will happen to Edward?"

"I have resigned."

"And what are you going to do with yourself?"

"I'm taking orders, as I always meant to do."

"Well, that's the end of Tolbrook."

"I'm sure Tom would make a very good clergyman," Amy
says. "At least he is a gentleman, and doesn't drink."

"But I never thought you would let us down."

"Blame Edward for that—not me."

And then Bill makes his remark about the rankers. "Edward is exceptional. That's not just my own idea—I've made inquiries from people who know. Anything we can do for Edward is worth doing."

I am silent in bitterness, not now against Bill, but against fate, my own weakness, what you will.

I seem to be thrust into a long tunnel from which I shall never again escape until I reach the speck of light at the far end. That light is my death. But the tunnel is not dark. On the contrary, it is lighted throughout by a kind of pale sad gleam in which everything is exceedingly clear and long familiar. I see the chairs, tables, pictures, and even my London office, with its worn carpet and ink-stained wastepaper basket, standing in dumb patience, as if waiting upon my decision. They have already that dejected look of things at a sale, where everything seems to say, "We are betrayed—there is no faith or trust in the world." I think angrily, "But what nonsense this is. Sentimental nonsense, and so is all this talk about the family tradition. We may have stood for something once. We kept up the Whig tradition and put evangelists into the living," and so on. "But that's all out of date, exploded—even if all the country houses go the same way as the Roman villas, they won't be missed. They may have been centers of civilization once, but they did not succeed in civilizing the barbarians—that needs bigger resources."

We have reached the flats. Bill, sighing deeply, shakes hands and says, "Well, Tom, I suppose, if you must, you must—but I never thought you were that sort." And Amy says cheerfully, "Oh, well, it's not quite settled yet is it?"

And from the lift she gives me an encouraging look, as if to say, "You'll try to be good, won't you?"

And as soon as the lift is out of sight, I fly up the stairs to Julie, whose presence in the building is not supposed to be known to Amy. I need consolation and support. Raging, I rush into her apartment and tell her of the plot to nail me to Tolbrook. "Bill's in it, too." For I like to be unjust to Bill.

Julie is wandering from one room to another, in petticoat and corsets, among heaps of silks and underclothes. She pays no attention to my complaints, and I demand angrily, "Has he been?" He, for us, is only Edward.

"No."

"Then what are you dressing up for?"

"I thought he might want to go out with me."

"Why, did he say so?"

"He often does after a party."

"And you haven't seen him for a fortnight. How can you continue with Edward?" etc. And I tell her that if she does not leave him, she will wreck her whole life.

Julie puts down one flowing garment and takes up another, throws it into the bedroom, and comes back again. Her habit of going about half-naked before me, like a Roman princess before a slave, always pleases me; even in my anger, I am gratified by a confidence, charmed by the woman's beauty. But the more warm my love of Julie, the greater my rudeness. For she never pays any attention to me, and I am like those Indian pagans who kick their gods when they will not hear their prayers.

"I can't understand you," I say, "making yourself so contemptible. It's revolting. Letting Edward use you."

"He uses you, too."

"Not any longer."

"Perhaps we were made to be used. I shouldn't like to feel useless. Perhaps I need Edward to use me and you need

Tolbrook to use you. What will you do without Tolbrook, Tommy; and Edward to badger? Won't you feel a little bit unimportant?"

"What nonsense," I say, but I feel a strange moment of uncertainty. I hear again Bill's shocked voice, "I never thought you would desert the old place."

"I suppose Edward is used, too, by somebody or something. He's getting more ambitious."

"I've done with him."

Julie looks at me. I am sitting on the bed among the dresses, which swell up on each side of me, and my feet, of course, do not reach the floor. Probably, in my frock coat and patent-leather boots, my high collar and formal tie, I appear a little absurd in this situation. Julie suddenly begins to laugh. She stoops down, red with laughter, and I see her breasts, now plump and round, within her wide-topped stays.

I do not usually mind being laughed at by Julie, but now, in that uncertainty which is rising so fast in my soul, I am more touchy. I exclaim angrily, "What are you laughing at?"

"If you could see yourself," she says, "the rebel." And coming up to me she takes my face between her hands and kisses me. "Don't be angry with me. I am suffering. I have been such a failure. Even in love. And I thought I knew how to love. I am only a burden and a nuisance to Edward."

"Then leave him."

"I've tried—but he says he needs me."

Suddenly Edward comes in. He is surprised to see me. "Hullo, Tom, are you staying?"

I am already off the bed. I answer with indignation, "Of course not. What do you mean?"

"I meant with me. Bill would like to see more of you," and then to Julie, "I was wondering, Julie, if it wouldn't be rather nice to have dinner somewhere out this evening, if you're free."

"I should love it," Julie says gravely. "But have you the time—ought you spare the time?"

Julie, I think, is always too serious with Edward. He would like a more irresponsible mistress. But he answers with a pretty speech about needing her company more than any amount of time, and we leave her to finish her dressing.

Edward, as soon as the bedroom door closes, drops into a chair and takes a book out of the nearest shelf. In one minute his expression passes through affectionate earnestness with Julie, blank indifference as the door closes, and becomes attentive as he opens the book. I ask him, "And what about this bill of Julie's? She's been half-mad with worry."

"I'm paying it. I told you I would."

"I thought you were broke, Edward. You told me so last week."

"So I was, old boy." He drawls, turning a page. "But a kind friend came to my help."

"It isn't Bill, I hope?"

Edward is silent.

"It was Bill then. I didn't think you would rob Bill, with three children and nothing in the world but the few hundred Papa left him."

"I'll pay him back."

"How?"

"Oh, I must sell, of course. In fact, I've had an offer for Tolbrook already—a surprisingly good offer—they'll take the timber at once."

"And what will happen to mother?"

"I thought she might go back to Cambridge. She's never really been happy in our wild parts. Listen to this, Tommy, I'd forgotten my Dorothy Osborne. 'This is all I can say. Tell me if it is possible I can do anything for you, and tell me how to deserve your pardon for all the trouble I have given you. I would not die without it.' And they talk about Madame de

Lespinasse's love letters. Give me a Dorothy—it's a thorough-bred to a neurotic poodle. Latin fire and passion! A cat on the roof. No, give me the English girl for power and breeding. And, mind you, I'll bet Dorothy beat any Pompadour at her own game, and did it with a style those puddings never dreamed of."

I say nothing. I am dumfounded. I can't tell whether Edward be the most selfish or the most admirable of men; so much above petty considerations of money, etc., that I can't even understand him. I stare at him in silence. I ask myself with a kind of dismay, "Isn't he afraid? Doesn't he fear some retribution—a bad conscience at least? Can one live without any decent principles?"

He does not even glance at me. He continues to read; his cheeks are flushed with pleasure; his eyes sparkle.

Julie comes in, dressed with a splendor suitable to her new stately beauty. And that growing softness of her figure seems to have invaded her glance, her expression. What had been passion and fire in the young girl was now more tender, more gentle and resigned.

"I am reading your Dorothy Osborne," Edward says to her. "Listen to this: 'I know you love me still, you promised it me, and that's all the security I can have for all the good I am ever like to have in this world. 'Tis that which makes all things seem nothing to it, so high it sets me, and so high, indeed, that should I ever fall, 'twould dash me all to pieces.' "

"I'm glad you like my Dorothy," Julie says, as if speaking of a friend. She is flushed with pleasure.

"Like her? I was in love with her from the first time we met—about '78 at Clifton, where my form master introduced me."

"Why is she so attractive?" Julie asks. "And how could she love that stick Sir William Temple?" And they begin to discuss the character of a woman dead for nearly two hundred years. "And yet they say she was very happy with him."

"A woman like that makes her own happiness. Besides, these were early times, you know—that vitality you get in her letters was everywhere. Look at Pepys."

They have forgotten me, and when I take my leave they turn toward me the kind faces of a grown-up brother and sister toward a small child returning to his toys in the nursery.

And as I walk in the park on my way home, I seem to hear not only Bill and Amy, and Tolbrook, but the very park trees, humbly accepting the dirt of London poured upon them from the smoky twilight. "You mustn't desert us, your own people. The humble and the helpless."

I remembered Edward's absent-minded voice, "They'll take the timber at once."

The next day I wrote to Edward, proposing to accept the agency, on proper conditions of pay, etc., and a proper security for the house. I lent him a thousand pounds, secured on the timber, in order to pay off Bill, and obtained a promise, for what it was worth, that he would borrow nothing more except through me or the firm. I joined the firm at once. It was still called Wilcher and Wilcher, although the actual partners were Pamplin, Jaffery, and Jaffery. Within a week I began to read for my articles as a solicitor. And all my reward for this sacrifice was a new heap of bills from Edward's creditors and the remark, in passing, from Julie, "You were born to fuss, Tommy. You buzz at me like a fly. But I suppose somebody must buzz."

79

"The point is this," I say to Ann, "somebody has to keep things up, and if Robert won't make a success of this marriage, you must."

"Why me?"

"Because if you don't it will be worse for you—much worse. Oh, I know it isn't fair," I said, for I was feeling angry against the injustice of things. "But so it is."

"Well, it's too late, uncle. This marriage has fallen down already. I haven't seen Robert upstairs for a fortnight. I don't even know where he sleeps."

"Then you must get him back. And don't talk of a marriage falling down. It's not a card house. It's a living relation—it's different every day."

"You ought to have been married, uncle."

"You think I know nothing about it."

"Oh, I know you lived with women—I suppose it's the same thing."

"Not at all the same thing—a completely different thing. You mustn't think there's any substitute for marriage—for the sacrament, the contract—the security."

"Security," Ann said. "Well, I've always got my job," and these unexpected words threw me into confusion and despair; they were like that little shake to a kaleidoscope which produces in an instant a completely new and unexpected pattern. I felt as if marriage, the home, all the most stable and valuable parts of social order had suddenly burst into fragments and formed themselves into something quite different.

In fact, this mere sentence alarmed me so much that I took occasion to say, that evening after supper, to Robert and Ann together that I had been intending to see Jaffery about a final disposition of my property, but that certain recent events gave me pause.

The children kept silence. Robert was smoking a pipe on one side of the parlor fire; Ann cigarettes on the other. Robert had the paper, Ann a book; but neither was reading. Since their late difference, they do not seem to like reading in each other's presence.

"You understand," I said, "that I should prefer to leave a

family house to continue as a family house—that is, to a united family," and so on.

The children were still silent. So I spoke about the importance of having some capital for farming; and a going concern, as at Tolbrook. And, in fact, I was preparing to suggest that, if they could adjust their differences, I should leave Tolbrook to them in trust for Jan, and the heirs male, when I noticed a certain look on Robert's face and its reflection on Ann's.

Now I had noticed this look once or twice before when I had spoken to the children of the division of the property; and though I knew it was a piece of folly, it always upset me. What, after all, could be more important than a man's will? I am ready to confess that I made my first will at the age of eight, when I left all I possessed to Lucy.

It was revoked, on the next day, I think, by a codicil leaving everything to the Zanana Mission when my mother became its local secretary. And I am proud of that precocity which showed, even so young, a sense of responsibility without which no one is fit to own even a money box.

"I see you think I am a kind of moral idiot," I said to the children, to all our surprise. For all at once I had lost my temper. "An old miser who can only think and talk about money and shake his will every time that he's crossed. But it's you who are the idiots, yes, perfect idiots—not to know that money is important—extremely important. I've had to do with money all my life, and I tell you that it's not only the root of evil, but the root of good, too." etc., and so on. "A few pounds more or less in a legacy may change a whole life—save some poor woman's happiness or her children's future."

But Robert continued smoking on his side of the fire until I had finished, and then took out his pipe and said that he quite agreed with me. "I could do with a million this minute, if it hadn't too many strings on it." And Ann lit another cigarette and said thank God for her job—it made her independent at least.

"O.K.," Robert said. "You're independent—and I'm free."

"What a good thing we're both satisfied."

"Satisfied with what? With the life of animals shut up in a dark room full of your own dirt—no love, no hope, no heaven, no regard for past or future. But the truth is that I ought to leave the place to Blanche. She may be a prig, but she's a Christian at least, and knows how to value the things of the spirit, and a family property, which is one of them."

But they were not even offended by my rudeness. So impossible it is for an old man to make any impression upon the arrogance of youth.

80

But I am right and they are wrong. Money enters into the whole fabric of society. Nobody attends to it, any more than they trouble about their own blood, until it runs thin or does not run at all. And when I was condemned to be a lawyer and money manager, I was put in the position of that heart which in a man's body does all the work and gets no attention or thanks whatever. The brain, the will, the passions, what do they care about that poor humble creature, pounding away forever in his dark prison, on the everlasting treadmill which gives to brain, will, etc., their light, and their life?

I say I had no thanks. But the truth is, I had less than no thanks. I had condescension or scorn. For, of course, as an essential organ, I was obliged to say to brain, passions, etc., just when they were in their most furious state of exaltation, "Take care—don't forget me—there are limits," etc.

In 1906, that year of revolution, I spent several hours and thousands of words, by telephone and letter, trying to make

Edward understand that he was bankrupt; and that his creditors wouldn't wait. But he answered me not at all, or with those
good-natured smiles which meant, "Poor Tom, he doesn't
comprehend great events even when they take place in front of
his eyes." Edward was waiting for a place in the new cabinet.
He could not give his time to lawyer's letters.

And, what was strange, I was held cheap, not only by Edward and Lucy and Julie, but by my own comrades in the ranks.

I was then thirty-eight, but not yet out of my articles, a
lawyer's clerk. I was one of a million London clerks who, in
top hat and black coat, beat every day to and fro in the dark
gullies of the streets, under a sky of smoke. The black houses
overhung us like the houses of the medieval city, grown
only in height and in dirt. The soles of our boots, the iron
shoes of the horses, made the loud monotonous music to
which, as it seemed, we marched upon a thousand errands,
which were one in object: to defeat some enemy. We were
like a besieged city, and the narrow faces of the passers, gray
like the dust, each absorbed in its own thought, were like
those of a garrison, under threat of terror and destruction. But
now the trumpets were sounding for the relief. The new age
was at hand, when all should be free, etc. And we believed.
The gloomy or reserved air with which we received these
tidings were not due as a hundred times before, to disbelief.
We knew that the time had come when prophecies should be
fulfilled.

Why, I don't know. Why do the people ignore political
threats, violence; the most solemn promises, until a certain
moment, when they suddenly agree among themselves? "This
time something is going to happen." It has nothing to do with
the newspapers or the political prophets. A dozen times in my
life all the prophets, the men in the know, have said, "Prepare
for the worst." The newspapers have declared, "We are on the
eve of tremendous revolutions." And the man in the street, the

farm laborer at the plow tail have paid no more attention than the sparrows and the cows.

And at another time when the prophets are buying Consols and the newspapers are declaring that the political weather is set fair, the little men say to each other, "This time something is going to happen." Is this the famous political sense which is supposed to belong to certain peoples? Or is it merely a judgment of circumstance closer to the people and the wage earner than to the clever men in clubs? Does something happen, on these occasions, which hits the sense of the common people, and the clerks on the buses, so that they find everywhere a unanimity of expectation?

We, the rankers, believed in those trumpets. But we looked at each other, just like rankers, as if to say, "All right, but what then? What have you and I got to do with these splendors?"

I remember one of the clerks at the office, a middle-aged man, saying to me, "Great times, Mr. Tom." He was a good Radical like myself; but then he added, "Not that they'll make much difference to the gas in our office." The bad lighting was an old grievance. And his look and voice both expressed the idea that for people like him and me, mere fusty clerks, the gas supply must seem more important than the most glorious of social revolutions.

81

And this feeling made me especially critical of Edward, and also violent in my politics. I demanded, in the same breath, the destruction of all privilege and a strict account of Edward's debts.

And Edward's financial position, at a critical moment in his fortunes, enabled me, or rather the firm, to impose terms. The first clause in our agreement, a clause not put into writing, was that he should leave Julie and marry Mrs. Tirrit.

We insisted on this. For only Mrs. Tirrit could satisfy the creditors, who were prepared to accept, on her verbal assurance alone, a delay of proceedings, and afterwards twelve and sixpence in the pound. They wanted fifteen shillings, but the lady refused them. Mrs. Tirrit was rich, but she was also a woman of business. She did not mean to pay for Edward more than was absolutely necessary.

This agreement gave the firm, and especially me, much satisfaction. Should I say that we felt a real pleasure in humiliating the glorious Edward? Lucy thought so. But I should be wrong and Lucy was wrong. We were not vindictive. We were only in revolt against the self-deception, the irresponsibility of our hero and master. We were the heart and stomach, saying finally to the poetic genius in the upper story, "Come now, please to remember that you also are human."

It was a shock, therefore, especially to me, to find that Edward did not break with Julie, as we had arranged, but merely kept away from her. Mrs. Tirrit heard nothing from him. And what was still more disquieting, he suddenly bought an enormous motorcar, for which, as we soon discovered, he had paid cash.

He was getting money from somewhere, and our whole arrangement threatened to collapse.

When I challenged him with trickery, he answered only that he had to have a car "for business purposes." He could not get through his work, that is, his tub thumping, without it.

None of us thought of Bill as the source of these funds, until I happened to meet Amy and she let out the secret.

Bill and Amy were just returning to India, and we had arranged to meet at Paddington so that I could see them off. I knew at once that they had something on their minds.

"Nurse has broken her leg," Amy said, and Bill at once closed in upon me. "This morning at half-past seven." Amy was carrying a six-month baby in her arms, her fourth, a daughter; Loftus, the third, aged two, was sitting among the hand luggage with an angelic expression on his round pink face.

Now, though I approve of large families, I could not help wondering how Bill and Amy proposed to bring up four children. William, at his public school, was already costing Bill more than he could afford. The very sight of Bill and Amy, therefore, surrounded by their family, always made me feel anxious, and perhaps a little impatient. I was tempted to ask how many more children they meant to have, and why. And in any conversation with them, I was apt to bring the financial aspect to their notice. "Broken her leg. That may be a serious liability. How did she break it—in your service?"

"It isn't about nurse—"

"It had better be about nurse—who's going to pay for the hospital?"

"It's Johnny," Bill says. But at this moment John comes running up with a large parcel. He is a thin little boy with Bill's rough hair and his mother's gray-blue eyes. Amy waggles her right-hand fingers at him in the air, under the baby's head, to show that she can still hold a parcel, takes the parcel, and says, "Is it true about Edward, Tom?"

The abrupt change of subject startles me, and I exclaim, "What about Edward?"

"Something about a tailor who wanted to summons him."

"Edward is very hard up," I say.

"I told you, Bill," Amy says mildly, and her tone gives me at once the information I am seeking. "Good God," I say, "you haven't been lending Edward money again?"

Bill turns on Amy, "There, I said you'd give it away."

"I didn't give it way. Tommy knew already."

"He certainly did not. Did you, Tommy?"

"Do you mean Edward actually took your money and asked you to keep it a secret?"

"It was a debt of honor," Bill says, "and it's none of your business, if you'll excuse me, Tom."

"I said you'd lose your money, Bill." Amy speaks with the patient mildness which always exasperates Bill. Her face is flushed, her hat is crooked, but her hair is neat and her expression is that of a policeman on point duty. I notice again that Amy has changed from the bride at whom we laughed, fifteen years before; but I should still laugh, from custom, if I were not so irritated.

Bill answers her, "You said we ought to do what we could for Edward, for Papa's sake."

"I said a thousand pounds was quite enough—and more than we could afford."

"You did not, excuse me. But what's the good of arguing? Edward had to have the money."

"Edward is bankrupt," I say. "He owes at least twenty thousand that he can't pay. And you're unsecured creditors. You'll never get a farthing of your money."

"H'm," Bill says, obviously disbelieving me. "I don't understand business. But Edward's career might have been ruined."

"Edward is a great man in politics," I say severely, "but in finance he is simply a dangerous lunatic. And you have enabled him to dodge the only settlement that could have saved him."

"Finance." Bill's air seems to say that finance is not of much importance to anybody; except little lawyers.

But before I can point out his mistake, the train comes in, and the couple are summoned to see their stack of luggage weighed and put aboard. Each has a different count. "Damn it all," Bill is shouting, "you've been counting the lunch basket. A lunch basket isn't luggage."

"Luggage is luggage, whatever it is."

"A lunch basket is gear—for the rack."

"But it's going in the train."

The boy John dodges round their legs. He continually puts

out a hand to them, then draws it back again as if fearing to be obtrusive. They look at him every moment, glancing quickly over him as if fearing to catch his eye.

"Want a job, Johnny?" I see the boy's look of apprehension. It is plain that he dreads being away from them even for a moment.

"Go and get me a paper. Here's threepence." The boy dashes away.

"You've probably thrown away that boy's chance for life," I say bitterly. "How are you going to give your children a start, without capital?"

Bill and Amy look at each other with a peculiar expression of anxiety. I think I have made an impression at last. I say, "Every pound you give Edward, if you have any more to give, is as good as another nail in his coffin."

"We were just wondering," Bill says, and I perceive that I am to hear the important communication that has hung over me from our first meeting.

"It's about Johnny," Amy says. "He's a little young for boarding school at six, but we couldn't take him back to India for two years. It wouldn't be worth it."

"It's getting him to Paddington," Bill says. "Nurse was going to do it. And then we thought of sending him with an outside porter."

"Of course, there'll be a master to meet him there."

All this a preface to a request which, after all, is not made. Bill and Amy, either from modesty or pride, we never decided which, are both of them extremely averse to asking any kind of favor.

"And we are just wondering—" Amy says.

"He wouldn't be a nuisance," Bill assures me. "He was a bit upset at first when we told him that he had to stay behind. But he's pulled up his socks in the last day or two. Poor little devil. He knows there's no getting out of it."

I say, with mild sarcasm, that if this is all that's troubling them, I should be delighted to take the boy to Paddington. They overwhelm me with thanks. Sarcasm has no more effect on them than rain on a couple of tortoises.

"If you *did* have time," Amy says, "you might perhaps give him a meringue. He's very fond of meringues. But really, Tom, it's a scandal to waste your time."

"Whist," Bill says. "Here he is. Not a word." And John dashes up with the paper. "Good lad, record time." But the boy's haste is obviously to return to them. Amy waves her left-hand fingers in the air and says, "I'd better have that, Johnny. Your father'll want it in the train." Johnny puts the paper into the hand, which firmly grips it under the baby.

The porter comes to report all the heavy luggage aboard. Amy and Bill turn to the hand luggage, and find that Loftus has been eating the labels.

"I said he was up to something," Bill cries, carrying the child like a sheep, hanging down between his hands.

Amy, not yet distracted, murmurs, "Never mind. It's flour paste."

"But what about the luggage—"

"Put him in with it—it will keep him quiet."

Bill thrusts Loftus into the train. With a filthy face, and pieces of label sticking to his mouth, chin, and cheeks, he looks at us still with angelic eyes, while a porter throws the hand luggage up on the rack. Amy and Bill count together, "One-two-three-four." "And the lunch basket," Bill says. While Amy counts five.

The guard is blowing his whistle, Bill says to me. "Good-by, old chap, and remember we mustn't let Edward down." Amy kisses me, warmly and unexpectedly, and murmurs, "You won't forget the meringue."

I cannot think what she means, till I see that both she and Bill are smiling at the boy. "Good-by, old chap." Bill shakes the child's hand. "And don't forget to write to your mother." Amy hands the baby to Bill, lifts John up and kisses him on both cheeks. She is still smiling, but her eyes and nose turn scarlet and tears suddenly appear on her cheeks. She hastily climbs into the train, and Bill hands her the baby, which at once wakes up and utters a loud cry. The train moves, and Bill dives through the door. I see Amy saying something behind the window. But I hear only the baby's screams and an affected voice beside me calling, "Good-by, Moms, my love to Paris."

Probably Amy has been reminding me about the meringue. The train has gone, leaving an empty hole at which both John and I gaze. Then I take the boy's hand and lead him to the station hotel. To my relief, he does not cry. I say, imitating Bill's cheerful address, "Well, old chap, that's over. Would you like something—a meringue?"

The boy, to my surprise, shakes his head.

"Oh, but I'm sure you'd like a meringue—a double one. They have wonderful meringues here."

He shakes his head again. I notice that he is trembling all over, his lips, his hands, his knees, even his body. His face is extremely white, and he opens his eyes with a look of amazement, as if he perceives something incredible.

I take him to a cab and we drive to Paddington. He sits quiet; and I think, "He's being brave, thank goodness. I'd better let him alone."

My bitterness against Edward has been followed by discouragement. I feel that I have been beaten in the struggle. I think, "I can't deal with Edward any more. I'll throw up the whole business. I'll go and explain it to Julie. I shan't blame Edward. I'll only say that he's too much for me, that I don't understand these politicians. I'm only a private person."

Suddenly I remember the boy, and I say to him in an encouraging voice, "So you're going to a boarding school. You'll like that very much. It's a very happy time."

He shakes his head.

"I liked it. I thought I shouldn't like it, but I really enjoyed it quite well."

I see to my horror that tears are trickling down his cheeks. He cries like his mother with a stoic face. And after a little reflection I encourage him, "Don't cry, old chap."

"I'm not crying," he says in a low voice. "It's my eyes."

We are at Paddington. But no master accosts us. The boy, thank heaven, has stopped weeping. I say hopefully, "Just time for something—a cream cake, or what about a cup of chocolate?"

"No thank you, uncle."

He disengages his hand from mine, and I look down to see if I have given him offense. But he looks up at me with a face which startles me by its perfect comprehension of my course of feeling. He says, "The master will be coming." He means, "Perhaps I'd better not be holding hands when this envoy from the unknown world of exile comes upon us."

The master arrives. He is a short, hook-nosed man with a friendly manner. He taps John on the head and calls him young feller—he beams at me and says loudly, "The worst is over, I see."

I can feel, rather than see, the expression on the child's face as he hears this; and I can feel the sense of loneliness and smallness intensified within him by words which mean, "These small animals needn't be taken too seriously." I feel for the child, but I cannot think what to do or what to say to him. The master waits a moment, looks encouragingly at us both, then at his watch. He remarks, "We've five minutes. What about a bun, young feller?"

The boys shakes his head and says, "Good-by, uncle."

"Good-by, my dear." I offer him half a crown. He takes it, and says nothing, not even thank you. The master, to my surprise, turns his back, and at once the child puts out his arms and reaches upwards. I understand his motive in time to stoop.

He embraces me and whispers in a voice which already seems to come from a distance, "Good-by, uncle. Thank you most awfully for everything." Probably a formula taught him by his mother, for use after parties.

Then he is walking away with the tactful master. I notice a half crown lying on the pavement, but I do not realize that the boy has dropped it until I am several yards away. And when I return for it, it has already disappeared. Some one of the group of porters and loungers standing opposite has picked it up, and when I look at them several of them stare back at me, with those wooden faces which say, "Think what you like—you can't do anything." I feel again a deep oppression of weakness, as if the whole of the civilized order about me, in which Bill and Amy walk so confidently and so rashly, and the young John carries his grief with so much dignity, is nothing but an appearance, a dream. And from the dream our unhappy people, especially Bill, Amy, etc., are about to be awakened.

I had an appointment with Julie, on Edward's affair. But now I went to her on my own, in the mood of the private soldier who says, "If they want hell, then to hell with it."

82

Julie, in the last year, had moved into a new flat, in West Street, just off Park Lane. I think her move had been an attempt to break with Edward. She herself had been urging him to marry Mrs. Tirrit. But if it was an attempt, it had failed. Edward had continued to visit her, sometimes every day, sometimes not for weeks.

I found her still in her bedroom at eleven o'clock. She kept late hours, night and morning. But to me the bedroom was open, and I sat down beside the dressing table while the maid brushed out her hair.

We spoke trivialities, about Edward's triumphs and an Ibsen revival in which Julie had been asked to take a part. "But I could not act Hedda Gabler—I should feel ridiculous waving a pistol now." Her eyes meanwhile asked me, "Why have you come?" She said, "I like your morning visits," meaning, "You have come for some special purpose."

The maid went out, and she said, "Edward has made up his mind."

"No, he's done nothing—except steal his brother's fortune," and I told her the story. "I'm leaving him. I shall go abroad. I want a holiday after all this. And you, Julie, you can't stay after this. Why couldn't you come, too—let's leave this miserable confusion once and for all."

"If he dismisses me, I should like to come with you, but I couldn't run away."

"You call it running away—when he has not kept a single obligation to you. It's he that runs away."

"No, he simply puts things off. And suppose he did really need me. He does sometimes need me, you know. When he is sick of politics."

"Yes, as a relaxation."

"Very well, a relaxation. That's something. We chatter about books and old friends—it doesn't seem very much, but I suppose it is a change for him. No, I'm tried. I wish he would make up his mind what he is going to do. But I can't go till he sends me away. The one thing is not to get muddled." And she spoke of some friend who had committed suicide.

"He wasn't tired of life or even unhappy, but he got in a muddle. He stopped knowing what he wanted. I remember he had some sort of quarrel about a dog which had bitten his wife; and he lost his front teeth in an accident."

I had never felt more admiration of Julie's wisdom and courage. We spent most of that day together, at Kew, which was one of Julie's favorite gardens. I remember the peculiar pleasure

I felt when she spoke of friendship. "It is the only thing worth having, but how rare it is. People talk about their friends, but how many have any friends? Most people go through life without friends, and they don't even know what friendship is."

"You have hundreds of friends, Julie."

"I had one once, but she died long ago."

I did not say. "But we are friends," because I feared her answer; which was bound to be sincere.

"She was a real friend. I could absolutely depend on her, and yet she was very critical of me. She used to abuse me like a pickpocket. It was she who made me act."

We were in the great palm house, and the tropical heat brought out the color of her cheeks and made her astonishingly beautiful. At thirty-two, Julie was growing more plump. But it suited her. She seemed like some dark Creole beauty while she strolled under the arching palm leaves and pondered, with downcast eyes. Her long lashes threw a green shadow on her cheeks. Little beads of sweat stood on her round forehead. "We had fearful quarrels, but they were good for me. She hated me to say that I was going to be a nun."

"Do you still wish it?"

"No, I don't think so. I should have to forget so much that I don't want to forget. I should feel so disloyal."

And in the midst of my admiration I thought for the first time, "Why shouldn't this woman be mine?" And all my uneasiness, my sense of insecurity, of the moral and social revolution which for the first time had become real to my nerves, formed one urgent wave of rebellious passion. It was the revolutionary movement, I suppose, in its private form. "I shall have her," I thought, "good and noble as she is. Why not?"

And I said in a voice carefully respectful, "I'm glad you're not going to leave us, Julie. We need you."

"Only the religious are happy in a world like this. But I haven't the right to stand aside."

"It would be very nice just to let things slide," Ann said. "But I don't feel I *ought* to let Robert walk right over me. It's bad for both of us." And that afternoon as we were going out for our walk she attacked him, most unexpectedly to me and, I think, to her. A moment before we had been anticipating our walk with some pleasure.

The weather was mild for February. In the morning it had rained, and the yards were flowing with pools and rivulets between the stones. But now the sun had come out and filled the sky with a dark blue-green radiance. It was like sea water in an aquarium lighted from some hidden source, and the big ragged clouds which floated in it seemed to be dissolving at the edges like gouts of yellow foam after a storm. The pools reflecting this sky were darker still, like great table sapphires, and the noise of water running from spouts and wall drains had the gaiety of fountains, so that one could not help smiling with pleasure.

But as we crossed the yard from the back door where we kept our winter coats, we came upon Robert. He was loading muck. The cart, oozing black filth at every crack, stood crooked, with one wheel raised upon the footway outside the stalls; and the horse, steaming from each curl of its winter fur, let his head and ears droop. Robert himself, in old khaki trousers, a leather jerkin, and long rubber boots, was dirtier even than usual. His nose and cheeks, frost-burnt by the hard weather before Christmas, were scarlet; and his eyes, among their redness, were bluer than I had ever seen them. I thought, "How Lucy would have delighted in this son of hers." And in the thought I enjoyed such a keen pleasure that I hardly noticed for the first minute or so that Ann and he were quarreling. As usual, they both spoke in the most casual tones.

"When are you going to make up your mind about Molly, Robert?"

"I made it up a long time ago. I like Moll. May be a bit obstinate, but a good girl."

"Stupid people are always obstinate," Ann replied.

"She's not so stupid. Only a bit shy. You make her shy."

"Then take her, Robert. She's just longing to fall into your arms. And you know you're always hankering after her—she's so nice and soft, everywhere."

"I wouldn't say—Molly is not so soft—she does a man's work here—she can carry her sack with everybody."

"Then go along, Robert, what are you waiting for?"

Robert looked at her for a moment, and then loaded another forkful into the middle of the cart. At last he said, "There's a few little points—what about the kid?"

"Oh, Jan would stay with me, I suppose. You would have plenty more with Molly. I'm sure she'd be a good breeder."

"Sure she would, and she wants 'em, too."

"She told you that, did she?"

"Yeah."

"So you really have been thinking of her."

"Well, Annie, you know how it is. A man often thinks of a girl, how she would be as a wife, not just his own wife; but a wife. Same as a girl thinks of a man; suppose he was my husband, how would that work out—taking the good and the bad and allowing for discounts? He's nothing in his face and he's small, but they say the small ones have more jump to 'em and last out better. But he's got a nice voice, and his nails are clean. Not meaning to marry him, but just running him through their fingers for a sample."

"Molly looked a little finger-marked."

"Now, I just wonder if that's a fair way to put it. It's smart, but it's not what I'd like to say of you. Seems to me a bit on the whisker side."

Ann had apologized and said that she was sure Molly was as good as she was fat.

"And not so fat either. She's got a good frame."

Ann took my arm and turned me toward the gate. "Then why not buy it—it's going for nothing. Only don't keep me waiting too long—I get tired standing the side lines."

"Yeah, it's tough on you." And he threw another forkful. We went out into the drive.

This exchange threw me into some agitation. It revived my anxieties for the marriage.

"Robert is a fine fellow," I said. "He has great strength of character."

"Oh, don't let's talk of Robert or even think of him."

We walked on in embarrassed silence. My alarm and agitation increased every moment. I felt that it was I who had committed some crime.

As we walked down the path among the bare trees, I looked at the girl and thought, "Yes, Robert is right. She has changed away from him." And not only in her dress, in her hat, her hair with its corded net, resembling the net of a chignon, her bodice, and her long buttoned coats. The Victorian dress, as she said herself, was a fashion. Her bodices were not real bodices—they were fixed with a contrivance of steel teeth which slid beneath her arms. Her wide skirt was not much below her knees and her stockings were flesh color. The dress meant little; the real change was in her thought, her speech, her ideas. Her churchgoing, perhaps, was only play, like her imitation chignon, but her housekeeping and house furnishing was not play. Her love for this place was true and strong. She spoke of home as only those speak for whom the word has gathered meaning. But simply because I felt more in sympathy with the child than ever before, I was afraid to speak to her, as usual, even about the old house, her father's life and work, the tragedy of his failure.

I perceived that there was some secret agitation in her soul, or at least her interior. But I could not tell its nature.

84

I don't know if I, more than others, am shut out from understanding of my fellow creatures. But their actions have usually surprised me. I cannot describe my astonishment when on the very evening of the day during which Julie and I talked so gravely about her duty she attempted suicide. She was found at ten in the morning, unconscious in a roomful of gas. I had a note from the maid and hurried round in time to meet the doctor and a policeman, who had broken in the door. The policeman wrote down particulars, the doctor listened with a stony face while I swore to Julie's carelessness and pointed out that she had not closed up her keyhole or the cracks of the window frames.

"The rug was against the door and the damper of the chimney was closed," the policeman said.

The doctor said nothing. It was obvious that he stood aloof from corruption in his professional and scientific honor. I made sure from the policeman that nothing more could take place until Julie was well enough to make a statement. And I hurried to Whitehall.

Astonishment had succeeded horror. But now anger united both in a resolution to bring Edward to his senses. If I had seen Edward immediately, I have no doubt that there would have been a violent scene.

But the anteroom at the ministry was already full of visitors, and Edward's secretary could promise only that I should be let in at the earliest possible moment.

Edward's anteroom was always full because of his unpunctuality, and because his friends liked to see him at the ministry, where on most mornings they could be sure of finding him. So that whereas in some great ministry, the Foreign Office or the War Office, one might find only two or three persons waiting, in Edward's there were often a dozen and more, either without appointments or kept half an hour beyond their time.

The secretary obviously found this arrangement quite natural. To him I suppose Edward was a person so important that his convenience came before that of all others.

And I felt the impression of power, not only in the matter of these people waiting on Edward, but even in the suspicious glance of doorkeepers, and the height of the room. For the anteroom, at least twenty feet high, which seemed much higher than its breadth, reminded one of those palaces whose giant magnitudes seem to say, "We are the habitations not of ordinary men but of ideals. Royalty, majesty, national honor live here, and as they are greater than any single man they need a bigger house."

I thought that I distinguished the same feeling in some of the visitors, who now and then threw a glance toward the high dirty ceiling as if to wonder if they had not underestimated the dignity of public business. Some others, obviously private visitors—a fashionable young woman, probably a comedy actress, to judge by her powdered face and her Dana Gibson figure; a well-known picture dealer from Bond Street; an old man with a farmer's complexion but a peculiar glance, colder and sharper than any I had seen, who was probably a trainer; and two young men who were certainly undergraduates—looked only at each other. A deputation from the constituency did not look at anything. They were used to the high ceilings which go with high responsibility. They had those looks of mixed ferocity and resignation common to all such official parties from the remote country, their jaws set with resolution, their brows wrinkled already with doubt, as if the sight alone of a busy office, in the great city, had caused them to reflect, "There may be other sides to our argument."

Upon me, so well used to such places, it had the same effect, and before I was summoned into Edward's presence I had

had time to reflect on his peculiar situation as a public man; his special burdens, etc., unknown to my experience. And I approached him with a circumspection and reserve of which, half an hour before, I would not have been capable.

I found him behind an enormous desk in a room not perhaps so large as that of the chief ministers, but larger than a small house. He sprang up and came to meet me at the door.

Edward was a junior minister of a young ministry, but he had already made it important in the public eye, by promises of railway reform, of tramways for farmers, of a reorganization of canals, of a new charter for dock labor. He had made himself popular and feared, and so he had increased his actual power.

Power makes most men cautious, reserved—or, at least, circumspect. Men in power have a special manner, and even a special look. Their courtesy seems to say, "Do not think ill of me," their look, "I carry burdens and secrets." With Edward, power seemed to have made him more friendly with all the world, and more indiscreet. It was only now, approaching him in the office for the first time, that I saw under the genial manners the air of preoccupation and apartness. "My dear Tom, I'm glad you've come—I'm afraid I'm awfully busy."

"It's about Julie."

"Oh, yes, but just a moment. Do you remember who owns the Queensport ferries? Some local farmers' committee wants a light railway instead—as you can understand everyone within twenty miles of Tolbrook has been putting up schemes to me. But I've an idea that this committee is the same gang that tried to get control of the ferries last year."

I told him that Julie had attempted suicide and might be arrested. His expression changed to a peculiar look of resolution. I did not see that look again until the moment when he finally recognized his failure. He said after a moment, "I can't stop her being charged."

"Come and see her. It might make all the difference to her statement."

He shook his head. "Wouldn't do any good."

"You mean you can't be bothered."

"I haven't time." He smiled. "Even the Transport Minister has certain small responsibilities," and he began again to talk about the light railways and the Queensport proposal.

I listened with despair. I thought, "This man is so completely spoiled and self-indulgent that he will not suffer a moment's discomfort to save himself from ruin. Yet he is so ambitious that he can hardly bear to be a junior minister, at forty-six." I said, "Why ask me about the ferries? You know they are quite adequate. A light railway would cost more and waste all the ferry equipment."

Edward patiently brought up more arguments to show that the railway, though more expensive, would be an improvement.

"You mean a change," I said, "and something in the papers to make people say that you are being energetic."

Edward smiled, and once more I saw the statesman beneath the old irresponsible. Even his smile appeared to say, "How can they understand us or our problems?" But it passed at once into his charming affectionate look, and he spoke, as usual, as if I had said something intelligent. "It does look like that, doesn't it, and of course there is something in it. A government has to show energy and do something, and that means making changes—sometimes, I dare say, unnecessary changes. But do you know, one of the things I'm beginning to realize in the last few weeks is that a lot of change starts by itself simply because there happens to be a new government. There's a change of feeling and expectation which is like a change in the weather. You can feel it. Of course, political weather changes every day, but this is like jumping from midwinter to midsummer in five minutes. And, of course, the expectation is always beyond what any government can do.

People want a new heaven and a new earth before the end of next week."

I listened with astonishment. At last I interrupted, "I can't wait. But if you may remember we came to a certain agreement. You have broken that agreement, by borrowing from Bill and by visiting Julie. Now you refuse to visit her when she needs you. Very well, you can't have it both ways. You must decide whether to carry out the agreement or to stick to Julie. Or I will throw up the whole business." I grew angry again. And I added some phrases about his shilly-shally and untrustworthiness.

He answered me with affectionate earnestness, "It's quite true, Tommy. I do put things off, and I've treated Julie disgracefully. But I'll decide today. I'll let you know before this evening. And you must let me know if it's all right about the inquest."

"And if it isn't all right?"

"I'll hear soon enough from my friends—good-by, old man. And don't think me too ungrateful for all you have done," etc.

I was too angry to wish him good-by. Yet I was confused as if perhaps I was not fit to judge a man who exerted power from such large rooms, and whose desk alone was as big as six ordinary desks. It seemed to me that what I called weakness in Edward might be strength, in the mysterious circles of power, and that he might know his own business in the world far better than I.

85

We were saved after all by the doctor, who, it appeared, was one of those who, at sixty-nine, gray-haired and worn, expected a new heaven and a new earth. When I called upon him again he greeted me, "I had not understood that that silly woman was a friend of Mr. Edward Wilcher."

"My brother, yes. They are very old friends. Lately there has been some little difference between them—my brother's political work gives him little time for society."

The doctor pursed his sharp lips. "A great work—these are great times."

"Women do not always understand the claims of a man's work."

"Never, never," his precise voice abolished Julie. "I read your brother's speech about the scientific age and a scientific government—a truly modern state."

And he spoke for a long time on the importance of the scientific approach to politics. I do not know what he meant, and I do not think he knew himself. Under his hard dry skin, behind his sharp eyes and mouth, he was another enthusiast carried away by some secret dream or impulse; to desire change, change; a new world at all costs. He had almost forgotten Julie when I brought him back to the subject. "If the case does get into court, you will be called."

"I shall say it was obviously an accident."

"What about the rug and the damper closed in the grate?"

"Leave it to me," the doctor said with the air of a cabinet minister. "I shall go round and see the young woman."

In fact, he waited at Julie's bedside until she came round. The policeman was also present, and made some protest against the doctor's first remark to Julie, that she mustn't be frightened. She had suffered an accident with the gas. But he took the case no farther. A police officer is not advised, in such a case, to stand against the medical evidence. When I was called into the room, the constable had already withdrawn, and the doctor was giving his last instructions to Julie's maid.

"Your friend has been very careless," he said to me, pursing his lips in a discreet smile.

"She has been well punished for it."

"The worst is over." He did not wink at me, but his whole

expression, his lively movement as he packed his stethoscope into his inner breast pocket, was like the wink of a triumphant conspirator. The old man felt, for that moment only, that he was an instrument of government, that he disposed supreme power. He drew me into the landing to talk again of Edward's speech. I had forgotten it; Edward had forgotten it as soon as it was uttered; but to this dry old man it was plainly the wisdom of the angels. I invited him to meet Edward, and he was moved as if by the offer of millions. "I have no claim."

"He would like to thank you."

"What for? Nothing. Don't mention it." He was blushing over the bones of his cheeks like a girl. "But I should esteem it a very great honor."

He left me astonished once more at the simplicity of good men, and Edward's prestige, achieved so easily and unjustly. "For what has he done," I thought, "except talk and make the right friends? And now he is a man of power, a ruler, and people like this doctor, honest good people, look up to him and trust him."

> God loves democracy; the proof is plain
> It cannot die; tho' hopelessly insane.

86

The sky was darkening in the east to the gray-black of heather ashes, a burnt moor. A few small clouds floated in this thick darkness, like grouse feathers. The sun was going down behind the moor, and, as turning our backs to it we came toward the house, the trees, still bare of leaves, were shining before us like gold wire, and Tolbrook was like a gingerbread palace with gilt chimney pots.

"Hansel and Gretel ought to be living here," Ann said.

"I never liked Hansel and Gretel so much as Alice. Too foreign. But I suppose they are both out of date nowadays."

"I like Alice the best," Ann said. "Alice has more character than all the others put together."

And I thought, "She has certainly changed. A year ago she would not have thought so, or spoken with the same conviction."

"But you would have thought the real Alice a terrible little prig," I said.

"I don't think so, uncle. I rather envy Aunt Lucy and Aunt Amy. They were born at a good time."

"All that is romantic nonsense. Lewis Carroll used to try to stop the new plays at the Oxford theater—he didn't like anything that might shock his Alices. His world is a long way off—farther than ancient Rome."

"I expect they were just like us," Ann said. "Only perhaps they had more sense."

"No," I thought, "not at all like you. You can't even understand a world that believed in heaven and hell. It was buried thirty years ago when church and state were overthrown. The cloth caps came to Parliament in 1906, and their cry was not for eternal life and the judgment of God but for the world's life and justice on earth. A revolution deeper than the French. Rousseau said, 'Trust human nature to do the right thing.' But now they say, 'By our will we shall remake the world, and humanity also.'"

The blue shadows had stretched across the fields and were rising up the front of the house until nothing was left except the golden chimney pots against a sky as dark as a lawyer's blue bag. "It is like a Christmas card," I thought, "except that it is real and I am seeing it, and it is far more beautiful than any picture. Because it is real, and so it must die. It is dying so fast that I can hardly bear to look at it."

"I don't mean that they were born with more sense," Ann said, "but there seems to have been more sense going round. It was easier to be sensible; nowadays, you have to find out everything for yourself. And before you know anything that matters, you're old."

I thought she was asking me a question, but I did not know what it was.

87

What do women seek in life as women? No man knows, because his whole body and his feeling of life are profoundly different. And because his experience is different, his mind and thoughts are different. I have always been attracted to women, as by a foreign country and a mystical religion. Once I dreamed of being an Indian sadhu, because I thought that by renouncing self and all possessions, all pride, I should enter into a final peace and joy. So I have felt of women; of Julie and Sara, but especially of Julie.

I was passionately in love with Julie, but what attracted me to her more than anything else was the sense of her nature. It seemed to me that in being Julie's lover I should enter into an experience at once noble and intense, a happiness both secure and exalted.

It is notorious that lovers have feelings of religious worship and reverence for their mistresses, and that sensual images are abolished even from their most secret thoughts.

But that was impossible for me with Julie. She had been Edward's mistress, and my passion was full of sensual images. Yet as in the visions of the mystics, these very images increased my religious sense of respect for a woman whose own instincts were as deeply religious.

Yet when Edward, not on the day of the ultimatum but a

week later, at last faced facts, accepted the terms, and broke finally with Julie, and at last she was free to be my mistress, I was seized with fear and reluctance. I no longer ventured into her bedroom. And because I thought of her with passion, I was as shy in her presence as the most foolish youth before some village girl.

I was glad of the excuse of business, to see her every day. For, as Edward's man of business, I had to make many arrangements about their joint property and about Julie's debts. So it came about very naturally that I spent part of every day with Julie.

Julie's attempt to kill herself was never spoken of between us. She did not insist to me that it had been no attempt, but an accident; she referred to it only once, "When I was so mad and criminal."

She did not let that moment of weakness affect her spirits. She was too proud. Or perhaps she was saved by confession and absolution from an evil despair. But I think she suffered, as by an illness or a wound, from its effects. She became more dependent on visits and company. And if I was prevented from seeing her, she showed disappointment. She turned to me in all her difficulties, more for company, perhaps, than for the assistance itself. Though, as it turned out, I was soon paying most of her bills. For she had refused Edward's settlements, and her marriage settlement was barely three hundred a year.

And as I came to do work for her at the flat after office hours, I had an excuse to stay late. Now and then, saying that it was too late to find a cab, I slept on her sofa. I do not know even now how far this was a deliberate contrivance, or the automatism of a steel filing which cannot leave the magnet.

On one of these evenings, Julie said to me, "It's nice of you, Tommy, not to make love to me. Most men would in your place."

"It's not that I don't love you, Julie."

"Do you really love me? I thought we were friends. We mustn't spoil our friendship."

"I've been in love with you for years."

And on the next evening, when I stayed till after two o'-clock and then proposed to sleep in the sitting room, she said to me while I was pretending to make my arrangements on the sofa, "Of course, Tom, if you would care to sleep with me, please do so. It is the least I can do for you."

I was silent in my embarrassment. Julie said gravely, "It would give me pleasure, too—I should like to feel that there was something I—could do for you—" and she opened the inner door for me, so that I had to pass through.

"It will please Edward, too. He's had it in his mind for a long time," Julie said. She was neither amused nor tragic. She pondered on the fact. "He told me years ago that you and I were exactly suited. He really believed it, you know, because he has no feelings for people, only for ideas—he labeled us both: type, religious; species, amorous and sentimental, and thought how nice it would be if, when he found me a nuisance, he could pass me on to you."

"No, Julie. I can't believe that." I was in her room and to my own surprise felt ready to faint with embarrassment and excitement. My head swam, my legs trembled. I was nearly forty, but still very naive.

"But we mustn't blame him, Tommy. That is Edward's charm—his independence—you can't blame a man for his charm. It wouldn't be fair. And if we are his victims, it is our own fault. It is because we enjoyed being fascinated—what is more delightful than to make oneself nobody, nothing, as light as a needle, and submit to some powerful magnet? Even now the feeling of Edward is like a vibration—it makes you quiver. But come, Tommy, you're getting cold—you can have Edward's pajamas. I have a drawerful of his things."

I stayed and, what was not strange perhaps, I was disillusioned in that moment. Rousseau describes the matter-of-fact conduct of Mme. de Warrens in offering herself as an instructor in love. Her calm good nature seems to have charmed Rousseau, but Julie's did not charm me. She was still the most attractive of women, the most graceful, but her whole action now, with its carelessness, its *sans gêne*, seemed to say, "I do this to please you, but it is a silly business." There was no exchange, no true intimacy of spirit. I recognized my bitter disappointment, the next day, and swore that I should not sleep with Julie again.

But Julie sent for me the same afternoon to explain some document to her, and I could not refuse to go. I saw her nearly every day. She expected me to do so, and every few days she would say, "Wouldn't you like to stay with me tonight?" or "Would you like to go to bed for half an hour before your train?" And if I excused myself, she would look at me with surprise and say, "Don't you like me, Tommy, in that way?" Then I was obliged to answer that I liked her very much in that way.

And I wondered at the simplicity of women, even so intelligent as Julie, who thought that the mere physical act, without mutual excitement or passion, or adventure, could have any importance or give an abiding pleasure.

88

Ann did not repeat her question. Probably she had not asked it of me, but of herself. And when we came to the house, she turned abruptly aside into Edward's study behind the stairs, now completely refitted and restored. "I love this room," she said, with unusual warmth. "How Daddy must have liked working here."

"He used it only in the last few years of his life. I'm afraid he wasn't very happy here."

"Robert says he was a bit too civilized—but that ought to be a good thing—at least for a man."

Now that Ann was herself unhappy, she began often to talk of happiness, and especially of her father's life—his easy success and his sudden failure.

"Perhaps his success was not so easy as it looked—he had courage as well as energy."

The girl pondered, sitting hunched up in the single chair before the empty fireplace, like Edward himself in his last years. "Plenty of people have courage."

"Courage to bear misfortunes. That's common enough. The only alternative is so unpleasant. But your father had the courage to make decisions. Even in party politics he took his own line. And that kind of courage is not very common."

"It's awful the way people are wasted—even brilliant people like Daddy—knocking himself to pieces on those old politics."

"But was he wasted? He helped to make a revolution."

"A revolution—to get rid of the poor old Lords. I'm glad it didn't come off. The Lords, at least, are harmless."

"Yes, because we made them so. But I suppose you modern young women are never taught anything about modern history, in your expensive modern schools," etc.

It is hard for me to be patient with young creatures like Ann, who say of our struggles, "A lot of noise about nothing." For, in fact, there are no political battles nowadays to equal the bitterness and fury of those we fought between 1900 and 1914.

It is a marvel to me that there was, after all, no revolution, no civil war, even in Ireland. For months in the years 1909 and 1910, during the last great battle with the Lords, any loud noise at night, a banging door, a roll of thunder would bring me sitting upright in bed, with the sweat on my forehead and the thought, "The first bomb—it has come at last."

For, to tell the truth, I was in terror of this revolution which I expected every day. Why then, you say, did I sign petitions, write ferocious letters to the press, which, even if they were not printed, expressed the most republican principles; and why did I help Edward in his own more violent campaigns? I answer that I don't know. I am amazed at my own actions; and I think I was often surprised even then. It was as though my muscles had fallen under the control of some central power, called democracy, inhabiting the English air and obliging me to do its will. Or perhaps I was only obeying some secret democrat planted, by tradition or some evangelical country nurse, in my own brain.

> Hard-breasted Nan snubbed Socrates. With zeal
> Her harder hand moulded the Greek ideal.

I can remember one night when after one of Edward's speeches we were both accosted in the anteroom of the hall by one of the more moderate members of the party, a Quaker manufacturer.

He remonstrated with Edward on a part of his speech which threatened bloodshed if the Lords did not give way. "I don't think, Mr. Wilcher, you meant to encourage actual bloodshed—but many people must have thought so. And we don't want to inflame dangerous resentments."

My whole soul cried out, "Yes, yes, yes," and yet I found my mouth assuming a politely superior smile. And I heard my lips say that a democracy must not be afraid of revolutions or it would cease to be a democracy.

And Bill, that stout loyalist, in writing to me about Edward's prospects, offered to bet that he would be first President of the British Republic.

The very idea kept me awake all night, or brought me strange and ridiculous dreams. Chatham, Castlereagh, Wellington, in full robes, seemed to hover over me with reproachful faces. I would even be haunted by coronets, ermine, and

woolsacks, without anything inside them at all. And all accused me of cruelty and meanness. "Why do you attack us, the
harmless dignities of old England?"

89

Freedom at any price. So cry all those
Who've had her once, paid through or with the nose.

When I think of these words, my heart still turns over. For
I not only feel the fearful truth of them, but I know it in
my own heart. I see again the horde of savage brutes pouring
out of St. Antony's ward to loot Versailles, and to insult
that king whose only fault was his gentleness, his hatred of
violence, his civilized distrust of everything extreme, osten-
tatious, vulgar, from Mirabeau's style of dress to his own
state bedroom. And what is worse, more terrifying, I feel that
I too could have served in that mob. As I sought the joy
of the Lord, so I could seek that joy of the devil. As I was
drawn to Julie, not only by her gentleness and beauty but by
the idea of her corruption, so I could have embraced the
fury, the lust, the cruelty of Marianne. Drawn to filth by its
filthiness, to villainy by its wickedness. Not to have any
scruples, any responsibility, any duties. To lie forever in a
sweet unrest, etc., upon the old hag's poison-dripping breasts,
and so on. In those days my tall hat, which, in our firm, partners still wear, or, indeed, I hope they do; my frock coat, which
was uniform among us until the death of George the Fifth,
who preferred it to the morning coat, seemed to weigh upon
me like that armor which in Venice torturers clamped upon
some state prisoner, to drive him mad with its constraint, its
weight.

"What is this freedom?" I thought. "This terrible power

which sooner or later overthrows all its enemies, and creeps like madness in the veins of a respectable lawyer of forty." I was terrified of this secret and stealthy power. And so I raged against the folly of those who opposed her.

And against Edward who, of course, was under Freedom's special protection, I could only express my irritation by attacking his extravagance, or his cynicism.

"Things are much too serious to be taken seriously."

"I hope you'll keep that to yourself. You have done yourself quite enough harm with your verses."

"But then, I should have hanged myself without my verses."

This was the time when he wrote about his own chief:

> Haul our great rebel's flag to Ritz's top
> The statesman's art is knowing where to stop.

It was sent to a friend who at once communicated it to his enemies. For no one, at that time, not even Lloyd George, was better hated. He was turned out of several clubs, and cut in the street. Old friends wrote to him calling him a renegade who had betrayed his class; a Judas who sold his honor; a hypocrite who, enjoying wealth, attacked the rich.

Edward was, in fact, very well off. For though Mrs. Tirrit had died a few months after their marriage in 1906, she left him almost her whole fortune for life, so long as he did not remarry.

But in politics, only politicians use their sense and keep their tempers; that is, in private. Edward's friends would hear no defense of a rich man who did not defend riches.

Their chief charge against him, as always in such cases, was, "He does it to get into the limelight." Undoubtedly Edward, in 1909 as in 1900, was more discussed than most of his colleagues. That is to say, he was talking himself into power.

Then in the first election of 1910 he lost his seat by fifteen votes. He was not offered another at once, because many seats had been lost, and the cabinet did not wish to take risks. Also, I suppose, Edward had his political critics and rivals. The more cautious who thought him too violent; the more extreme who did not like what they called his dilettantism—that is, those tastes and pursuits which, for Edward, were the culture he was fighting to preserve.

Suddenly he went away to France for a holiday. We said, "He is biding his time." And, in fact, a month or two later, when a seat fell vacant, he was offered it by the local committee. He did not accept it. And we said, "The time has not come." For, in fact, the Lords and the Commons were still negotiating.

And then we heard that he had married a young girl. I hurried to Paris, full of foreboding.

I found Edward in the royal suite of a great new hotel, with American lifts and half a dozen bathrooms. He was already surrounded by artists and writers. New and extraordinary pictures stood against the walls.

"What are you thinking of?" I asked him. "Surely it's madness to be out of England now. There might be a crash any day."

"They know where to find me if they want me. Meanwhile I think I owe myself a holiday. I haven't had a real holiday for thirty years."

90

We thought Edward would ruin himself with debts or women. We never imagined the real catastrophe, that he would retire from the battle to enjoy that civilization which he has given so much energy, so many years, to defend.

"A bit too civilized." Robert's words. The very voice of his time in judgment on ours. I thought it nonsense, but now, as I stand in Edward's room, I feel not its truth but its meaning.

> I knew Versailles, said Talleyrand; nor since
> Such tolerant grace of life. True! traitor-prince.

What was Edward's charm; and Julie's and Mrs. Tirrit's, so different in character? A universal tolerance, based on a universal enjoyment. They were faithful to friendship, to kindness, to beauty; never to faith. They could not make the final sacrifice. They took a holiday at the wrong time; or could not bother to keep up with the new arts; or, like Mrs. Tirrit, did not face, in time, the doctor who would say, "You must have an operation." They would rather die in peace than live in pain.

I argued with Edward for an hour, but at the end he would promise to come back to England within the next weeks only if there were an actual deadlock between Lords and Commons, or the Prime Minister sent for him. "And now," he said, "what about those papers?"

For I had brought some papers to sign. Edward was raising another mortgage on Tolbrook, for which, by good luck, my firm had been able to find the money.

Edward himself appeared to be living at the rate of many thousands a year. But no one could conceive where he was finding the money. His new wife, daughter of one of those cosmopolitan families who live in hotels, by nationality half-Belgian, half-Irish, by education English and Parisian, was not rich. Her parents spent too much upon themselves to give her much dowry.

She came in, one of the most beautiful girls I had ever seen. Her hair was like the glossy rind of a chestnut; her eyes were a sea blue; her only fault was a too pale skin, and too rounded cheeks.

Edward jumped up to receive her; she showed her pleasure

in a smile unexpectedly frank and unsophisticated. Her dress, her turnout, her manner were those of a woman of the world. Her smile, her glance, her speech were naïve. She said to me, "Tell Edward that he must go home and teach this stupid old government a lesson."

And, in fact, to my surprise the new Mrs. Wilcher was my ardent supporter. But though I expressed my support of her views, I did so in a guarded manner. My late ardor had suddenly acquired caution. For I could not help reflecting that the influence of so young a person might be imprudent.

Edward paid no attention to either of us. He had picked up his wife's hand, which was singularly small and of a perfect shape, unusual in very small hands, and while pretending to admire her rings was admiring its beauty. She let it lie in his palm, but continued to discuss his affairs with me. "What I say is, he's got a duty to the people. Even if they have treated him badly."

"Your rings need cleaning, Lotty dearest," Edward said. "What are diamonds without a drop of ammonia?"

"He told me there was going to be a revolution, and now it's come he's playing round here with all these fancy painters instead of taking his proper place at home."

"Fancy painters," Edward said laughing. "She means some of the greatest in the history of art. Look at this, Tommy"; and he showed me an extraordinary daub of misshapen women among trees of metallic green. "Cézanne."

The girl did not look at it. She said in her lively voice, in which the earnestness of a young girl seemed to struggle with the secret gaiety of a bride, "Art is very important, I know, but these are historical times when our oldest institutions are being turned right upside down. Why, there might be a republic next week, and how would Edward look then?" And she spoke of the importance, to a statesman, of being on the spot when a revolution began. She quoted Mirabeau. It was obvious that

she was well educated, and yet she had kept that kind of simplicity and vigor which good education so often destroys.

Edward, standing beside her, continued to play with her
hand, took off her rings and put them on again, yet with such
finesse that he did not embarrass either of us with the idea of
amorous folly. He seemed to be laughing at himself as well as
the argument.

"Politics is not my affair, Mrs. Wilcher," I said. "I came on
business; but I quite agree that this is supposed to be a great
opportunity for the more extreme wing of Edward's party."

"Oh, no," Edward said, "they didn't like my speeches about
abolishing the Lords. Our party is not quite so ready for the
revolution as you might think."

9 1

I was alarmed for Edward, but I thought, "He knows his own
political business better than I do. He understands the real
workings of party politics, and perhaps he would not like to explain them even to me."

So when Julie asked me if Edward had not injured his career
in going abroad, I answered, "Not at all. He has shown them
that he has some sense of his own value. I told him that it was
quite time they gave him something better than the Transport
Ministry."

"All the same, I'm glad he's not making those speeches.
How I hate all that socialist stuff."

"My dear Julie, as Harcourt said a long time ago, we are all
socialists nowadays."

Julie was profoundly conservative and pessimistic. The
porter was caught stealing her silver, but she would not prose-
cute. "Nobody believes in God any more, so why shouldn't
they steal? And I'm so sorry for that lad, he's so young and poor

and so eager for life. You can see it in his eyes. The flats pay their people so disgracefully. I don't see that we have any right to nice things while a young man like that can't even afford to keep a woman."

"That's what Edward thinks."

"But they teach so much spite and envy—they're making all the world miserable and squalid, instead of only part of it." I laughed at Julie's politics. She never understood the democratic process. But I was delighted in her flat, in her company.

The flat was not that one to which I had hurried in 1898, a young man full of amorous excitement in the thought of an actress and a mistress; but everything in it was the same. The white-paneled woodwork, the Beardsleys, the Whistler pastels, the Japanese prints, the author's copies from the nineties. The same cloisonné cigarette box stood on the sofa table beside a book, always open and face downwards. Julie was always in the middle of a book, usually an old one. I have seen "Stories Toto Told Me," by Corvo, lying on that little table for three months. Yet I, too, was always pleased to turn the book over and read where she had read, looking through her eyes into that world of the past, always tranquil, always beautiful, like a mime show.

These rooms had for me the quality of Julie's own character and mind, something which belongs only to a civilization in its perfected form. Its simplicity, its lack of pretension, of any strong character, even of strong color, its good taste, which seemed unconscious, and which was, in fact, the consequence merely of Julie's integrity, had also the calm of profound reflection. The books, the prints, the small bronzes all expressed ideas of life, which were simple only in form, like Julie's beauty, her dress, so expensive and carefully thought out, or her talk, which conveyed so many subtleties.

In Julie's flat I felt the repose of comprehension. I was known there even by the books. I was accepted like the cat,

and like the cat I felt myself at home. But I was no longer fascinated. I saw too plainly Julie's weakness: her idleness, her
habit of dependence.

Julie did not love me, but in a surprisingly short time she
came to need me. She needed even to worry about my tastes
and my pleasures. So it was that she became the pursuer and I
the pursued. Yet willingly pursued for many years. Julie's flat
gave me, I suppose, what husbands find at home, a private and
stable world of their own.

And Eeles' death, early in 1912, of fever, seemed to remove
the only possible threat to this domestic bliss. Julie grieved for
him more than I had expected, but not in a manner to distress
our comforts. In two months I could congratulate myself that
the man was forgotten.

But one evening Julie said to me, apropos of nothing, "I suppose we could now get married, if we liked."

I can't describe the effect of these words. They deprived me
the power, not only of speech, but of thought. I could not even
form an answer. And after some moments' embarrassed silence, I got up, made some excuse, and though it was my night
for staying, went away. But from Paddington thank God, I had
the presence of mind to send two pounds of chocolates with a
card expressing my love.

If I had not been inspired to this simple act, I do not think I
could have borne the recollection of that crisis in my life. For
the upshot was that I did not see Julie again for more than a
year. I wrote. I took care of her business, I paid her rent, etc.,
but I could not bring myself to meet her. In cold blood, I perceived that, after her unlucky speech, I had no alternative but
to marry her or to brutalize these relations, which had become,
though troublesome, civilized by a mutual accommodation.

My conduct may seem absurd and even pusillanimous. I
can't explain even now why I felt so convinced that it was impossible to marry my mistress. But I have this excuse, that by

this time Tolbrook had come almost entirely into my possession. It was saved. And I felt perhaps that to bring a Julie to Tolbrook would be an impiety to my father's house, now in my care.

92

Mrs. Ramm came to tell me that tea was ready. She appeared a little surprised to find us still wearing our hats and coats in the half-finished room. And we were perhaps equally surprised. Ann, crouching still over the empty fireplace, straightened her back and pushed up her spectacles; I, half-propped against the library ladder, asked, "Is Master Robert in yet?"

"No, sir, he's gone."

"Gone. Where?"

"He went out with a bag, sir. He said you would understand."

"Oh, I see," Ann said, "he must have had that phone call he was expecting."

This did not deceive either Mrs. Ramm or myself, who could see that the girl was astonished.

"I wonder has he gone off," Ann said at tea.

"Gone off—impossible. He wouldn't do such a thing." For I was naturally taken aback. "How could he leave the farm with no one to take care of it? And what will he live on?"

"He might, all the same," Ann said thoughtfully. "Just to show me where I get off."

I did not believe for one moment that Robert had taken so decisive, so violent a step, without preparation or capital. But I was distressed by the very idea. I could not eat. "You ought to be ashamed," I said, "to speak so of your husband."

"But don't you think it's true, uncle?" she asked. She seemed perfectly tranquil. "No, perhaps he is not vindictive, but only likes to teach people a lesson." And after reflection she continued, "The truth is, I suppose, that he wasn't a born brute, but he thinks he ought to be a brute. He's like these Nazis and Fascists, who behave like beasts on the highest principles, as if it were a new religion to give philosophers castor oil, and knock people's teeth out for being Christians, and rub women's faces in the mud."

"Robert—what nonsense—he would never rub anyone's face in the mud. He is all against these Nazis as you call them."

"He put his fingers on my mouth the other day and made a face—it's the same thing. And he's very rough in other ways, too. He's always teaching me to be a woman. But I suppose it's something to do with the Time spirit."

"No, no," I said, "that's enough." For I could not bear to hear any more out of the German boxes, at such a time. "Robert is a good-natured boy, and very hard-working. And don't you think that we could do without him. He's taken all the responsibility here," etc. For I was not only disturbed in my conscience; I felt already a thousand new problems pressing upon me. "And if Robert has taken a holiday, I don't think you have any right to blame him." Seeing all at once that the girl was very white, and conceiving that she must be distressed, I went to bed. But not to sleep. For the more I thought of the situation without Robert, the more I disliked it.

"Robert," I thought, "has changed everything—he has picked his own men—how am I going to run a modern farm with a lot of youngsters who go about in blue overalls with oil-cans in their hands?" And I felt again the tragedy of revolution, that it can't be reversed. "No, nothing can be put back again—a man who is out of date is out of time."

93

And early in the morning I found myself in Robert's little orchard, on the site of the old shrubbery. The cold spring wind blowing round my legs and up my dressing gown awoke me. I was glad that some instinct had made me put on a hat. How I had got out of the house at such an hour I could not imagine. The place was familiar to me. But now to my startled eyes it appeared unnatural, a magic copy or original form of that reality. I seemed to have been transported into another world, of celestial beauty, but cold and unfriendly. Robert's little trees, in flower, were like standard roses of a new and extraordinary kind; the grass seemed to wear unnatural green; the sky, a blue so pale yet piercing that it alarmed me like a new sky, which is far more unexpected and terrifying than a new earth. Even the birds, which were making so much noise that they deafened my very thoughts, seemed to be of a new species, more bold, harsh, and excited than earthly birds. Exalted spirits of birds, impudent and furious with passions. The very beauties of the place, the glitter of flowers, the scents, the waving branches, the colors as delicate as pastel and radiant as cut jewels, increased my panic. For I felt that I did not belong among them.

But suddenly a gust blew down a few raindrops, and at once the ground grew solid under my feet. The sky faded to the usual pale blue of a cold spring morning, whose blue is mixed with thin cloud. And I saw beyond the hedge the great trembling mountain of the lime, with its leaves like green flowers. For the imagination, apparently, it does not rain in heaven. And seeing that one of the little new apple trees was dead, among the white bouquets of the rest, I thought, "I must tell Robert."

And then instantly I remembered that Robert had gone, and felt the pressure of that event upon my brain. I heard again the cow mooing which had perhaps brought me from my bed. For I had certainly heard her in my sleep and been oppressed by the agonizing dream which affected me so often in the old days, that the cows had not been milked.

"Yes," I thought. "It was that cow brought me out of bed. I suppose she has only been separated from her calf." But I went to find her in the shed, and afterwards I walked through the yards. All seemed in order there. A window flew up and a door opened. A boy rode into the yard on his bicycle. He was yawning to an enormous extent but, seeing me, shut his mouth quickly and opened his eyes. I approached him and wished him good morning.

"Good morning, sir."

"You've come to get the cows in?"

"No, sir, I've come to fetch away the drill."

"Who is in charge of the milking?"

"I don't know, sir."

He retreated backwards from me and I saw him looking at the windows as if for help. Probably he had been told that I was mad. Now in such a case, as I know by experience, it is useless to attempt any kind of intimacy. For if you talk sense, the other says to himself, "Madmen are all like that—they are as clever as monkeys. They pretend to be like anyone else, till they can get close to you and bite your nose off or strangle you," and, of course, if you don't talk sensibly, they say, "Oh, poor chap, he's getting worse every day."

But the incident did not improve my spirits. "How," I thought, "am I going to attend to all these new duties if people treat me as a lunatic? It's enough to drive a man mad."

And when I went into the house to tell Ann that no one was in charge of the cows, I found her at the telephone, in pajamas, with her hair strangely screwed up in curlers. Mrs. Ramm stood by, and the two, between Ann's cries down the instrument, conversed in low anxious voices.

"What are you doing, uncle?"

"Nobody is looking after the cows, and it is nearly time for prayers."

"Farley is acting as foreman."

"Old Farley—Robert wouldn't like that."

"He knows the place, and you said you liked him."

"But suppose Robert comes back?" For I was still convinced that Robert would come back.

"Then he can make his own arrangements," and she began to call down the telephone, "Hello, hello, Queensport. Is that the Labor Exchange? Hello."

"Does Farley understand this new kind of farming?"

"It's not really new, uncle. I always thought Robert rather old-fashioned. He doesn't keep in touch with research. Don't you think you ought to go and dress? Why are you carrying your clothes?" It was true that I had my coat and trousers over my arm. But as soon as I saw this I remembered the reason. "I thought they might be forgotten—I was going to brush them myself."

"Don't worry, uncle. They'll be brushed."

Both the women wore that expression which means "Don't fuss." I thought that there was every reason to fuss. But it was no good saying so to Ann and Mrs. Ramm, who had already made up their minds that old men are fussy.

And when I went to the nursery for prayers, there was the child Edward Wilcher, whom they call Jan, crawling about the floor, alone and unattended, with knives on the table and a bright fire in the grate.

The truth is not that old men are fussy but that they have learned from experience how much the young trust to luck, until some disaster falls upon them, by their own fault. And at that moment, of course, they cease to be young. They, too, become anxious and careful.

The flames of the lime, like burning salt, were so bright in the morning sun that they shone even through the calico blind and made a green light on the nursery wall. I pulled up the blind to forget anxiety in admiring this beautiful tree, so long beloved. The boy began at once to haul himself up by my dressing gown. He is now, at fourteen months, a rapid crawler, very strong in his limbs, and he likes to balance himself on his legs against chairs, etc. He has become, as I hoped, a handsome child, with his grandmother's eyes and his father's hair; and he continually bursts out laughing with an expression which says, "I can't help it." He looked up at me now with that intent gaze of a small child who is beginning to distinguish human beings from other tall objects, as creatures able to move and act, to make noises and to communicate to him unexpected feelings.

The relations between this child and myself, if I may say so, are established on a footing. His mother and father, like other young mothers and fathers, have been under the illusion that I could not handle children and did not like them. This is absurdly far from the truth, which is that children, and especially this beautiful child, so like Edward in beauty, Lucy in energy and courage, give me an intense delight, but a delight mixed always with a deep anxiety. I feel, "I mustn't hope too much. I must be careful what I do or say. A careless word, an abrupt action may injure the delicate muscles, pervert the virgin brain."

As a young man I have often jogged a small child on my knee; but I know a man who killed his own son at the game of ride to market.

Therefore, when Jan approached me, Ann or Robert were wont to cry, "No, no, run away. Don't let him bother you, uncle."

But as I say, we understand each other. The proof is that the

child always does come to me, and his glance clearly distinguishes me as a friend.

And now in his look, his clutch, I felt a pleasure, strange to
me for many years. I did not forget that sense of anxiety and
tension which had upset me during the night, but it became
reasonable. I felt, "But all this is justified. Tolbrook may be a
great nuisance," etc., "but it fulfills a purpose. It is necessary.
It is a complete thing. It is living history." And the responsibility that lay upon me became at once heavy and exalted, to be a
master of a house, with children; that is a high dignity.

When Ann came in, I told her that Jan had been left alone
with knives and fire. But she was absent-minded. She said that
perhaps we'd better have prayers quickly because a new milker
was coming to see her.

"Is it wise to take milkers from a Labor Exchange? How do
you know what bad characters may come about the place, and
ruin your cows?"

"This milker is from the village, and we had to have one.
Molly has gone."

"She can't have gone with Robert."

"So they say, and why not? After all, it's what we expected.
Have you got your books?"

The boy gave a sharp angry cry to catch my attention, and I
hastily looked again in his direction. One must be prepared
with children to attend to several things at once. At the same
moment Mrs. Ramm and the two girls who are all her staff in
these degenerate days came in to prayers. He turned his head
then, almost round, like a parrot, to stare at the newcomers,
sat down without bending his legs, and instantly crawled toward them. But Ann caught him, took her place, set him in her
lap and turned toward me her face with the look which meant,
"Time for the next thing."

I feel in these days the new importance of the prayers. For
the girl listens with a new attention. I dare say she is suffering.

I choose my reading with care, and I throw my heart into it. It is an exhausting effort, but I am sure that I ought to make it.

"Save me, oh God, for the waters are come in, even unto my soul. I stick fast in the deep mire where no ground is.

"Let not the flood drown me, neither let the deep swallow me up.

"And let not the pit shut her mouth upon me."

When I say these words, my own heart contracts with pain and terror. I think, "What sad old man, what broken-hearted woman, sinking into the last darkness, uttered that cry of despair? And what is to be my own fate in the next months or years?" And I pray not only for Ann but for myself and for all those who have walked in the shadow of that death.

"Draw nigh unto my soul and save it;

"For Thou, oh Lord, art the thing that I long for,

"Thou art my hope, even from my youth.

"I am become as it were a monster unto many; but my sure trust is in Thee.

"Oh, let my mouth be filled with Thy praise; that I may sing of Thy glory and honour all the day long."

Then God, indeed, gave happiness, and I thought, "Am I not indeed blessed among men, with this honest girl for a daughter and this child, to bring once more to the old house, and my old age, the revelation of God's mercy and love."

My heart was unlocked from that fear, the darkness was drawn away as by the sun which glittered on the wet window-panes; and when I rose from my knees, I went toward Ann meaning to say to her some word of encouragement. But she with the boy under her arm was giving directions to Mrs. Ramm about the spring cleaning, and it was only the boy who, twisting his neck to look up at me, noticed my approach. He did not smile, but his expression was full of curiosity and intentness; his hand, stretched up toward my sleeve, was asking, "What is this new thing?" And in the same instant he was whirled away to be dressed. Mrs. Ramm hurried one way, the servants another. Downstairs I heard the telephone ringing. And all at once Jan next door in the night nursery uttered a loud howl of rage. I felt that the top of my head would blow off. But I thought, "This is life—I have just thanked God for it. If I am to fall dead in a fit, at least I shall have fulfilled a purpose."

9 5

Children bring turmoil to a house because they are full of energy and invention. They love life and they can communicate that love, which is the body of faith.

But I don't suppose Lazarus enjoyed his resurrection, and I remember that in 1912, when Lucy came home to Tolbrook with her young son Robert, then aged two; and soon after her Amy arrived from India with her two youngest, John, twelve, and Loftus, eight, together with a friend's child, Francie aged two, I complained bitterly that the last refuge of peace had been destroyed.

This was a time of misery for all who loved decency and reason in human affairs. The Irish threatened civil war; the suffragettes were burning letters and beating policemen; and the air was filled from all sides with the threat, "If you do not give us what we want we shall make life impossible for everybody." I was a strong supporter of the nationalist and suffragette cause. For I said, "Freedom must be served." But I was much disturbed. And when I came to Tolbrook for rest I found the house rocked from top to bottom because there was no Scotch oats for Robert's breakfast.

Lucy, I suppose, was suffering. Her husband had gone abroad on a world preaching tour with Ella and left her behind. She would not admit the least criticism of Brown, but I think her nerves were in pain. Amy, for her part, had just lost her youngest child, the only daughter, and grief seemed to have the effect of making her more slow and obstinate. Lucy used to say that even to watch Amy cutting bread made her mad. "She looks all round the bread first as if it was a field of battle. I suppose Bill would call it a reconnaissance."

Moreover, Lucy and Amy did not agree, at any point, about the management of children. Lucy was a martinet. She would spring from some uproarious game and exclaim to young Robert, still rolling on the floor and kicking up his short fat legs in delight, "Now then, young man. That's enough— off with you," and if Robert did not immediately obey she would snatch him up and walk off with him to bed. If he fought her then she would at once slap him, not angrily, but with a cool determination to hurt, which shocked Amy. When Amy or I protested she would say, "I'm not going to spoil the boy."

"But, my dear," Amy would say, "Robert is so good—I wish only that Francie was half so obedient."

"He hasn't learned yet when it's time to stop playing," Lucy would answer, "and unless he learns it now he'll never learn it."

But though Lucy was a stern mother she was far more particular on some points than Amy. I remember a savage battle because Amy and my mother, left to look after the young children, had taken them driving into Hog Lane, which was the Tolbrook slum. My mother was used to give most of her charity to these very poor people. I think she was shy of the superior cottages. And for years she had visited Hog Lane two or three times a week. Amy saw no harm in going with her and taking the children.

My mother, now over seventy, had taken great delight in the grandchildren. I suppose she had lived a very lonely life at Tolbrook for the last nine years. She saw me only at week ends, and then I was always busy and usually worried,

especially by her accounts. Probably the reopening of the nurseries had given even more pleasure to her than to me. True,
she spoiled the children. "A typical granny," as Lucy complained. But even Lucy admitted the right of an old woman to
spoil babies.

Now all her old anger against the mother with whom she
had fought for so many years, that mysterious woman's war,
returned in one wave, "What!" she cried to me. "Robert in
Hog Lane. But, of course, mother would!"

Lucy had come in from some Benjamite meeting, and I
think that religious fervor always heightened her intolerance.
She flew to the nursery, where my mother and Amy were taking off the children's coats and talking to them in the manner
of the nursery.

I remember that this also irritated Lucy against both my
mother and Amy. "Listen to them," she would say. "Doting."

And this was unfair. Amy never doted. She always seemed
to amuse herself with small children, rather like a slightly
older sister. And although my mother, to our surprise, had suddenly shown a new manner, a new briskness, it was not silly
but merely a little comic. Among any children, whatever they
were doing, she would stoop down and utter a series of short
ecstatic cries, as if enchanted by their cleverness. Though I
think sometimes she did not really notice what they were doing. And so now, as she drew off her darling Robert's coat, she
was crying, "There now, that's one sleeve—isn't he a clever
boy. And now the other. Oh, he can do it himself—he doesn't
need Granny," and so on.

Lucy snatched the child out of the old woman's lap and exclaimed, "You want to kill the boy, I suppose."

My mother looked up with astonishment and confusion.

"You know they've got diphtheria in that filthy place—and
worse things than diphtheria—but of course that's just why
you would take Robert there."

My mother began to struggle to get up, and I went to help her. I thoroughly approved of Lucy's objection to Hog Lane for the children, but I was shocked by something in my mother's face. I can only describe it as guilt and terror. "Rubbish, Lucy!" I said. "Mama didn't think, that's all," and I took my mother to her room.

"Why do you let Lucy speak to you like that?" I said. I was angry with her for her patience. "It's abominable."

"Perhaps she was right—there may be diphtheria—I should have considered."

After that she came little to the nursery, and seemed to avoid touching the children even in Lucy's presence.

When I reproached Lucy for her violence she answered only, "I've no patience with Mama's groveling to those guttersnipes. We've got one or two like that among the sisters, and they're the most hopeless jellyfish of the whole zoo."

Amy, however, continued to take Francie to Hog Lane. And when Lucy abused her, in startling language, she answered placidly, "It's not their fault they're dirty—they're that kind of people," as if speaking of some foreign race.

"It is their fault. They're dregs. They wouldn't stay in Hog Lane if they weren't. It's just because they're dregs that mother kowtows to them."

So Amy, with her eighteenth-century idea of the world set in castes labeled the church, the bar, the poor, etc., seemed more democratic than the evangelist Lucy, who judged rich and poor by the same iron standards.

And when I was most exasperated by Lucy's violence, or Amy's obstinacy, and their long-drawn battles of gun against fortress, I would come in and find them romping with the children on the floor, creeping about on all fours, and barking or mewing or snorting, in a ludicrous manner. And the two middle-aged women with their gray hair, their deep lines, and stiffened bodies, the one too thick, the other too gaunt, would giggle as wildly as the children, until they were crimson and helpless, and rolled over to let the children crawl over them. And this undignified spectacle gave me a strange and keen kind of happiness which was mixed with pain. As if there were something incurable in the world's suffering which was also its secret root of joy.

9 6

Lucy, as one might expect, had a hearty contempt for Francie. She disliked little girls and probably all women. But Amy expressed a warm admiration of Robert.

It was our joke that Amy, watching Robert one evening in the bathroom when both the small children were sitting on their pots, said thoughtfully, "After all, you can always tell that Robert is a gentleman. It's his expression, I think." The "after all" was a reflection on Robert's paternal ancestry, which gave Lucy great pleasure for years afterwards. Robert was an energetic child, obstinate but always good-tempered, and with all a small boy's power of amusing himself. Lucy had a passionate but critical attachment to him.

But the worst quarrel between Lucy and Amy came from a strange accident. Robert fell into the lake and was rescued by John. This boy liked to wander about alone. And he was lying in a field when he saw Robert running down from the house. Robert, who had just learned to walk, loved to escape from his mother. He disappeared among the trees. But John, remembering the lake, came running across the fields, and when he could not see Robert, looked for his footprints in the muddy bank, dived in and brought the child up, not even yet unconscious.

Lucy, when she discovered the facts, said to us, "That boy's too good for Amy. He's got more sense in his little finger than her whole family from Adam," and she began to make much of John. She took him riding with her, and bought him an expensive camera for which he had been longing. For Lucy, whose money had been invested, by my advice, in building land near Ferry, was far richer than Bill and Amy, who were always in debt.

John had grown into a tall fair boy, more like Edward than his own parents. I had taken to him at once, and, indeed, at this time began that warm friendship which gave me so much happiness and pain for many years. I would take occasion, even then, to talk with the boy about his studies, and I was glad to find that I could help him in some points of Latin syntax, etc. And I was charmed to see his devotion to his mother. A natural and proper thing, but always delightful. One would say that John, who had not seen Amy for five years, had fallen in love with this heavy plain woman. He would color when she glanced at him; he would lie in wait for her; he would grow suddenly talkative and lively when they were going out together; he would secretly buy her presents and surprise her with them.

Amy, for her part, was visibly delighted and a little nervous. She would speak brusquely to the boy like a shy, young woman, who does not know how to manage a love affair.

It was Amy's ambition that John should go to the varsity. I don't know how this strange idea had occurred to her, for Bill strongly opposed it. Bill wanted him to go to Woolwich and be a sapper, "The finest job in the world, bar none. You ask anyone who knows." But at the moment Amy was in possession of the field of battle—that is, John's mind. And she often urged him to his work.

Then Lucy would say, "A good thing if he doesn't get a scholarship. The varsity is the ruin of boys. Don't you listen to anyone, John. This is your holiday, don't forget that. I tell you what, we'll go for a picnic on the moor, behind Torcomb; I want to see some people round there."

John and Amy, who had planned to go sailing together at Ferry, looked alarmed. For a picnic on the moor meant that they would be left to look after Robert while Lucy visited some outlying Benjamites. Neither Lucy nor Amy kept a nurse; Amy was too poor and Lucy would not trust any nurse with Robert.

"But John was taking me for a sail," Amy would say.

"You can sail any day, but this is the day for the moor."

And, in fact, Amy and John never had their sail. Either the weather was too calm or too stormy; or if there were a fair breeze, Amy had to look after my mother, or John had to look after the children.

John, like his mother, was a born family slave. He was reliable and good-natured. Amy, for her part, having once been useful to my mother, found herself indispensable.

My mother was the opposite of a tyrant. But she needed a nurse, and especially after this difference with Lucy she could not bear strangers near her. She would rather endure solitude or risk a fall; much rather die in peace. But she could not be allowed to die, and so one of us always stayed with her, and it was usually Amy.

For I was busy, and Lucy, I think, could not bear to be with the mother whom she had treated with such cruelty and injustice.

97

When I intervened on Amy's behalf to point out how important it was for John to get a scholarship, Lucy answered me, "Why shouldn't you pay with all the money you've made out of Edward?"

I knew that this was a deliberate provocation. Yet I always lost my temper. I would cry, "That's an abominable slander," etc., and I should have liked to kill Lucy. Her poisonous tongue made wounds that nothing could heal. No one was more quick and clever in twisting malice and truth, falsehood and injustice, into one burning dart and feathering it with a plume drawn from the victim's own breast. She had a devil's genius in striking at the very roots of the soul and paralyzing its nerve.

It would flash upon me, "It's true. I have got Tolbrook from Edward and now the London house as well. It's true I carried out the separation between Edward and Julie. If I had not done so they would almost certainly have drifted together again. And Julie did always encourage Edward and help him in his career. She gave him a refuge; she gave him absolute loyalty. Yet, if I had not arranged the separation, Edward would have probably been ruined, and if I had not saved Tolbrook it would have been lost to the family."

And my reward for years of heavy soul-destroying worries is to be thought and called a usurer.

The love of possessions. It is spoken for a reproach, and I feel it like shame. But what are these possessions which have so burdened my soul? Creatures that I have loved. The most helpless of dependents. For their very soul, their meaning, is in my care.

A woman loves her baby in its weakness and dependence, but what is more dependent than a house, a chair, those old books, a tree?

In these savage family quarrels of 1913, I would clap on my hat and go out to walk under the trees. And gradually I would feel their presence. I would even stop to touch their bark, as I had seen Amy, after some quarrel with Lucy, take Francie upon her lap. She, too, was unresponsive, but Amy had consolation in her.

All the Tolbrook trees, even so far as Tenacre, now a desert, were like children to me. I knew their shapes from every side. They were present to me even when I sat at a table, and the loss of any one of them, by storm or decay, was a pain to me even while I did not recognize it. I would feel, perhaps in the midst of conversation, a sudden discomfort. "What's wrong—what have I forgotten?" and then, "Was it that speech this morning of Lloyd George at Limehouse, or the German's new battleships, or that suffragette beating the policeman with a whip, or my mother's bad cold?" and then suddenly it would come upon my mind, "No, of course, it's that elm which was blown down last month in Pool's Paddock—what a gap."

9 8

All the trees were dear to me, dearer than my own life, and perhaps my soul's good. But specially the great lime. I had always known it. Its delicate branches against the winter sky, its thin quivering leaves in summer had stood before my bedroom window and the nursery windows on the same floor for all my life. They were among my earliest memories. In illness, I had watched their moving shadows on the wall and seemed to breathe the scent of their flowers. On moonlight nights of summer, too hot for sleep, I had lain awake and seen the criss-cross of the outer sprays, drawn by the rising moon, gradually pass across the ceiling and down the wall, till they reached my counterpane and feathered it like a wing. Sunlight falls upon a lime as upon no other tree. It pierces the oak as with red-hot arrows; it glances aside from the elm as from a cliff; it shrinks from the yew as from a piece of darkness; it tangles itself in the willow and seems to lie there half-asleep; among the crooked apple branches it hangs like fruit. But over a lime it falls like a water made of light, the topaz color of the moor streams, and full like them of reflected rays, green and sparkling.

Only to stand beneath the lime was such a delight to me that often I turned aside to avoid that strong feeling. Especially in summer, when the tree was in flower, pouring out that sweet scent which seemed to float on the falling light like pollen dust on the moor waterfalls, and every crevice was full of sailing bees, I shrank from an excitement so overwhelming to my senses. The organ noise of bees, like vox angelica, the scent which made the blood race, the slow smooth fall of light in its thousand rills, over the living flesh of this beautiful and secret creature, enticed at once the eyes and the imagination. Within that burning tree I felt God's presence. And there I bathed in an essence of eternity. My very consciousness was dissolved in sensation, and I stood less entranced than myself the trance; the experience of that moment and that place, in the living spirit.

And though I had sworn to hate Lucy for the rest of my life, I would find myself, half an hour later, strolling arm in arm with her through the garden, in the midst of a serious discussion about my mother's health, or the gardener boy's bad morals, not in forgiveness but simply in forgetfulness. The wound was there still in my breast, it would hurt for the rest of my life among thousands of others dealt me by Lucy, but I did not notice it any more than a rushing stream feels a new stone cutting its tide, or a growing tree suffers from last year's bullets fired into its bark. I was alive in that family weather, cordial to all living things, the good and the evil.

99

When Edward suddenly arrived in England and told us that in six months we should be at war, I was not only incredulous, but angry. I said if war broke out, it would be the fault of such as he, alarmists and warmongers. We did not quarrel because it was impossible to quarrel with Edward, but I gave him no support in his campaign for preparing the country.

I persuaded myself that he was trying to make a new position for himself, and to form a political group.

"You'll divide the party," I told him.

"What will happen to the party when the war starts?"

"Come, Edward, even the stupidest soldier knows the consequences of war in modern Europe—the destruction—the ruin of all that we have built up." I dare say Tolbrook was in my mind.

"That's the great attraction," Edward said, "at least to certain energetic minds. The engineer, for instance, he likes to start afresh from a blueprint. And the artist, he likes a clean canvas."

"It isn't a matter of epigrams and paradoxes." I was annoyed with Edward.

"No, it may be rather a serious matter for us. We've never allowed for the artistic temperament. The Kaiser has it—and it flourishes in Vienna."

Lottie stood some way off examining Ann in a new dress. Like other very young mothers, Lottie treated the small fragile Ann rather like a toy, to be dressed and undressed. The baby had her own trunks, her own maid, as well as the nurse. But she was a delicate creature and spent most of her time in Amy's lap, listening to Amy's very small stock of nursery rhymes.

Lottie called to us across the room, in her voice which was still a schoolgirl's, full of life but with little inflection, "Got your answer yet, Edward?"

"No, I didn't." Edward had written to some party conference, announcing his intention to speak.

"I said it was no good writing. You tell him, Tommy." She came toward us. "He's being too nice to them. That lot don't understand Edward's niceness. He must be really nasty before they take any notice."

"It's not quite like that in England," Edward said smiling.

"And as for the conference, I mayn't have time for it if the P.M. sends for me."

"Is the Prime Minister sending for you?"

"I dropped him a hint when I arrived. I can a tale unfold, but not on paper, and not to the embassies."

"The Foreign Office? All John Bull must know
This writing on the outer door: F.O."

Lottie quoted, startling us both.

"My dear Lottie—that's not for publication," Edward said.

"I don't care," said the young woman. "It's time some of those old fogies did get a shock. And if you don't do it, Edward, no one else will."

Edward began to smile, charming and nonchalant, but the girl exclaimed in a peculiar tone, patient and yet implacable, like that of a keeper who sees a young spaniel shirking the gorse. "No, no, we're going right in with both feet—that was the promise—or are you lying down on me again?"

"Certainly not. A shocking suggestion," Edward said, checking his smile. "No, no, I'll give 'em an ultimatum—and hang the risk of party splits."

And, warmly encouraged by Lottie, he held meetings on his own account, wrote letters to the press, joined the militia, and was photographed, in uniform, for the illustrated papers. He even spoke for the Navy League.

All this made me very angry. I said "Edward is a clever fool. See, he has suddenly got tired of his holiday and his art and wants to play at politics again. But he is a typical party politician; no sense of responsibility. He is blinded by ambition, by that secret demon which infects all politicians, whether they like it or not."

And when Edward's meetings failed, and the *Times* refused his letters, I did not know whether to be more angry with the country for humiliating our family great man or with Edward for stirring up, as I thought, war fever.

100

My life, which these children think so flat, might be described as three great waves of passion and agitation. The first rose in my youth, out of that inland sea, and gradually grew higher, darker, heavier, more dangerous, until, in the great war, it fell with one tremendous crash. And after that war, out of the confused choppy ocean of my middle age, arose another wave, not so high as the last, but faster, wilder, and blacker, which finally dashed itself to pieces in a swamp and became a stagnant lake among rotting trees and tropical serpents. From which Sara, like a mild English breeze, came to rescue me, by blowing away the vapors and sweeping me off from that oozy gulf into a third wave, a bright Atlantic roller, smooth and fresh, which was just about to come into port when it struck upon a sand bar and burst into foam, bubbles, spray, air, etc. But like the waves you see from all these western cliffs, never finding rest.

I believe I have been more agitated during this last week in Tolbrook than any time since before the last war. For one thing, there is a new war fever about; and this time a true fever, a disease, a distemper of the blood. I can't bear to read all this stuff about Hitler and the Nazis, as if that set of cunning rascals were likely to contrive their own ruin by provoking war. Thus I cannot look at the morning papers. And, for a second thing, it seems that Robert has actually gone off with Molly Panton, a thing I could not believe.

Ann has now all the evidence she wants from Robert himself. The couple have obtained work in a Lincolnshire farm of large acreage, where they are acting, apparently, as humble workers. The girl is in the dairy, Robert is a general farm laborer.

And when I express my wonder that Robert should leave Tolbrook for such a position, Ann says only, "It's just like him."

"What is like him?—he is a skilled farmer, and a very ambitious one."

"It's this Adam and Eve idea," Ann says, "which is going about. When Adam delved and Eve span. Men must work, if possible, in a muck heap, and women must weep, if possible, into a new baby."

"What fearful rubbish—what is all this? Do you mean Robert models his life on Genesis?"

"No, but Genesis came out of the ideas of people like Robert."

"My dear Ann, you are a great donkey—to talk such stuff. It's the kind of stuff which poisons everything with its stuff. Because it sounds like sense." I was angry with the girl. And she answered me:

"Yes, perhaps it is nonsense. After all, what do I know about Robert—I couldn't even keep the creature happy."

"Come now, that's enough—and what is this garment you're wearing?"

For she was in a kind of cloak, at eleven in the morning.

"It's only a dressing gown—I didn't dress properly, because I was going to work at the papers," meaning, I suppose, Edward's papers. She has suddenly resolved to write a life of her father, a project which I encourage. For I always wanted to see Edward receive justice from posterity, and I wished, too, for Ann to have some occupation. Nothing, I felt, was worse for a girl in her situation than idleness.

"A dressing gown," I said, "to write in. But that's an exploded idea. It went out even before my time. Good authors don't write in dressing gowns. And I hope you're not going

about the house in that ramshackle state—for it doesn't suit
your style at all." And I pointed out that her best point was her
figure, at least from the waist upwards, and that she would be
foolish to forget it.

The girl then went and dressed. And coming down again,
she said to me, "I mustn't fall down on this job, too, must I?"

"What are you talking about—your book?"

"No, I meant giving satisfaction as a niece."

But I could see very well that she was amusing herself at
my expense. Which I do not mind, so long as she does not become a sloven. Which, for a girl, is the quickest road to damna-
tion. Quicker even than drink.

101

Edward's papers, my own memorandum among them, astonish
me again by the wrongness of my ideas on every conceivable
subject, and the rightness of his. But I should not be surprised.
I am simply stating the fact that Edward was a man out of the
common run, and I was not. And therefore, of course, I acknowledged his general superiority, as any fool must do, and
yet found every single particular thing he did foolish; as fools
always do.

"All this war agitation," I told him, "is doing you no good
at all—it's only annoying the party chiefs."

"What will happen to the party when the war breaks out?"

"Oh, if you're counting on war, you'll be mistaken." I had
so nearly said "again" that Edward colored slightly and I felt
myself redden.

The fear of war now so possessed me that I hardly thought
of anything else. One day in town I met Julie and Edward together, near Berkeley Square, just outside the discreet little
teashop which at one time was a rendezvous for what Edward

called the three-quarter world—women like Julie, ostensibly respectable widows, or wives with husbands abroad, and their lovers or keepers.

I had not visited Julie since that unlucky proposal after her husband's death. We had exchanged some birthday letters, but it was already becoming understood between us that we had separated for good. I had even arranged a settlement which Julie, less proud than she had been seven years previously, accepted.

I had congratulated myself on the success of this difficult negotiation, which had left behind it neither bitterness on Julie's side nor any deep regrets on mine.

The sudden and unexpected meeting might well have startled me. Yet it was not until we had walked as far as Julie's flat and had spoken for some time about a recent speech of Lord Roberts, who, of course, I looked upon as a dangerous firebrand, that I noticed the silence and embarrassment of the others.

I thought, "What! has Edward gone back to her—he can't be such a fool." And at the same time I was enraged that so trivial an anxiety should intrude upon this terrible crisis. I said, "Where are we going—West Street?"—where Julie's flat was.

"No, it hadn't been suggested," Edward said, after a moment. His caution further irritated me. I thought, "Heavens, he doesn't think I'm jealous, does he?" And I said, "Where then?—it's rather cold for the park."

"If you'd like to come up," Julie said, and before I remembered that I had, in fact, not intended to enter Julie's flat again, I found myself in my usual armchair, before the usual bright, too large fire, surrounded by the usual pale clean colors and delicate scents.

Julie, on the other hand, did not lounge in her chair, but sat upon a piano stool, at a great distance from me. Edward stood awkwardly by the fireplace, and his whole attitude, I thought, even the way the collar of his coat stood out from his neck behind, forming a little pocket, expressed a sense of defeat, and surprised humility. "I suppose he came to Julie for consolation," I reflected, "because Lottie is too hard on him." And I became more and more indignant with him. "If only you would stand up to people like Roberts," I said. "That would have been the way to make yourself indispensable."

Edward started and said, "But Roberts is right—we aren't prepared for war."

"War—war—why do you harp on war? Nobody wants a war."

"Don't you think so?"

"What?" I was astonished.

"I should say a lot of people are always ready to welcome a war. Of course, they don't say so. They usually say the opposite."

"Most people," Julie said.

"Rubbish—what nonsense—speak for yourselves."

"First there's the young—the sporting ones," Edward said. "And the young carry a lot of political weight because they are energetic and have so much time to give to politics. Papa and Mama have other things to do—like paying their bills."

"I can feel war coming," Julie said. "And it's quite time."

"Do you want war, Julie?"

"We deserve war—we think of nothing but comfort."

"Yes," Edward said, "there's another group of war welcomers. I'd forgotten them—the people who feel that the world is wicked—that it deserves punishment." He sat down and picked up the poker, but at once laid it down again and glanced at me. The gesture and the glance were that of a man who has begun to ask of his smallest action, "Is that wrong—does it tell against me?"

It made me perceive, for the first time, the extent of Edward's failure. For one measures failure commonly by its effect upon the one who has suffered it. I felt, "If Edward is shy of my opinion, how vast must be his fall." And with a sick heart I said, "Yes, the fire could do with a poke."

"People are right," Julie said from the back of the room. "It is quite time the world was punished."

"There you are," Edward said, "Julie thinks we ought all to be shot or ruined. The good want war because they want to suffer and the bad want it because they want the other people to suffer." He spoke without his usual animation, but in Julie's melancholy tone, of one who accepts fate. "Plenty of people are ready to take any risk to themselves so long as they can get their revenge on somebody else—often some purely abstract enemy, like Germany or France, or England. See how the Irish nationalists delight in hatred of England—which is a pure abstraction."

"But we know there is an evil will," Julie said, "and the evil will delights in all evil."

The room was growing dark and Julie, on her piano stool, was only a white form in the twilight, with one bluish cheek and shoulder where the light from the uncurtained window fell upon her from one side. Edward and I, in the golden light of the fire, seemed to be in a different world, and I think we both felt it. Edward jumped up and said, "Have my chair, Julie—aren't you cold there?"

"No, thank you—it's too hot." And she said in the same voice, "After all, we are evil ourselves—we have plenty of bad thoughts."

"Not you, Julie. You are the best friend anyone could hope for."

"No, no," in a voice so passionate that both of us were silenced.

I thought, "She wants Edward, and she is angry that she can't have him—she has always been in love with Edward," and I became still more impatient with these triflers. I said, "All this seems to me pretty wild stuff. The question is simply, is war inevitable? *I* say, so far from being inevitable, it isn't even natural. And if it does break out it's our own fault for not stopping it."

"Another large group," Edward said, touching the poker but withdrawing his hand again. "Another large group," he resumed, "probably the largest of all, is the people who are dissatisfied with their lot—the failures." He paused and I felt that he had plumped the word out in defiance of embarrassment. I was so irritated against him that I nearly exclaimed, "That is *your* reason for believing in this war." But thank God I was able to control myself. I seized the poker, to rescue it from Edward's hand, and poked the fire before I recollected that I had no longer the master's right over that fire.

There was a long pause. The fire had now sunk to a red glow. It illuminated only a few square feet of the beautiful Persian rug; Julie's book, lying face downwards, *The Hound of Heaven*, in a first edition; and Edward's boots, which were not well cleaned. The rest of the room was felt rather than seen; and Julie was only a shadow among the thick uncertain shadows of furniture in the background. But the sky through the dark frame of the window had become brilliant with the strange light of a London dusk, neither blue nor green, gloomy but limpid, like a clear sheet of glass, apparently transparent and profound but showing no star. It was like some vast shallow jewel lit by a cunning arrangement of lights hidden behind it. Its beauty gave no sense of expansion to the spirit, but only oppression. And I actually found myself on my feet with the thought in my mind, "I could catch the last train and be at Tolbrook before midnight."

But instead I proposed to turn up the light.

"I don't think I want the light," Julie said.

I noticed again something strange in Julie's conduct. "Why does she sit there away from us, and how did she come to meet Edward in the tearoom? It must have been by appointment—

and probably not the first time if I caught them together. I pass that corner every day, but all the odds were against my catching them on the first occasion." And then at once I dismissed the whole thing from my mind. "I suppose I'm in the way, but what does it matter—let them sleep together if they like. I've no time for such nonsense while these lunatics threaten war."

"They're pretty numerous, too," Edward murmured.

"Who are numerous?"

"The failures—the dissatisfied. About nine-tenths of the population, I suppose."

I laughed. "So, according to you, nine people in ten want war."

"Oh, not all the time, of course, only now and then. It's only when they have a majority all at once that you get trouble."

"According to you, we ought to be at war all the time."

"Luckily modern war is expensive and complicated and needs a lot of organization. That's its one advantage, if it is an advantage. In the Middle Ages any baron could make war any afternoon. Many did. But now war can't be run except by a special department, and so you don't get quite so much of it."

I got up. I could bear no more. "It's no good talking to you, you can't be serious on any subject. I've got twenty minutes for my train, so I must fly. Don't let me take you away."

Edward got up. "Yes, it's quite time I rid Julie of this nuisance. You're not going down home, are you?"

"Yes, I thought so." For I had resolved to catch the train.

"I might really come with you; apparently there's nothing for me to do in town. I suppose there is a dining car on the train."

"But perhaps Julie would rather you stayed."

"I thought you were going to dine with me," Julie said.

But Edward excused himself in somewhat lame terms. He seemed too dispirited even to use his social resource. And we took a taxi to the station.

We spoke no more about the war danger. I was too much annoyed by what I called Edward's cynical frivolity.

Neither did we speak of Julie. I could not be bothered, at such a time, to tread tactfully among complicated sentiments.

102

But one consequence of this meeting was unexpected. For in the next week when I was back in London I found myself, at five o'clock, at Julie's doorstep. It had been, till six months ago, the usual hour for my arrival. And in some fit of distraction I had reverted to the habit. But now, since I was there, I went up. Julie was in. She received me with a kind of calm, gentle surprise which gave her, I thought, a stupid look. Indeed, I thought, seeing her again, that she was growing plain. Her plumpness was unbecoming. Her pallor had an unhealthy look. Her eyes and forehead were full of fine wrinkles. And while we were waiting for tea I felt sorry for her. I thought, "She is finished—she has let her life ebb away," and I said with a roughness which surprised my own ear, "You should take more exercise, Julie, you're getting too fat."

"Yes," she said, sitting with bent head, and one hand gently stroking the back of the other, an old trick. "I am really ashamed to think how I spend my time. I don't know where it goes to."

I could have told her that. It went in long meditation and trifling tasks. Julie was thinking all day long, even while she dressed herself, ate, or wrote a letter, of some friend in the past, someone who had loved her or whom she had loved, or ought to have helped.

"You should take up some useful occupation," I told her.

And Julie answered, as usual, with good nature, "But what could I do that was really of use? I thought of district visiting, but you know I could never talk to poor people to do them any good. I tried once and found myself agreeing with one poor wretch that it was no good trying to keep clean."

"No, you wouldn't be any good in doing anything unpleasant. But why not act again?"

Julie shook her head. "No, leave me my memories of the time when there was great acting and great plays to act."

Then we began to talk about this great period. I knew nothing of the stage. It may be true that, as Julie believed, the only time when there had been real enthusiasm for the stage, and great acting, had been in her youth. It is not probable. I did not quite believe it then. But I liked to listen to Julie's chat, and to hear her quote, to see her animated, and so we passed the evening, and I stayed the night.

I do not know why or when I decided to stay. Perhaps I did not decide at all. But finding myself at peace for a moment, in that quiet familiar room, I could not take myself away from it. And idly sought that other pleasure of the past. Yet I knew even then that this act must change all my relations with Julie.

But I said to myself of Julie, as I said to Edward, "No, I can't really give my mind to such trifles in a time like this." And when, by her silence, however melancholy, she permitted me first to stay and then to enter her room, I affected to be carrying out the old routine. I allowed myself to believe, when I climbed at last into her bed and took hold of her and arranged her body to suit my purpose, that I was performing a trivial act which might, for a moment or two, take from our minds the weight of our anxieties. But the truth was, I was trying to fly out, by that door, from oppression and fear. And Julie's gentle acquiescence hid from me the violence of my deed.

And I flew from Julie at the end of the week, from her talk about Henry Harland and the rest, to the tense and balanced life of Tolbrook, where Lucy and Amy still bickered and did each other mutual service, where Edward was still waiting to be summoned into the cabinet, and Lottie, in her sharp school-girl's voice, nagged him every day for submitting to neglect.

She would say to me in Edward's presence, "The trouble with Edward is he's too proud to make a noise as if he wanted something, but I don't see he's got much to be proud about yet."

The girl's youthful sincerity, which was so charming, could also wound, and we could see that Edward was henpecked. Yet what was pitiable and I think humiliating to himself was his need of Lottie. He received her sharp abuse with an uneasy smile, and repaid it with compliments and expensive presents; he followed her everywhere and seemed unable to let her go out of his sight.

But Lottie grew more bitter. She was enraged against Edward. For she had thought him a great and important person. And now he had turned out, as it seemed to her, defeated and patient under defeat. In a young woman, scorn is hatred.

She had a trick of quoting against him his own writings, and one day, in the presence of his mother, Lucy and myself, and several visitors, having complained that Edward would not give to the press some private knowledge injurious to a minister, she quoted to us in the clear elocution of the well-trained young person:

> "Statesman and scholar, he disdains to try
> The hero's role before the scholar's eye.
> A statesman still in judgment, smiles at praise
> For trifles which amuse a scholar's days.

Modest in triumph, silent in defeat,
No littleness could tempt his vast conceit."

Edward, with the perfect manners, which were all he had
left to carry him through humiliation, smiled and said, "Oh,
yes, so-and-so," mentioning a well-known statesman "but I've
thought once or twice since that his graceful attitudes may be
due to nothing but shyness."

"So-and-so modest—no more than you are, Edward!"

"But don't you think he might be nervous of losing what
fragment of self-respect remains with him after thirty years in
politics?"

"Self-respect. You really make me tired, Edward. You're just
too soft." And suddenly she jumped up and left the room.
Moreover, some days later she left the house, taking Ann upon
a visit for which Edward was not asked. And remained away
for the next two months.

104

I did not notice the progress of Edward's despair, which advanced, like a fatal disease, imperceptibly.

I was too busy, too distracted by the daily conflicts of
Tolbrook, and the political crisis, to think of Edward oftener
than at a week's interval.

I was now fighting against the smallest preparations for
war. I was like the man who is so frightened of cancer that he
will not go to the doctor for stomach ache.

There was a new navy bill that year, and some of the local
Radicals were protesting against it. I had already split with the
local committee, but I joined eagerly with these groups of anarchists and pacifists. I even paid out of my own pocket for ad-
vertisements in the newspapers saying that the government

policy was leading us into war; that we should offer friendship to Germany and not provocation.

I was glad when Bill and Amy came to live near us, not because he was my brother, but because I hoped for his support. We were very anxious to secure army men for our platform, and I hoped that Bill, who was, after all, an old-fashioned Christian, would come out against the navy bill. He had also a grudge against authorities. For after a fall from his horse two years before he had been put on half pay, and lately, in spite of his protests, invalided on pension.

"I'm fit enough," Bill said, "but I'm sick of this nonsense. No more boards for me. Amy and I have had enough of wandering. We want a home before we die."

And, in fact, they took on lease, with the option to buy, a small and hideous red-brick cottage on the Queensport road, beside the Long-water Estuary. They had nothing but Bill's pension, and three children dependent on it. Willie was a lieutenant, but he still needed an allowance. The other two were at school.

It seemed to me an act of madness for such paupers to buy property, when Tolbrook was open to them. I wondered if perhaps Edward had paid them his debt.

But Lucy, who knew Edward's secrets, wrote not. "How could the poor boy pay anything when he hasn't a penny of his own." Her explanation of Bill's rashness was simply that he had no money sense. "He's never had any idea of what things cost. He and Amy were mad on having this place of their own, and they couldn't restrain themselves."

"They won't have it long if Edward's war breaks out."

And, even as I shook hands, I asked Bill if, as a soldier, he could advise any nation to plunge into a European war.

"I don't know anything about it," Bill said. "I'm out of touch, you know. I say, you've been a long time coming to see us. What do you think of us?" Meaning by "us," apparently, the house. "Not too bad in front, after all, when we've put up the porch. But, of course, it's not Chatsworth or Hatfield."

They were full of that excited impatient hospitality of a young couple who have set up house for the first time. " Come and see my range," Amy said. "It's old-fashioned, of course, but really far better than those flimsy things they make now."

"Oh, the range," Bill said. "Tommy doesn't want to see ranges. Come along to the garden. Of course, it's really only a rubbish heap at present—old bottles and brickbats."

"According to Edward," I said bitterly, "you won't be able to enjoy even brickbats and bottles for more than another six months."

"But does Edward really know? Is he in touch with anyone on the staff? Look at that lovely bit of ground. All sloping south—and real good stuff under weeds."

And I could not get Bill even to discuss the war danger except from a professional point of view. He had a story that the Germans wouldn't make war that year because of a new Russian gunsight, just coming into production, and because the French army was getting too good, and because we had a wonderful new rifle just going into production. And when I lost my temper and asked him if he thought Europe was about to be ravaged because the German general staff wanted to play with its new toys, he answered, "Not quite—but it's their job to know the best time for a war," and then urged me to admire his jonquils.

It was a relief to me to meet John, who was at home from school for the Easter holidays. John had taken his scholarship, among a famous band. I felt that he was to be an honor to the Wilchers, and I delighted now in his gentle manners and sensible looks. I thought, "He, at least, will understand me." And I said, "You don't want a war, do you, John?"

"Is there going to be a war?" he asked, and in the same

breath invited me to see the new landing stage, at the end of the garden; and his boat.

"Many people seem to think so," I said, "and by thinking so, they are creating a certain danger."

"There always seems to be a war somewhere, doesn't there? She's got nice lines, hasn't she?" showing me a little tub of a dinghy lying below the garden. "But of course she's completely rotten under the paint. You could put your finger through her. Would you like a sail?"

At once, feeling perhaps that I was not inclined for a sail, he added, "But perhaps we had better wait for a better day, with more wind. And besides, the paint isn't really dry."

"Yes, perhaps we had better wait," I said, for I had already touched sticky paint with hands and umbrella.

"The wind is getting up though. There's a flaw now—and it's going the right way." The boy pointed at a thumb mark of breeze on the smooth Longwater. "But, of course, it's only a flaw."

The struggle in his mind between longing to use the boat, his own first boat, and common sense was hard. He said sadly, "I only painted the rudder this morning. And there's no tiller."

"That settles it," I said. "What a pity. I should have liked a sail with you, very much."

"Though I could steer with an oar. Yes, uncle, why shouldn't we try after all? You could sit on a newspaper."

"It would stick to the paint and ruin all your beautiful work."

"Oh, I don't mind that, I can easily do it again. Just wait while I run for the gear."

And he took me for a sail, which, just as we had expected, was a complete failure, and caused in us both the highest degree of chagrin and embarrassment. I became covered with paint; there was no wind. And while we drifted along the shore of the Longwater from one mudbank to the other, the poor boy, extraordinarily sensitive to another's feelings, frowned and said repeatedly, "I am most awfully sorry, uncle. I'm afraid it was a bad day for a sail, after all."

"Not at all, John. It's the wind dropping. That's just bad luck."

"Oh, I knew there wasn't any wind. I was a perfect ass. I can't imagine why I chose such a hopeless day."

He was almost in tears; and I, exhausted by inventing consolation, was at last silent and almost as dejected as himself. Fortunately, when we came back at last, he recollected that I had not yet seen a wornout millstone, discovered in the kitchen garden. He showed it to me with pride and said, "We don't know what to do with it."

"Perhaps a miller could find some use for it."

"Oh, no, we must use it somewhere—after finding it like that," as if he owed a duty to this foundling.

I felt ever more attracted to this sensible affectionate boy who felt a duty even to broken millstones. I was deeply touched by his attentions. And I sought his sympathy. "You don't believe in war, John. Wars have never decided anything. They are the most useless kind of madness."

The boy reflected thoughtfully, "War has never decided anything," and all the way to the house he seemed to reflect on my words. But as Amy came out to greet him, he said to her, in a heartbroken voice, "No wind, Mums, and the sail isn't big enough yet."

"I must sew on another strip."

And at tea, while John and Amy discussed the plan of the new sail, Bill, who did not take tea, told us, as an illustration of the dangers of war, a long story about some patent improvement in the Maxim gun which had been offered to the British staff and refused. "May cost us the war," he said gravely. "Yes, pretty big responsibility these chaps had, whole of the empire, millions of lives, depending on 'em."

I was defeated. I could not even argue with Bill. I could only remark, when John was listening, that perhaps if there were fewer experts on the machine gun, there would be fewer wars.

"Unless they were all on one side," Bill said.

105

Amy had approached me privately about Bill's health. His digestion was giving trouble. Would I persuade him to see a specialist?

But I have always been doubtful of specialists, and I was not on good terms with Bill. For I could not bear his fixed intention of making John into a soldier; I advised Amy to try carbonate of soda, and I took every opportunity of conversation with the boy. But I was rarely able to be alone with him. For as soon as I was seen at the cottage, Bill would thrust a spade or fork into my hand and set me to work. During that spring of 1914, I spent nearly all my week ends at navvy's work. Amy and I would dig, Bill, who was not allowed to dig on account of his myterious pains, would be nailing trellis on the arbor; John would be whitewashing the back of the house in an absent-minded manner; and Loftus, sent to weed, quietly doing nothing in some corner.

And if I spoke of the dangers of militarism, for John's ears, Bill would say only, "It's a tricky question. Damn the arbor. It's a regular swindle. They said it was ash and half of it is dead."

"You wanted the cheapest," Amy said.

"Excuse me, you wanted the cheapest. I wanted to go to the army and navy."

I said that it wasn't safe to buy from a firm we never heard of. "That's very nice, Johnny. Now the bit under the window."

"You said we couldn't afford five pounds twelve for a luxury—look at that boy, look at him." This in a tone of despair.

John, in fact, had paused in the middle of a stroke with his brush. I thought that he was reflecting still upon my theme, until I saw that he was leaning through the kitchen window to read the newspaper spread upon the kitchen table. The brush was still pressed against the brick wall, but it was motionless.

Amy's back was turned to the house, but, as if feeling a danger, she now quickly looked round, and called out, "Mind your brush, Johnny, it's dropping."

But Bill's shout drowned her. "*John*, what the hell are you playing at?"

The boy jumped, and the brush moved. Bill grumbled loudly, "Regular bookworm. Can't resist a bit of print. I don't know what's going to happen to him."

But afterwards, when I asked John what he had found so interesting in the newspapers, he answered that it was an article about Captain Slocum.

"Who was Captain Slocum?"

"He sailed round the world in a twelve-ton yawl." The boy was surprised that I had never heard of this hero. And when I remarked that the European situation appeared very dangerous, he answered only, "I suppose it always is—at least rather."

"Don't be so sleepy," I said. "A boy of your age should take an interest in things. And European politics are going to affect your whole life. Very much so."

He reflected for a time, and then said, "But I suppose the political people are looking after this."

It was as though I had heard again the voice of Amy saying that no doubt her insides knew how to look after her baby. John, too, appeared to be a private person.

But now I was frightened by the privateness of such as Bill and Amy and John. I answered angrily, "And who is looking after the political people? Did you never hear of democracy or imagine that it had duties as well as rights?" etc., etc.

"But I haven't got a vote, uncle."

"What does that matter? Any sheep can vote. The thing you've got to do is agitate—agitate. Look at your Uncle Edward."

And the boy with his peculiar detached tone of a sixth-form boy murmured, "A scene of agitation."

"Of course, what do you expect with people what they are—especially political people. Besides, that's the way democracy does work—the biggest agitator wins—it's a battle of noise and impudence and egotism." And, in fact, I found myself speaking of democracy with great bitterness. So that I stopped in some confusion.

But the boy was calm and aloof in his private world of reflections. "The art and craft of government," he murmured.

"But, of course," I said, "it's the only government for us in England—in fact, it's the only reasonable government anywhere, because people can agitate and make nuisances of themselves when they feel like it. And if you don't let them, they'll get into worse mischief in revolutions and general throat-cutting."

1 0 6

Tyrants hate Truth, death takes them by surprise,
Hail Democrats, who love the larger lies.

When I suggested to Ann just now that this would make a good heading for her war chapter, she answered, to my surprise, "You don't like democracy much."

"My dear girl, I've never faltered in my belief in democracy."

"Yes, you believed in it, so did Daddy. But you didn't like it. I used to think that democracy was rather popular in those old days."

"Democracy in those old days, as you call them, was the

creed of the whole nation."

"So it is now. But everybody abuses it all the time—I only wondered if you did the same in the last century. I want to get the angle."

"Oh, yes, the angle," and I felt as if the cool refreshing breeze of exact scholarship had blown on my forehead, already growing warm with indignation and excitement.

I did not know that a woman was capable of this careful approach to a historical problem. I had almost written too careful, too balanced. Ann has spent three weeks on her war chapters, and she is busy two or three hours a day. And if I cannot praise her style, which is that of a medical journal reporting a case of infantilism, I have to remember that the young of this age do not study Pater and Newman, as we did in the nineties. They have their own models in the *Police Gazette*, etc. Ann's curt sharpness, as of an examining prison matron, is not due to condescension toward Edward and myself and other antiques. On the contrary, if the girl has a bias, it is in Edward's favor.

"I suppose," she said to me, "they wouldn't have Daddy back in the cabinet because they were afraid of his brains."

"Or perhaps they didn't like his ferocious attacks upon them. As he used to say himself—a government is not so inhuman as people think—it hates to be abused."

"They could have taken him back after the war started."

"Yes, perhaps they were always doubtful of him. They may have felt he wasn't single-minded enough. They didn't like his writing, especially things like essays and criticism. Just as the Tories never liked Balfour's writing philosophy."

We were sitting in Edward's room. It had become our favorite in the mornings, when it caught the sun. And in the evening, when the tall curtains were drawn and a clear fire burned, we often talked till long after midnight. We agreed that it was the warmest and pleasantest room in the house. For in the last seven weeks, since Robert's departure, Ann, by the aid of my memory and a good decorator, had restored to it almost all the elegance of its high day. The shelves were once more full of books. Edward's writing table stood in the window. And on the walls hung his portrait, a drawing of Lottie with Ann sitting in her lap, and a reproduction of two French impressionists which had once belonged to him. Even his inkstand, his pens, his crops and sticks were in their places. For I had put all Edward's things away at his death, labeled with his initials.

It gave me great pleasure to see this beautiful and dignified room restored to use and life. It was a room which, unlike Julie's, spoke of courage and enterprise. The strange but brilliant pictures, which still gave me a certain discomfort, the strong color and bold decoration, the solid furniture and noble books, both from the most manly and lively century of our history, these were an inspiration. They said, "This is a place not for retirement but for counsel with strong minds and meditation upon great examples." But a keener pleasure was to see Edward's daughter, in his own armchair, sitting at home once more among his own possessions, so piously gathered by her energy; and his grandson playing on the floor with blocks which had been cut from a bough dropped from Wesley's oak, for Edward's great-grandfather.

Some old books and chairs, a child's blocks; are these things to give happiness in a world of miseries? No more I suppose than the features of an old friend in a world of strangers.

But with what joy does a man of my age see a friend's face; a man, that is, who is exceedingly lucky to have one friend in the world.

Indeed, I am enjoying such happiness in these summer weeks that I can hardly believe myself to be Tom Wilcher, that life-battered gnome. Peace has come to me, as I suppose it always comes, by surprise, and out of the very midst of storm.

And this happiness, which I have never enjoyed before, a calm gentle home-keeping happiness, is none the less precious to me because I am old.

For I have discovered that old people, even such old people as myself, with bad health and worse consciences, can enjoy life with as much appreciation as a child eats his breakfast, or Jan, here, sucks a lollipop. And this happiness is not grounded in delusion, or some deceit, put upon me by the family contrivance. For Ann herself declares the same contentment. She said to me only last evening, "I've never felt so at home in any place before. But, of course, I never had a home. When mother married again, I went to school in Chicago. And then it was Lausanne, and as soon as I had got money of my own, I cut away and went to London. I wanted to live in one of the real cities and mother was in New York, and I couldn't do medicine in French. The first time I wrote London, England, on my notepaper, I felt as proud as if I had had a big success. In spite of the other eight million."

I was thinking that Ann, after all, was very like Edward. No feature was the same, only the hair and the eyes. But her voice was like his in a female edition, and she spoke often with the same tone, as if secretly amused at her own follies.

"But are you sure that chair was really the one father used for the writing table?" she asked me.

"Almost sure—it was very like it."

"We must be quite sure or the charm won't work."

"You shouldn't talk about faith arising from chairs as if you were a savage. Faith is an act of the intelligence, as you ought to know," etc.

For I value very much the girl's intelligent and honest mind, which, I see very clearly, has brought to me much of the relaxation of this peace, so novel and delightful to my soul. And so I find her follies the more deplorable.

"Good writing isn't a matter of chairs, but hard work," I said to her, "as your father knew very well."

But she had already returned to the inquiry. There was a Lottie in the girl, the perpetual schoolgirl, as well as an Edward. "I suppose politicians are always suspicious of an original mind, that's why governments are always behind the times. And army staffs. A real genius, like Napoleon or Marlborough, always makes them look silly. But, of course, he has to get power first, and that usually takes a revolution."

I suggested that Edward, though a clever man, was hardly a genius; and, secondly, that geniuses might be dangerous in government. "What you want is a steady conscientious kind of man."

"Lawyers and bankers."

"Quite so. I am not ashamed of my trade—not at all."

"But I wasn't thinking of you, uncle. I don't think of you as a lawyer—you are much more a religious man."

"And why should not a lawyer be a Christian—or try to be one?"

Ann did not answer me. It was a modern trick of hers to break off a conversation when she chose. Probably, in her modern school, just as she never learned how to enter a room, or to keep her back flat, or to make herself charming, she was never taught how to begin, maintain, and conclude a real conversation. And the pity of it was that she was very teachable. When I saw her sitting bunched up, with her nose and spectacles poked into a book, I showed her by demonstration what a figure she cut: "Like a monkey on a stick with a pain in its stomach."

"Thank you, uncle, I know I'm rather stoopy," and she did really make an attempt, once or twice, to sit up.

I was greatly touched by this response to interference which was, of course, extremely tactless.

"You are a good girl," I told her. "You never harbor malice."

But she did not answer me. She was too deep in her book of political memoirs. Probably, of course, her patience is merely contempt for my opinions. Be it so. I enjoy now, because of that patience, whether from the heart or the mind; because of that efficiency, whether devoted or merely professional; because of that tolerance, whether due to charity or indifference, a happiness that I have never known before. So that often I feel guilty and ask myself, "Can this go on? How have I deserved such peace, at Tolbrook of all places? And with this painted chit from the laboratories."

107

Our only quarrels now were on the subject of Nazis, etc. For Ann thought that we ought to come to an arrangement with Germany in order to avoid war. "There is no danger of a German war," I pointed out. "The real danger is civil war. France, Spain, and Italy are divided from top to bottom between Catholic right and Communist left," etc. "Yes, we may well have more wars of religion, which would indeed destroy civilization."

"Would that matter very much?"

Now this is a question that always enrages me. And I told the young woman what I thought of her. "You ought to have more sense. You're not a born fool, at least. Or don't you have any idea what civil war means? In Germany, during the Thirty Years' War, more than half the population, about fifteen million people, died of starvation or disease, or murdered each other," etc. "Nothing is too bad and too cruel for men who have been turned into brutes. Yes, and it's the young people like Robert and you who might bring about this awful misery simply by talking nonsense about our civilization having no value."

She did not answer me, and I thought, "There now, we're quarreling. And it's your fault, you old fool. You ought to be more careful. But what is one to do? Why must these children always talk rubbish? Why must they make everything more confused and more perplexing?"

But Ann, after knitting half a round, answered only, "And, of course, there's the Maginot Line."

"I agree with you, my dear. History will say that Maginot, that modest little soldier, was the greatest of all. He made civilization safe, by making European war a doubtful and dangerous enterprise."

108

My own words filled me with wonder at the survival of civilization, by trifling strokes of luck, by the narrowest escapes. For what is it, a fabric hanging in the air—a construction of ideas, sympathies, habits, something so impalpable that you cannot grasp it. You look for its friends, and you find that it has none. Nobody cares for it any more than they care for the ground under their feet or the air they breathe. And it survives in spite of this mass of ignorance, selfishness, spite, folly, greed, hatred which makes up the ordinary political life of the world. As Edward wrote:

> Descent from apes. Quite so. But please to crack
> This nut, professor. How long climbing back?

We are apes and worse than apes. We know the light and turn from it. We do evil for the secret delight of it; not because it is delightful to our senses, but because it is evil. It was this terrible truth which I had grasped in the years 1913 and 1914, before that last and most savage of wars. I saw the enormous power of evil, and the weakness of good, and in my terror I ran about like a man who has just noticed that his house is in danger of collapse. I begged everybody, "Not so loud—don't shout—don't stamp your feet—for God's sake don't quarrel—keep quiet," and I pointed to the large cracks in the walls, the holes in the roof, the glass flying from the windows. And to my horror, some of the people began at once to shout louder and to stamp on the floors. When Edward spoke of the secret and everlasting conflicts of life, I called him a cynic, and when Julie reminded me of the evil will, I was angry with her. But now I felt that evil will. It seemed to me that millions delighted in wickedness, a little wickedness, and that when all these little spites pushed the same way, war must come and civilization must fall.

109

But, what is strange, the moment war broke out all my terror and foreboding disappeared. I ran to the recruiting office. I was one of those who stood for fifteen hours in Whitehall, with thousands of my kind, men of all ages, of all classes, trying to enlist in the new armies. And I neither felt nor met despair. On the contrary, I felt an extraordinary gaiety and lightness of spirit, and round me I saw and heard the same gaiety, smiles, jokes. Everyone was friendly, talkative, and, what was new and strange, too, everybody was making a joke of what he had left. One man said, laughing, "God knows what's happening at the office—I thought I was busy today." Another answered, "Yes, that's it, isn't it? I was saying yesterday that I hadn't had time for a holiday since last year, and here I am for the duration." Young City men with their hats on the backs of their heads leaned against the wall, and their whole attitude seemed to say, "To the devil with care and decorum." Neither was this

the spirit of refugees, of beings suddenly flung out of old settled routine by some catastrophe. I saw such after a mine disaster—they were as crushed in spirit as if the earth had fallen
upon them; even the children were gloomy, bewildered, with
the sudden wrinkles of old age. These men were lively, watch-
ful, receptive, all their faculties and their tongues active; you
would have said that they were going on a kind of holiday; or if
they were, after all, too serious, too tense for summer visitors,
then upon a religious holiday, a pilgrimage.

And in forgetting anxieties, in forgetting things, all these
men seemed to notice people more. I, who had been walking
through crowded streets for years without noticing a single
person, now felt interest and sympathy toward all my neighbors. I wondered about their lives, their feelings; I wanted to
talk to them, to hear them speak. So it was all round me; one
heard everywhere lively, friendly conversation. Everyone was
ready to talk, to confess himself. And I thought of Chaucer's—

> Sundry folk, by aventure y fall,
> In fellowship, and pilgrims were they all.

We were all sent away. The War Office was not ready for us.
But I went from the queue as from a place of revelation. I
thought how mean and small my life had become, and I had
never noticed it.

Others felt it, too. The nation was dedicated. No one was
ashamed to speak of honor, freedom, love, and truth. Churches
were filled and soldiers wrote of religion.

110

I was sent to France in 1916 as a stretcher-bearer. I was too old
for the infantry, and I refused a commission. But the last weeks

of that bitter winter in the Somme trenches gave me pneumonia and left me with a damaged heart. I was invalided out of the army in September, 1917, and came home to Tolbrook after more than a year's absence. I had been happy in the army at war. I had lived among grumbling and that private soldier's wit which makes of all life, its glories as well as its miseries, something obscene or contemptible. I, too, had spoken of a dead comrade as a stiff or a landowner, and called the cemetery the rest camp. I enjoyed being called Pinkeye, Little Tich, or Shorty and told that I had the duck disease because of my short legs. And when I used speech which filled every sentence with obscene images, I was expressing not anger but a secret desire:

> All women bitches, liberty a lie,
> So soldiers, who for home and freedom die.

We were like monks who have foresworn the world, who have no responsibilities in it except to save it by the devotion and sacrifice of their lives. But while we threw dirt upon that which we loved, we exaggerated its virtues. So in London I was shocked by the fat complacent faces of profiteers, by the crowded restaurants and the imbecilities of the stage, by the swarms of young girls walking the streets, not even for money, but for pleasure.

At Tolbrook, indeed, I seemed to find dignity and peace. Lucy had gone back to her husband on his return from abroad, just after the outbreak of war. The nurseries were closed and I was no longer waked in my room along the passage at six o'clock in the morning by Robert singing in his bed, or trying to shake it to pieces. The housekeeper was competent, the food very good after army food. My mother, though at seventy-eight bent and crippled, was apparently content in her daily routine of prayer, reading, and correspondence with mission friends.

But now, for some reason, I could not find serenity in her room. When I read to her or prayed with her, I would feel its stillness like a tension of the nerves. And the silent attention of the old woman, with her white thin face, seemed to ask of me an effort that I could not give. The effort, I suppose, of a comprehension, a sympathy that she had never had from any of her children, except Edward, who rarely troubled even to write to her.

And if, removed by experience of war from Lucy's masterful influence, I began to feel in some dim way that my mother, whom I loved and reverenced, had yet suffered the cruelest injustice at our hands, by the mere whim of her daughter and her own sensitive pride of spirit, I had not the patience, at such a time, to break an old, and therefore easy, routine of formal affection.

I found myself restless and troubled. I missed not only my friends of the war but something which had belonged to us all from the day of our enlistment—a peace of the spirit. I had left noise, dirt, and servitude at the front, expecting peace, and I found that peace had stayed with the servitude. And I began to spend nearly all my time at Turner's Cottage, as if some of that peace might be found with Bill, simply because he had been a soldier.

Bill now looked very ill, with white hair and a gray face. I could not have recognized him except for his pugnacious jaw. But he refused to discuss his health or a doctor. "Doctors! What's the good of doctors? What do they know about anything? Nothing. Come on, and I'll show you my apples. Good solid path, isn't it; fifteen inches of broken brick under it. Made it myself last year. There you are, how's that for three-year trees? Hi, Amy, there's some windfalls."

And Amy, coming in her stately manner, would gather up the windfalls as if retrieving an empire.

I was shocked by Bill's looks and by his whole attitude toward his responsibilities. I took occasion, as soon as I could get him alone, to point out that he must consider his health. "Suppose anything happened to you, Bill—we're all mortal—what would happen to Amy and the children?"

And Bill, after a long pause, answered in a meditative fashion which I noticed for the first time, "Well, Tom, I look at it like this. We're all in God's hands."

Then suddenly laying a hand on my arm, he drew me toward the end of the garden. "Have you seen our new view?"

But I was in no mood for seeing views. I could not help asking myself who would pay for Loftus and John, still at school, if Bill died. "I dare say I'm as good a Christian as you are, but we have to think of children's futures," etc., etc. And then I suggested that he should make Edward pay his debts. "Edward owes you more than two thousand, and he could pay very well—he's spent that on presents for Lottie in the last six months."

"No, no," Bill shook his head. "Poor old Edward, he's worried enough." He was still drawing me toward the end of the garden, and when I protested he said mildly, "But you believe in providence, Tommy."

"Of course I do, but I think it's our duty under providence to use some foresight," and so on, and I repeated my arguments about seeing a doctor, and overhauling his financial position.

But Bill did not even attend to them. He remarked that providence had intervened on his behalf many times. For instance, "when Amy didn't die of that miscarriage on the trooper"; and "when we got this place so cheap." And then suddenly pointing, "There you are, I always said that the willow ought to go. Fine tree, but we took a chance, and look at the result. Magnificent!"

What enraged me against Bill was the suspicion that his talk of providence was only a kind of trick to avoid responsibility. I thought, "To a man like Bill, untrained in logic or self-criticism, the doctrine of providence is simply a temptation to avoid the trouble of thought."

"Just forget your mud pies for a minute and think of your family," I said. But Bill looked at me with his vague meditative eye, as if I had not been there, and before I could say more John came out from the house. He had just returned from some reading party on the moors. At first sight I was disappointed in him. He had shot up into a tall, thin boy of seventeen, with his hair in his eyes and a stooping back. He had lost his looks. His forehead was too high, his nose too long, his eyes too small. He told me that he had been reading the *Republic*.

"Plato," Bill said. "Yes, I must look into Plato. I always meant to do some philosophy. But just now potatoes is what we want," and he laughed, as if surprised by his own joke. "Get a fork, Johnny, and break up that strip of grass." And he called out to Amy, "Now, Amy, that's not two spits —a spit and a half is about the size of it. Deep trenching is the thing—all the books are definite on that point. And we'll need our potatoes pretty badly if the war is going on another year."

John murmured "The war is always with us."

"Well," Bill said carelessly, "I suppose it's got to go on till we win—or they'd win." And he said to me, "John is a bit of a pacifist, you know; been listening to all this 'Stop the war' stuff."

"But you aren't a pacifist, John," Amy said, contradicting Bill. I noticed that Bill and Amy now avoided argument, except by this indirect method. And they showed new affection for each other. I saw them walking arm in arm on several occasions when, no doubt, they thought themselves unobserved.

"I don't know what I am," John said, languidly raising a very small fragment of dry earth on his fork, and looking at it with a bored air. "But war doesn't seem to do very much good—not obviously."

"Good," Bill said. "No, did anyone say it was any good. You might as well ask, what's the good of cancer?"

At these words, Bill paused. Amy became scarlet, John very white. And I felt a terror as if something unbearable had happened. But Bill continued in the same mild tone. "No, I don't see it's any good. No one wants a major operation, I suppose, or a war. But if you ought to have one, you've got to have one. It's not going to rain, is it?"

We all looked up and declared that it might rain. Or it might keep up. And the digging continued. It appeared after all as if nothing had happened. Bill's pause had no significance. Amy said something about the roots. Bill, who was not allowed to dig, advised a mattock. And I thought, "It was only my nerves. Dyspeptics like Bill always look wretchedly ill and live to a good old age."

111

Two of John's friends, from the reading party, came to tea. Both had the same slouch, the same long hair, and they talked about the *Republic* among themselves, in a mild and absent-minded fashion. I was infuriated against them all. I said, "What, has this apathy, this decadence, struck even into the schools?"

And I made some sharp remarks about the men in France, suffering every horror, while at home scrimshankers amused themselves with summer holidays. None of them answered me. On the contrary, afterwards, while we stood watching John prepare his boat for a sail, they were polite to me, in their absent-minded fashion. They asked me about my experiences in France; they sympathized with my illness. They seemed like elder statesmen condescending with a fractious child. But suddenly I heard one of them say to John, "My last sail, I suppose."

And John answered, "Have you heard?"

"Yes, I report on Monday."

"What, are you joining up?" I asked.

"I'm called up, sir," said the boy.

"What unit do you mean to choose?"

"I suppose they'll decide that."

"Doesn't make much difference," John said.

"No, I suppose not," said another.

Then there was an unexpected silence, and, looking at the boys, I saw upon all their faces a strange expression, preoccupied and, as it were, waiting. They reminded me of those faces one sees in railway waiting rooms, at once resigned, impatient, bored, and suffering, of harassed travelers who have missed their connection, and expect nothing but disappointment from their journey.

It occurred to me suddenly to ask, "Has your school had many casualties yet?"

"All last year's sixth have gone," one of them answered, speaking to the air.

"Seventeen out of nineteen," John said from the boat. "But they say Jimmy won't die. He'll only be blind. Anyone got a piece of string?"

I felt ashamed and I began to feel shy among these boys, condemned to death. I spoke of their magnificent services in the air force, etc. They listened politely, but without comment, and John said, "Come on, boys, I think she'll hold now—and if not—"

They got in and sailed away, leaving me upon the bank. I had not been asked to join them, and I was glad because I should have felt like an intruder.

I was ashamed, and my love for John returned with a force I had not known before. I said, "What right have I, with two-thirds of life behind me, to criticize these boys, meeting their hard fate with such unassuming courage?"

I proudly accepted John's confidence when he offered it to me. I delighted in that good nature of a boy who had still the humility of childhood, without its selfishness. So free from touchiness that when, in the midst of our talk about the Greek way of life, etc., I ventured to urge that a haircut would give much pleasure to his father and greatly improve his appearance, he answered at once, "Do you really think it worries father?"

"Very much. And me. It gives a wrong impression. It makes you look aesthetic—one would think you are trying to seem like an artist."

And he went to Queensport that same day to visit a barber. True, when I saw him the next morning his hair did not seem to be any shorter, except at the neck behind, but he seemed to think that it was shorter, for he asked me if he would not pass for a convict, or a soldier.

"Has it been cut?"

"Yes, I told the man to cut it short," in a tone of mild surprise.

I gave up this problem. For I saw that hair, for some reason, meant so much to the boy that he could deceive himself about its length, and that even barbers understood his secret desires.

We were sailing in his cranky little boat, a pursuit which caused me acute misery. For wet, especially in the seat, always gave me rheumatism; the motion of a boat, even on a calm day, made me ill; the necessity of continually getting up and moving across to the other side of the boat, and ducking my head under the boom, at the risk of my hat, broke up every conversation and exasperated me extremely; and, finally, I could conceive nothing more stupid than to proceed by zigzags, from nowhere to nowhere, for the sake of wasting a fine afternoon. Neither, if I might mention such a point, though it is probably unimportant, have I ever been able to understand why there was no accommodation provided on small yachts for things like sticks and umbrellas; whereas land conveyances, such as gigs and even governess carts, always have a basket designed for their proper storage and protection.

Yet when John asked me to sail with him, a common accident, for it was his only idea of entertainment for guests of all ages and both sexes, I never refused. For I felt it a privilege. And I would have sacrificed more hats, umbrellas, and suffered even worse attacks of lumbago to keep the regard of so honest and candid a soul.

It was during these happy weeks of John's holidays that I resolved to make him my heir. I could not think of anyone more likely to do the family honor, and to maintain its tradition.

113

And in this perception of John's unique quality, in my deep attachment to the boy, I began to understand for the first time the anxiety of parents in wartime. I recognized in Amy's face, sometimes when she looked at John, the expression of a feeling which never ceased its steady pressure upon my own soul. A slow, perpetual fear, mixed with a kind of desperation.

It was useless for me to say, "The war will be over long before John is old enough to fight." Nothing removed that pain.

And just as I understood Amy, I began to understand also the real motives of some of our neighbors who opposed the war, and demanded a peace of accommodation.

True, I did not agree with them. I was already a keen supporter of that great idea for a League of Nations which has since done so much to give Europe security and confidence. I can even claim to be one of its earliest advocates. I was the first to form a League committee in our district, and to address public meetings on the subject.

It was at such meetings that I first discovered how unreasonable and bitter people can be when they are frightened. They would not listen even to my proof, that their very fear, for sons, husbands, lovers, was the justification of my argument. That war must be put down by force.

Perhaps in those early days I placed too much emphasis on the force needed. As it turned out, little has been required. But I was astonished at the violent opposition which I encountered.

When I asked some women if they realized that they were throwing away the lives of young men yet unborn, perhaps their own grandchildren, etc., by their pigheaded unreason and senseless Antinomianism, I was actually assaulted, etc.

But I am afraid that many of my meetings ended in disorder. For I was in a highly nervous and excitable frame of mind.

So also I was led into a foolish quarrel with the curate in charge at our own parish church.

This man denounced the whole idea of a League, with sanctions, as an imperialist plot to exploit victory and humiliate Germany and Austria.

I therefore approached the fellow, a lanky tallow-face from Cambridge, asked him to tea, and brought up the subject of evil. I suggested that the modern church did not lay enough emphasis on the positive nature of evil, etc. He answered that in his view the Church ought to go in for socialism.

I saw, of course, that he was trying to evade my point, and I put it to him plainly, "Do you believe in the devil or don't you?'

To which, twisting up his mouth into a conceited knot,

he answered that, even in the Fathers, the reality of the devil was not so strongly developed as laymen supposed. He was regarded rather as a negation of God, or a general name for the characteristics of man's fallen nature, and so on, a heap of heresies.

"Excuse me," I said, "but I heard you argue, from the pulpit, that the best proof of a personal God is the existence of the good will in man, of love, charity," etc., and so on. "The usual thing, and quite right, too, nothing could be better." For I wished to do him justice and to show that I was not prejudiced against him. "But if so, surely the evil will in man, his lust, spite, and cruelty, his love of supporting a bad case by mere argument, out of pure conceit" (for I thought I might touch his conscience here) "are proofs of the devil's real existence—and a pretty devilish existence, too, at the present moment of the world's history."

But it proved useless to argue with the fellow. He answered, according to rule, that good will was a principle of unity, superior to individuals and pointing, therefore, to a Power superior to all individuals; whereas spite and hatred, etc., were self-regarding vices in the individual, factors of disunity requiring no higher power beyond—all the usual sophistries—and I remembered too late that it was always useless to argue with dishonesty which would not acknowledge the plainest facts. So I said, "This matter is too serious for logic chopping—the point is simple, do you believe in your own confessed creed or not? Do you believe in the devil and the need for fighting him and for supporting any measures, military or otherwise, to defeat his purposes?"

"The devil," he answered in his abominable accent, "is said to be a gentleman, and therefore probably supports the government, so that I certainly disapprove of him."

This horrible levity upset my temper, and I said that the matter was scarcely one for raillery, and that if he were not my guest, and entitled to special consideration, I should be obliged to tell him what I thought of his hypocrisy, manners, appearance, etc.

He withdrew then at speed. For I admit that I had now lost my temper and uttered some abuse of which I was afterwards ashamed. But it was untrue, as reported in the village, probably by the wretched creature himself, that I had threatened to mutilate him. Though it has occurred to me since that emasculation would have been the appropriate fate for one who had performed a similar operation on the doctrines of the Church.

I had silenced the Judas, but he was not to be defeated for, as I might have reflected if I had not been led away by the dispute, he was already sold to the devil's service, who had armored him already with the impenetrable brass of intellectual conceit. He actually preached against me. I could no longer read the lessons in church, and finally was obliged to cease from attendance. For I could not take communion from the hand of a blackguard who had betrayed the creeds, and denied the devil, at such a time of crisis.

This separation from my beloved church was a great grief to me, and I blamed myself for my impatience with a wretched nincompoop who was perhaps, from education, incapable of that moral courage necessary to acknowledge the evil nature of man as well as the good.

My excuse is that my friends were being killed and, above all, I felt that secret fear which is a much more powerful motive than the strongest principles.

John was barely seventeen. Amy and I congratulated ourselves privately that the war would be over before he was called up. But in the spring, by giving a false age, he succeeded in joining the air force. His explanation was that all his friends were fighting, or dead.

The fear in which those live whose sons and lovers are fighting is like deep water; it is calm as well as deep. I don't think Amy and I ever expressed to each other the least anxiety about John. It was Bill, to whom John was now a hero, who said, "It will be a damn shame if Johnny gets killed. The country can't spare boys like Johnny." And Amy would answer mildly, without even a change of color, "We really could be getting the lettuces planted—it's so mild."

We did not talk or think of Johnny getting killed; we only lived with the fear, the feeling of it; almost the certainty of it. My mother remarked once on my habit of leaving at a moment's notice an excellent dinner and splendid fire at Tolbrook, in order to travel four miles through muddy lanes to a cold supper and freezing drafts at the cottage. "That's three times this week, and poor Amy never has warning." I wondered at myself. But I perceived at once the attraction; I wanted to share with Amy a feeling which she alone in the world possessed in the same force.

It was probably raining. I could not ride a bicycle and was obliged to use the trap, without a cover, and the yard pony, a sluggish beast shaped like a beer barrel, with a trot like a carpet beater. I remember still those nights, as one remembers scenes from a time of crisis—the streaming rain, blowing in my face, the clouds smoking through a sky like the last day; the hoofs rattling and splashing on roads which were unseen in the black shade between their high banks. Until some green and ghastly ray, darting down between two clouds, suddenly flashed upon them, and showed them like rivers of Tophet, liquid sulphur winding through hellish rocks of darkness. And when at last I would come in sight of the Longwater, it, too, would have a diabolic aspect, unexpectedly bright, as if from an infernal and pallid fire; seeming composed not of water but of some heavier liquid, perhaps molten beer bottles. An image that should please my temperance friends. And these heavy waves, flowing all in one direction with a deliberate movement, formed, I thought, a kind of reproof, as of satanic order, to the turmoil in the sky and the agitation of the bare trees, dashing and rattling their branches overhead and flinging down their subsidiary showers like a crowd of hysterical ghosts from some churchyard of the drowned.

Under such a storm the cottage appeared ridiculously small and flimsy. I would always feel surprised at first sight of it, and say, "That can't be it. That's the boat shed." And it was like that pleasure with which we look into a toy house and find it occupied by a complete family and its furniture that, when I had put the pony in the coalshed, and thrown Bill's own rug over it, I would knock at the door and see, as it sprang open, Amy's little maid, and Amy herself, at full size, among tables, chairs, and lamps, etc., and to hear from within Bill's call of welcome.

Such arrivals, for some reason, always animate a company, and for some minutes we would all hold out our hands to the parlor fire, laughing at nothing and congratulating each other on an encounter which happened four times a week. Then Bill would say, "All right, old girl. I see you telegraphing—Tom doesn't want anything extra except beer, do you, Tom?"

This was because Amy was attempting, by various grimaces over his shoulder at the maid, just inside the door, to express complicated messages about the cold meat and the remains of an apple tart.

Nothing, of course, could prevent Amy from going to the kitchen to provide a meal of which half could not be eaten, and her obstinacy would cast a first shadow upon our hospitable feelings, on both sides.

Bill would say, "Can't do anything with Amy. Might as well try to push an elephant off a bun," and we would sit silent, for we were always a little shy when left alone together.

Then at supper, with Amy's return, we would revive and gravely discuss the weather, the war, the rations, and John's last letter.

Although the eldest son, William, was now a staff captain in the regular army, and had greatly distinguished himself, I can't remember that we often discussed his letters, which were, I imagine, few and dry. He was, I think, a young man whose manners, by their cold polish, which belonged rather to the Rifle Brigade than the R.E., had always given his parents some uneasiness. And I have heard that in the regular army during the generation between 1902 and 1914, possibly by re-action from the scrambling ways of the Boer War, the manners of subalterns did assume a reserve, an aloofness, which was not qualified, like the arrogance of the old guard, by any ideal enthusiasm for Bible reading or imperial responsibility.

Bill or Amy would always inform me what William thought of the war, what the general had said to him, and what he had suggested to the general, with the manner of those who conceal their pride in a possession which is also a national property. But in John they delighted frankly, like those who show their own back garden with wonder that so modest a plot can produce real flowers and edible fruit.

We chattered and we laughed. Amy, whose laugh was a private convulsion, as if a silent earthquake was heaving at the rocky bondage of her stays, would make her chair creak so loudly that Bill would cry, "Easy, old girl—take the sofa if you want to laugh. It's stronger."

And even while Amy laughed I could feel her fear. It had grown to be part of her. It had changed the shape of her lips when she laughed, and the expression of her eyes.

It was preparing us both for the news of the disaster to the Fifth Army in 1918; John was reported severely wounded and a prisoner. On the evening when Amy told us this news I felt not despair but a kind of relief. I said to Amy, "He's got a chance," and in Amy's voice, replying that the German doctors were said to be quite good, I heard exactly the same note, like an echo. "After all," we thought, "he may escape." The darkness of our fear made that hope seem almost like a rising sun.

115

I had been reading *The Student in Arms*, the story of a young subaltern soldier who, like John, had felt it his duty to offer his life for the free spirit. I found such comfort in the book that I took it to the cottage.

I soon wished that I had been more prudent. It was a custom at the cottage for Amy to read aloud in the evenings, and now she read us *The Student*, which I knew from cover to cover.

Amy was a bad reader. And Bill had developed an extraordinary absent-mindedness, which made a severe trial of our patience. Bill at that time was a very sick man who could barely walk across the room without support. Yet he would continually get up in the middle of one of Amy's sentences to look out of the window to see if the sky were clearing, or to make sure that some sapling was still firmly tied to its stake.

And I now began to notice that the garden had become an obsession with Bill. I suspected that most of the time when he seemed to be in deep meditation he was reflecting only upon shrubs, bulbs, or a new layout for his roses.

Amy would read: "Here are two contemptible fellows, a philosopher without courage and a Christian without faith." And Bill would take his pipe out of his mouth and say, "It's stopped."

"What's stopped?"

"The rain—no, it hasn't," and then, "Johnny might have said that—it's true, too."

"Do you think so?" I would ask. "Is John a convinced supporter of the Church?"

"But he's very philosophic—takes the rough with the
smooth. Poor chap, he's had to."

"Good heavens, Bill, but that's not what the book means. It
means that a philosopher must be honest even if his conclusions expose him to ridicule or lead him into pessimism."

"Yes, the rough with the smooth. What a gust. Thank God
the leaves aren't out."

"But Bill, it refers to a duty, not a way of life," etc.

"Isn't duty a way of life—probably the best way?"

"Yes, yes, but let's stick to the point," etc., and it would
end by my telling Bill that he didn't know the meaning of
words, and so on. Amy would then complete my exasperation
by saying, "I think Tom's right. John was not really so philosophic. Too particular about his food. But he was always quite
fearless." And she would take off her spectacles and look at
them thoughtfully. Amy had lately been obliged to use spectacles for reading. But she did not like them, and complained
that she could not see through them. To which Bill would reply, "Then try without them."

Amy would then put on her spectacles again, screw up her
eyes, make some extraordinary grimaces, and begin to read
like a child, one syllable at a time, until she forgot herself in
the interest of the work. "Death is a great teacher—from him
men learn what are the things they value."

"Something in that," Bill would say. "Yes, it must be a bit
of a surprise to get to the other side. I dare say it will be consid-
erably different from what we imagine."

"But what he means, Bill, is that in the face of death a man
gets a new scale of values."

"I don't see that. Besides, it isn't true. When you're up
against it you get the same kind of values, only more so. My
God, I remember when I stopped that potleg in Ashanti, how I

longed for a pipe. I thought I was a goner that time. But all that's old stuff now. Know anything about root-pruning, Tommy?"

"No, but I dare say they do it at Tolbrook."

"We dug up John's plum tree and cut off its roots," Amy said, "but it's dead."

"My idea," Bill said; "my funeral entirely." He seemed to make this admission not as a duty but because he wanted to dwell on the misfortune. "But it was all in the book."

Hoping to divert him from the reading to the garden, I tried to continue the subject. "Which book was that?"

"Let's finish the chapter, old man. Carry on, old girl."

"In the time of danger all true men are believers—they choose the spiritual and reject the material."

"I think myself it was a bad tree."

I burst out laughing, then, and Bill, taking his pipe out of his mouth, asked me in surprise, "What are you laughing at?"

"You."

And I was alarmed at the same moment that he might be hurt. But he answered only, "Is that all," put back his pipe, and said, "Carry on, old girl, you stopped at the word material."

116

And remembering those nights, so wearing to patience, so sweet to memory, I took down the *Student* from my private shelf. "It was a great book at that time," I thought, "for it expressed the best feeling of the time—the sense of duty, of sacrifice; the desire for a better world," and when I opened it that hope, that desire rose again from its pages with all the sadness and the power of the young man who knew he was to die. It moved me again, and I thought, "If only I could get Ann to read it, would it not enlighten her spirit?' "

For I was worried about Ann. She looked ill and anxious,

and yet she would never rest. She would sit down to read, jump up to telephone to some dealer, run out of the room to see that Jan was asleep, and then begin checking the day's accounts, all in the same five minutes. She was always tired, always busy, and yet I never saw a smile. A new line was growing between her brows, and when I said to her, "Don't frown, you're making yourself ugly," she did not even hear me. "And you ought to rest more—you give yourself no peace."

"Peace," she said, as if the word had become old-fashioned, and even sentimental. "When there's time, uncle," and she would run off again.

I laid the book open on her workbasket as if I had put it down in a fit of absent-mindedness. But she threw it on the floor to reach my socks.

"My book," I said.

"Did you want me to read it?" She picked it up. "Who is Hankey?"

"He was a young officer killed in the last war. Some people think he was one of the greatest losses we had. His books gave new faith and happiness to thousands."

"In the last war?" She was still in her war chapters. "I must read that."

Ann kept the book for a week. Each evening she sat still in front of the fire, reading with such concentrated attention that I had great hopes of her salvation. But one morning after prayers she gave it to me and said, "Your book, uncle. I'm afraid I've kept it rather a long time. But I've so little time now for reading."

"What did you think of it?"

"It does give a new angle on the period."

"I didn't recommend it to you as a historical document, but to do you good, if possible. To make you understand something that you don't seem to understand, that the only door to happiness is faith."

"I suppose that's why it does seem a little dated—the bits about faith."

"Don't you want to believe in anything, you foolish girl?"

"Well, uncle, I'm rather busy just now."

"Hankey says that if you're doing what is worth doing you ought to enjoy it."

"Well, I don't. I hate this farming job. It's never done, and it's getting worse."

"Because you fuss. You try to do everyone's work. Where are you off to now?"

It was time for our walk, but she was dressed in an old pair of dungarees.

"To look at the byres. I can't leave them to Farley."

She went into the byres and afterwards to the fields. I saw her riding away on the yard pony. We had no walk, and she forgot even that I had missed my walk. She sat at luncheon still in her blue dungarees, and after a long troubled reflection she said, "I don't trust Farley one inch. I knew he was always against what Robert was doing, and now he's trying to undo it all."

"Perhaps Robert went a little too far."

"Robert did a good job here. I'm not going to have it spoiled by an old fool like Farley, who doesn't even know that he's a mass of stupid jealousy."

"You're very hard on people, Ann, as well as yourself."

"Am I?" She was naïvely surprised. "No, I don't think so. I don't think I'm hard."

She continued to reflect upon my remark, for half a dozen times in the midst of those anxieties which troubled her all day she would say, "No, I don't think I'm hard. I know I spoil Jan." And again I saw the look of anxiety and doubt as of one struggling with abstruse and complex problems. "I may be a fuss-pot, but that's not the trouble. I just don't know things thoroughly."

In 1919, immediately after the armistice, the child Ann returned to Tolbrook, where she was alone with her nurse and my mother. But my mother's memory was failing. She did not recognize people, and often called them by the names of the dead. Edward was in Constantinople with the staff; his wife was in France with an American canteen.

The house was very quiet, for Ann was a silent and reserved little girl. A woman came every day to give her lessons, which she learned very easily, and yet with anxiety. For she would always make me hear her.

She would appear before me silently, in the evening, and wait till I spoke to her. Then she would say, "Please, uncle," and hand me a lesson book. And I would ask, "What are the chief rivers of England?" or "What are the chief events of the reign of Alfred the Great?"

At once the child seemed to grow even paler, wrinkles appeared between her eyebrows, she fixed her gray eyes on the sky through the top of the window, and began, carefully, to repeat her lesson. She was always right, yet she hesitated often. Seeing the child's anxiety and self-doubt, I sometimes ventured to prompt her. But I found this was a bad policy. For she would flush and cry, "Oh, no, uncle, you mustn't tell me."

"But, dearest child, I wanted to help you."

"But you mustn't, you mustn't," stamping her foot. "How can I know if I really know it? Now I shall have to start again."

Once or twice, at a prompting, she broke into tears. And I gave up the practice.

Yet I believe we were great friends. It is hard to tell if children truly care for one, unless one is clever at pleasing them. I am not clever with children; I can't tell stories, and I am shy of intrusion. Yet Ann would greet me always with warm affection, and though she was independent and liked to go walking by herself, she would often accept an invitation to come with me. Then she would take my hand and seemed to feel a kindness.

Our walks were largely silent. She was not communicative. And on those evenings when I sat reading to my mother I had often to remind her that the child was in the room.

She would sit on the floor cutting out war pictures for a scrapbook; or drawing, with so little sound that it was easy to forget her presence.

Yet if I or my mother happened to say, "Where is this or that, spectacles, book, the newspaper, the blotter?" the child would at once rise up, find the object, and silently bring it to us.

"Dear me!" my mother would say. "Ann is like a little imp the way she pops up."

And just as Ann knew where everything in the house was to be found at any moment, she had always the latest news of her father and mother. She remembered their letters to the last word and, with the aid of the governess, followed their movements on a map.

She would say, "Daddy is at Cairo now. It's fearfully hot there." And ask, "How do you get fever? Is it a microbe?"

"I don't know, my dear. But there won't be any in Cairo. It is very civilized in Cairo."

"They have lepers there—and plague. The French soldiers had plague in 1796. What is plague like?"

"Your father is quite safe from plagues."

"Yes, of course," she would say with her usual politeness.

"An old-fashioned little thing," my mother once called her, in her own hearing. But a week passed before Ann asked me one day what it meant to call a person "old-fashioned."

"Quiet," I said.

"Nurse says it means prim. What is 'prim' exactly?"

"Nurse is talking nonsense. It is a very good thing to be old-fashioned. It means serious and thoughtful."

"Well, I should like to play with somebody, but Francie only shouts." For Francie was visiting at the cottage.

It was true that Francie was a noisy child. When Amy brought her to Tolbrook she would rush at Ann and shout, "Come on, Ann, let's play at something."

"Yes. What shall we play?"

"Oh, anything—come on."

"Let's play tig."

For answer Francie would hold up her skirts, put her head between her legs, and stick out her tongue. Francie was an accomplished buffoon. But Ann did not laugh. She was always surprised by Francie's jokes, and she would say, "Is that a game?"

Francie would then pull Ann's hair and rush away. Ann would run after her, catch her, and retaliate. The delicate, slender Ann was extremely strong and courageous. She would chase the biggest village boys if they dared to abuse her. Thus the stout Francie would soon be in tears. She would run for protection, and the embarrassed Amy had to console her.

When I reproached Ann on one occasion for making Francie's nose bleed, she answered with the same anxious look, "What ought I to do?"

"She's your guest. You oughtn't to hit her."

"But she was chasing the yard cats."

The yard cats were Ann's special friends. Half-savage like all farm cats, living a wild life among the barns and stock, they would come running to Ann as to an envoy with a flag of truce.

"You should tell her not to."

"I did, but she didn't care." And, after a pause, she remarked with a sigh, "Francie is a difficult child. I would rather go to see her and she can entertain me."

Amy, however, did not ask Ann to the cottage. For she had taken a strong dislike to her on Francie's account. Amy was capable of unreasoning feuds, and they were deep and strong. I dare say she hated Ann when Francie, once more defeated in battle, came weeping with the puzzled Ann hovering behind, not sure whether she had done right or wrong.

118

William, now acting major, with a D.S.O. and M.C., was killed a few hours after the armistice in one of the last actions of the war. And there was no news of John. I was afraid to go to the cottage. I stayed away, on various excuses, for a fortnight. I can bear my own grief, but I can't bear that of other people and I dared not meet Bill and Amy. I knew that they would talk about their sons.

This was a time of great dejection. I had not cared for William, but I could not help feeling that his death, at the beginning of a distinguished career, was a fearful waste to the family.

Even the disappearance of the curate at Tolbrook, on promotion to a very good living, could not raise my spirits. I seemed to see all round me, what no one had expected after the great heart-searchings of the war, general apathy and disintegration.

In church, where once more I was enabled to read the lessons, I found suddenly a small and apathetic congregation; smaller than I could remember. The young did not come any more. The young wives whose husbands had been at the front, the boys and girls whose fathers and brothers had been in some navy ship, now stayed at home or amused themselves. Many of the old faithful who before the war had never missed a Sunday were dead, and no one came to fill their places. And suddenly a great many voices were heard accusing and demanding, or jeering. For the first time I met young men and girls, the generation of John, which had been too young to fight, and found in them that cynicism which I did not know how to answer. For they said, "The war was a bad joke played on us by a lot of old fools," and when one answered, "The war is over and you have your lives before you," they said, "Life, oh, yes," as if they were making another joke.

It was the cynicism of the young which shocked and frightened me. It was as though the spring leaves, deliberately, for some secret and devilish purpose, distilled poison in their own sap and withered on the twigs.

We heard by wire that John was coming home from a German hospital and Amy and I hurried to London to meet him. But in all my excited joy, I still felt a private terror that he too might have caught this disease of the will.

We scarcely recognized the young man who, laughing, limped up to us on the platform and embraced us both. We had last seen John a schoolboy—clever, affectionate, but still a boy. We walked now, rather shyly, beside a man of the world. Even his conversation had changed. He no longer seemed, like a boy, to carry about secrets from which, at unexpected moments, some cryptic speech unwound like a strange plant out of a wall. He spoke in lively tones, easy and self-forgetful.

"And how are you, John?" Amy exclaimed, as we made our way through the crowds.

"Oh, very well. And they say I won't even limp—I only need some massage."

But two minutes later, Amy, not being able to think of anything else to say, asked, "And how are you really?"

"Never better, Mums."

He looked round at the station, that place where one never sees a cheerful face, and said, "I never thought I'd see this again. Very nice. Very nice, indeed. It's a gift."

"And how are you really, Johnny? Really and truly?" Amy's voice and look expressed her wonder at this son become so suddenly a man. Her question seemed to say, "Shall I understand the words of this delightful stranger?"

"Very hungry, Mums darling, and fearfully greedy. I want a really expensive lunch. And it's on me. I'm rich, you know. Or I shall be when the army pays up what it owes me."

And when I spoke to him at lunch about the cynicism, the moral defeat of the new generation, he answered, "Our lot aren't worrying—life is too nice."

"What do you think about this talk of a social revolution?"

'I don't know anything about anything. But I've a sort of feeling of earthquakes about. I think we ought to have oysters, don't you? Don't be alarmed, Mums, I know you don't like oysters, but my plan is that you shall ask me to eat your share for you, and after a time, out of pure filial feeling, I shall give way."

And at the cottage, so far from being bored, cynical, he amused himself all day with the gramophone, his books, and country walks.

And I said to my friends in town, my partners in the London office, "All this talk of the revolt of the young is largely a newspaper sensation, got up to hide the flatness of the news. The best of the young, the ones with some intelligence and force of character, are extremely sensible people and most delightful to know. For instance, I have a nephew," etc., ctc. And I dare say I bored them all with my talk about John.

119

The only shadow upon this very happy time was a sudden worsening of Bill's illness. In a few weeks he became a skeleton. His face was clay color. He was so weak he had to be wheeled about in a chair. He could not even smoke; his pipe made him vomit.

And now, when I delivered an ultimatum that a specialist

must be obtained, he told me that he had seen a specialist years before. "They had an op you know, that time my horse rolled on me, and found it wasn't ribs at all. Hopeless. Sewed me up again. Gave me six months, and that was five years ago. Good work, old boy. Five years."

"And does Amy know?"

"She found out pretty soon. She's smart, Amy. You can't keep her in the dark very long."

What astonished me was that Bill had known of his condition when he took the cottage. I asked myself, "How could a sensible man be so imprudent; or is he, like Edward, simply depending upon me?" My anger revived. And that I could not reproach a dying man increased my resentment.

But so it was that in a few days I seemed to become accustomed to Bill's dying. I dare say the reason was partly that neither Bill nor Amy seemed to pay any attention to it. And so I found myself arguing and joking as before. And I pointed out to Bill how irresponsible he had been, in lending his money; and in case he might be thinking of me when he spoke of providence, I mentioned that war taxes had practically ruined me.

But Bill answered only that these were funny times and the devil only knew what was going to happen to anyone or anything. "Mama says she will pay for Loftus' schooling, and Lucy thinks she can get John a job through one of her Benjamite friends."

"What sort of job—Lucy is probably thinking of a grocery shop. And I could take John into the firm."

"A good idea," Bill said, in his absent-minded manner. He was sitting in his chair outside the house on a March afternoon, cold and gray. His excuse for being out was a few small breaks in the clouds through which the sun sent down narrow pencils of light. Half a dozen of them were always traveling slowly across the fields like the rays of some explorer's apparatus. The groups of bare trees, fields, or cottages, suddenly illuminated by this magic lantern, had the air of creatures suddenly awaked from hibernation. They seemed to say, "Let us alone. We may have been cold; but we were at peace."

"The prettiest spot in the country," Bill said suddenly, pushing out his putty-colored face from his rugs and turning his yellow eyes about. I was startled by the contrast between his easy acceptance of my offer and his enthusiasm for the place. I said, "And I won't charge any premium."

"Thanks, old man. Just wheel me down the path, will you? I want to show you something."

I wheeled him down the path. I thought: "Is he really so selfish or can't he think of anything but his gardening and his views?"

"Our premium as you know is usually pretty high," I said.

"Yes, old man, it's good of you. But John would make his way anyhow—there you are," showing a gap through the trees which revealed almost a mile of cold, troubled water, olive colored, laced with yellow foam, and various low hills, squared out between black hedges into fields of dark purple or dark blue-green. The few willows opposite were tossing their long branches in the wind as if trying to warm themselves. "Pretty good," said Bill, "but just wait till the sun comes out."

"And what's going to happen to Amy if you go? But I don't see why you shouldn't have another five years."

"The M.O. says three weeks. Excuse me, old chap, but your foot is rather near that sapling. Don't do to knock the bark off. That's a weeping willow. In ten years this will be the prettiest spot in the garden, or Queensport for that matter."

And I found myself promising Bill that I should secure the cottage for Amy. "If necessary I'll advance her enough to buy the freehold."

My own words surprised me. And I still do not know what had suddenly made me feel small and mean beside the improvident Bill with his absurd passion for a small garden. My wonder at the improvidence remained, but it was thrust aside by the sense that to Bill dying, a few trees, flowers, etc., planted and established by himself, a view opened, might have a special value and importance.

Bill himself showed no change of mood. He said in the same detached tone: "It would be a good spec." And then, as if asking for my approval: "The idea is, you come down here on a hot day and have tea under the new willow and you'll have the view in front of you all the time. My idea is that you need two or three different tea places in a garden."

"A very good idea. A splendid idea."

"And look at the view—right across the estuary. Bold Head and even a bit of the sea outside. Just right incline three paces. There you are, with the sun on it. A spot of real true blue, or is it green today? Here, move me over, will you. Ha, I knew you could see the coast-guard station. Amy said you couldn't. I call you to witness, Tommy." And then he remarked with strong and deep satisfaction: "I always said this place had never had a chance. I think we've done it pretty well, on the whole."

"Very well, Bill. I hope it will be a home for Amy and the boys for the rest of her life."

"It might and it mightn't." Bill reflected a moment and sucked his lips as if smoking. "Of course, old boy, I should like that a lot but I haven't counted on it. And if you try anything, go carefully, very carefully. Fact is, Amy doesn't generally want to do what I want to do. She's been the finest wife a chap could hope for, as you know; I couldn't have done without her. But there it is. We all have our little ways, and that's hers. She reacts. So I haven't set my heart on anything like a permanency here. In fact, I don't expect it." He spoke as if he might have expected to live, in spirit, at the cottage for eternity. "But I think you'll agree it's not a bad job. It was worth doing."

"It's one of the most beautiful gardens I ever saw."

"Oh, well, I'm not a gardener. Not a real expert. I just had an idea about the place."

120

Bill died suddenly three weeks later. But Amy would not accept the money, even on the most businesslike terms. She said in effect: "If I borrowed all this money from you I'd never know how I was going to pay it back."

I accused her of being too particular, and we had a little argument. For Amy was an obstinate woman. "A sister," I said, "should not object to being under a small obligation to a brother."

"A debt is not an obligation," Amy said. "It's money."

"Legally, my dear Amy, it is an obligation."

"That makes it all the worse."

"You haven't answered my argument."

"But we're not arguing, Tommy. You can't deny that it's about money. And there's no arguing about money. Money's money."

I tried another line of approach. "All the same, Amy, Bill would be very upset if you sold. He loved this place."

Amy turned scarlet. I saw that she was getting upset. She said: "Do you think they mind what we do?"

Amy's picture of Bill leaning out from some material heaven to watch her doings startled me, and I answered: "I meant only that he wanted you to carry it on."

"He would never want me to do what was wrong," Amy said.

"But he himself suggested an advance."

"Bill was always rather careless about money. He said I ought to trust God more, but I said that wasn't the same thing as getting into debt. Not when you've got children. No,

365

Tommy, I'm sorry." Amy was growing calmer as she perceived her own conviction. "I know I should never be comfortable about it. Even if Bill doesn't understand."

So the lease was sold, and I saw the strange spectacle of Amy, whenever she came to Tolbrook, going down to Queensport to look over the hedge at Bill's apple trees, to see how they were growing. She was very pleased with the new owners for their care of the place.

121

I took John into the firm as I had promised. And he did extremely well. He had a scholar's memory for detail, and a scholar's conscience for exactness. He was apt to be unpunctual, but even in that fault he improved after I gave him, for his Easter present, a good alarm clock.

Loftus had entered Woolwich that year. He had always meant to be a soldier. Amy therefore came to make the family home with John. She took a small flat for him in Bloomsbury; and he appeared well content with her very limited ideas of entertainment. Amy, of course, was extremely happy. Her expression while she presided at John's table was ridiculously like that of a middle-aged bride.

I had planned that John should live with me. But I saw more of him than Amy, both at the office and on our daily walks. Almost every fine day we walked together in the park after office hours; and I believe that John enjoyed our conversation as much, or almost as much, as I did.

Of course when I say that, I allow for that grace of temperament in the boy, who was never, to my knowledge, rude to anyone in his life. It is possible, therefore, that I bored him with some of my middle-aged chatter, about old times, and the political situation, or even about theology. But it was John who urged me to publish my book on the need for a new statement of the Christian belief, with special regard to the positive power of evil and the real existence of the devil. And our discussions on the subject gave me the happiest evenings of my life. I write advisedly. I enjoyed with Lucy a keener delight but never that serene mood of happiness with which I strolled beside the beloved boy in the evening of a London day and spoke with him on the common ground of great subjects.

We would wander sometimes far from our course on the rough grass. The noise of the city, ceasing to be an interruption, became a friendly ground bass to the chirp of the sparrows, the obbligato of London sheep. It seemed to say: "You are at home in a world which is all domesticated, where even nature serves only for the walks of friends and lovers." The London evening sky filled with sober radiance was like a Dutch picture, by that most home-loving of people, whose very sketches seem to distill the peace of family hearths into dumpling bushes and meditating cows.

The very blackness of the trees, on which the spring buds glittered like emeralds, was familiar, like the thick domestic smoke upon an old fireback. I had pitied the London trees, like wild birds in a cage, but now love was mixed with pity, and I would say to John: "Shall we go on the grass?" in order to pass beneath the trees. And he always agreed.

"We've plenty of time," he would say.

"Yes, you're young—you have all your life before you," etc. And I would say something about his gifts and the great openings afforded by the modern world. For I always liked to nurse John's ambition. And I remember he answered once in a phrase that might have been Edward's, "Yes, I suppose you always get a good many openings after a bombardment, very large ones, but rather muddy at the bottom."

"My dear boy, the career is always open to talent, and work."

"Oh, of course, I was only joking."

It would begin to grow dark. The lights of Piccadilly became visible through the trees, and in the old bow windows of Park Lane, filling for the season, blinds were drawn. John would take my arm, perhaps to guide me, for I was apt to walk into trees or railings in the twilight. But the gesture, even if its motive was partly utilitarian, to save trouble, was also that of a true affection. John was interested in my preservation from accident. It gave me such pleasure as I could not express. "My dear John," I would say, "I mustn't keep you. I am sure you have a party somewhere, with charming young ladies only too anxious for your attendance."

"No hurry, uncle. Mind that tree. Yes, I think you're right about openings. There will be plenty of chances when the smoke clears away a bit. Of course, just now everything is a bit unsettled. And the big noises seem to be chiefly big noises."

For John, as much as I did, disliked the superficiality and pretension infecting not only politics and literature, art and manners, but even the Church, in those disturbed times.

122

My remark about the charming young ladies pursuing John was not without a purpose. For once or twice a young woman had called for him at the office, a creature whom, at a first meeting, I took for a young prostitute from the cheaper streets. Her figure was slim and flat, her face disproportionately large and round. In repose, with its small features, large blue eyes, and brassy hair, it reminded one of those dummies put in hairdressers' windows. But it was seldom in repose. Gladys was always jerking her head, twitching her little mouth, rolling her eyes, and humping her shoulders. In conversation she would wriggle her behind as if it itched; and frequently she plunged her hand into her breast or down her back in order to scratch herself. Her voice was the chatter of a colobus monkey; her laugh the shriek of a cockatoo. She was daubed like one of Edward's pictures; and her nails were always dirty.

I did not care for Gladys, but when I suggested to John that she was scarcely the kind of girl to be brought into an office of our standing, he answered with amusement and surprise, "But Gladys is not that sort, uncle—her people think no end of themselves, I can tell you, and she went to school at ———" —a famous school of which I cancel the name, in justice. "What don't you like about her? Of course she's got up a bit and she runs on a bit—but that's only the fashion. She's really rather a good soul, and she has a lot of guts, too."

"I see them only too plainly," I said. "But I suppose stays are out of date, like my prejudices."

John smiled and answered that Gladys did not need stays; her figure was so good. "She's always in first-class condition, as I dare say you've noticed. She does her exercises three times a day."

I met him everywhere with Gladys, even at Julie's. I had not wished John to know Julie. He met her only by accident one day when I had taken her to the theater. And I did not introduce them. But he asked me about her, and insisted on calling. And then it appeared that he knew very well in what relation she stood to me; that all the family were aware of it. He charmed Julie and he was charmed by her.

"You can see," he said, "that she was magnificent in her great days," and I could not tell him that Julie had had no great days, and that she seemed to me much deteriorated from her little days.

Julie, during the war, had worked with enthusiasm at a soldiers' club, serving in the canteen, and also giving little recitations, etc. And she was still visited by the many friends, among all ranks, whom she had made. She kept open house, and she was drinking too much. And when she found herself misunderstood, or even robbed, she would say, "Anything I can do for these boys is not too much. How could it be?"

And in these words so calmly spoken one felt something mysterious and false. Falseness now seemed to be taking possession of Julie. It peeped from the most unexpected corners, as bats and rats suddenly show their whiskers in the crannies of palaces too long unused.

The rich material was there, the dignity, the sincerity, but all began to seem meaningless and therefore tawdry; as palace velvets, when the palace becomes a show for trippers, begin at once to look like plush. The slender tragic actress had changed into a theatrical poser, who was apt to give a little performance at certain cues, such as the words friendship, courage, loyalty. And like all such performers on the carpet, without her lime-lights, she seemed amateurish. What John took for the grand manner of a former age was simply the flummery of any age.

And she made such a fuss about John that I was ashamed for her.

Now, to my astonishment, I saw her offering the same attentions to Gladys, who, for her part, lay on Julie's sofa most of the evening, her feet in the air, her skirt to her thighs, smoking thirty cigarettes, drinking half a dozen whiskies and telling us about her boys, how often they had tried to rape her, how nearly they had succeeded, how she had got rid of some of the others, who were too dull, or ugly, or poor, or who didn't know enough to attempt a rape.

All this time John sat by, looking from Gladys to us with the expression of one who says, "Admire this wonder—"

I did not know whether to be more amazed that John should bring a girl whom he at least thought respectable to visit a kept woman or outraged by her manner to Julie.

I could barely keep my temper until the pair had left, before I asked Julie how she could endure such conduct. "What are you thinking of—allowing John to bring that nasty little beast here and encouraging her to behave like that?"

"She is indeed a horrible little creature," Julie answered. "But she is a friend of John's and I owe it to him to make his friends welcome."

"Nonsense; we owe it to him to open his eyes about Gladys."

"I hope you won't be so foolish as to interfere between John and one of his girls," Julie said. "They'll only laugh at you—or perhaps stop coming here. And I don't want to lose John's friendship."

"Laugh at me," I said; "let them." But I was angry with Julie, and I exclaimed, "Really, Julie, you are getting flabby. What is the good of us if we don't stand by what we believe? Do you think it is a good thing for girls to paint their faces like the lowest strumpets and go about in short skirts or even short trousers and drink and swear like bargees?" etc., etc. "We may be old fogies," I said, "but we have some standards and I am not going to desert them simply because they happen to excite amusement among a few ill-taught children."

And I spoke to John, who, as I had expected, took it very well and apologized for the girl. "She was a little tight, of course—but she had no idea of being rude to Aunt Julie—she admires her tremendously," and so on.

The idea that this sensible boy might be so stupid as to marry Gladys had never entered my head until Amy came to me one afternoon at the office. "Have you seen this girl that John is in love with?"

"In love? He didn't tell you that he was in love."

"No, but he is," Amy said. She looked so solid, so stupefied that I perceived her desperation.

"Rubbish. Have you seen the creature?"

"Yes, I met them at luncheon. John invited her to the flat. He's bringing her to Tolbrook on Monday, to see Edward."

"All that means nothing, Amy. You don't understand these young people nowadays—they form all kinds of friendships, without the least intention of marriage."

"I don't think she likes me, either," meaning apparently that the luncheon party had not been a success.

"You needn't be worried," I said. "John has had plenty of girls. But I'll give him a hint, if you like."

Amy was persuaded at last to go home. But she had made me nervous. I began to reflect on the imbecility of young men with girls. And by the next day I was in a panic. I went down early to Tolbrook to obtain Edward's help in this dangerous crisis. "Of course," I said, "there's no question of an entanglement, but the girl is a bad friend for the boy. She encourages him to be casual. And you might let John see what you think of her. You have a lot of influence in that quarter."

123

Edward had remained in uniform for a long time after the war. He had some post in the local demobilization office. Perhaps he had liked to feel that he belonged, even in so small a way, to administration. But now for some months he had been retired; and he had already fitted up his study behind the stairs, where I now write. He had decided to give himself to literary work, an autobiography, a political history of the last thirty years. All of us, especially my mother, encouraged him in his ambition, saying that it was exactly suited to his capacity. But Lottie had refused to come back to him, and, what was unexpected, he seemed astonished by this blow. He would not even speak of it, and when my mother, with that humor which still flashed amid the ruin of her mind, like a jewel among debris, would say, "Our princess is still looking for her red carpet, I suppose," he was visibly wounded.

My mother had looked forward with delight to Edward's return. The little old woman, now so bent with rheumatism, and so diminutive that even among us who were not tall she seemed like a dwarf, once more showed a kind of coquettish gaiety. She seemed to flirt with Edward, and uttered those little ecstatic cries which we had not heard for many years. But this excited happiness made me nervous and alarmed Edward. I was used to think of my mother as a saint, troublesome in her unworldliness but always to be respected. I did not like to see her behaving without dignity. And Edward was wounded by her jokes.

She herself soon realized that he was uneasy in her company. She said to me one evening, when I read for her those last prayers without which she would not face the night, "Edward has grown very touchy these days. Have I said anything to hurt his lordship's feelings?"

"Perhaps, Mama, he wouldn't like to hear you say that."

She answered with wonder, "But does he really mind what I say?"

"Yes, I think he does. You see, he feels that he has disappointed us all."

"But I'm not disappointed in him. I think he is much nicer since he left politics. I could never bear that Chamberlain man." My mother was speaking of the radical Chamberlain of forty years ago.

"He thinks you laugh at him."

"So I do, but surely a mother may laugh at her own baby—her eldest." She thought for a moment and said, "But I must be more careful. I shouldn't like to hurt the poor darling." And within five minutes, when Edward came to say good night, I heard her say to him, "And so our Prime Minister has torn himself away from the cabinet." She called Edward's new room the cabinet.

Edward paid only duty visits to his mother's room. And

after a few protests to me, a few exclamations of surprise and pain, she accepted this new deprivation. She said only once, "It is strange for us both to be lonely in the same house." And looking at her then, with the great bony orbits of her eyes, like those of a skull, I thought I had never seen a face more sad and more resigned.

And even then I thought only, "It is sad to be old and weak and troublesome." I did not perceive for many years the long slow tragedy of a woman, obliged to accept the niche that her children, thoughtless enough, had made for her; and to live in it, as life prisoners live in a cell. But that, I dare say, is the common fate of women like my mother, whose very love makes them feel guilty because they could never satisfy its demands, whose pride of soul prevents them from complaint or self-pity. They are the proudest and the humblest of creatures; the most lonely and the most self-reliant. To her dying day my mother discharged those duties which she had laid upon herself; visits, a correspondence which often kept her up half the night; personal charities, the accounts which were always wrongly added. I do not suppose she thought of herself as an unlucky woman, who had married the wrong man and had a family as strange to her breeding as young wild cats to a Persian.

124

My mother never became an eccentric. If she could not sleep she lay patiently in her bed, or read a book. She was too considerate of others, too proud, to give way to singularity. But Edward, in his loneliness, soon fell into strange habits. He would spend half the night walking, or even driving, across the lanes and over the moor roads. Shepherds and the cowmen going out to first milking were startled by the sudden appearance of a horse and trap coming down from the moor, with reins dragging and the driver sound asleep in his seat, held from falling only by his driver's apron.

When they waked him and warned him of his danger he would always deny that he had been asleep, and then, addressing them by name, ask after their families and speak of the beauties of the moor at this time of the morning.

Edward had that art, so necessary to a politician, of remembering faces and names, even for twenty years, after a single meeting.

"But you do go to sleep," I told him. "And it's very dangerous."

"Of course I do, but it's the only sleep I get," and he changed the subject. He could not endure any talk about himself.

"My health is excellent," he would say. "This is just the life that suits me. I can get on at last with some real work."

"Your history?"

"That and perhaps a novel or so. No one has written a real political novel—giving the real feel of politics. The French try to be funny or clever, and the English are too moral and abstract. You don't get the sense of real politics, of people feeling their way; of moles digging frantically about to dodge some unknown noise overhead; of worms all driving down simultaneously because of some change in the weather. or rising gaily up again because some scientific gardener has spread the right poison mixture. You don't get the sense of limitation and confusion, of walking on a slack wire over an unseen gulf by a succession of lightning flashes. Then the ambitious side is always done so badly. Plenty of men in politics have no political ambition; they want to defend something, to get some reform—it's as simple as that. But then they are simple people, too, and it is the simple men who complicate the situation. Yes, a real political novel would be worth doing. I should like to do for politics what Tolstoy has done for war—show what a muddle and confusion it is, and that it must always be a muddle and confusion where good men are wasted and destroyed simply by luck as by a chance bullet." And then he said to me, "I'm not referring to myself." Edward was extremely quick to know another's mind and I had been thinking, "Poor Edward, he was knocked down by such a bullet."

He smiled and said, "My case was rather different. I retired from the stage too soon, or too late, as you prefer. Like most circus performers and prima donnas. Like most people, in fact."

But during the daytime, at least, he seemed to work with purpose, and affected a strict routine. Breakfast at nine, correspondence till eleven, with a secretary from Queensport, work afterwards. At half-past four Ann, dressed in her smartest frock, was brought down to his room for tea. And he would receive her with that affectionate grace which he always showed to women until he knew them too well. He placed a chair for her, stood till she was seated, and adjusted her cushions.

It was her duty to preside, to pour out the tea. When I was of the party, I could not bear to see the child's nervous anxiety, both at her entry and during the meal. Her fingers trembled so much that the cups rattled while she lifted them; and sometimes the milk flew in drops out of the jug. But Edward would say, "Why do they always fill milk jugs too full?"

The child would answer, "It wasn't too full; it was my fault"—with indignation against herself.

Edward would make conversation suitable to the occasion, about her walks, her lessons. But soon forgetting himself he would depart from lesson-book history.

"Yes, but we don't really know anything about Alfred's politics. The fact is, all made-up history is nonsense. You want to go to sources, especially letters and memoirs. What a tragedy that so much of them are lost. Why do men like Creevey leave their papers to their women—wives or mistresses, it seems to come to the same thing. A woman who has lived with a man always sees him under the same species, Homo, uxorious, carnivorous. She can never conceive that in the world's eyes he may have a different value."

All this would embarrass me for the child's sake and I would try to remind Edward of her presence. "All this is not very interesting for Ann."

"Of course it is," Edward would say. "Ann understands these things as well as anybody. Don't you, sweetheart?" with a smile which made the child color. And she would answer, "Yes, please, Daddy, do go on," and turn paler than before, in terror of some question which would reveal her ignorance. Yet once when Edward forgot an appointed teatime, and had gone out walking in the fields, I found Ann at six o'clock, in her best frock, with the table still spread and nothing touched, in such a passion of tears that I thought she would do herself an injury.

I tried to comfort her. "My dear child, I expect your father will be in soon now. Let me ring for some fresh tea."

"No, it's too late. He won't want it now."

"Then let us have some."

"But you've had yours in Queensport."

"You must have some then."

"No, I couldn't." And then, controlling herself, she got up and said sedately, "It was my mistake. I got the day wrong. I must go and do my prep, if you'll excuse me, uncle."

She never allowed the least reflection on Edward. And when sometimes he remembered to say good night to her, she would for once forget that strong anxiety which weighed upon her whole life. Then I saw her face smoothed of all its unchildish lines. Nothing showed then but an abounding, eager love and she would throw her arms round his neck with abandon.

125

Edward agreed with me that no other single cause was more influential in a man's life than his marriage. Nothing more disastrous than a bad one. And he promised to support me against Gladys.

And when Gladys and John arrived, and I presented the girl, he made occasion to remark that politics was like marriage, those who were out wanted to get in, and those who were in complained bitterly of its slavery. "But we do not take them too seriously."

"But surely," John said, "you are glad to get out of that gang?"

"I like to pretend so. I assume the graceful attitude of the man who has just been thrown out of the window."

Edward and John were old friends with tastes in common. And while they were quoting Horace and Catullus, I saw Gladys' greedy, cunning eyes, looking from one to the other with that expression which, in a woman's face, means "What fools, what bores—when are they going to look at me?"

And she broke in loudly, "Poor little me, my education stopped at English."

Edward smiled and bowed. "Who said that the world is women's book? I always thought it would be better to say, a charming woman's book. For the world opens itself to charm, but it's apt to close up before a red nose or a fish mouth." Edward, in paying a compliment, had the fashion of the earlier time. He embedded it in a little speech which gave it general value and prevented it from embarrassment to the receiver. My father had used to say bluntly, "You're looking well today, never saw you prettier."

I had heard John say to Gladys, "Hullo, piece, you look like a virgin in the desert—meaning the cocktail."

Apparently the young woman preferred the new style for

she said to Edward in her loud, raucous voice, "Is that a short way to tell me I'm a mess?"

"Not at all. Quite the reverse." And Edward, instantly adapting himself to her outlook, took the young lady by the forearm and said, "You are far from a mess, as you know very well. I really think I must cut John out."

"That wouldn't be hard," said she, grinning and becoming all at once soft and flexible; so that she seemed about to fall into Edward's arms. "But what a naughty man it is. You've had some, I can see that—thousands, I suppose."

"Not at all—I have been only too lucky at cards."

And he began to flirt outrageously with the girl, who ended by sitting on his knee and ruffling his hair, etc. "Here's to Ted and to hell with John—too bloody pleased with himself, anyhow. All right, John, you think it's funny to see me get off. But you wait."

John in fact was laughing at the scene. Every moment he turned his eyes toward me as if to say, "What a child it is— how charming." And on Edward's face I saw the same smile, forty years older.

But, what was strange, neither was cynical. In both, so like each other except that Edward had the more regular features, one saw the same good-natured indulgence. And again, in the midst of my impatience with Edward, I felt that sense of a disease, creeping through all veins, of every age and sex. And I brought up the subject of the corruption of the time. "These night clubs—did you see that last prosecution—and they say Berlin is worse."

I had hoped that Gladys would now show her true colors, and I was successful. She laughed and said, "Nunky is shocked at us."

"Yes," Edward said, "unless he is envious of us."

"But why must this corruption overwhelm the whole of Europe at once?"

"It is always so after a war—people want a holiday, or perhaps I should say an unholy day."

"But is that true? This gloomy corruption, this moral defeatism, the exaltation of selfishness can't give much pleasure," etc. I saw them smiling at me, but I was all the more determined to make my point. Gladys jumped off Edward's knee, put an arm round my neck, kissed me, and said, "You're just right, old dear. We're a bad naughty lot—but we do get some fun. And if we didn't, someone else would."

"True," Edward said. "One doesn't like to miss one's share, even of headaches."

Tea was brought in and Ann entered the room in her stiff old-fashioned frock. I saw her look at Gladys with a kind of horror. She had never before seen a painted face. They were still unknown in our neighborhood.

Gladys, for her part, showed that contemptuous indifference toward Ann which I had noticed in girls of her age and time. She had, in her own words, "no use for children."

Edward made Gladys a bow and said, "The bride will pour out for us."

"The bride—here, what are you getting at? Do I look so bedded? Well, I warned John."

Gladys, who seldom laughed, but often smiled, with much good humor, now smiled upon us all as if to say, "We're all friends here, aren't we?" Then she sat down at the tea table and Ann retreated to the farthest corner of the room.

I asked Ann afterwards what she thought of Gladys, meaning to warn the child against so bad an example. But Ann said only, "She's from London, isn't she?" She seemed, as usual, to be storing knowledge for use.

"I hope you will never paint yourself like that."

"I wonder where she gets it?"

And I dared say no more. For, I asked myself, "Is there any door by which this corruption cannot enter, even into a child's mind, by way of her serious and candid respect for knowledge?"

126

It was useless being angry with Edward, as irresponsible as John himself. And in my alarm I saw nothing for it but a direct attack. I wrote and told John that Gladys would be the worst possible wife for a lawyer, and happening, on the next day, to meet Gladys herself in the vestibule of the office, when she was waiting for John, I asked her if she did not think John was staying too late and drinking too much. "You mean no harm," I said, "but you are doing harm. The boy is not giving his mind to his work."

She merely gazed at me with a blank face and half-open mouth, an arrogant pose which means in such persons "What is this freak?"

"I suppose you think I have no business to interfere," I said, "but John is my godson, and I don't want to see him ruin his life before it's well started."

Then suddenly she became animated, jerked her shoulders one way, her behind the other, laughed in my face, and said, "That's all right, Uncle Lucifer. You needn't be afraid for your precious infant—it's not John would be ruined if we clicked," and she told me she wouldn't dream of marrying a man who couldn't afford even to keep a car.

The strange appellation, Lucifer, startled me so much that I did not know how to answer. It was only afterwards, from Julie, that I discovered it to be a reference to my legs, or rather trousers. My good city tailor quite agreed with my dislike of seeing men drape their legs in two skirts, and my trousers were cut on the old manly basis, to show the limb. The infantile mind of Gladys had found this reasonable fashion, or rather principle, amusing; and she was accustomed to refer to me as Lucifer legs, or more formally as Uncle Lucifer.

And before I thought of some suitable comment on her statement, that marriage, in her view, was simply a question of cheap motoring, John came downstairs; she blew me a kiss and said, "Take care of them, Nunky, London wouldn't be London without them," and walked off on John's arm.

1 2 7

I hear people talk of the modern girl, the new generation and so forth, but two women more difficult than Gladys and Ann can't be imagined. Is it wrong to suppose that young people like John and Gladys, brought up among the slogans, etc., of war, grew up different from those like Ann and Robert, in the next generation, who began to think for themselves among the confused problems which started up on every side with the peace?

When Lottie sent for Ann in 1920, to go on a visit, I remember the child's pale set face as Edward and I saw her off, with her nurse, at the station. She had not seen her mother for three years and knew nothing of her. She was leaving the father whom she worshipped. But she did not cry. I suppose she had already learned, in that time so hard for children, that tears were unpopular. Grown-ups had no time for consolation. She seemed only to shrink, to grow thinner and more fragile, more plain, as she stood holding Edward's hand; and when she had kissed him, for the last time in her life, she turned away quickly and climbed into the carriage as if in flight.

But even then she did not cry. As the train moved, I saw the narrow, pale oval face, as white as paper, behind the window glass, and the peculiar intensity of her look at Edward. She was frowning as if to concentrate on something that she could not grasp. She was not sure, even then, that she had enough of him to remember. I suppose for all her love of Edward she had never come very near to comprehending him. And now I see that concentrated frown again when the woman stands before some new task, some new problem. Yesterday it was the question of breaking up some fallow; or rather, the question whether Farley's advice was to be trusted. Today, at luncheon, she said to me abruptly, "Molly's going to have a baby."

"What Molly?"

"Robert's Molly. Robert wrote this morning."

I was shocked. For I had always hoped for a reconciliation between the young couple. "Then I suppose you will have to divorce him."

"Yes, but this baby must have started here—three months before Robert went off with the girl."

"I'm not surprised—you practically invited him to go off with her." For I was much upset by the idea of this divorce.

"I never thought Robert could do such a thing—I wonder where they did it."

"Robert has behaved badly, but so have you—I can't think how you could be so stupid—throwing away a good husband like that."

"A good husband?"

"He might have been a very good husband. He had a sense of duty—that's the main thing. But of course you don't believe in nonsense like a sense of duty. You never found it in your test tubes," etc. An unfortunate speech which I have regretted.

But Ann answered only, "Yes, I suppose I wouldn't take high marks on men."

"The only thing you seem to understand are textbooks which are always stuffed with nonsense," but seeing then her look of anxious perplexity, her pinched cheeks and troubled eyes, I felt sorry for the child, and told her that on the whole I blamed Robert more severely, etc. Which was not true, but perhaps justifiable in the circumstances.

But she is still, three days later, pondering day and night. You can see the questions passing round and round her brain, like colored chemicals in an apparatus. "How did Robert do such a thing—whose fault was it? Shall I never get to the bottom of all this?"

And so her predecessor, the little girl of ten, looked at her father eighteen years ago. Edward, as I noticed as we came home, had a look merely of surprise and resignation. He had not expected this blow to hurt so much. He did not ask why he had suffered it. But, in fact, one can say that the loss of wife and child killed the man. He had not seen Lottie for four years, and he had paid little attention to Ann at Tolbrook; but when Lottie now asked for her divorce, and for Ann, he gave up all pretense of a desire to live and to work. I urged him to fight at least for Ann, but he answered, "What sort of a father have I made? No, it isn't my role."

He ceased even to read, and spent whole days strolling about the grounds, or sitting, almost motionless, in his chair. When I told him that he ought to be finishing his book, he would answer, "It's not worth finishing. Amateur stuff. I know enough to know that I don't know enough. Even the foundations have shifted. And I'm too old to begin a new education."

"You're not old at sixty-three, Edward."

"We don't make old bones, as a family—we live too much on our nerves and senses. And there's nothing so aging as failure. Why, I can hardly get round the lake; and look at my fingers, stiff and swelling in every joint. *Dégommé.* To come unstuck. The perfect word."

He was sitting in his room, and though it was September he had a fire in the grate. His thin body had always felt the cold.

"But Edward, don't you think it is a pity for people to talk so much about earthquakes and avalanches and so on—it's only the sensational newspapers and the politicians, translated into schoolboy Byronism. It's just something to say—"

I spoke with warmth because I had just been discussing this subject with John, during the week in London. And I had been struck as well as pleased to find that John had agreed with me.

Indeed, I was enjoying at that time, in my renewed friendship with John, a resurrection of hope and enterprise. I had instituted in the office the new reform of wearing short coats; and also of typing instead of engraving our wills, bringing us up to date in both respects. And with John, I was on the closest terms of intimacy. We would even discuss Gladys and agree that, in spite of certain good qualities, she was not a suitable wife for a lawyer, in a firm of our standing. And, what had surprised me, Gladys bore me no malice for my intervention. She seemed to treat the whole affair as a joke, comparable with my trousers, collar, waistcoat, etc., in which she never ceased to find amusement. She would greet me as "Uncle Spider," and ask me how I got my feet through "them." "Or perhaps you start at the bottom and go to the top instead of from the top to the bottom," and I would smile at these mild but rather vulgar jokes in order to preserve the harmony of our band.

"I don't think," I said to Edward, "that young men of sense (meaning, of course, John) are fairly represented in the newspapers—they're not so silly. It's only the half-educated—the class that does swallow print, who talk about a futile world," etc.

"A large class," Edward said, "perhaps the majority. Yes, it's interesting to see how revolutions actually come about—how they cast their shadow before them—no, not a shadow"—Edward visibly elaborated the material for a couplet—"a bar of heat. It's as if a furnace door has been opened—the furnace where new societies are forged, and the heat at once begins to melt everything, even a long way from it, things which will not be ready for the crucibles for a long time—ideas, institutions, laws, political parties, they all begin to lose their firmness."

I had often heard Edward on this subject. He had thought to

see the same process twenty years before, and I was about to remind him of the fact. But I remembered suddenly an old couplet of his:

> Men, women, laws relax. When Angelo doffed
> His coat, they say, the waiting stone turned soft.

And suddenly the idea came home to me and I was frightened. It seemed that the very ground grew thin beneath me, and everything about me began to change form, to dissolve. As if there were an infection of change in the very walls, books, and Edward's bent figure, white hair, and hollow cheeks.

Edward tapped the bars with his poker; outside it was growing dusk, but his curtains were not drawn, and a warm breeze languidly moved their folds and made a tassel swing against the pane. They were still cutting in some field across the paddock, and the reaper as it circled made a regular crescendo, from the sound of a distant bee to the noise of a stick rattled on a fence. The voices of the boys and young women who were putting up the stooks, or stitches as we call them, came through on the lazy wind like the last social chirping of birds at twilight when they have stopped feeding and think of finding their roosts.

It was the kind of evening when, at one time, I had loved to be at home. But already I was assailed by a thousand anxieties, the fear of rain which might damage my harvest, the wretched prices for corn. And the voices of the boys reminded me only of a most impudent robbery, in the last week, of all the pears, still green, on one of my best trees. I thought at the same moment, "That binder hasn't been paid for; those boys are getting worse every year, regular young criminals; this breeze smells of thunder; has Farley yet had the thatcher on the wheat stacks?" And at the same time, curtain, binder, boys, stacks, even the wind seemed to fade, by Edward's talk, into the mere colors and sounds of some mysterious historical play.

"All that is very pretty," I said suddenly, in a voice so loud that I startled myself. "But it is only simile," and so on. "What exactly is this mysterious process of what-do-you-call-it, melting, softening?"

"I suppose it is simply expectation of a new order," Edward said. And I thought he was enjoying himself, as always in an abstract inquiry. "It is an intelligent anticipation of the wrath to come. But, of course, it affects people differently—Julie sentimentalizes, and John, it appears, marks time, or perhaps he has simply withdrawn gracefully. Every revolution has that handicap—that as soon as it starts a lot of the best brains in the country go out of commission—I mean those with independent judgment, the really scholarly and scientific brains, the ones that a revolution needs above every other."

"John has been slow to settle down—it's only natural after all the excitement of a war."

"No, he is standing aside. People like John feel that they aren't wanted—that there's no place for them among the turmoil, the chatter, the spite, and the nonsense of all sorts—he was born to serve some independent truth—he could have made a first-class researcher or scientist," and so on. I listened, but I could not attend because the binder had stopped and the voices out there in the field were all talking at once. "It's broken down again," I thought. "That means that the barley won't be finished tonight—" and I kept on saying to Edward, "There's something in that perhaps," or "All this is based on a premise that I don't accept," but I was actually distracted. And the end of it was that I could bear suspense no longer. I jumped up, took my hat and umbrella, and hurried down the field. Great raindrops were already falling. The sky over my head was dark blue. The sulphur-colored clouds that I had seen from the window rushing eastward occupied only half the sky, on the east. I walked, therefore, in the bright evening sun, and the tumult of the clouds, which looked like a mass of troops and people in headlong retreat through huge rollers of dust and smoke, resembled a moving picture. The wind had dropped, the leaves stood motionless; I was surrounded by an immediate silence so deep that the falling drops sounded as loud and startling as bullets, and their drops fell from no visible cloud; out of the blue sky. But when I looked closely at this sky, it seemed unnaturally dark and thick, the blue of wood smoke.

I thought every moment, "Now it is going to break." And as I do not like thunder and was fearful that the lightning might strike the steel point of my umbrella, I hesitated whether to go back to shelter or forward to the binder. But my feet decided for me. They carried me forward at a round pace, and on consideration I approved their resolution. It was no time to avoid a plain duty.

The thunder did not break. Instead, the drops increased in number and suddenly became a flood. The trees, the hedges, and the fields, the sky itself and all its gesticulating silent mobs wavered like reflections in a stream, suddenly touched by a breeze, and then dissolved into an air which was largely water. I found myself alone among warm cataracts, with no distinction of material for the senses except the variety of noise: the dashing of leaves, the roar of boughs, the hissing of a copse, the rustle of hedges, the tinkle of drains. Which proved so delusive that in the thickened twilight I lost my way and found myself walking in the stubble, mixed with new clover, of a field already cut; an accident not surprising on such an evening. But now of such bewildering effect that, as I stood, with every clover leaf pouring its waterfall into my boots, I felt as if the very earth were liquefying under my feet, as if the familiar trees, fields, and sky had actually melted into some primitive elementary form, and that the world of German philosophy, in which everything can be anything else, as the philosopher pleases, had actually realized itself in a universal nothingness, whose very color was uncertain. And I, the very last individual being of the old creation, though still solid in appearance, and capable of supporting a hat, as I ascertained by touch, trousers, umbrella, etc., as I perceived by sight, was yet already wavering in essence, beginning to lose the shape of my ideas, memory, etc., preparatory to the final and rapid solution of my whole identity.

I do not mean, of course, that I continued in such a delusion. It was the weakness of a passing second. Yet it caused me to feel again how insecure are those chains of assumption by which we conduct our lives; how easily broken; how necessary to be anchored to a faith which, being of the mind and the spirit and so forth, can defy the corruption of sense and the shims of fashion.

As the rain thinned to the consistency of a shower bath, I recognized the field and in the same instant saw a corn stack in front of me. The oats. Only half-covered with a worn-out rick cloth.

"That will cost me fifty pounds at least!" I thought, and went to find my manager. But he, as usual, had a dozen good excuses, of which the chief was the invariable one, that I didn't provide enough rick cloths.

"Why, then, didn't you thatch?"

"Well, sir, it didn't seem worth while when we were threshing next week." A nice young man, whose very politeness and genteel accent seemed to say to me, "Why worry—especially about the oats?"

128

My mother died in her sleep, and it turned out that she had left everything to Bill's children; nothing to Amy. Apparently she thought of Amy as provided for by Bill, and her pension. John, therefore, received three thousand pounds.

Gladys at once proposed to marry him. John, I thought, had been cured of Gladys, and his reception of her proposal assured me of it. He told me that he didn't think it would work.

"Of course it wouldn't work—she would drive you mad with her noisy sillyness."

"It's not that—but she's used to a lot of attention and a good deal of society. And I've got my exams. I can't really spare the time for honeymooning."

A month later he married Gladys in a registry office and invested his legacy in a small motor-repair works belonging to one of her friends. She obtained the use of half a dozen cars by this master stroke. The works were in a small and dismal village near Birmingham.

John, since Gladys did not like housekeeping, took the upper part of a house there, and Amy went with the couple as housekeeper.

I found John dawdling through a few hours' work a week, in which he had no interest whatever. Gladys was out motoring all day with her young men. Amy alone seemed completely happy and useful, cooking, shopping, and even scrubbing for the household. She was obviously puzzled by Gladys, but gave her warm praise. "She's not a bit jealous—I see John as much as I like."

I asked the boy how on earth he had come to marry Gladys. And he answered vaguely, "I'd gone about with her a lot and she seemed to want it."

"Good heavens! Is that a good reason for throwing away your life; and I thought you were taking so much interest in the law."

"Well, uncle, I suppose it's not very certain that the law will go on much longer, I mean in its present form. Or the estates we look after."

And having, in this one phrase, demolished the ancient and

majestic structure of English law and English property rights, he added, "But, of course, everything is a bit shaky just now."

Of John's two partners, one Gladys' friend, a middle-aged man who had already made a war fortune, did not appear at the works more than once a week, for a few hours. The other, a young man, like John, lately demobilized, was working twelve hours a day, but drinking all night. He was a great red-faced boy, his eyes already bloodshot with drink.

"Five years of this," he said, "and I'll be able to do something worth while."

"What do you want to do?"

"Copra. In the South Seas. Get away from all this. Have my own schooner. But I wish you'd get that fella John to pull his weight. He always gets his nose in a book. Too much bed work, too. That bitch Gladys gives me a bad pain."

Two months later the slump ruined the firm and both the partners. The red-faced boy shot himself. John became a motor salesman in a London firm; and Gladys took work in a fashionable flower shop. She was said to be popular with young men, and out of hours she always had the use of some young man's pocket and car. On one occasion she and two young men were arrested for insulting behavior, in a small country village, and it was shown that all three had been sharing a room at the inn. John went down to bail them out. But when I expressed to John my horror at this wretched life, without sense or order, he answered with his usual cheerful nonchalance, "But have we done so badly, considering?"

"Considering what?"

"Oh, everything. We've never been actually on the rocks and, of course, Glady is a trump—when we're stuck, she just turns to—"

"Are you going on all your life like this, living from hand to mouth, in a flat; don't you want some family life, children?"

"Well, things are a bit uncertain, aren't they, and I don't

think Gladys is particularly keen on children. She'd rather keep her job."

And sometimes I grew angry with him. "You're a drifter, John. You're getting nowhere. And you could have made a career for yourself, you could have been somebody."

"Well, I suppose they also serve who only stand and sell—though of course dustmen take a higher place. I often feel I ought to be a dustman and do a really civic job."

The country flat had consisted of three rooms. But in town they had only two. I entered one day upon a ludicrous scene. Amy was lying in the sitting room upon a couch much too short even for her short figure. She resembled a very large blue skittle with a red knob, balanced miraculously on the top of pink sausage. Gladys and John were looking at her, the first with the expression of one who examines a doubtful cod in a fishmonger's; the second with embarrassment. Amy turned her head from one to the other. "It would do very well—I'm perfectly comfortable."

"You don't look comfortable."

The question was, could Amy sleep in the sitting room. I said at once that it was impossible for Amy to sleep on that couch. I was outraged by such a suggestion. Amy, after all, was Bill's widow.

"That's what I say, Nunky," Gladys said. "She'd stick out both ends and get double pneumonia in her feet."

But Amy was indignant. "I used to sleep on much smaller beds in India. I'm quite comfortable." And thinking perhaps that her appearance lying down was not a good argument for the couch, she put her feet to the ground, sat up and looked at us. I was struck by her intense anxiety, which seemed rather comical in the circumstances. With her round face, her little round forehead deeply marked with orderly wrinkles, her fixed gazing eyes, she might have been a portrait of desperation carved by a Dutch dollmaker.

And yet, as I observed with surprise, Amy had somewhere found a real dignity which, at this unfavorable moment, or because of it, was somehow revealed to me. It consisted perhaps only in resignation to the blows of fate, and a flat back.

Her desperation, so comical to me, suddenly acquired some excuse. For now, to my surprise, Gladys said, "Then that settles it—we couldn't fit a bigger couch into this dog kennel."

John and I protested with force. I at once measured the floor with my umbrella, which was exactly one yard in length, with inches nicked on the handle. I have all my umbrellas made to this pattern, which has shown its worth in many a family discussion.

So I proved now that there was room for a six-foot couch in the window.

"We'll get a box couch," John said.

"And where shall I keep anything without the cupboard?" Gladys asked.

"We can have a couch with a drawer and put the pillows there."

"Then we'll all be living in our drawers, unless I park my frocks in the car and sleep with Doggie." Doggie was one of her friends.

Amy said that she couldn't put Gladys out, to which Gladys answered that, on the whole, she would quite enjoy a change of husband.

John now proposed to look for a three-room flat. "If you can find the rent," Gladys said. And, of course, the end of it was Amy's expulsion. The wife in such a case has the last word. And Gladys had long resolved to get rid of Amy. She was tired, so she confided to Julie, of hearing her think about John.

I do not know if I understood the nature of Amy's disaster. I remember that I was desperately worried just then, by the financial situation, the bills, the taxes, the cost of repairs at Tolbrook, and the whims of a new housekeeper. I could not ask

Amy to Tolbrook, because of this housekeeper's strange condition of temper. But I had the grace to take her to the station.

Her belongings seemed to be reduced to one trunk and a string bag, and when I asked her if she had no more, she answered, "I had to cut down a bit. There wasn't room in John's flat. It's rather a blessing when one's on the move."

"Where are you going?"

"I thought of Broadstairs."

"You know someone at Broadstairs?"

"No; I've never been there—but Mrs. Johnson, she's the widow of Bill's first colonel, has given me the address of a boardinghouse; she says it gives the best value on the coast."

"A rash statement," I suggested.

"Well," Amy said, "she's been a widow for twenty years—you'll write to me sometimes, won't you, Tom—about Johnny? He's never been a very good writer himself."

129

Edward caught a mild influenza that winter which quickly developed into pneumonia. He seemed to have made up his mind that he was to die. Yet he was more cheerful than he had been for years; he chaffed his doctors when they told him he was in no danger; he flirted with his nurses. And on the last morning of his life he congratulated me. "You knew what you wanted, Tommy, and you made for it, from the beginning. It's the only way. The new age can only use specialists."

"But, Edward, you can't compare my work with yours. You have made history. I have been a small cog in the machine."

"You gripped something. I hit the air."

He died unconscious the same night. And when I was sorting and bundling his papers, among a mass of unfinished work, I found these verses:

Life tragic to the soul; to mind a joke
Now tragi-comic, gives its cruelest stroke.
Grief for the dead, tho' sharper it returns;
That grief which only grief, by grief, relearns,
Tempers the heart in which it beats and burns.
But that comedian who sold comic truth
For laughs, and missed the laugh; age playing youth
To seem a doting fool; those heroes' scars
Who shot themselves in aiming at the stars
Of glass, third class, can find no anodyne
Hurt pride in its own pride still seeks to pine;
Self-ridicule puts poison on the knife
And leaves a wound that festers all your life.
Now dead ambition which no rot can sink
Bloats on the soul corrupting in its stink;
Not time destroys the old but creeping spite
For all they fought for, in a bungled fight.
For fame along the street, June's summer gush
Choking the sun with gilt, the leaves with plush,
For triumphs lost which won would still be mean—
They die of laughing at their might have been.

I had read them again in the last month when I handed to
Ann for her father's biography all that material which I had
kept against the day when posterity might do him justice. Today when I went to Edward's writing table, so neatly arranged,
I found them in the rejected basket under the samples of oil
cake, twine, and seed which have now begun to appear among
Ann's correspondence.

"Why don't you like those verses?" I asked her, when she
came in to see if tea had been brought to me, and to make up
my fire.

She took the paper by the tip of one finger and thumb in
her hand, which was her chief beauty. Not so small as her

mother's, but with those tapered fingers and smooth joints which very small hands rarely possess. I saw now not only that the hand was dirty from some farmyard work but that the skin of the fingertips was cracked and the fingernails were broken.

Ann put the paper close to her shortsighted eyes, read, frowned, and said, "A little too fussy, don't you think; it sounds as if he took it all too seriously. I don't want people to think that about him."

"Ah, of course, our times were not very serious." I spoke with irony.

"Yes, it will have to be a period piece—to get the proportions right."

"A period piece, for Edward—"

"All that old politics looks so small from this end of the telescope—and when politics gets to look small, it looks mean, too. But poor Daddy wasn't mean—no, it's rather tricky."

"My dear child, your father was a century before his time. That was his tragedy. Even his supporters thought him extreme—he used to talk about abolishing marriage."

"Yes, that's what I mean. That's how they used to think. I shall have to look up the early Communists, too."

She put down the paper and called through the window, "Farley, Mr. Brown says I'm quite right about those milk records and I want them tonight." She went out, saying angrily that if Farley pretended to be deaf it would be a good excuse to get rid of him.

Ann does not seem to find it odd that her correspondence about the divorce should include bulletins about the farming at Tolbrook and almost continuous advice from Robert.

Edward's verses were still lying where she had left them weighted down with a sample packet of a new sheep-dip; and I felt that not only Edward but I too was receding into a past which was irrecoverable. I looked round at the little room and before my eyes it seemed to change from Edward's familiar study into a museum piece, detached even from Tolbrook by its new paint and its old books, so carefully revarnished.

To Ann, I am a museum piece. I can't tell whether she guards me from Blanche and from Sara, from all those agitations of the outer world, because she sets some value on my life or because she has a sense of duty. Probably her motives are not only unknown to me but beyond my comprehension.

We can understand new ideas in the world, but we cannot share new feelings. In the last terrible years of Julie's degeneration I found myself still climbing her stairs, like a convict who, in a world changed out of recognition, turns back to the jail which he knows.

The feeling in that room was known to me, and though Julie and I disliked each other, we understood each other's words. But when Gladys or even John spoke to me in those years, I was not sure that I understood. I was not deaf, but I felt the uneasiness of the deaf, who strain to comprehend something which eludes them.

One day John, in a moment of confidence, said to me, "Of course, Gladys has her own morals—she is almost systematic."

The word "systematic" seemed to offer me a chance I sought, to tell him that Gladys was consistently unfaithful. But John's next words, in a dreamy voice, were "Yes, she's rather strict, in her own way."

"She seems to make it a rule," I said, "to get drunk three times a week, at Julie's—you are all drinking too much." For I was greatly troubled by these drink parties at Julie's flat. Two or even three times a week they would meet and drink together till late at night. Yet they did not meet for drink, and certainly not for conversation. They seemed to be driven together by a force outside themselves, like the gravity which makes loose balls roll together at the bottom of a bowl. It was, I think, because they had nothing to give each other, except bare company, that they drank.

And when I reproached Julie for these beastly habits, she would answer with dignity, "I've never been drunk and I've never seen John drunk. Gladys is drunk every night but that's not my fault and at least I keep her off the streets."

And, in fact, Julie did not get drunk. She became only blowzy and red. Yet I can't remember a more horrible sight than to see her, still a dignified façade, and Gladys, with her sparrow's character of lechery and impudent courage, and John, scholar in the very spirit, sitting in that room which still seemed beautiful and civilized, drinking and talking together the endless nonsense of the half-drunk.

Each became a parody of his own nature. Julie's dignity was turned into pompous hypocrisy; Gladys' frankness became obscene, imbecile; John's good nature and unselfishness became sloth and boredom. He would lie across a sofa, unbuttoned, his long hair falling down his perspiring face, and throw out, with lazy grin, some classical allusion which the others neither understood nor heard. Unless Gladys catching it up could turn the sound of it into an obscenity.

Julie, in the morning, when her head ached and her whole flabby body seemed to be dissolving in self-pity, would say to me, "I could kill that little fool Gladys, but John is so weak. She kept him away all last week because I told her that in my time only harlots painted their fingernails."

130

Yet when we had absolute proof of Glady's infidelity, in Julie's flat, she refused to let me speak to John. "You will simply drive him away."

"It is a duty," I said, "perhaps the best chance to save the boy from that Delilah." And I wrote to him.

The proof was clear. Julie's maid had surprised Gladys and

the middle-aged dealer whom she called Doggie on the sofa to-gether. I told John that he could divorce his wife at once.

I received no answer to my letter. But a few days later Gladys came to Julie and me, just after luncheon, and told us coolly not to interfere in her affairs. "Why, you silly old sods, when were you born? If it wasn't for me and my friends, like Doggie, John would be in the workhouse. And let me tell you I've been a bloody good wife to him, as well he knows. Good-by and sleep well; that's for John, too." And she went out.

"You see what you've done," Julie cried. "Can you never stop meddling?"

"Is that what you call meddling," I said, quite furious with the woman, "to try and rescue John from that vampire?" And in my rage and alarm, I put on my hat and took a taxi to John's place of business. It was one of the smaller shops, of the high-est distinction. Its showroom was furnished luxuriously with fine rugs, cut chandeliers, palms, and so forth. John was en-gaged with a client, a woman. But his fellow salesman knew me and did not trouble me. I pretended to examine the cars. John affected to enjoy his work, but it always made me uneasy to see him humoring his clients, whether they were of his own class, who were excessively polite and smiling, as with their servants, or some rich woman of a lower class, insolent and mannerless. At the moment, he was dealing with two such women, mother and daughter—a fat beast with the bulging jowls of a French pug and a skin like a leper, whose expression, as she looked round, was so ridiculous in its arrogance that one would have laughed at her if it had not been for the cruelty of her stare, her crooked mouth; and a young girl with the smooth mask of profound stupidity, ignorance, and conceit, painted to give the idea of luxurious perversity. But it was marked already with the peevish ill-temper which goes with small minds and petty selfishness. Both women wore furs and jewels of great value.

"How much is the landaulette?" the old one snapped at John, throwing back her head in order to droop her thickened eyelids at him. The boy answered her with smiling courtesy; the grace of an ambassador which, no doubt, she took for servility. And the young woman meanwhile stared at him with unblinking eyes. You could see the idea passing in her infantile brain, "What sort of animal is this—I suppose he is a man of a sort."

The old woman was poking her leper's finger with its soft bleached skin into the upholstery.

"Special process. I've heard that tale before."

"We use nothing but the finest hides—if you would like to see—"

"Are you telling me that I am a fool?"

And the young one drawled, "It's not his fault, mother—he's only doing his job." All this in tones which reached and were meant to reach the whole shop, including myself and three new visitors, of the better kind, now surrounding the other salesman and chirping to him their gay inquiries and little jokes, like old friends from the country, or canvassers seeking a vote.

New arrogance, for some reason, always wishes to display itself to the greatest possible number of people, and to disgust them.

Or perhaps only to take revenge, like this old creature, for some secret meanness eating out the soul.

"But I knew your cars were rotten," she screeched. "Everybody knows they're rotten." A statement which caused the other party, carefully not looking in her direction, to redouble its bonhomie with the second salesman.

At last the hag went out, and the daughter stayed only to drawl again at John, "Thank you, but I'm afraid we want something rather better."

I hurried to his side and he received me with the usual affectionate smile. "Hullo, uncle."

"Can I see you at tea?"

"Why not now—?"

"I thought it was against your rules."

"The manager's out. Let's get in here." He opened the door of a large limousine, and we reclined on the wide seats, as soft as a bed. It was impossible to sit upright upon them.

"What abominable people," I said to John. "How do you bear them?"

"Did you think so—the girl was rather pathetic, poor dear. Did you notice her bad teeth—she probably affects that poker face to hide them."

"No, I didn't. I could not bear to look at such a creature. How can you stay in such a job?"

"Perhaps it's all I'm fit for, uncle—at least nowadays." I knew the boy had deteriorated at a terrifying pace. In his yellow dry face and pouched eyes I saw already the corruption of weariness. But his acceptance shocked me. I said, "Rubbish, you only have to pull yourself together, and find an object in life."

He was silent, idly swinging the tassel of the car. Silence and gesture meant that I was talking nonsense. We both knew that he had failed to find any object in life big enough to engage his interest. And taking new resolution for my desperate enterprise I said, "Gladys came to see us this afternoon."

"Yes, she told me she was going."

I was startled by the boy's careless tone and his glance at me. It was a glance full of cold boredom which seemed to put between us an immense distance.

"Did she tell you why?" I asked.

"Something about her friend Doggie, and a scene at poor Aunt Julie's."

"D'you approve of this man?"

"He's a friend of Gladys—he doesn't bother me much."

"But, John, as a husband—"

He interrupted me. "I don't worry about him. Gladys' affairs are too complicated. And, as you know, we get on pretty well, very well—she's not had such an easy time."

I did not feel horror at a speech which meant that John was indifferent to his wife's unfaithfulness; I felt only confused and, as it were, out of my element. The car which enclosed us, like a drawing room on wheels, terrifying in its elaborate luxury; the seduction of the cushions, which seemed to draw me down into an attitude of defenseless acquiescence; the heavy air, scented with some perfume which also seemed to impregnate the leather, silk, carpets; their very dust which revolved in the pale sunshine, filtered to us through four layers of plate glass, all seemed to belong to a civilization which, like John, found me superfluous.

I said, "I don't want to make trouble."

"No, no," he said, "of course not—all for the best."

But I was glad when the manager returned and we were obliged to get quickly out of the car and break off our interview. I felt as I went away that harm had been done though I could not tell what it was. And in fact, my friendship with John came to an end. Neither he nor Gladys visited the flat again, and when I went to find him, though he was as charming as before, he was plainly embarrassed by my persistence. No doubt he had to choose between me and his wife.

Strangely, it was with Gladys that I regained acquaintance, on our old terms of mutual forbearance. For when a few months later John lost his job, I helped her to support the household. And when in the next year he was run over by a car in Bond Street, we made arrangement together for his removal to a private ward of the hospital and for special treatment.

In those days I grew almost fond of Gladys. She seemed devoted to John. One would have said that his death would break her heart. He died, and she went at once to live with the man she called Doggie. She laughed at my disgust; "I know how to manage Doggie. He's such a dirty dog, I don't mind what he does. And I think I owe myself a good time."

"Can you have a good time with that man?"

"My God, yes. He's got about five thousand a year and he'll spend it, too, if you give him a fair deal, or he'd better," and she said to me with a contempt which I could not reproduce, "You've got me wrong, Nunky—I'm not going to the devil. I've got a good grip on things. I'm not like that old soak, Julie—I'd be ashamed."

1 3 1

A Rock, his faith, defying all the shocks
Of time and tide; and dead like other rocks.

When I think of John, I am still frightened. How does faith fail? Why does its sap cease to run? Not by age or disease. John was young and strong. When I said prayers this morning, I said to myself, "I must love these words, I must rejoice in truth." But in that act, I felt my spirit withdraw from them like leaves touched by frost, some devil's breath from the perverseness of my will.

I looked at Jan kneeling in his mother's lap. For though he can't speak, he has learned to pray. He imitates me. At first he used to clap his hands together, not being able to distinguish between clapping and praying. But now, having looked closely at his hands, he puts them carefully together, and when he has done so, takes them apart again several times, to look at them again, as if he might find something in them.

I said to Ann this morning, "He will thank you some day, for an experience that is already becoming part of his very nature."

Ann looked doubtful, and her doubt at once infected me so that I asked myself, "Do I mean anything by those words?"

"I don't suppose it can do him much harm. Robert won't approve, but we needn't mind about that."

"Robert won't approve?" I asked.

"He wants me to go and meet him about the divorce, and I shall have to take Jan."

"My dear, you can't meet that woman."

"I don't intend to—could you manage for a week end? Mrs. Ramm knows your routine."

"I suppose I shall have to."

Both of us, no doubt, were feeling a certain depression. Ann said, "What a life." Her anxious glance was fixed on the boy. He was running silently about the room in his combinations, turning and twisting unexpectedly, like a gnat dancing on the air.

"At least you will get the thing over," I said.

"Perhaps, but it's getting rather complicated."

The boy stood on one leg opposite the fireplace, and raised the other as if trying to perform a figure of ballet. His face was absurdly affected. Then suddenly he stood still, bent his knees and his neck and looked at the floor. A pool formed on the rug; Ann darted at him. "You naughty boy, what on earth made you do that?"

She whisked him away to the night nursery. His glance backward over his shoulder was at the pool, with an air of tranquil curiosity. But though urine was the worst thing possible for the blue drugget of my new rug, I could not help laughing.

Why does a child make gaiety spring in the heart, even with its mischief? Because he cares for nothing. He does not know the complication of the world. And Lucy, a hard and obstinate woman, could always throw power into my soul by the same innocence. She did what she chose. I remember the day, soon after John's death, that I met her for the first time in years at Queensport station.

She was white-haired, shrunken, with cheeks so thin that one saw through them the shape of her gums and the dry corded muscles of her jaw. Her nose like a finch's beak, hooked, yellow, and shining. The blackened skin round her eyes gave them the piercing brightness of lights behind a dingy curtain.

"But you're ill," I cried.

"Rubbish." She kissed me with that passionate eagerness which she showed always when we met after a long separation and, leaning back from me, exclaimed, "You're just the same," smiling as if to say, "and just as ridiculous."

"What's happened?" I asked her. "Is Brown off again abroad?" For I always hoped that Brown would once more go to India and leave her to me for three or four years.

"Nothing's happened," she said sharply. "I've just come home for a little." Her sharpness showed that she did not want to give me her reason for so sudden a return. And in fact I never heard it. Whether she knew that she was gravely ill, or whether, as was likely, she acted upon an impulse deeper than reason—the instinct which makes a wild animal struggle toward its hole, even in the blindness of its death agony, Amy and I agreed that she came home to die.

"Then you must have been ill," I said to her. "I never saw you so thin."

Lucy gave an impatient jerk of her chin and looked about her. "But what have they been doing here—where's the stationmaster's garden?"

"They cleared it out to make a place for motor buses."

"They would—the fools."

"The buses had to go somewhere."

"I don't see why—who wants the buses?"

"Brown doesn't believe in modern progress?"

"Progress downwards, through the stink of oil and tar. Hell is fired with petroleum," and, seeing me laugh, she said with her cool fierce glare, "What are you laughing at?—that's Biblical —and all this nonsense is Biblical, too. These are the days of trial—when the devil has a free hand. But I suppose you're too blind to see what's going on under your nose—or you don't want to see it."

"There are some things I don't like, certainly."

"Only some things," said Lucy coolly. "What has old Nanny Pinkham done to her cottage?—she's ruined it, the fool—it looks like a cheap teahouse."

"Mrs. Pinkham is dead. Someone from town uses it for week ends. Are you getting any converts, Lucy?"

"Not many. How glorious it is today—just right to come home on."

It did not seem to me a glorious day. It was November, with a sharp northeast wind and a mackerel sky, as cold as sea water, sprinkled with foam. The cows stood with their backs to the wind, and their red coats darkened when the hair was blown the wrong way. The banks were full of dead weeds, black and red, tangled in gray bennets. The muddy road was full of shallow pools like tomato soup, which threw up drops as high as our heads. And the trap, dipping and rolling in old ruts and new holes, nearly jerked us out of our seats.

"Thank God," Lucy said. "They haven't put down this beastly tar in our lanes—in the north, every road is black— devil's roads."

"I heard that your Tolbrook congregation was less than it used to be."

"It's finished. Old Mother Brown was the last."

"So the Benjamites also feel the religious slump."

"Each week brothers have fallen away. There's the moor now—did you ever see such a color—blue-black fire—I try to remember it but I never can."

"Why does a religion die, Lucy? It's very strange when you think of it. Why do people cease to take any interest in God?

Even the simple people who know nothing about theological quarrels."

"The people only want something for nothing," Lucy said. "We are well rid of them, as I tell the master."

"Then your sect will die."

"I believe. And the master, bless the lamb."

"You aren't a religion."

"Drive, Tommy, drive. Get her head up—make her go."

"It's very rough here." But I touched the mare, and in her surprise she cantered a few paces, rocking the trap like a small boat in a rough sea.

Lucy burst out laughing. "Make her go, Tommy. Oh, how I love that rattle of real iron tires on a real road—I haven't heard it for years."

"Your Benjamites will die out, Lucy."

"Well, what does that matter? Besides, there are still two or three hundred of the true believers."

"Not very many if you are the only ones to be saved out of the whole world."

"I think it is a good many, considering what the world is. How many ought to be saved out of a thousand million lice and bugs?"

"You shouldn't talk like that, Lucy."

"What are you afraid of, Tommy?" Lucy turned her laughing face toward me. "Your people can't hear me. You're like an old maid, when Consols go down to fifty. A pity you never married. But I suppose you were afraid of a wife."

Lucy brought me no consolation, no encouragement. Yet already it seemed that the heavy weight which had oppressed me was lifted. And her glance round the hall as she entered Tolbrook, her peculiar shiver of delight, as she grasped herself by the forearms and turned up her sharp chin to look, her cry, "So here I am again," made me laugh and gave me a sudden exhilaration.

I also found myself looking round at walls so familiar that I had not looked at them perhaps for years, except to ask if they needed repairs; and I had suddenly the indescribable sense of life rising in my soul, of power.

There is a drawing of the raising of Lazarus, by Rembrandt, which expresses, as no words could do, that sense. He looks at the people standing round his grave with a face of haggard amazement, as if he is saying, "This is what it is to be alive, and when I was alive, I did not know it."

Once more I walked with Lucy through the rooms, through the yard and the familiar fields, and at every step we recalled some childish event.

And through Lucy's eyes I saw again the richness which had been given to us, the fortune of those who have had a lively childhood and who have never lost their homes.

Lucy made it for me by the power of her spirit, which created again that beauty. For I did not see then that beauty must be made again and that when love dies the form that expressed it is also dead.

132

Ann left this morning, in snow, a quick heavy fall which has given us a blue sky. All the rooms in the house are filled with its reflection. It is as if the sky itself had entered into them, bringing an air more pure, a stillness more serene than any known on the earth's surface. Here in my mother's bedroom, long dismantled, I seem to float in another world, far detached from the turmoil of history and full of another brightness, another tension, than the fire and conflict of human life. I could believe that my mother's spirit has returned to this place in which her heart suffered, in private, so long and uncomplaining a martyrdom; in which her spirit created for itself so strong a fortress, transparent to our eyes and therefore indestructible even by Lucy's fury. The heavy mahogany furniture, the four-poster have gone. My tenants preferred twin bedsteads from the Tottenham Court Road. The great bed was too stately for their modesty. It asked too much. It imposed a grandeur which was insupportable, and therefore laughable to nice people whose modest idea was that unassuming comfort in which every luxury and indulgence can be enjoyed without even the sense of privilege; with the warm security of maggots in a dustbin, under yesterday's ashes. My young millionaire from London plumed himself on his lack of ceremony, on not even possessing a dress coat.

Only the plasterwork remains from the magnificence of the past—some absurd cherubic angels blowing trumpets and playing dulcimers and zithers on the ceiling, who, in this borrowed light of the sky, seem to give out from their bulging cheeks and dinner-plate halos a faint radiance of pale-blue light, as if some angelic essence, transmitted from above, made them recall their birth, in an age of romantic faith.

"Excuse me, sir." Mrs. Ramm is peeping round the door.

"Yes, yes, yes." I jump off the bed.

"It's Mr. Farley about the dairy boiler—he says it's leaking."

"Go and ask the mistress—let him write to her."

"When is the mistress coming back, sir?"

"I don't expect she's ever coming back," I say, to my own surprise. And I walk past the woman and go down the corridor, as if I am busy. I am not going to be troubled any more about burnt boilers or sick cows, or stopped drainpipes or damp walls. I am too old. I have my soul to make which ought to have been made long ago.

And perhaps it is a good thing that Ann has gone. I was getting spoiled with company. I had got used to chattering with my nurse. So that now I miss her and wander from room to room, as restless as a hungry man who keeps walking because he is afraid to sit down and accept starvation.

It is easy to lose the art of being lonely, and fatal to an old man, the last of his generation, who, if he wants any warmth in his heart, must feed his own fire. For whom loneliness must be a natural condition. A thousand times in my life I have called myself a lonely man. Even while Lucy was alive, but estranged from me, I pitied myself for a lonely and worried old bachelor. But in fact I did not know what real loneliness meant, for even when I was not thinking of Lucy, or thought of her with anger, my soul knew her presence and her life. Even when I hated Lucy she was my sister, dear to my very bones.

And perhaps it was a premonition, in my secret feeling, of her loss that made me more furious against her in the last month of her life than ever before. Within a day of her arrival we were quarreling because she would not see a doctor. And I remember my rage while I stood in the hall and shouted to her on the stairs, "Die, then, if you like, but I'm damned if I bury you here." A scene that now, while I stand in this silent hall, filled with the pale snow light, as of a house long dead and changed into a ghost, can still move my flesh with horror, and with bitterness.

Lucy, in return, threatened to leave Tolbrook. "You won't need to bury me anywhere. I'll bury you first."

Yet both of us were equally furious with Amy for breaking in upon our family reunion. She wrote to Lucy: "If you won't have a professional nurse, let me nurse you. I have had a good deal of experience, you know, especially of fevers."

I was especially angry, because my only hope of seeing proper treatment for Lucy was a trained nurse; and now, of course, she said that such a nurse would be a waste of money, since Amy was available.

I dare say her real motive was contempt and disgust for the body which thwarted her will, and irritation with Amy. She said in effect: "If Amy thinks she can nurse me, let her try the experiment on me and we shall see how it turns out."

I had not met Amy since her expulsion by Gladys. And I think she rarely saw John himself in his last years. We exchanged letters at Easter and Christmas, but between while I sometimes did not know her address; years had passed without my counting them, and now when Amy came to Tolbrook, from some south-coast boardinghouse, I was surprised to find her changed. She did not seem to stoop, but she had a rounded back, broad and soft, and she complained of breathlessness. Her hair was the silver white of an old woman; and she had an old woman's deliberate cautious movements, exasperating to the older Lucy. But she would never sit down if there was anyone to be waited on. At Tolbrook she was once more the servant.

"She's stupider than ever," Lucy would say. "It's really a wonder what she thinks about."

And in fact Amy never read a book or a newspaper, beyond the morning's births and deaths. Only sometimes, when she was forced to be at rest, on a journey, or in the evening before the lamps were brought in, when it was too dark to sew, one saw a look of confusion and wonder on her face. Her eyebrows would go up, her lips purse, her hand would go to her cheek; she would gaze at the fire with the expression of one who asks, "What am I doing here—how have I passed through such things?"

It was at such times that Lucy would utter her sharpest speeches to Amy, saying, "Is that shirt meant for Tommy or Loftus?"

Amy would then start and take the offending shirt out of her basket. "For Loftus, dear."

"Loftus in a pink shirt—he would sooner die."

Loftus in fact was an extremely smart and correct young soldier, who on his rare visits had charmed us all and especially Lucy. I think Lucy, as well as Amy, had paid his debts. And she seemed always to be defending him against some imaginary critic.

Amy, having adjusted her spectacles three times and looked with mild indignation at the fading light, would say, "Do you call it pink?"

"I wonder are you color blind, Amy—that would explain a lot."

Amy, understanding that this was a criticism of her taste in dress, would answer mildly, "Bill always liked me in blue and I always think it looks nice in itself."

"Bill hated you in blue. And he was quite right—it makes you look like a beetroot in sugar paper."

"Queen Alexandra was fond of blue and she had very good taste," Amy said. "Of course she wasn't my coloring."

"You don't think that matters," Lucy said, angrily twisting her shrunken yellow face.

"Yes, but people can't very well object to blue," Amy said, meaning perhaps that the Queen had justified blue and so she was entitled to please herself by wearing blue frocks, even if they did not suit her. Amy's peculiar logic, her dress, her deliberate manner, her cheerful ignorance all irritated my poor sister to extremity; I think, above all, she was irritated by Amy's silent uncomplaining grief. She herself had never hidden her feelings. She liked to talk about her dead, to express her bitterness or her pleasure. Dying, she could still make jokes, talk nonsense, and laugh; quarrel with me about trifles; or fly out against some old enemy.

With Amy she quarreled a dozen times a day. She was the worst possible patient and neither obeyed Amy's rules nor took any remedies. Yet if Amy was out of sight she would ask for her. The two women were inseparable and deeply concerned in each other.

"I can't understand how Lucy could bring herself to live with a man like Brown," Amy would say. "So coarse and common and not even faithful to her. She is so fine. She does not really care twopence for anybody. If only there were more like her." And Lucy would say of Amy, "It makes me rage to see her so lonely. Bill had no business to die like that. But, of course, she killed John by letting him marry that filthy creature. And, after all, she doesn't know how to appreciate life. Too slow."

These words of Lucy, even then, gave me a shock of pity, and I asked her, "Have you been so happy, Lucy?"

"Happy?" she answered briskly. "Yes, I am so happy to be at home again that I could dance—"

"Yes, at home."

"And with the master, too, praise the lamb—I've been happier still with the poor master. Yes, it's been glorious sometimes—to hear him speak, and feel how he moved those savages; it threw a glory on the whole world. I'll never forget one meeting—it was last winter—he carried us all away; even that pig-woman Ella was sobbing, and I was flying in the air. And afterwards we walked through the frosty lanes and the dumps like mountains, it was a Welsh mining place—the finest mutton you ever tasted. I only wanted some homemade jelly." And, laughing, she said, "How I love being alive—I can't imagine myself dead and the world going on without me. I should like to be the wandering Jew, and go on forever."

We were walking through the lower floor, which was now the farthest extent of Lucy's exercise. She could now barely drag herself with the help of my arm or Amy's through the four rooms and back again. We were economizing in fires for lack of servants and the house was very cold, especially in the winter. Often we both wore overcoats, as if for a journey into the fields, and I remember that Lucy would stop in the big room and look out of the windows at the sleet falling on the grass blackened by rotting leaves, the streaming trees, and the clouds hanging down in long gray rags like torn sails, and say, "Isn't it grand to be out," as if the carpet were grass and the pictures, the chairs and sofas about us were natural objects.

She loved especially the rattle of sleet or hail on the big

windows, and when I reminded her that she had always hated cold and, above all, wet weather, she answered sharply: "What nonsense, Tommy. I never hated any weather at Tolbrook."

"I wish you hadn't gone away from us."

"So do I, but I had to, and I must go back next month. The master wrote yesterday."

"But that's impossible and wrong. You can't go back. It will kill you. Why should you go back? Robert will be coming next week—back from school."

"My dear Tommy, you don't propose to lock me up here."

"You'll have Robert here. You know you can't go back. You only suggest it out of perversity."

"Rubbish, Tommy. I must go back because I'm needed." And the old dispute broke out with more than its old ferocity. For as we grew older we grew more rough. We did not mind hurting each other. And this was not because we were hardened to blows but because we were more desperate.

I wanted to say to Lucy now all those bitter things which I had kept silent and hidden. "You are the complete egotist, you live only for yourself."

And Lucy answered, as usual, that I was a mean smallminded creature, who had crept away from life into a woman's pocket. "You hung upon me, and then it was that poor creature Julie. I'm not surprised you drove her to drink."

She was too weak to let go of my arm, and while we disputed we still walked slowly through the rooms.

"I may be disgusting," I said, "but you are a spoiled obstinate vain woman who has made a god out of herself. Yes, you think you are a martyr to religion, but you are only worshipping yourself and sacrificing to your fearful pride."

"Yes, a coward—a mean stupid coward!" Lucy gasped, hanging on my arm to keep herself from falling.

When I recall that quarrel my muscles contract. I jump up from my chair and exclaim aloud. I shiver as at the recollection of a crime. Why did I lose my temper with a sister who was more dear to me than anyone in the world? Why did I hate her so that even to her death I was furious against her and continually tried to hurt her?

Our quarrels were not easily made up. We knew how to hurt each other. We should have fought for days if it had not been for that old rule of my father's that all family quarrels must be made up before the last bedside prayer.

That rule had not applied in the time of our separation. Some of our fights had continued for months, and even years; like the battle of the chair. But strangely, when we were in a house together, we obeyed it. I can remember sitting in my room feeling against Lucy the savage anger which she alone could rouse in me. Yet I did not go to bed. It was as though I could not go. I did not think, "I must not pray until I have made it up with Lucy." But the compulsion lay upon me as if the very air of the old house had within it an order of tradition, a platonic form, shaping my conduct.

So at last I said to myself: "I suppose I'd better say good night to the woman—she's really not responsible." And I got up and went to her room. But before I had opened the door it sprang open before me and Lucy stood there laughing and holding up her arms. It was strange to see in the little old woman, dried as a mummy, with her witch's nose and chin, her fierce eyes, the gestures of the beautiful young girl, frank and coquettish. "I heard you coming, Tommy. I knew you would have to come—because of Papa."

Even then that malicious delight in my defeat might have driven me away. But Lucy, seeing me hesitate, grasped at my arms to pull me into the room, crying: "No, no. You must stay and talk to me. Do you remember—"

And we talked half the night, like children, with our arms round each other's waists; so bound together by love that we seemed to have but one heart and one delight between us.

What was that heart, that delight, in two creatures so different? It was something deeper than the love of man and woman, brother and sister. It was the very soul of the home, of the family; it was living history. My father lived there still, not in himself, but in what he had given to our memories, and to our minds which seized upon them. When we laughed at some old trifling joke it was with a laughter which carried us away, out of ourselves. And when we spoke of Edward, of Bill, of our father and mother, it was with a love quite different from what we had felt for them alive. It was something that we had never known before, greater and deeper than ourselves. We were enchanted, and we cried together: "Why did we never appreciate our father enough? Why did we never see the stanchness of Bill?"

And when at last we separated we kissed each other with warmth which said, "We are the last; we mustn't lose each other."

Yet our quarrels broke out again on that same day. We were obliged to quarrel, by that very sincerity which belonged to our family feeling. And Lucy, when she gave me power, gave me anger.

We were quarreling bitterly within half an hour of her death. Lucy, for the last time in her life, lost her temper with me and cried: "What have I got to do with Bill? He was really ill, and I am not. I certainly won't let any of your doctors poke me about. And I won't drink any of Amy's poison. If she hasn't enough sense to let me alone, she certainly hasn't enough to cure me."

A few minutes later we found her lying on the floor in a faint. We lifted her into a chair, and Amy ran to send for a doctor. "This is our chance," she said. "She can't stop us now."

Lucy opened her eyes suddenly and said: "I wasn't really fainting," like one who denies that he has been asleep.

"You're very ill, Lucy. You mustn't move."

"I don't want to move." And then she said in a surprised voice: "I suppose I'm not going to die."

"No, of course not, Lucy."

"I feel very queer. . . . I can't see properly." And her voice was full of indignation and surprise. "I do believe I'm dying."

Her agitation was so great that I had to keep her from struggling out of the chair.

"I won't, I won't," she said. "Why, I'm not sixty yet. And Robert coming home. Let me up, Tom. You fool, let me up." She was trying to shout at me, but her voice was failing.

"But you must keep still, my darling," I begged her. "Don't exhaust yourself. You'll be all right soon. Amy has gone to call the doctor."

"Nonsense. I tell you I'm dying. Don't let her come in. We don't want any strangers." She was pushing out her hands as if to thrust someone away, trying to force her voice, which was not louder than a raucous whisper. "Tommy, promise me, keep Robert away from them . . . they don't understand children . . . and make a gentleman of him. He can do what he likes afterwards, but first, a gentleman . . . keep him at school . . . Latin . . . with a proper education . . . you'll find I've left enough money." And then putting up her arms, "Promise me, Tom, quickly. There's no time—quickly, Tom."

She fell into unconsciousness again and never recovered from it. She had a kidney disease which might easily have been cured by treatment. Fortunately, the doctor arrived before her death, and gave us a certificate without a post-mortem.

133

I not only missed Lucy; I was deprived of her as one is deprived of some essential organ. Virtue had gone from me and from the house. It was now that Tolbrook began to frighten me by something more than loneliness. I felt for the first time in its quiet corridors what I feel now, the weight of a deserted and childless home. As if some old unhappy creature hung upon my shoulder, with the crushing force of masonry.

Ann has written me two letters. It appears that this girl is one of those who do not know how to show affection, save with a pen. But this very kindness convinces me that she will not come back. My happiness with her was illusion. "She got tired of Tolbrook and of me," I said. "And why not? A clever girl buried in this hole with a dull old man." I thought that she had come to love Tolbrook, but her sentiment for the place was only a passing interest. She came to family prayers to see how Jane Austen's characters felt, and she set the old rooms in order to know her father better. And she knows neither him nor me. She belongs wholly to the young world, curious, scientific.

> Professor B, profound in his acumen,
> Knows everything, as eunuchs know their women.

I miss the boy's voice, his bare feet running in the passage, from the bathroom to the nursery.

When living and dead inhabit the same house, then the dead live, and life is increased to that house. In Ann's eyes I saw her father, and sometimes in her voice there was the tone of Lucy's courage. In the child's step, how many children ran along the upper corridor. But when the living go from a house, then the dead are cut off in their death. And death stands in every room, silent and unmeaning.

The servants are watching me. When at night I can't sleep and go to Lucy's room, or to my mother's, now entirely empty, I hear boards creak and voices whispering. No doubt Mrs. Ramm has orders to wire or call the police if I should try to escape.

And at dawn, when I fall down upon a chair and sleep, I

have such terrifying dreams that I would rather not sleep at all. This morning I dreamed that Tolbrook itself was growing smaller and smaller. The walls closed in; the roof came down upon me. The house became a coffin and it seemed that I had been shut up in it alive. The undertakers were screwing down the lid. I heard even the grating of the screw in the hard wood and tried to cry out that I was not dead yet; to strike up against the coffin lid. But my arms were pinioned and my jaw was tied. I could neither speak nor move.

And what was most terrible all my body, quite apart from me, seemed full of bitterness against me. As if every cell were complaining, "What has he done with us? We are betrayed."

134

I waked up, streaming with cold sweat, in the salon. I had been lying in a broken-down armchair opposite a binder, whose arms seemed to quiver at me, like the whiskers of some devilish insect, asking, "What is this intrusive creature?" It moved and stretched out a monstrous eye upon a thick stalk. I jumped up and saw that this eye was Mrs. Ramm's head. She had been hiding behind the machine. She said to me in a trembling voice, "You ought to be in bed, sir—you're not well."

"Agnes Ramm," I said, "if you go on watching me, I shall push you downstairs."

I could see that this frightened the fool. She went off at once to send a report to her mistress. I went upstairs, dressed in my town clothes and packed a bag with my notebooks and a clean shirt.

Then I turned back the carpet and opened the bell trap. And again I was able to congratulate myself on my foresight in keeping always a store of change. There was in the trap over forty half crowns and a dozen florins, dropped down the crack, no doubt in mistake for the nobler coin, on a dark evening, or when there was danger of surprise. There were also twenty-seven letters to Sara, written since her silence and kept for the address, which had, by some means, been withheld from me. These letters I also packed—they contained much private matter—and divided the silver between my pockets and the toes of my pumps, which, stuffed with socks, form an excellent traveling cashbox.

I then went down the nursery stairs and out of the nursery door into the rose garden. It was not yet seven. No one even imagined an escape, carried out with such speed and resolution.

And since I did not need to go for cash to Queensport, where I should certainly have been recognized, I was able to take a bus direct to Plymouth where I safely joined the mainline express.

I can't describe my astonishment and delight in this escape, in the rapid motion, so long forgotten, of the train. The telegraph wires hopping by like frogs; and the great trees, still bare, sailing down the wind like the rigged ships I used to see towed into Queensport.

"After all," I thought, "I am a Wilcher—I am like Bill and Lucy; like my father who spent half his life in camps and lodgings. It is in my blood, which is all English. The Latin, the Celt strike root; they want only to make a home somewhere; and if they must wander they take with them always a dream or legend of home. But the English soul is a wanderer, a seeker. You find it in every corner of the world, dressed in some local imagination; studying Chinese antiquities, or ready to assure you that salvation is in the Hindu yoga. The English have taught every nation to admire its own culture—they go to the Pacific, and say 'Glorious people, keep your nakedness and your sacrifices, they are far preferable to our own miserable governments and ideas'; they go to Africa and become Mohammedan; they sail among the South Sea Islands and say, 'This is paradise and here only I have found civilized people, beautiful and kind, wise and holy'; they are enraged when they see some barbarous race put off its beads and its wildness and study English and wear trousers. Then they cry, 'What are you doing in trousers, you poor wretch? Why do you put on that hideous dress of degenerate Europe?' and so on. No," I think, gazing from the window at a flying village on its green carpet, "when I wanted to be a missionary, when I dressed up like a Hindu to talk about the Indian wisdom, I was fulfilling my destiny. And that house which I loved and hated so much has been my treacherous Delilah. It brought me back from God, from India, from Sara. But not again."

In fact, I was in London before two o'clock, and no one stopped me at the station barriers. I had escaped.

My plan was to go to Holloway and obtain Sara's address from the chaplain. And within two hours I had the address in my hand. Owen's Lane, Lewisham, an easy journey. I took a room for that night in a central hotel, a great barrack with many hundred rooms; for I knew that if the family pursued me they would seek me in one of my usual stopping places in Kensington.

135

I was again in London; but, as never before, a stranger, a man without a home. I have said that it was the art of a woman like Sara, a servant bred, to make herself a home everywhere. But now I saw that to the wanderer all the world is home. He is the least homeless of men because he possesses all, the earth and the sky, the houses and the trees, with the eyes of a home-keeper, and all men and women are his familiars.

This was the secret I had discovered when, at the outbreak

of war, I stood in a row with the other volunteers and found that we were friends. We had left our homes to be at one in the family of those who have thrown themselves naked upon fortune.

In London I found cold and bright weather. The sky was as pale as glass and the few small clouds seemed like snow flocks or the tops of hidden Alps whose lower slopes were hidden in a blue-green mist. The pavements rang in this cold air like bells and on every side one saw pink cheeks, pink noses, and sparkling eyes and teeth. I could not help laughing as I walked through the streets, for I thought, "It is said that war hangs over this unhappy world, that the people are full of foreboding and uncertainty. But see these young men in their spring overcoats, these girls laughing among their furs and chattering like pies, what is politics to them but nonsense in the papers. They think not of danger or death, but life."

And I felt one with them. I was young again, without a care. For that is what it is to be young; to be careless. The young are born pilgrims. Babies, as soon as they can walk, begin to explore the world. As every nurse knows, their first idea is to escape from their keepers. They are free born and look upon the whole earth as their possession. To be free is to be young.

And as I walked through Trafalgar Square, under the glittering mountains of the sky, I kept smiling at the people, who seemed, as far as I could tell through my spectacles, to smile at me. I even felt an inclination to say to them, "I have come to town to get married. Yes, I am starting a new life, with the woman I love; or, more strictly speaking, a woman I sometimes love and always esteem," and so forth. Just as formerly, when I had stood among the queue of war recruits, in 1914, I had wanted to tell the story of my life to anyone who would listen to me; and I myself had heard with pleasure a great many rather long and somewhat dull confessions.

And at last my confidence did overflow into speech. I found myself talking to a gentleman in a brown bowler at the corner of Pall Mall, opposite the Athenaeum. Possibly I had been attracted by the hat, whose peculiar color revealed an expansive nature. I was saying to him that it was a fine evening for so early in the year; that London was looking its best. And then I told him that in fact I'd come to town on a very pleasant errand, etc., not unconnected with matrimony, and so on. The old gentleman, who was obviously an important person, answered very reasonably that it was a fine evening, and a good idea. He wished me luck, etc. But his eyes, which were very round and prominent, said that I was either drunk or foolish.

This warned me that I was in no position to be unconventional. But so it was that ten minutes later I found myself again in conversation with a newspaper seller outside the National Gallery.

To him, adapting my words and manner, I said that it was tiptop weather for a holiday. "And, in fact," I said, "I'm on the loose—I'm taking to the roads from now on." And since the man remained silent and serious I added, to show that I had spoken in joke, "I speak figuratively, of course."

Almost at the same moment I seemed to remember the man's face, that he knew me, and that he was planning some means of detaining me. "Ridiculous," I said to myself; and smiling, I made a further remark about the gypsy in every human soul, etc. But the man, who had a peculiarly white face, continued to stare. And suddenly I began to feel alarm. But I was walking away with dignity when I almost ran into a policeman.

Now since that unhappy time, from which Sara rescued me, when I actually came into the hands of the police, I have always had peculiar feelings in their presence. When a policeman looks at me, I never know quite what I am going to do. And this time I jumped, and then, gazing at the man, said in a loud voice, "I can see you know who *I* am."

The man, who was, I suppose, coming off duty, and had, like so many policemen, a very short nose, looked at me attentively, but with that careful lack of interest which police-men show on such occasions. He answered at last, in an unex-pectedly brisk lively tone, "No, sir, I'm afraid not."

"My name is Wilcher," I said. "Thomas Loftus Wilcher, and I've just made a remarkable smart getaway from my fam-ily who thought they were going to shut me up in a—But never mind. Good afternoon"—and I walked off with even more dig-nity, though I was almost fainting with indignation. I was furi-ous with the police, with everybody. And when I got to my hotel I went and locked myself in my room. I did not come out even for dinner. And I thought, "Nobody in this world under-stands anybody—nobody except Sara. For Sara has charity in her soul."

136

It was that misunderstanding which made me a criminal. For one day, just after Lucy's death, I happened to be walking in the park; and such a weight of desperation fell upon me that I wanted to cry out or kick the railings.

It was a Friday. Always the worst day in the week. For first, it was that day, before I went to Tolbrook, when I realized that once more I had not been able to get to the end of anything. Unfinished work was piled upon my table; and more problems awaited me at home.

And all this work was like draining water in a sieve. For the whole social fabric was obviously dissolving. The European currencies had already collapsed; and we, in England, were ask-ing ourselves how long we should be an exception.

Secondly, Friday was the day of my visit to Julie. And there was no doubt, since John's death, that Julie and I hated each other.

Yet, because of this hate, this tension, I must be particu-

larly careful not to give her cause for offense. And all our inter-
course must be guided by a fixed routine; as, during the war, in
some dangerous areas of the front line we had been guided by
cords stretched from one piece of cover to another.

So I had always to enter with an air of gaiety and to cry,
"How are you, my dear?"

Often Julie would not answer me. Sometimes I could not
even see her. For she would sit for hours silent and motionless, doing nothing, in a half-dark room. It was only after a moment, while I looked round, possibly with relief, that I could
distinguish her in some corner, a pale bloated mass which I
had taken for a heap of cushions.

The room was still kept neat and clean by Julie's devoted
maid, but it had become revolting to me. I would say to Julie,
"What, sitting in the dark, my dear—let me turn up the light.
Oh, I see, you've been reading some Moore, *A Drama in
Muslin*."

"No, I wasn't reading it—I know it by heart."

"Nothing new from the library?"

"Nothing good—everything is so dull."

But often she would not answer me at all. If she had been
drinking she was always in an angry mood and could not bear
to speak to me. I knew that she brought men in, not the young
soldiers, who like the poets of thirty years before had found
wives and jobs and settled in life, but various dependents or
failures. One was a broken actor older than myself; another
was an ex-stockjobber, who had been in prison. But even when
these hangers-on were present, Julie showed no animation or
pleasure. I would find her drinking with one or another in silence; and they would look at me with contempt and irritation, as if to ask, "What do you come here for, to interrupt us
in our contemplation?"

Sometimes Julie did not speak to me for weeks; yet every
Friday or Saturday I would stay the night with her. Why did I

perform an act become so hateful to me? You say it was habit. But habit is not whim. My habit of going to Julie once a week was also her habit. If I broke mine, I broke also something of hers. And I could not know how that break would affect her. I said to her once, "If you would rather I didn't come in, you have only to bolt your bedroom door."

But she did not bolt the door. And I continued to go to her bed, for fear of some worse catastrophe to us both. For I felt in Julie already that sullen rage against the world which in the end brought her to an asylum.

I used to urge her to go to church. "You are a believer, Julie," I would say. "You have faith—how long is it since you went to mass?"

And she answered me in her slow voice, which had still the dignity of its elocution, "I don't go because I don't choose to go."

"But isn't that a mortal sin in your church?"

And suddenly furious, she would cry, "Why can't you leave me in peace?" These fits of rage were terrifying in the gentle, calm Julie. I would swear, after each outburst, that I should never see her again.

But the time had not come when Sara, by bringing back to me some joy in life, gave me power of faith to take that fearful risk of a breach with Julie, which confronts me still with the question, "Did I murder Julie's soul?" A responsibility to be borne only by the living faith which knows in the heart, "I have done evil but I may yet do good."

I dared not leave Julie then and so, as surely as the week end returned, I would go back to her.

But on this Friday, to my great relief, I found myself twenty minutes early for Julie. I sat down on a free seat. But such was the pressure of my agitation in these days that I could not sit still for a moment. I jumped up at once.

It was a fine evening in late spring. The tulips were open

and there were many strollers gazing at those unflowerlike objects; civil servants, typists, etc. Now, I did not usually notice people at all in those days. I was enclosed in fears, I had sunk into the darkness of anxiety, and there was no Lucy to light within my cell the flame of rage or love. But as I jumped up, I collided with a group of passing girls. I apologized and one of them smiled. And now as I walked up and down, I could not help noticing all these girls who crowded the path. I noticed their ugly hats, their short unbecoming frocks, which revealed so many ill-shaped legs, and especially their faces, which seemed so bored or merely blank. "In my young days," I thought, "no girl permitted herself to look like that in public; arrogant, or blank. If she had not the sense to seem attractive, then her mother instructed her."

Especially there was one young girl, in a scarlet hat, who passed me three times in ten minutes, with a face so blank and stupid that I could not bear it. She had no more expression, as Lucy would have said, than a new potato. Only her eyes showed some mild intelligence as they examined the dresses, the shoes, stockings, hats and, finally, the faces of other girls. Yet she was not ill-favored; her features were neat, her complexion healthy.

"Good gracious," I thought, in my exasperation, when I passed her for the third time. "Look at you, young and passably good-looking, and nothing to trouble about, and all you can do is to gaze about you like a Dutch cheese. Wake up, for heaven's sake." And then I thought, "But, of course, she doesn't know how to wake up. She is some quiet little typist, who passes her time between a dull office and a prim little suburb. And she has come to the park with some vague notion of seeing the dresses and the flowers, and perhaps having some adventure. Or, if she doesn't think so, the little donkey, that is her real motive. She is secretly hoping for an adventure."

And then at once I thought, "Suppose next time we passed

I said something to her—some little compliment, or perhaps something more particular, even a little startling."

"Pooh," I said to myself, "you old fool—she would just think you a nasty old man or she would call for a policeman. And, besides," I said to myself, "I shan't see her again. That's four times. Even a goose like that can't walk up the path for a fifth time, with a face like an unaddressed envelope. No, no," I said to myself, "you won't see her again."

I turned round and looked sharp about me. But I could not see her until I had nearly reached Hyde Park Corner. And then, suddenly, I caught sight of her absurd red hat and pink nose. She was sitting on a free seat beside the path and looking at the passers. And the next moment I found myself on the same seat, almost touching her. My heart was beating so that I could scarcely breathe. But my jaws grinned, and I muttered something. I saw the girl's eyes fixed on me with the same mild curiosity. She said, "I beg your pardon." And I began to pay her compliments, and also to tell her how nice it was for her to be young, and to have all her life before her, and so forth. In fact, I was simply amazed at myself, especially when I went on to say that no doubt she would find a nice young man soon, who would teach her how to make better use of her time—and so on.

All this time she was looking at me with the same blank expression. Only her face grew gradually redder. All at once, she raised her hand and knocked my hat into a flower bed. Then she got up, faced me, and still with the same wooden face took her dress by back and front and gave a little jerk and wriggle, to get it down. And she walked off.

I picked up my hat and ran after her. "And now, I suppose you will call the police."

But she only looked at me severely and answered, "I should think you'd better have someone to look after you." A nice sensible goodnatured child, with good principles. Probably a member of the church. I felt such esteem for her, mixed with my exasperation, that I didn't know whether to pinch her behind or kiss her hands. However, she jumped suddenly on a bus, and I found myself alone on the pavement.

The surprising episode left me so confused and excited that I had walked almost to Apsley House before I perceived that I was wasting time. I then looked at my notebook to discover my next engagement, and I saw, of course, in the correct day, among a mass of pencil memoranda, a *J* in ink underlined twice in red. And I recollected that this was Friday, my day for Julie. I can't describe the sense of disgust and futility with which I then hastened to West Street and, entering with an air necessarily more brisk and friendly, because of my lateness, cried, "Good evening, my dear—I'm afraid I'm a little late."

Lucy used to call me a hypocrite. But this was a typical piece of incomprehension. Any man who was not a brute must have pretended some kind feeling to Julie; and since she was still a sensitive and understanding creature, the imitation had to be good. And so it was the more troublesome to me.

137

I was not only astonished at my conduct with the young girl in the park; I was horrified at myself. For I had used some phrases to her which were calculated to shock her modesty and which, it seemed to me, I had chosen for the purpose. To wake her up. To excite her. To make something happen, for myself as well as for her. I could not believe how such words had passed my lips. But two nights later I was talking in the same manner to a woman who might have been one of my own servants. For it was twilight and the place was my own street.

How I began this conversation I do not know. I found myself, as before, beside the young woman and in full speech before I knew what I was doing. And again my last words to her were, as she escaped into a house, "I suppose you will tell the police."

For I have no doubt that part of the fascination, the spell which this new life of adventure cast upon me was the danger of ruin and disgrace. They say that if a service be only dangerous enough it will always find volunteers. I must not say that I wanted to be arrested. Many times in the next weeks, after one of these enterprises, I would lie awake all night shaking in terror at every sound and saying to myself, "That's the police." And next day, mixed with my self-loathing, there was triumph, as if I had won a great success against the laws of the country, and decency, and everything that I respected. And as my adventures became more bold and more scandalous, so the loathing and the triumph increased.

Part of that triumph, which proved it to be the devil's, was in its distortion of the whole moral world. Having abandoned the pure light of heaven, I saw not merely my own bad deeds but the whole world of my action, illuminated by the fantastic glare of putrefaction. So now I delighted in opposing a suggestion in the firm that soft collars should be permitted in office hours; not, as formerly, out of loyalty to the old Westminster collar, which I wore myself, but because the senior partner, old Pamplin, was inclined to give way on the point. I enjoyed telling Pamplin that he was growing slack in his ideas. For he was a great upholder of duty, Church, and state. And the times appalled him. Every week, with his beaked nose and round blank eyes surrounded by wrinkles, he seemed to grow more like an owl startled by the collapse of its barn and the intrusion of daylight.

The old man, in his gloomy slow voice, would say to me, "England is finished—no sense of duty anywhere—no honesty—the only question anyone risks, what can I get out of it?" And I would answer that on the contrary I thought the country was doing very well. "All these new houses, new schools—it's astonishing. Democracy may be bad at war, but it is good at peace," etc.

"I don't like your new houses, and what do they learn in the new schools—egotism, materialism; to grab, and to do the least work for the most money." Pamplin was the kind of Tory of whom Edward wrote:

> Leave politics to us, the tories cry,
> For politicians cheat and rob and lie.

Now the truth was that I myself felt such uneasiness about the state of the country that I was ready to jump into the Thames; but now, out of mere perversity, I would purse up my mouth into a devil's grin and say, "It seems to me that, as a democracy, we ought to be carrying out even bigger changes. For instance, in the law," an idea which, of course, made the old man turn quite green with fright and anger. For he loved the old law almost as much as I did.

In the same way, I enjoyed arguing with the vicar that what we wanted at Tolbrook was the real old-country sermon on hell-fire; nothing but hell could do the farmers good. And then I would go out and look about in our own country lanes, to catch some factory girl coming home from Queensport on her bicycle.

I find in my commonplace book this quotation, which I must have written down at the very time when I was pursuing this strange and horrible life.

"The soul which is deprived of its essential activity, in works of faith and imagination, quickly corrupts. Like all spiritual things, enclosed within the prison walls of fear and doubt, it grows quickly monstrous and evil. It is like a plant shut away in darkness, which, still living and striving, throws out, instead of green leaves and bright flowers, pallid tentacles, and fruit so strange, so horrible that is like a phantasm seen in a dream; something at once comic and terrifying. The dumb stupid creature appears suddenly to be possessed of a devil's imagination."

The devil loves to look upon his own corruption. Despair is his secret joy.

138

I had my narrow escapes. I was assaulted and threatened. A young man who intervened on one occasion when a young woman showed offense attacked me with a stick; but I nearly ran him through with my steel umbrella. I remembered Edward's old advice, founded on history, that, with the white arm, the thrust has always defeated the cut. So in this little battle the force of evil, better instructed, utterly defeated that of virtue, which was left breathless on the ground.

At last, of course, I was caught. Somebody followed me home, and the police came to warn me. They also warned my family. I received a shock. I swore to reform and for some months I did not offend. And then one evening I found myself in a situation more disgraceful than any before. What astonishes me now is that I was not locked up in these years before Sara came to save my soul alive. For I took ever greater risks. The demon that possessed me could find pleasure only in defiance.

My family, and especially my niece Blanche, formed the plan of shutting me up. Sara, at a later date, warned me of it; but far from making me more cautious, I think the warning increased my rashness. I actually welcomed the visits of Blanche's specialists, villains hired to sign away my freedom. I did not know, and I do not know now, what qualifications these creatures possessed. They are a special class. I suppose that in the queer monstrous growth of a modern state they have been developed in one of the darker corners, to fulfill the functions of getting rid, in an easy and respectable manner, of old people who have become troublesome to their families.

Blanche's favorite was a little young old man with a face like a Manchester terrier. His hair was flaxen, his huge eyes were water colored; his sharp nose was as pale as if powdered; his hollow cheeks were pale green. He was dressed also in a suit of pale yellow tweed, with pale lemon-colored boots; and he talked to me about his farm in Surrey, his Guernseys, his Punches. But all in a little pale voice; and looking all the time into the air as if he were thinking of something else, a sad memory.

Of course, I told him that I had been the victim of coincidence and that the girl had made advances. That is common form in these cases. Neither of us believed it. But it served to break the ice. Every situation has its polite routine, imposed by its own forms, and the form for a patient of my type is to say, "I have been the victim of a miscarriage of justice."

"Yes, essackly. Of course." The poor little creature sighed. "Quite so," and then he proceeded of course to the next step. "It's very natural, of course, to feel a certain attraction—at any age. A pretty girl, yes," he sighed again and his eyes wandered over the ceiling. Then he murmured, "I used to like breaking things myself. Yes, a good smash—I saw an old lady yesterday who had broken all her china and torn all her clothes off and walked down a crowded street, in the rain."

"And I suppose you're going to lock her up," I said, getting angry. I knew it was dangerous to support the old lady. But I was tempted by the danger, by the pale eyes of the little terrier, which now turned upon me their cold pale surface. "What nonsense," I said. "I know exactly how she felt. She thought, 'Here am I, a nice respectable old lady in a black silk dress, and two petticoats, and stays and drawers, with lace edges, and chemises and all the rest.'" The terrier, while I went through this list of feminine apparel, kept on gazing at me and his eyes seemed to grow more and more like the gelatin which my clerk used to make a copy of circular letters.

" 'Here I am,' I said, 'a respectable old lady, and all my brothers and sisters, and nephews and nieces, think that they have me safe, stuck down in this parlor, and tied up with strings and buttons and busks, so that I can't be anything else but a respectable old relative, until I die and leave them my money. Yes, they think they have got me boxed up for life, and almost as good as in my coffin. But they're wrong, I'm not dead yet. I've got legs and arms. I've got a body. I'm a human being after all. See.' And off came the silk dress, the stays and the petticoats and the buttons and the strings, and there she is walking down the street as naked as Eve. I wish I had been there to see." And I burst out laughing. All this was so dangerous that it made my blood tingle. I trembled with excitement. I thought, "Shall I pull his nose? That would do it." But all at once he said to me, "Yes, exactly. I know the feeling. It's quite natural. Quite a lot of people get into prison for no other reason. They even confess to murders they haven't done, you know."

"Oh, I've heard of that."

"Anything to break the pattern," he said. "Personally, I go in for rock climbing."

"Rock climbing?"

"Yes, it keeps the nerves on the stretch. It acts as a safety valve for all that superfluous energy—and it breaks the pattern. Asylums, you know, have plain walls."

He sighed and said, "Of course, there are graffiti—errand-boy type. The walls have to be washed down fairly often."

I hate men who use foreign words, and I grinned angrily at him.

"Why not? Mad people all go that way—it is too much sex that inclines to insanity." Another very dangerous suggestion.

"No," he sighed. "I think they only draw their diagrams to break the proprieties—having nothing else to break."

We then had a very reasonable and pleasant little talk, about various forms of insanity, perversion, religious mania, etc. I suggested that according to his views the ideal religion would be something quakerish or perhaps anabaptist, without any forms at all.

"Not altogether. The free religions produce some of the most violent cases—the older church tends more to private perversions or melancholia. Protestants go in for homicidal mania, and Catholics for hysteria."

"So the ideal religion would be free church one week and catholicism the next."

"Possibly." This was the highest extent of his agreement to anything. "Or perhaps a judicious mixture of routine and stimulation."

"Your conclusion points to my own religion, the Church of England. So that even pathology defines it as the best religion."

"Perhaps. But the question is slightly out of my depth. I am a pathologist, you understand."

"Yes, that is also a religion—but, if you'll permit me, a bad one—a mere polydiabolism, or perhaps I should say, a para-polydiabolism, since even your devils are figments, roughly adumbrated in bad grammar and worse logic."

"There is much in what you say." In fact, we parted with mutual esteem or, at least, toleration and suspended judgment.

If the terrier had been paid to drive me mad and then certify me, he was either very stupid or a great fraud. For I was certainly on the very edge of pulling his nose and shouting "Boo" when he began that sensible and reasonable conversation.

To change the pattern. To get into prison, into an asylum. You would say whole nations grow suddenly bored at the same moment and tear off their clothes to dive into vice, or, fascinated by some dark unknown sea, draw nearer and nearer to it, walking on the very edge of war and destruction.

> All breaks, all passes save God's cry to men,
> Break all, die all, that ye be born again.

139

No. 24, Owen's Lane, was a terrace of small single-fronted houses in worn yellow brick. It was an old street but in good repair. Doors were painted, bells had been polished. As a judge of property I could see that it belonged to a good estate, probably a large one, and let to good tenants.

I will admit that I felt strangely confused as I rang the bell. My heart was beating violently and the effort was painful and alarming. No doubt any man's heart may beat at such a crisis in his affairs, but it does not remind him that all his affairs may end at any moment.

The door was opened by a fair young man wearing dark-green trousers and a tweed coat. He looked at me with suspicion and said, "And who may you be?"

"Does Mrs. Jimson live here?"

"She does. What about it?"

"I should like to see her, if you don't mind. My name is Wilcher."

"I thought so. Well, you can't see her. I know all about you, Mr. Wilcher, and you're not going to come near Mrs. Jimson again, if I can help it."

"But she's expecting me. It's all arranged."

"Who arranged it? You wrote. That's not arranging. It takes two to make an arrangement. You take my advice, Mr. Wilcher, and go away before worse occurs."

"Excuse me," I said, "I came to see Mrs. Jimson, and I mean to see her."

"Don't you come in this house or I'll throw you down the steps."

I now began to feel myself growing angry. At the same time I reflected that anger was very dangerous to me and my cause. A heart attack would render me quite helpless and defeat me.

"Young man," I said, "I don't know who you are, but I must beg you to mind your own business and let me take care of mine."

"Mrs. Jimson is my business, like any decent chap's. That's enough for you." Then he quickly closed the door. Luckily I had already placed my foot in it.

"I won't get off," I said, for I was now quite infuriated, "until Mrs. Jimson tells me to go."

There was then a moment's silence, and it suddenly occurred to me that Sara was also behind the door. I heard something like a whisper. And I said, "Are you there, Sara? If so, let me in at once."

There was another silence, and I thought I heard a board creak, as if Sara's heavy body had retreated down the passage. Then the door was flung back and the young man waved his hand in my face. "Get off, I tell you, or I'll call an officer."

This mention of the police, of course, enraged me greatly. And I shouted, "I won't get off—I'm coming in." And I jumped into the hall. The young man was taken by surprise. I had pushed him a yard or more before he began to push. I had now lost my temper and I was pushing so hard that I might have pushed him right down the passage. But at this moment my head began to swim, a frightful pain constricted my heart, and I was obliged to stoop down into a very ignominious position.

I then found myself sitting on the doorstep. The door itself had closed behind me, and I perceived that I had been pressed back. Luckily I did not faint. Having taken a dose of Ann's medicine which was always in my pocket, I went to the inn at the corner of the street and wrote from there a note to Sara, explaining that I had come to fetch her, enclosing a check for five pounds, and asking her to join me at the hotel that afternoon or the next morning. I delivered this note into the letter box of No. 24 and returned to my hotel, where, I am bound to admit, I passed the rest of the day in much agitation.

I dared not believe that Sara had betrayed me, that she had really allowed me to be driven from the door. On the other hand, why had she not answered my letters or sent her address? I fell into much dejection. The hotel, the streets, which had seemed so encouraging on the day before in their life and bustle, had now a stupid look, as if, after all, they meant nothing.

The evening papers were full of some new threats from the man Hitler, and new dangers to peace. But I could not make head or tail of them. One said that Germany had great grievances which ought to be satisfied; another that Hitler could never be satisfied; a third showed an American caricature of the British lion having its tail cut off by Germany and Japan.

I sat in my room all the afternoon waiting for Sara. She did not come, and I could not rest. I lost myself in corridors. I wandered through enormous halls with roofs of colored glass, where thousands of people in dark gloomy clothes and black hats sat drinking at little tables. And all their faces seemed to wear the same expression, "I am I, that's all I know about it."

I came into a great drawing room with a bright fire, but nobody was in it. One evening paper lay on the carpet. There were no pictures in the room. It seemed like a waiting room without a purpose, with no journey beyond it. I was tired. My legs would scarcely move. But I dared not sit down in one of the great chairs for fear my heart would stop. I could not die in a waiting room.

Where am I going, I wondered as I faced again that huge

field of dark coats and white faces, corn high, silently drinking from cups and glasses, each as solitary as a stone on a beach.

"And where are they going?" I thought. "Do they know? When Chaucer wrote of pilgrimage, in England, then every man knew where he was, and where he could go. But now all is confusion and no one has anywhere to go. They leave home only to sit under glass roofs, in black overcoats and black hats, with faces so private and cunning that you are afraid of them."

A pilgrim is not a lost soul, I thought, nor a wanderer. He is not a tramp. But these are lost souls who don't even know that they are lost. They read three newspapers a day saying different things, and then they put on their black overcoats and hats and come to some place like this, to look at each other's hats and coats and to feel nothing, to say nothing, to think nothing, only to wait. And all the time, something called history is rushing to and fro and changing the very shape of hats and coats and trousers and collars.

I did not go to bed. Motors roared in the streets. And from the court there was the hum of some engine, discreet but relentless. I seemed to be bound in the midst of complicated enormous machinery. And I felt that at any moment the room itself would be called upon to play its allotted part; it would begin to revolve; its walls would close and crush me to death; or it would sink slowly down, into the earth, to be passed again through the fire.

140

In the morning a note came from Sara, apologizing for my treatment on the day before and asking me to come and see her at ten o'clock. It was for me like a resurrection. I took a strong dose of Ann's medicine and went again to Lewisham. The medicine had the effect of making my heart beat too fast, so that I was extremely giddy and once or twice I fell down. But I kept on smiling and laughing at the people so that they helped me up and did not think that anything unusual was taking place. In any case, I perceived that they could not tell, merely by seeing me fall down, that I had run away from home.

The young man, Fred, again opened the door, and this time he began at once to shout at me. But before he could attempt to push me down the step, I heard Sara's own voice. She came downstairs as fast as she could, calling out, "Now Fred, now Fred, don't be so silly."

And pushing past the young man, she said to me, "Oh, sir, I am so sorry. Never mind what Fred was saying. You know you're always welcome. If you would come into the parlor."

She was older than I remembered her. Her hair was gray and she seemed broader and redder. Her arms, which were bare to the elbow, were of surprising thickness and weight. But her eyes still expressed that lively good nature; her voice, that delight in a friend which had long ago endeared her to me.

"Come in, sir. If I may say so, you don't look quite yourself. But who does this weather? All these colds about. A green Christmas and a full churchyard. I said so to Fred and we've had three funerals in the street this month alone."

Speaking so, she had hustled the young man to one side. He, for his part, seemed ready to oppose her and said, "Now, Sara, you know what I said."

"Why, yes, Fred," in that caressing voice which I had heard so often, "I know—I won't forget. Now if you'll just go off and see that nothing boils over," and she guided me into the parlor and shut the door on the furious young man.

"He's on the railway," she explained to me. "Night work, and he ought to be in bed by this time. But I can never get him into bed. You know what these young ones are—never want to go to bed and never want to get up. But such a nice fellow. And so good to me, too. Well, you see—" and she laughed, while she dusted down a chair for me with her apron. When she laughed, she shook all over. "You would think he wanted to eat any other man that came near the house. Why," she said, sitting down, "you wouldn't believe it, sir, but he wants to marry me. Of course he's not so young as he looks. These fair ones cheat the wrinkles—forty-two and two little boys. They're at school now or I'd like you to see them, sir. Like little angels to look at, but, as Fred says, the other thing for mischief."

"But, Sara," I said, "what about our arrangement? You know that I was going to take you away. What's all this about Fred?"

"Oh, you needn't mind him, sir," Sara cried, laughing. "He's easy. And as for your kind offer to me, sir, I can hardly believe it yet. But you always were the very best of men to me, whatever Fred may say, and indeed I don't deserve half what you did for me or would do—" and she ran on, speaking of me in so affectionate and grateful a manner that I could not help laughing. "Come, Sara," I said, "we all know that you're a great flatterer."

"No, indeed," she said, very seriously. "I couldn't flatter a good heart, for we all know that good hearts like honest tongues are few and neither gets its proper due. And indeed, sir, you've been an angel to me and the only thing is whether you haven't thought too much of me, and might be disappointed."

So then I forgot all her fatness and her coarse cheeks and her new habit of saying sir at every other word, and I sat down beside her on the sofa and told her that I could never be disappointed in one so truly good. And so on. Indeed, I grew romantic and said much that would look ridiculous in print. And Sara said that, in that case, she would have me; only she must have a week to pack. "A week," I said. "How can I wait a week?" For I thought that long before that the family would discover where I was.

But Sara was all compliance. And the end of it was, she would go and pack that minute, and send Fred out to get rid of him.

Then she brought me a tray with tea and cake, and a glass of brandy, and told me to rest quietly until she came again to tell me that the coast was clear.

141

And now I was too inspirited and too impatient to rest. As I moved about in Sara's room, I was amused by my passing jealousy of Fred. "What right have I," I thought, "to be jealous of anyone? And is it not just like Sara to make this new nest for herself, and adopt this new dependent."

I recognized on the mantelpiece two little figures, in white Sèvres, one without a hand and the other mended in the neck, which had certainly come from Tolbrook. And this also made me laugh. "How that would shock Blanche. But with Sara, how natural. We were letting the house. Why leave to tenants these charming figures which they would not miss?"

And as I turned from the figures, I seemed to recognize a chair. Surely it had been in the attic at Craven Gardens. A hideous object of carved oak, with rows of little spindles in the back. And I was astonished. How on earth, I thought, did that chair come to be transported from Craven Gardens, which was, in any case, burnt out four years ago, to a cottage in Lewisham?

Four years ago I was shocked to find that some of my trifles had passed into Sara's keeping. But now I was not only amused; I felt a secret exultation in Sara's impudence, and more than impudence. Something far deeper. Something that had come to me also from Lucy. A freedom. An enterprise. And looking round, I saw a dozen more objects from forgotten corners of Tolbrook and Craven Gardens: an engraving of Wellington at Waterloo; a glass picture, cracked in four places, of Cherry Ripe; a little tripod table with one foot broken short. Apparently Sara had permitted herself to take nothing that was in use, or in good order. Everything was cracked or chipped. A woman of principle. And by this strange route I pierced again into the living Sara, with her peculiar attitude to life. As one who faces a powerful but stupid enemy with the ready invention of a free lance and the subtlety of a diplomat.

I remembered the first time I came to know Sara's quality as a life manager. It was during Robert's school holidays. My nephew, from the beginning, struck up with Sara a friendship which alarmed me. For at that time I knew nothing of the woman except what I had heard. Young Jaffery, as we called him, though he was my own age, had engaged her for me, and he had described her in his own detestable language as "a bit flyblown."

"She's been before the Bench for cashing bad checks, and before that she was living in sin with a so-called artist, who also has a police record. But they say she can cook and she's the only one who is willing to go to a place like Tolbrook at the wage you suggested. On the other hand, she can't afford to be particular about conditions." All this meant, of course, that I myself had not too good a character, after recent scandals; and that I was also a skinflint. For Jaffery was the kind of fool who, in order to be smart, could not resist being offensive.

But, having only Jaffery's description to guide me, I had always thought of Sara as a bad lot. Though I soon found that she was a good though extravagant cook, and a sensible housekeeper, I did not care for Robert to be too intimate with her. And when I caught him running to the kitchen, I would say, "Mrs. Jimson is busy. You mustn't order her about like that. It's not her place to wait upon small boys."

"Oh, Sara doesn't mind," he would answer. "She likes it,

the old trout." And this very roughness of manner and speech seemed proof of the contagion I feared. I said to him severely, "She's not an old trout. She's a responsible person. You ought to know by now that servants have a right to proper respect."

"I like old Sara," he said. "I can do what I like with the old nose."

"What do you mean, old nose?"

"She's rather ashamed of her nose. So I call her old nose," and he burst out laughing.

Robert had been a great anxiety to me. For I was responsible for him to Lucy, and yet I had never succeeded in getting close to the boy. I had not seen him for some years before Lucy died. He had been at school, and in the holidays Lucy had either sent him to the seaside with Amy or gone visiting with him. She never let him come near the Benjamites if she could help it.

After Lucy's death, I went to see his schoolmaster, and the boy was brought in to me, short, thickset, small for thirteen, with his father's build and his mother's look. He was said to be lazy at his books but good at English. His English verses were the best in the school.

I explained to him that he would live with me at Tolbrook. That his father, who had but lately set out on his world mission, had approved this arrangement.

He listened to me with his peculiar intenseness and said nothing.

I had seen him at his mother's funeral standing beside his father among a group of Benjamites. He had shown then an unexpected violence of grief which drew me to him, as to one who had loved Lucy. And so I spoke now of Lucy's wish that he would work hard and complete his education at one of the great schools.

He listened and said suddenly, "I want to go to so-and-so—it does engineering," mentioning a school I have never heard of.

"But your name is down for so-and-so," I said.

"Yes, but I want to be an engineer."

"You can be what you like, but first you must have a good education. The school you mention may be good, but I know the one I've chosen is good and I can't take risks in such an important matter."

He said no more, but he looked at me with Lucy's obstinate expression. And his report was bad.

But when at Tolbrook I told him that it was a disgrace, he answered cheerfully, "I thought it might be pretty rotten."

It was impossible to tell if the boy were irresponsible or only careless. He was noisy and dirty in the house, he never opened a book, and if he were reproached for any fault he showed a face like wood and said nothing. But it was difficult not to like his gaiety, his spirits, his friendly air. He would come to table with filthy hands and begin at once a friendly conversation about the weather, the crops, or the local gossip. An eagle had been reported over the tors and so-and-so had missed a lamb. Such-and-such a farmer had bought a reaper and binder, but it had stuck in his gate.

And I could never tell that his lively talk was not merely a device for preventing some remark upon his hands. For if I should say, "Robert, your hands are dirty," he would not answer. You would suppose that he had not heard me. And such cool obstinacy alarmed me, for I thought, "What will become of one so confident and unteachable?"

142

It was Sara who prevented what might have been a disastrous quarrel with the boy. Robert asked me one day if he might mend the clock in the back hall, an old thirty-hour grandfather clock of the Stuart times. Its single hand had not moved in my lifetime. I answered that the relic was too fragile; it should be left alone. A few days later, on examining the clock, I found that the works had been removed; only the face was left. The hand had been pegged to a board.

I taxed Robert with taking out the works and he admitted the deed.

"But didn't I tell you not to touch the works?"

"Well, uncle, they weren't any good, were they?"

"That depends on what you mean by good—they were a valuable movement by a famous clockmaker—now I suppose they are ruined," and so on. And I told him to put them back at once.

But he did not do so. At this open rebellion I was at my wit's end. If I gave way, I perceived that the boy's character, already headstrong, would be entirely wrecked. And how could I enforce a decision? I could not use violence for, even if I had been able to contemplate an act of cruelty, it was against my principles. I therefore pointed out to him that without mutual trust we should both be unhappy; and in this case, at least, he was in the wrong. For the clock was mine and so forth. The boy answered that I need not worry about the clock, because he would make it go. And there was a sharp dispute, in which I spoke severely of his obstinacy and lack of good will.

The boy then disappeared. Imagine my alarm when he did not come to luncheon or tea or supper. I sent out the men to look for him. And finally, in despair, I consulted Sara.

"Don't you worry about young Master Robert, sir," she said. "He'll come back for supper. And I've got the bits of the clock all safe."

"The bits of the clock?"

"Why, yes, sir—the poor little man took it all apart and he can't find how to get it together again. He's been terribly upset about it."

"And where are these bits of my clock?"

"Well, sir," and the woman looked at me as if to say, I suppose you must know. "The truth is, that they're in my room."

"In your room? Your bedroom?"

"You see, sir—I thought if I gave him a tray for the wheels and things, they'd be under my eye, and I'd know he wasn't losing any of them."

"And also, I suppose, your bedroom was a place where I wouldn't be likely to catch Master Robert doing what I told him not to do."

Sara then turned very red and assured me that she had no idea of such a plot. But I told her that she was spoiling the boy and that her bedroom was no place for him. In fact, I had almost decided to send her away on the spot.

"Show me the clock," I said, "or what's left of it." She took me to her room, and I saw on her chest of drawers, which was also her dressing table, the lid of a cardboard box filled with the remnants of the clock. Tools lay on the only chair, on the window sill, and on the floor, which was strewn with chips of wood and metal. A vise was fixed to the washstand, and in the chamber pot, standing in the basin, spindles and wheels were soaking in dirty paraffin. For a moment I was too much disturbed by this last familiarity between the couple, that Robert should make free of such a utensil in a servant's room, and that Sara should permit it, so to speak. And Sara's own conduct increased my embarrassment, which may have been absurd, but was I think justified. For, instead of ignoring the object, she held it out to me to show me that the wheels were in safekeeping. "They're all there, sir—I thought I'd better leave them in the oil because of the damp. I'll see they don't get lost and when Master Robert goes back to school, any clockmaker can put them together again. And I'm sure, sir, he never meant any harm—it's only that he couldn't bear to see any clockwork about and not make it go. You know what clockwork is to boys, sir—it just goes to their heads and there's no stopping them. So I thought I'd see he came to no harm. It's what they say, 'One way in by the door, and ten by the windows'; and

Master Robert's so easy and good-hearted, you can turn him which way you like."

And, in fact, it now began to strike me that Sara had managed a difficult problem with some skill. She had saved the clock.

"And do you know where Master Robert is now?" I asked.

"Why, no, sir, not just now. But he'll come back, never fear. Only of course he's a bit upset and perhaps if no one said anything about the clock."

"You spoil Master Robert, Mrs. Jimson."

"I hope not, sir. But as they say 'Yesterday is neither a maid wed or a man fed.' And I was just wondering—if nobody should say anything. It's not that Master Robert wouldn't understand that nobody was saying anything—on purpose. He's sharp enough." Sara's grammar became confused, but as I found out at a later day, the confusion of her grammar was always the mark of a clear intention. I understood her very well, and gave her to understand, discreetly, that if the clock could be restored, I should not be severe on Robert. And it turned out that all this time the boy was eating a large supper in the back kitchen. What's more, he returned next day to our usual routine, without offering either explanation or apology. Yet I could not help feeling that a serious crisis had been avoided by Sara's tactful management. The clock was duly replaced. And several years passed before I discovered, or rather, one of my tenants discovered, that a great part of the works was missing.

143

And long before that time Sara had become indispensable to me. I had learned to appreciate the quality of a woman who could devote herself not only to a willful small boy but to chairs, tables, carpets, and even vegetables. I have heard her object to a kitchenmaid that she did not know how to treat a potato.

One forgot the thick, coarse figure, the rough features, in the light of a spirit which gave always encouragement. From the beginning I had noticed one good quality in Sara, her regularity at prayers and church. But I knew she had been well brought up by a God-fearing mother and thought her piety merely habitual. I came to discover how strong and rich a fountain of grace played not only in the energy of her religious observance but in everything she did, and in her most casual remark. All was colored by these country maxims, so often in her mouth, which rise from a wisdom so deep in tradition that it is like the spirit of a race. Never sigh but send. Hot needle and a burnt thread. Give me today and I'll sell you tomorrow.

And yet Sara had her faults. She had her obstinacy. I remember that she made up her mind that the pictures wanted washing; and though I forbade her to touch them, she washed them all, with soap and water, in my absence, and afterwards excused herself on the ground that she had misunderstood me.

Then we looked at each other and I said, "I told you not to wash them."

"I think they look brighter, sir. I polished them off with a new potato. Now if you could get someone to put a touch of varnish on them, they would be twice as gay."

She had her own mind. She kept her own counsel. She was devoted but she was never servile. And I rejoiced in her quality which belonged to my own people, whose nature was rather affection than passion; whose gaiety was rather humor than wit; whose judgment did not spring from logic but from sense, the feeling of the world. Only to hear Sara's step in the passage was a reminder of the truth, which was the taproot of her own faith, that we were travelers in the world, enjoined to live "like men upon a journey."

144

Now, whether it was the tea, the brandy, Sara's good fire, or
happiness and peace of soul—or all together—I went to sleep
on the sofa. I had not slept for two nights and I slept well.
When I awoke it was nearly one o'clock, and I was extremely
startled to find myself in the strange room, dark and quiet,
with a pain in my legs and the fire going out. And what was
still more bewildering, as I looked about I seemed to be carried
all at once to a hundred different situations of my past; I
seemed to fly into pieces. I looked at the rug and I seemed to
see a baby crawling over its Turkish reds; I looked at the tablecloth, which was however only half a tablecloth, and I was
playing beggar-my-neighbor with Lucy, amid cries of rage; a
brass oil lamp on a tall stem started from the corner to remind
me that under its discreet shade I had flirted with a fat schoolgirl in pigtails, Amy. And at sight of the mirror my mustache,
shaved off forty years ago, grew again. I stroked it and said to
Edward, with Bill's mustache manner, "My dear boy, if you
must poke the fire, do it properly. Give some thought to it."

And at the same time, I was listening to a murmur of voices
in which I seemed to recognize first Lucy and then Edward, but
mysteriously changed. "No," I said, becoming more wakeful
and putting down my legs. "It is Robert and Ann."

I jumped up, now very wide awake, and rushed to open the
door. But as I opened it, Sara bustled in, in fact, walked straight
into me and nearly knocked me down.

"What are you doing, Sara?" I asked her. "Who have you got
there?"

"It was only Fred, sir, I was just trying to make him have
some sense. Gracious, look at the fire. And you'll need it for
your dinner. I mean your luncheon. There, I'll pull up this
chair, and the little table. Don't worry about Fred, sir. If you
stay quiet in here just another five minutes. He's got to go on

duty; and, oh dear, what a trouble he's been. Why, would you believe it, a boy like that, for so he is a boy to an old woman like me—I hardly dare to go out of the house, even to do my shopping or to fetch the beer. They say widowers don't make jealous flesh, but Fred is as touchy as a hedgehog."

So she ran on, talking of Fred and Fred's children, and his delicate chest, and his colds, and even his favorite dishes.

I had heard Sara chatter but I knew that she was not a foolish woman. She could hold her tongue when she chose. So I looked at her and listened to all this talk of Fred with surprise; until, meeting her bright brown eyes fixed upon me with so much candor and affection, I saw, as through the brightness of a clear window, both obstinacy and cunning gazing out at me.

I had long recognized in Sara, among her great virtues, very great faults, of which the chief was a resolution to have her own way. Indeed, you can hardly call it resolution any more than you can say of a tree that it has a resolution to grow, or of streams that they are determined to run into the sea. She was as persistent as a natural force. And to that persistence all her virtues as well as her vices were made to contribute. She could use her kindness, her affection, as well as her talkativeness, for her own purpose, whatever it was.

"What are you doing, Sara?" I said. "What are you plotting? I know all your tricks—you thought I didn't see them before, but I knew all the time that you were as cunning as an old monkey."

Sara turned very red and opened her eyes as if in alarm, but she continued in the same voice of cajolery. "Oh, sir, I know I did deceive you; indeed, I behaved very badly to you."

"Yes, yes, but our arrangement, woman—what are we going to do?"

"Yes, of course, sir, our arrangements—" Sara stopped with such a peculiar glance at the door that I too glanced toward it. I had expected to see someone come in. "Yes, sir," Sara said, "of course we shall have to arrange things, won't we, and you needn't be afraid of Fred. He's a bit sudden sometimes, as they say, but you couldn't find a better boy anywhere, no trouble at all—for goodness knows it's not his fault if he has a delicate stomach."

At these words my head turned round. I shouted out, "You are deceiving me, Sara. I thought you so good and religious, and wise, but you are nothing but a cunning greedy creature, a regular peasant. I suppose you have caught this boy Fred just now, as you caught me, and catch everyone—yes, that's what you do. You pretend to be so religious and modest and respectable, and all the time you're leading a man on, and heading him off."

And I rushed at her. I had never hit anyone in my life, much less a woman; but at that moment, so had Sara maddened me with her talk and her honest look that I believe I should have hit her. I meant to hit her on the nose.

But my head continued to turn round, the darkness came in front of my eyes, and instead of hitting Sara I tumbled over a chair and she caught me from falling.

"There, there," she said, carrying me across the room like a child and putting me on the sofa. "You shouldn't, sir—it always was bad for you. Yes, it's just what you say. I've been a bad woman. Well, I know it. Though I hope they taught me better at Holloway. There, sir—don't get up. You're really not fit to be going about, and if you wait a moment, I'll—but there they are. Here's Master Robert, sir, at last, and his nice little wife."

Robert and Ann came into the room and I saw Robert kissing Sara and apologizing for their lateness. And it turned out that Sara had wired for them on the day before, and her message to me had been a trap. I did not forgive her and I told her so. Yet she showed not the least remorse but continued to chatter about Fred, and dear Master Robert and his nice little wife. "I'm so glad he got a clever little wife like that for I always thought that he would go marrying some great lump."

Ann and Robert had brought a taxi with them and I was glad when they had carried me into it and taken me away.

But when I spoke of Sara's treachery, Ann answered that Sara had behaved with great good sense. "I never much liked the idea of your Sara," she said, "and I don't see the attraction now, but she's certainly got a head on her shoulders."

"How long has she been living in this place?"

"I don't know. I gather she went as housekeeper to a widower."

"I don't think he'll be a widower very long."

"I don't know about that," Robert said. "Sara's refused him several times."

"How much has she refused him?"

"Well, what does it matter at her age? Poor old Sara, I should think she might be allowed a little fun. And I'll bet she makes Fred happy."

"Yes," I said. "I'm sure she will. And there is no doubt that she has acted with good sense. I shall write to her and tell her so. And if she would accept a wedding present, I shall ask her to choose a piece of furniture from Tolbrook. A sofa, perhaps. Her sofa was a poor thing. I suppose it belonged to Fred."

Ann and Robert looked at each other as much as to say, "He's wandering." And I began to laugh. I thought, "All the same, this is the end of me."

"Where are we going?" I asked the young ones.

"Home," said Ann, "as soon as we can. But I don't think you had better go much farther today, uncle."

They did not ask me any longer about my own wishes. And I did not protest. It was somehow understood among us that I had no right to protest. I had become a dependent member of the family, like Jan, for whom these responsible persons, Ann and Robert, would make all necessary arrangements.

So I was carried to a nursing home, where I spent the next six weeks. And then back to Tolbrook, where I was again under strictest orders.

145

It is September. I have been out of bed for a fortnight, but it seems that I have enjoyed a family life for a long time. To an old man who has admitted that he is finished, the years fly, but each day is a gift of heaven. To streaming windows he says, "Once more I see the beauty of your melting lights and hear an English shower." He greets each spring and harvest as a piece of good luck.

Robert is threshing in the great salon. He did not ask me if he could bring a threshing machine into the house, but I was waked yesterday morning by what seemed to be an earthquake. The floor shook under me, the windows rattled, the plaster fell from the ceiling, and the air was filled with a loud, roaring sound, with explosions and cracks like rifle shots. But before I could get out of bed, Ann opened the communicating door between our rooms and said, "It's only the threshing—Robert said he was beginning after breakfast. But I suppose he couldn't wait."

"Is he coming to prayers?"

"I'll send out and tell him."

And in a few minutes Robert, still in his blue overalls, comes into the nursery. For since we have returned home again, he has been as regular at prayers as Ann. I even think he is more serious than Ann, for I can feel his attention. I do not ask why this miracle has happened, or how Robert and Ann were reconciled. When on my first day out of bed I saw the girl, Molly Panton, forking the new straw into the bull pen, I exclaimed to Ann, "What, is she here? And what about the baby?"

"The daughter's here, too."

"Good God, what are you thinking of? What will the people say?"

"Robert doesn't seem to mind. And I suppose she's too stupid to mind anything."

"You had no business to allow such an arrangement—it's perfect madness."

"I had no choice. It was one of Robert's conditions."

"So Robert made conditions?"

"Trust Robert."

"No apology, no explanations?"

"He said he wanted to keep an eye on the daughter, and he'd never get anyone better than Molly with cows."

"And what were your conditions?" I asked, feeling ready to shake the girl.

"I didn't make any. I saw it wouldn't do."

"Why, it's incredible. What are you made of—are you Robert's doormat—have you no pride at all?" etc. For I was disgusted. "And have you reflected that you've wrecked your life—and probably Robert's? It's ruin for a boy like that to get his own way."

"Well, he has got a way and I wasn't sure I had, and you know, uncle, it's not a final arrangement. We're just going to try how it works—there's no promises on either side."

"I see, everything left to chance and luck, and you expect it's going to work, as you put it. The work will be yours."

"Yes, it's going to be rather a job, but up to now everyone has been a model of discretion—even Robert."

"Discretion," I said, and then I could not help laughing. "Very well," I said. "I'm an old fool—I don't understand anything, but I thought you modern girls had some pride."

"Well," Ann said, "I am rather inclined to be proud of this arrangement—even Robert can't say I've been prejudiced. And as for Molly, you know, uncle, I feel rather sorry for her. I still don't know why she wants to hang about." A touch of feminine spite which gave me a little solace, for I felt that, after all, the girl was not completely incomprehensible to me.

"I dare say," I said, "she hopes for another baby."

"I dare say," Ann said, in a mild tone. "But it's not going to happen yet. Robert did promise me that—only one at a time," and she added, "Otherwise Robert himself would look ridiculous. Not that he cares. But I do. Or, I think I do."

The scientific inquirer peeped out again, and indeed every time I think I have come close to this girl's nature she recedes from me again into a distance that I can't penetrate.

She is again pregnant. I gather she is already in her fifth month, so that she lost no time in what she describes as the Lincoln negotiations. But if perhaps she has a Delilah of the more scientific kind in her composition, she does not betray her to me. She appears, more than ever before, preoccupied with some problem, and as before, in her pregnancy, she is careless and troublesome to us. She will not take her emulsion, etc., and insists on going out alone, unless Robert or I can catch her.

She worries us both. Her face is yellow and appears shrunken. New wrinkles mark her eyes and forehead. She labors through the fields, she throws back her head and hollows her back to carry her burden, and fixes her eyes on the horizon. She does not notice the apple-scented lanes, the bright crops, the trees heavy with leaf, trembling under the warm breeze. When, to distract her mind, I invite her to admire the season, she answers vaguely, "You aren't tired, are you? You mustn't get tired." And when I speak of her writing, of her father's papers, she says, "I suppose they will have to wait."

In the news she takes no interest whatever, much to Robert's indignation, who declares that there is going to be a war. "And serve you all right if you won't take the trouble to look facts in the face."

"But if you look them in the face," Ann says, "they get nervous and pull another face. I see the glass has gone back—it's just as well you're threshing under cover."

"It is lucky," I venture to remark, with some irony, "that the Adams brothers used the classical proportions of the double cube. There's no other drawing room in the county would take a threshing machine."

And both of them turn to me with the politeness of those who have forgotten a guest.

"Well, yes, uncle, it's just the place—might have been made for the job—and if one or two ceilings shake a bit loose it was quite time for 'em."

"You really are better today, uncle. We must go for a real walk."

146

But Ann, though she walks with me, prefers, I think, to be with Robert. And since I like to be with her, I spent all this afternoon in the salon. The huge machine, like a species of Roman siege engine, towers in the middle of the floor, driven by a tractor among the broken laurels. The driving band passes through one of the beautiful windows from which the panes have been knocked out of the sashes. The carts are backed in turn along the west side, brushing the painted walls. And behind Farley, who is feeding to Robert on the top of the machine, I see over the middle window a rural trophy in plaster of delicate scythes and sickles, sheaves and hayforks, tied up in pale blue ribbon. But the thick chaff dust, which lies along every panel molding like yellow snow, is already hiding their beautiful detail, characteristic of Adams refinement.

Farley's head, when he takes his stand upon a new load, almost brushes the cupids on the ceiling, painted among the fine Adams plaster by Angelica Kaufmann. They seem to be flying round the old man's bald brown skull like cherubim round one of El Greco's saints. He feeds with deliberation, throwing each sheaf where it is wanted, and the expression on his dried-up face, wrinkled as an old fencepost, is that of an eternal patience.

The girl Molly lifts off the filled sacks and twisting up their loose necks drags them across the floor with her huge arm to the side door, where Robert, by taking out a panel and knocking down the bricks, has made a loading platform. The grinning and horned Pan who, in white marble, plays upon his syrinx under one end of the magnificent mantelshelf, famous among the scholars of architecture, carries on one horn some laborer's luncheon, tied up in a red handkerchief; and round his waist, mixed with the marble flowers and grasses, hangs a bunch of real onions on a string. His grin reminds me of Robert's smile.

The whole building—floor, walls, and roof—shakes and thunders, and through the mist of fine dust rising and falling in the air on every draft long bars of yellow sunlight decline, hiding the far end of the room in a blue shadow.

Ann has placed herself on a pile of sacks between two windows. She has a book open on her lap but does not read. She knits and looks occasionally out of the window, or at Jan running about among the mountains of chaff which rise below the thresher, or at Robert high up on the machine; but always with her preoccupied air, like one who looks at a passing landscape, a strange child, a figure on some distant mountain.

In a pause of the roar, while the tractor is stopped to tighten the driving band, she says, "That child is full of fleas from the draff." And Robert's voice answers from among the gods and goddesses on the ceiling, "He may as well get used to 'em now."

The two old men, who are shoveling this draff away to keep it from swallowing up the machine, look at the child with mild speculative faces. They are those old laborers, twisted and knotted almost out of human shape, lame, stooped, with distorted arms and crooked, swollen fingers, who are seen only in harvesttime, when they creep out again into the sun to do some humble task which does not need much strength.

Jan runs up to one of them, seizes his broad draff fork by the shaft, and, trying to shake it, looks up, laughing. The old man looks down without a smile. His face, like Ann's, seems to express a deep preoccupation, neither sad nor cheerful, but questioning.

Ann calls, "Come here, Jan, you mustn't be a nuisance."

The boy looks round and then rushes away to the other side of the thresher to hide from her, and to do what he likes.

Ann continues to knit. It is Robert who comes down from the thresher, takes the child from under the wheels of the cart and carries him back to his mother. "Keep him here, will you? That band would cut him in two."

"He won't stay, you know."

"Make him stay—you don't want him killed, do you?"

"Stay here, Jan."

Robert climbs the thresher by the wheel and gives the signal. The machine once more shakes the room, and the grain pours out of its filters into the sacks. Jan runs off, looking back at his mother with a broad smile of delight which says very plainly "I don't mind *you*." Ann gazes at him with her absent expression and says nothing. A moment later he is creeping under the cart wheels.

I sit in the armchair, a tattered bergère in white and gilt, last of the drawing-room furniture; and the very ruin of this beautiful room is become a part of my happiness. I say no longer, "Change must come, and this change, so bitter to me, is a necessary ransom for what I keep." I have surrendered because I cannot fight and now it seems to me that not change but life has lifted me and carried me forward on the stream. It is but a new life which flows through the old house; and like all life, part of that sustaining power which is the oldest thing in the world.

Tolbrook, so Jaffery says, is losing value—it is already not much better than a farmhouse. But is it not a fall back from death to life?

Robert, I suspect, is more Brown than Wilcher, a peasant in grain. But he does not destroy Tolbrook, he takes it back into history, which changed it once before from priory into farm, from farm into manor, from manor, the workshop and court of a feudal dictator, into a country house where young ladies danced and hunting men played billiards; where, at last, a new-rich gentleman spent his week ends from his office. And after that I suppose it was to have been a country hotel, where typists on holiday gaze at the trees, the crops, and the farmer's men with mutual astonishment and dislike. Robert has brought it back into the English stream and he himself has come with it; to the soft corn, good for homemade bread; the mixed farm, so good for men; the old church religion which is so twined with English life that the very prayers seem to breathe of fields after rain and skies whose light is falling between clouds.

That was Sara's religion, which served her like her pans, her rolling pins, her private recipes for clearing soup and saving a burnt stew; a wisdom and a faith so close to death and life that we could not tell what part of it was God's and what was man's sense—the sense of the common English, in a thousand generations.

I need not strive to send into Robert's heart and Ann's mind some arrow of conviction. For when I read to them in the morning, the old prayers, and they kneel at their familiar seats, they are already in the way of the country faith. For that is not an argument. It is an act and a feeling.

When therefore Jaffery and my niece Blanche protested against the change in the house, I told them that Robert had my support.

Jaffery laid this trap for me. He wrote to me reminding me that I had given instructions for a new will some months before but never signed it. He asked me if I should like to sign it in private. So I sent him a message by the gardener's boy. He was our agreed messenger when I did not want to excite curiosity in Ann or Robert or the servants.

Jaffery arrived suddenly at a corner of the drive and took me to his Queensport office. I left a note to tell Ann that I had to see an old friend. This was true, for Jaffery was officially an old friend.

I found on Jaffery's table a long row of papers tied in pink tape and many bundles of letters.

"What's all this?" I asked.

"Your wills and instructions. From your own boxes; seventeen completed wills from the London office, five at Lloyds Bank, seven at the Westminster Bank, and three here."

"Yes, I kept them in case of any legal questions. As you know, a destroyed will may be proved. I don't like destroyed wills. Better to cancel them."

But I was annoyed with Jaffery. I could see he was playing some trick. He is a smart man and smart men are always doing foolish things, especially at some serious moment.

"I only want to see the last, to cancel it, and the new one," I said severely. "You can pack up all the rest."

"There you are," and he unfolded certain packets.

These in fact were my last three wills and the new ones, not yet signed. The first left everything to Loftus and Blanche, the second left £2,000 to Robert and £500 a year to Ann and another £100 for every year that I should live after she took charge of me. In a codicil I increased this sum to £200. Then there was a will, made after Robert's flight, leaving Tolbrook to Ann as trustee for my great-nephew Edward John Wilcher Brown.

Now, by my last instructions, I was leaving the landed property to Robert absolutely, and £5,000 to my niece Blanche.

Frankly, will making has been a responsibility from which I have too often recoiled. The burden was too heavy. To do justice between so many conflicting rights and needs.

Neither was I in good fettle for such a task. For, first, I was upset by Jaffery's folly. And no sooner had I sat down to read the draft than Blanche came running in. The woman was breathless and crimson from running, and yet she cried, "What luck to find you here, uncle. I just looked in." Plainly Jaffery had sent for her.

I was angry at this plot and told them that if Robert wished to use Tolbrook for a farmhouse he might do so.

"But, Uncle Tom, you don't realize—" The big woman still panted with haste and anxiety to use this lucky and important moment. "He doesn't care one farthing for Tolbrook or you, and neither does that creature Ann. They only came back—"

"Excuse me, Mrs. Wilcher," Jaffery interrupted. "We hardly know the full reasons." And I think he made some warning signal to the woman, for she went on, "No, Mr. Jaffery, I will speak. For my uncle's own sake. And you know very well they wrote to you about a nursing home. Yes, uncle, they were going away together, to South America I believe it was, and they were going to put you into a home—"

"That's very likely," I said, looking with surprise at the woman. For I saw that she wanted to please me, to ingratiate herself; and yet she was already eager to hurt me.

Blanche's chief fault in life is too great love of justice. She resents too much injustice to herself. And hating injustice, she seeks always to punish those who do injustice. So that now she wanted to please me and to punish me at the same time. "They were going to shut you up," she said, "and the only reason why they didn't do so—"

"Really, Mrs. Wilcher." Poor little Jaffery, for all his airs of the dashing country bachelor, is a creeping little man in his soul. "You shouldn't impute motives."

"Impute, what nonsense, Mr. Jaffery," cried Blanche, who fears nobody. "You showed me the letter yourself. Saying that uncle was so ill they'd changed their minds and would come back and see him out. The very words, uncle, see you out. They're just waiting for you to die—and Master Robert goes to church to keep you in a good mood."

"Well, Blanche, it's certain that I must die, and I suppose I can't last very long now. My heart plays very queer tricks and my feet are too big for all my old shoes. And, as Sara used to say:

> When your head begins to swell
> Jack Ketch will pull your passing bell.
> But Christian feet when they grow long
> Seek to reach the churchyard throng.

And now I see it is getting late; I'm afraid I must go home."

"But, uncle, you don't mean to let them do what they like? You don't want to see Tolbrook sold just to anybody?"

Blanche made a rush as if to seize hold of me and prevent my escaping from her, but stopped halfway on the recollection that I was ill or mad or both, and might therefore cheat her by falling dead or uttering some violent nonsense.

"Good-by, my dear Blanche," I said. "You have done quite right in telling me plainly that I can't live much longer. I suppose you couldn't state a month for my death?"

"But, uncle, I hope you will live for years, and if you could only turn that couple of harpies out, I am sure something could be done. There are wonderful treatments now; Loftus is completely cured of his rheumatism by a bonesetter who broke his neck."

"If I want you, you can be sure I'll send for you," and I went away as quickly as I could, because I felt so much ashamed of cheating her of Tolbrook.

Jaffery, as he drove me home, kept saying that we had done nothing, after all, about the will.

"It doesn't do to let these things slide," he said.

"Yes, I'll let you know. But it needs some thought."

For I began to feel very strange. And, in fact, before I reached the Manor, I went to sleep and didn't know how I had got rid of Jaffery, or reached my bed, until the next afternoon.

148

I waked up to see Ann's shrunken anxious little face and swollen body perched on a bedroom chair beside my pillow. She was sewing and frowning through her spectacles at her work. She is a slow but careful needlewoman, having learned to sew, I imagine, only in the last year. Seeing that I was awake, she said, "What did you do that for, uncle? Mr. Jaffery could have come here if it was so important."

I could see she was longing to know what I had been up to; and indeed, I suppose it is a pretty serious matter for these children what I do with my property.

I said to her, "Robert has no capital and I suppose you haven't saved much."

"Nothing." She frowned at me as if to say, "What's going on now in the old lunatic's head?"

"Do you want to go to Brazil?"

"No."

"Are you going?"

"If Robert goes, I suppose I shall have to. That was the bargain. Brazil or Lincolnshire."

"Lincolnshire. Why on earth Lincolnshire?"

"Robert rather fancied the farming there."

"Are you so happy with Robert?"

"I wasn't happy without him. And I had the children to think of."

"Only one then."

"Robert says there's going to be five, at least."

"Robert, Robert, Robert—isn't there any Ann left?"

"Well, uncle, I rather agree with him there—if you have a family, I think it ought to be a family, for the family's own sake."

"I see, so you've arranged everything. And as soon as I'm out of the way, off you'll go. How long have I got, do you think?"

"You'll have to be very careful. You very nearly didn't come round yesterday, after Mr. Jaffery brought you back."

"Well, am I going to get up again?"

"Not just yet, at any rate."

I was angry with the child, and I was going to say, "You are very cool about it." But when I looked at her I thought, "She is unhappy, and perhaps she is lonely. Or why does she want to sit with an old nuisance like me? The young may be younger than they were in my day, but they grow old more quickly. In a world without manners or reserve they find too soon that loneliness of spirit which I found only in my old age." And I said to her, "If you didn't dip your face in a flour bag and put that raspberry jam on your lips, I should like you much better."

But she did not seem to hear me. She is as obstinate as a mule, as Lucy, as Sara, as Amy; she wouldn't wash her face to get Tolbrook. I lost my temper and said to her, "It's no good waiting. I'm not going to tell you what I did at Jaffery's. So go away, for goodness' sake. And give me some peace from all of you."

Then she went out so quietly that I was perfectly enraged against the whole race of nurses who oppress us with their patience.

149

Of course, I am very unfairly prejudiced against Ann. It is absurd to be angry with the girl for painting her face. She is really a good girl of whom I am quite fond. There is certainly a good deal of the conservative in my composition. I never read of an old house pulled down but with a pain in my very heart. The loss of Devonshire House gave me my first touch of angina. And still that long wall of dirty yellow brick in Piccadilly, with its two gates, and the low plain house behind them seem to my memory more beautiful than all your European glass, steel, and concrete.

I walk once more before them, in a new frock coat. The gates open, and I see the old duke, with his sleepy eyes, his heavy beard, his huge hat. The duke is my enemy, for he has deserted Gladstone, and I am then a violent young Liberal. But I am taken by surprise, my hand springs up of itself, and I take off my hat.

The duke is equally startled. He slightly moves his eyelids and takes off his own hat, with an awkward hasty movement of the shy man who hasn't prepared himself. We pass with mutual astonishment. And then I recollect myself, and begin to abuse the duke to myself, saying, "If Home Rule is lost, then the Lords will be responsible for all that happens in Ireland."

But I feel strongly as if the duke and I are joined together in some private relation. I am laughing at our confusion, our bows. I tell the story to my friends at Oxford and make fun of the duke. But I am still enjoying him, as a piece of history, of England.

For the truth is, I have always been a lover rather than a doer; I have lived in dreams rather than acts; and like all lovers, I have lived in terror of change to what I love. Time itself has haunted my marriage bed like a ghost of despair. And on the day when I possessed Tolbrook my keenest fears began. It was not till I was a pillar of the old order that I felt how the ground trembled under my feet, how close beneath the solid-looking stone was the primitive bog.

When I was small, we children often played in the linen room. We used the big square baskets, with their leather corners, for galleons and fought out the Armada under the shelves. But one day at the end of a game someone, probably Lucy, tipped me heels over head into a half-filled basket and shut down the lid. I remember still my first surprise, my laugh, my expectation of something delightful, a new game; and then, when nothing happened, and nobody answered my cries, and I found that I could not open the lid, my panic.

I knew that this was a joke and yet I felt that I was going to be murdered. That my brothers and sisters had planned to get rid of me and leave me to choke and starve. When I screamed for my mother and she did not come, I believed at once that she, too, was in the plot. She was tired of me.

People think that a child's faith is absolute, because instinctive; therefore very strong. It is not so. Because it is unreasoning it is easily upset. A child does not live by faith but by forgetfulness. It forgets itself so quickly that it forgets its terrors. But those terrors are more terrible, more far-reaching, than any grown-ups because of that childish ignorance of security. For me the very earth was not solid, it might swallow me; the water was not bound by the nature of a liquid, it might rise in one wave and chase me up the steepest mountain; the sky was not emptiness, it was full of demons; the night was not an absence of light, it was the presence of a thing, a creature, which shut me off from all who loved me and hid me from all help, in order that it might jump upon me and strangle me. As I say, even my brothers and sisters, who seemed to love me, my mother who spent her life in caring for me, were capable, to my faithless mind, of turning upon me and murdering me.

In one of these baskets—yes, I know even the basket, because it was the only one with a lock, and it is there still, as good as new, or rather, made better than new, cleaned and polished and oiled by the faithful, busy hands of Sara, whom my faithlessness attempted to murder; in that basket more than sixty years ago I suffered a torture so extreme, so fearful that it twists my heart now. Even this moment I feel a pain that might kill me, but I do not care if I die; I do not value life. Let me not fly from this real sense of life, too; this pain, for childish suffering and for the child itself, so far from me that he is no longer myself but a different being. And through the child, it is a pain for all childhood, so easily hurt, so helpless. For no power can protect a child from his own ignorance. No kindest nurse, no farsighted anxious mother, assuring it every day of love and sympathy, can give its weak half-formed brain the power to judge of truth and falsehood, of the real nature of things. The strongest assurance from the most loving familiar lips will be abolished in one instant by a smile from another child, the bark of a strange dog. What surprises me is not that I screamed in the basket but that I did not die there, that my childish heart and brain could stand such shocks of agony without bursting. I do remember that I did not recover from it for some hours or perhaps days. I could neither eat nor sleep, and I had one night, I dare say the same night, a kind of fit which caused my mother to fear that I should be an epileptic. The doctor was sent for and, wise man, listened to a plea which my father had refused, that I should be allowed to sleep in my mother's bed. My father did not believe in coddling children and he had, in this special case, another reason to stand in my way. He did not want my mother to be troubled by a restless child, during her own light sleep.

But now he gave way, and for two or three nights, so blissful that they remain ineffaceable in my memory, I took my father's place in the big bed. I still see, with a child's magnifying eye, its posts diminishing toward the immense height of the ceiling, with its plaster cherubs, or as I thought of them, fellow babies, playing their Christmas trumpets. I remember my fascinated delight in the glossy red satin lining of the curtains, and the tall mountains of pillows, like a tor under fresh snow, which stood over me when, having slipped to their foot, I waked in the morning. I was in paradise. And yet I knew, even then, that, kind as she was, my mother suffered me with difficulty in her bed; and that she had never cared greatly for my plain face, my awkward ways, my spectacled eyes. I got on her nerves, as they say. It was by mere contact, I suppose, that I regained, on my mother's breast, the power to live, to believe, taking it directly from that warmth, that life, which had given me life already. As I took from Lucy, from Amy, and from that little maid whose name I can't remember, from Bill, from Sara, some direct communication of their energy, their confidence.

150

It is almost comic to see Ann's anxiety while she goes in and out. It has made her so restless that she can't even read. No doubt some rumor has come to the house. She knows that Blanche was at that mysterious conference. And Mr. Jaffery is always appearing in her conversation.

No doubt she thinks I am spiteful to keep her in suspense, with the spite of the old. But I feel no spite. I simply find myself prevented from discussing with her this matter, which is the last fragment of my privateness. And what a flatness afterwards.

> One flesh, one mind, in wishing to be two,
> For two can love again, as strangers do.

Today, after fiddling about for ten minutes with my pulse, temperature, pillows, etc., she plumped out, "I suppose Mr. Jaffery wanted to see you about your will." Then she turned red; or rather, two patches as big as pennies appeared on her cheeks under the powder. I wish every girl who powders could see herself blush magenta. Nothing is more ugly.

I almost burst out laughing at the girl's naïveté. But I answered after a moment: "No, I canceled it. If I die now, there won't be a will. Everything will be sold, the house, farms, furniture, pictures."

"But, uncle—"

Ann was now redder still. The mauve patches were as big as pen-wipers. She looked at me with eyes full of dismay. "Did you want the place to go—isn't it a fearful pity?"

I saw that she was really fond of the place, that she was going to suffer at its loss; and so to upset my mind again. And I thought that I was entitled to some peace on my deathbed. So I answered rather more sharply than I intended, "Whose fault is that—if you let Robert take you away and Jan away to the ends of the world—in Brazil or Lincolnshire?"

She stood silent, shaking her thermometer but not looking at it.

And I thought, "She is really a good-natured girl. And we all treat her rather badly. I am treating her badly. But she is strong, and strong people always have troubles piled upon them. Weak people even like to worry them and throw new burdens on them. When you say to children, 'This toy is made so that you can't break it,' then they are sure to treat that toy as badly as possible."

So, when we used to send Amy to buy something for us in Queensport, we always gave her the most careless instructions: "You'll get it easily—plenty of the shops have it." Even though we ourselves had failed everywhere. But to any of the maids or to my mother we gave the most exact and careful particulars.

1 5 1

When I heard that Amy was dying, I couldn't believe it. It was the year of the great strike, and I was oppressed with terror. I thought that at last civil war had come to destroy the very soul of England; its kindness. I found her in a dismal little boardinghouse on the south coast. I had never visited her there before; I thought I had no time. Neither had I reflected that Amy was now a poor woman. Her son, Loftus, was indeed already well off for he not only had his share of my mother's estate but had inherited a large sum from her sister, his godmother. But he, no more than I, perceived that his mother was almost in poverty. She did not mention it. And both of us, I suppose, were preoccupied, Loftus with his polo in India and myself with the state of the country and the decline of religion.

"My dear Amy," I said, when I saw her bare room, looking out on a coalyard, "I'd no idea you lived in such a place."

"The people are very nice," Amy said. She was propped up in bed with pillows and barely able to turn her head. "And there's a good attic." She had had rheumatic fever, and now her heart was failing. A nurse sat beside the bed, a red round-faced woman in gold spectacles. She had been giving oxygen at intervals during the night and I remember the first thought which occurred to me, "How strange to take so much trouble and to go to so much expense only to keep poor Amy alive."

The thought came to me, but I did not accept it, because I knew now that Amy was dear to me. Yet so strong was custom that I could not help feeling ready to laugh at the old woman.

"A good attic," I said. "Have you another room upstairs?"

"No, the boxes," she whispered. "Such a nuisance in lodgings."

I remembered that Amy had spent almost her whole life in trains, in lodgings, or in other people's houses. She had come to see everything from the traveler's point of view. "Yes, I can see that an attic is useful," I said.

"And water in the room," she whispered.

"Oh, they all have that now."

"All the difference."

"Yes, water in the room." I wanted to laugh at this extraordinary conversation. "Saves servants, it probably pays."

"Wash things—in your room," Amy whispered. "Landladies don't like bringing hot water," and she added after a moment, "naturally."

"Naturally, of course."

"And washing—such a difficulty—when you have to move quarters."

"Yes, I can see that."

"Very lucky find this place—gas ring, in corner. Make my own tea."

"Yes, that's a great advantage."

"Bill—great fuss about his tea—liked to see the water boil."

"Was he—did he? I've missed Bill. We've all missed him."

"All nonsense—that women can't make tea."

"Did he say that? But Bill was very fond of you, Amy. He used to tell me what a good wife you were."

Amy was silent for a moment and the nurse got up to feel

her pulse. Amy looked calmly at her and shook her head as if to say, "Don't bother me."

"Have you a good vicar here?" I said, seeking for an appropriate subject.

Amy shook her head. "Very high."

"I thought you liked the High Church."

"Not with bells. Too foreign." Her voice began to fail and she turned her blue eyes toward me with that look of shy good nature which I had not seen for forty years. "What a nuisance for you—to come down."

Suddenly I felt that I couldn't bear to lose Amy. My throat choked; my eyes smarted. "You're not going to leave us, Amy. All you want is a good long rest. It's wonderful how hearts respond to a good rest. You must come away with me somewhere."

Amy shook her head. "Got to die sometime," she whispered. "I've been lucky—thirty years with Bill—and the boys, so much happiness." She waved her hand and made a pluck at the air.

The nurse quickly put the mask over her face. She murmured to me, "Very weak."

But when the mask was taken away again, Amy spoke quite briskly and strongly, "Yes, the curate came, but I sent him away again. He's a pacifist, like that man at Tolbrook. I wouldn't have him —I said, 'what about his oath?'" Amy, I imagine, thought that clergymen took an oath of allegiance.

"You sent him away?"

"I couldn't stand him—talking about Bill."

"What did he say about Bill?"

"About me seeing him soon."

"I hope we'll all be together again soon, Amy. And Bill has been waiting for you."

I said this for comfort to the poor woman, but her expression did not change. Like Bill himself, she seemed to take little concern in what happened after her death.

She reflected a moment and said, "I never could understand how Bill stood them."

"All sorts to make a world," I quoted Bill.

"What we want—Christian soldiers."

"Bill took after his father—he was always rather evangelical. Now, Amy, if there's anything you want done—here I am."

Amy reflected. "Thank you, Tom. I think I've done everything—I wrote to Loftus yesterday and I told the undertakers."

This information took me so much by surprise that I could not answer. Amy continued, "But you might see they don't put in any extras. The estimate—in my blotter. You know what undertakers are."

Her voice was now failing again and the nurse started forward. But Amy made an impatient gesture. "All right, nurse," and to me she said, "You'll stay to lunch."

"Well, Amy—" I hesitated. "I left my bag at the hotel."

"But I've arranged for lunch. Veal. Your favorite."

"My dear Amy—it's very kind of you."

"I really wouldn't like to disappoint Mrs. Biglow—a special favor—to me—and she's so busy, this time of year."

I thanked Amy and promised to stay to lunch. She lay still for a moment and then she said, "I'm going now, Tom."

In my distress, I did not know what I ought to do. Amy and I had rarely embraced and now we seemed too old to begin. But Amy had her usual expression of calm reflection. She murmured thoughtfully, "Yes, I think that's all—except, oh, yes—my summer stays at the cleaners."

"My dear Amy," for I was shocked that she should waste her last moments in this way.

"Yes, but they're C.O.D. I don't want Mrs. Biglow to be bothered—she's rather excitable—May—the new season."

As Amy said this her face changed and the nurse brushed me aside and put the mask over her face. But she was too late.

Although Amy was kept alive, by injections, for another hour, she did not again speak.

I found that I had very little to do for Amy after her death. She had arranged for her own funeral; to Tolbrook; and even for the inscription on the stone which marked Bill's grave. "And his wife, Amelia Alice, born Madras, India, April 14th, 1871. Died . . ."

And when the trumpets blew, the walls fell down flat.

1 5 2

When Lucy died I had felt the pressure of confusion, as if I had lost with her a guiding force of revelation; and now, when I thought, "Amy is gone," I felt afraid. For when we had said at Bill's death and John's death that Amy was saved by her faith in the resurrection, we had been wrong. I don't know what Amy believed, but her faith did not need theology. Its strong roots were in a character which nothing could shake.

When we laughed at Amy as a young bride, left alone in our household of clever young people, she withdrew into her pride. But she was brave by nature, she did not sulk in it. She used it only for her home and her refuge. For her pride was not vain; it was nothing more than the ordinary self-respect which all brave people have by nature. She set no great value on herself and so she had no self-pity.

And now lying here, I miss Amy more than all those whom I have known. I know why Amy sent away that curate and why she would not let me talk to her about the consolations of religion. She did not want them; perhaps she did not altogether like them. Perhaps in her shrewd mind, as simple and strong as Sara's, she was skeptical of heaven.

Amy and Sara, countrywomen both. They didn't submit themselves to any belief. They used it. They made it. They had the courage of the simple, which is not to be surprised. They had the penetration of innocence, which can see the force of a platitude. Amy's "got to die sometime" has been on the lips of every private soldier since the first army went into battle. For her it was still profound.

To Amy, death in this true shape was a familiar, and she received him like an afternoon caller. But to me here death is a wonder. When I look now at the last horizon, I see him rise into the sky, more illuminating than the brightest sun, colder than the arctic moon; and all the landscape is suddenly altered. The solid hills melt into cloud; and clouds affirm a reality.

Familiar shapes are changed before my eyes. And seeing these strange patterns, these immense shadows reaching to my feet, I say, "I never knew this place before. I have lived like a mole in a run, like a cat in a kitchen."

153

There is nightshade in my medicine, and I think Ann gives me too much. It makes me feel as if I were turned into an airplane, throbbing and floating on the air. It gives me so many ideas at once that I feel confused. Just now I saw Ann looking at me with a startled face and I knew that I had been talking and laughing. But her sad expression made me angry and I said, "Why are you so closed up? It's pure obstinacy at your age."

I could see Ann thought I was quite mad. She smiled in a hesitating way and shook her head. "Yes, you're just determined not to feel any kind of pleasure. It's the nonsense of the age. Every age had its nonsense and this age likes to be hard and careworn. But I've no patience with a girl like you—you have plenty of faith—but you refuse the happiness."

"I'm afraid I'm not much of a Christian, uncle. They didn't catch me young enough."

"What does that matter whether you're a Christian or not?" I said. And I was so much surprised by my own words that I suddenly began to smile, like someone who has made an epigram by accident. Ann began knitting again so that she needed not to look at me. She was disturbed by this smile. Once people think you're mad, your most ordinary actions seem mad; like picking up a pin in the street, or smiling at your own thoughts and discoveries.

"Yes, what does that matter—faith has nothing to do with Christianity. Look at Sara and look at your Aunt Amy. Yes, look at Amy. She had a happy life, she said, and she was quite right. I envy her. But her religion was nothing to her happiness—it was simply regimental. She was happy because she had strength. She became a woman of power. She didn't need anybody or anything—in fact they needed her."

"You oughtn't to talk too much."

"That's impossible now—to talk too much. Why shouldn't I talk?" and I began to laugh at Ann's face. I could see she was even frightened. The first time I had frightened her. "But you think I'm talking nonsense."

"I'm sure faith is a very nice thing to have," she said.
I wanted to shake her. But instead I said in a soft voice, "But you have it, my dear—you have it. How could you go back to Robert without faith? Yes, you are very strong—I dare say stronger than Robert. But he is for happiness—why, you can hear him whistling now in the yard. He lets himself be happy when he feels like it. But you keep up this play of carrying a world on your shoulders. The world is at your service—you have only to enjoy it."

I stopped to see what I was saying. Ann got up and left the room so skillfully that I did not notice that she had gone till I turned to her again. She has the idea, I think, that she upsets me, and that if she tactfully keeps out of sight I shall be more likely to make a fair will and give Robert some capital for a new start.

154

I admired Bill for taking death with such excellent manners. But now I see that he was doing something quite natural and inevitable. When death rises high above the horizons, the landscape draws in its shadows. It becomes flat and ordinary. Its details are even insignificant. But there is room for more of them and, like small copies of the real, like miniatures, they become more dear. As I lie with nothing to do but feel the world agitating round my bed, not only the fields about this house are present to my mind's eye but the moor, the Longwater, Queensport, and beyond them all the villages and towns of my country, with their spires and towers and chimneys standing under this broad daytime of eternity, their streams reflecting its face, in the innocence of creatures dependent on the whims of the spirit. And the dirty back lanes where I found Lucy, the pond into which those Tory rascals threw me, in the war election, the squares and streets and parks of London, become as familiar to me as the rooms of this house.

I walk upon the fields of the whole island as upon my own carpet, and feel the same exasperation against them for being a perpetual burden on my regard; I love the noble buildings as I loved these old chairs and tables, with anxiety and irritation. For I know very well that they are not being properly looked after. I love this island as I loved Tolbrook; and tremble for it; and perhaps I shall be happy to get some peace from both of them. They have broken my heart between them.

What does it matter who gets Tolbrook; it is only one room of my house. I really have no time to make a will. I shall probably die without one. Then Blanche, Robert, and Ann would get each in equal share, which is probably a fair division. For Blanche has the best claim; Ann has the most need; and Robert is Lucy's son.

155

A small boy is whistling in the yards, on three notes. He is pretending to whistle a tune known only to himself, and he thinks that everyone is deceived; whereas it is perfectly obvious that he has only just learned to whistle and doesn't know any tune. I have heard him often during the last fortnight and he has enraged me. But now he makes me laugh so that I shake the bed and get a pain in my chest. What do I care about the other world? One dies and learns. Probably these young people who don't believe in heaven are right. Perhaps I have been talking nonsense to Ann, and pestering her to no good. If so, I shall not tell her.

What did Amy care for heaven? What do I care, so long as I lie in Tolbrook churchyard? I shall ask them to bury me without a coffin.

The truth must be confessed, that I am an old fossil, and that I have deceived myself about my abilities. I thought I could be an adventurer like Lucy and Edward, a missionary. I shouted the pilgrim's cry, democracy, liberty, and so forth, but I was a pilgrim only by race. England took me with her on a few stages of her journey. Because she could not help it. She, poor thing, was born upon the road, and lives in such a dust of travel that she never knows where she is.

> Where away England, steersman answer me?
> We cannot tell. For we are all at sea.

She is the wandering Dutchman, the pilgrim and scape-goat of the world. Which flings its sins upon her as the old world heaped its sins upon the friars. Her lot is that of all courage, all enterprise; to be hated and abused by the parasite. But, and this has been one of the exasperating things in my life, she isn't even aware of this hatred and jealousy which surrounds her and, in the same moment, seeks and dreads her ruin. She doesn't notice it because she looks forward to the road. Because she is free. She stands always before all possibility, and that is the youth of the spirit. It is the life of the faithful who say, "I am ready. Anywhere at any time."

Or perhaps, to be honest, I should say that she is a bit of a Protestant and therefore a bit of an anarchist, and so forth. Which characteristics may be discovered in one or two other peoples of similar stock, history, etc., who are also apt to find themselves in new lodgings at short notice; with new aspects from the windows of their spirit, and new bugs, fleas, etc., in the mattress, to keep their bodies on the jump.

I never liked lodgings. I was too fond of my dear ones at home. And what if they were trees and chairs and furniture and books and stones?

Material love. What is material? What is the body? Is not this house the house of spirits, made by generations of lovers? I touched in my mother the warmth of a love that did not belong to either of us. Why should I not feel, when I lie in English ground, the passion of a spirit that beats in all English souls?

Ann came in to put me to bed for the night. She found my notebook on the bed and silently removed it. She did not reprove me for breaking her order to lie flat and do nothing, and in her silence it was understood between us that whether I die today or tomorrow does not matter to anybody. But for her that is a defeat; for me it is a triumph.

"You look as if you'd swallowed a safety pin," I said to her, making her look at me with Edward's eyes, which should be gay. "You take life too seriously."

"Don't you think it is rather serious?"

"My dear child, you're not thirty yet. You have forty, forty-five years in front of you."

"Yes."

ABOUT THE TYPE

The text of this book has been set in Trump Mediaeval. Designed by Georg Trump for the Weber foundry in the late 1950s, this typeface is a modern rethinking of the Garalde Oldstyle types (often associated with Claude Garamond) that have long been popular with printers and book designers.

Trump Mediaeval is a trademark of
Linotype-Hell AG and/or its subsidiaries

Printed and bound by R. R. Donnelley & Sons,
Harrisonburg, Virginia

Designed by Red Canoe, Deer Lodge, Tennessee
Caroline Kavanagh
Deb Koch

TITLES IN SERIES